Dear Reader,

Arabesque is proud to ⟨...⟩,
a fictional account of four courageous and committed heroes
serving in the Air Force, Army, Navy, and Marines. We know
that you will come to admire and fall in love with these proud
African-American military officers: Major Zurich Kingdom
in *Top-Secret Rendezvous,* Colonel Neal Allen in *Courage
Under Fire,* Captain Haughton Storm in *The Glory of Love,*
and Colonel Nelson Wainwright in *Flying High.*

The **At Your Service** romance series is the story of their
lives and the women they love . . . filled with patriotism, ca-
maraderie, romance, passion, and intrigue! Each novel will
draw you in and not let you go, as you come to appreciate the
honor of each hero, as well as the commitment of the people
they care about. The series is a fictional account meant to
capture the essence of those serving our country, and as such
we have taken creative license with the cover photography
and the stories we know you will enjoy.

BET Books began planning this unique series honoring
African Americans serving in the military in the Spring of
2002, not knowing that events would unfold in the war with
Iraq in "Operation Enduring Freedom."

Now, more than ever, we hope that you enjoy this series
yourself, or buy the books as gifts for someone special. We
welcome your comments and feedback, and invite you to
send us an e-mail to **BET Books@BET.com.**

Best regards,

Linda Gill
Vice President and Publisher

THE GLORY OF LOVE

For the next twenty-four hours, Roxanne would tell herself that what happened between her and Storm was a build-up of stress, frustration, and plain old lust. She would try to convince herself that her desire for him was nothing more than her surrender to the pulse of the jungle, the breath and cry of the wild, the allure of sand and sky. In the heat and humidity of the island, her need to mate was strong. It couldn't possibly be love.

Her eyes told him everything he needed to know. He could reach over, stroke her nipple, knead her flesh. She would moan and come to him. He could turn to her, press his manhood against her belly. She would open for him. His penis throbbed, ached ferociously for her. Coaxing her would be so easy. But he could not, or rather *would* not. The first move had to come from her. The chasm between them was ten years old. He had caused it. If the void was to be sealed, it would be Roxanne's decision. He wondered if her body would obey her mind and heart.

She turned to him, the flame of desire burning through her veins. "Let's get this lust thing out of the way."

Confusion furrowed his brow. "What?"

"We aren't going to be able to concentrate on the game until we get this lust out of our system."

She grabbed his face and pulled him to her. Roxanne reveled in the press of her lips on his. It had been so long. Oh God, too long. His arms came around her. Swallowed her. And for the sensation of his wet skin against hers, she would disappear in his embrace, only to reappear in his eyes and sparkle there like a diamond in the night.

THE GLORY OF LOVE

Kim Louise

ARABESQUE

★BET BOOKS™

BET Publications, LLC
http://www.bet.com
http://www.arabesquebooks.com

ARABESQUE BOOKS are published by

BET Publications, LLC
c/o BET BOOKS
One BET Plaza
1900 W Place NE
Washington, D.C. 20018-1211

Copyright © 2003 by Kim Louise Whiteside

All Kensington Titles, Imprints, and Distributed Lines are available at special quantity discounts for bulk purchases for sales promotion, premiums, fund-raising, and educational or institutional use. Special book excerpts or customized printings can also be created to fit specific needs. For details, write or phone the office of the Kensington special sales manager: Kensington Publishing Corp., 850 Third Avenue, New York, NY 10022, attn: Special Sales Department, Phone: 1-800-221-2647.

BET Books is a trademark of Black Entertainment Television, Inc. ARABESQUE, the ARABESQUE logo, and the BET BOOKS logo are trademarks and registered trademarks.

First Printing: August 2003
10 9 8 7 6 5 4 3 2 1
Printed in the United States of America

This book is dedicated to my son and good friend Steve Allen Whiteside, Jr. I'm so very proud of you, and I love you with all of my heart.

ACKNOWLEDGMENTS

A bounty of thanks goes to Jairus "Bear" Anderson who never met a video game he couldn't beat. Thanks for being you, for being in my life for so long, and for answering all the weird questions I asked about games. An author once said, "To write is human; to edit is divine." To Chandra Sparks Taylor for her divine red pen. Thank you for making my words shine and my stories sing. To Denise Livermore, who is a wonderful writer. Thanks for supporting my work and being such a glorious inspiration. To George Richmond for his pilot insights. Thanks for helping me to straighten up and fly right. To my mother, Lola Relford, for smiling and saying, "Baby, keep going." You'll never know what that meant to me. And last but not least, my son for inspiring, and being excited about, the possibilities of this book. I don't need a PR agent . . . I have you!

Prologue

Franklin "Amadeus" Jones had gone completely mad.

Carl Baer stared at his lifelong friend with a rancid mixture of pity and revulsion.

"What do you think, Carly?"

Carly! He hated being called that. But he'd put up with it for the twenty-five years that they'd been friends. Carl swallowed, forcing a bitter rise of bile back into his stomach. Yes, he admitted; he'd put up with a lot.

Carl's nerves flickered with unease. "I think it's time to get him back before the toxident wears off."

Amadeus cackled, and then strutted around like a peacock, as though the world were in his hip pocket, as though they all weren't living on borrowed time.

There were three other men in the motel room. Amadeus's muscle, looming quietly in the shadows. They had helped to incapacitate and carry the soldier. After they got him on the bed, they bound him so that Carl could *do his thing*. The injection had taken only seconds to administer and the man on the bed started talking soon after.

Amadeus had hurled a barrage of questions at the soldier. Pulling out his innermost feelings had been like extracting a tooth, and Amadeus played the masochistic dentist role to the hilt—drilling, picking.

Needling.

He acquired more information from the soldier than he could ever use.

"Look at him, Carly. A warrior. A killing machine. They

don't come any better than Chief Storm, here. He'll be perfect. Don't you think?"

Amadeus hadn't lost *all* of his faculties. He was right about that at least. The roan kiss of Nubia. The hard detachment of a warrior. Bulky. The guy tied down on the bed looked as though he could rip a man in two with his bare hands and had probably done so on several occasions.

"He will be formidable," Carl admitted. He was gripped by one of those instances when he couldn't stop staring at his friend. Pillsbury Dough Boy complexion and bright yellow hair. He was the only individual with albinism Carl had ever known personally.

Drool glistened at the corners of Amadeus's mouth. "What about the sample?"

Carl pulled a long thin syringe from a case. The surgical steel glinted angrily in the harsh overhead lighting. As a scientist, what he was about to do had thrilled him once. And God help him, aspects of it still did. But the implications of his actions felt like hands choking him sometimes and made him physically ill.

Amadeus turned to him before he had time to mask his wave of repugnance. The pale man drew closer. Just a soft whisper above skeletal, his body gave new meaning to the word gaunt. He always dressed more like Beethoven than his namesake, and Carl could smell the scent of mental decay rising like rotting flesh from Amadeus's pores.

He closed in. That thin mouth and those tiny teeth grinning. Desperation sparked inside Carl and he slapped Amadeus quickly across the face. Knowing his own strength, he was sure the blow sounded much worse than it felt.

To no avail. The grin was still there. Still moving toward him. Carl closed his eyes for his punishment, but what he received was a cold kiss on the cheek from lips that weren't quite there.

He shuddered.

He'd always been afraid of Amadeus, especially the light flickering just behind his eyes that made him look like a wolf on the verge of being rabid. He hadn't wanted this friendship. But they were *both* freaks. They'd been outcasts since birth and had found each other.

Like the man lying on the bed, their fate was sealed.

One

He would need surgery soon. Commander Haughton Storm lay low in the dry night air, obscured by brambles and thin lifeless bushes. Just when he thought he'd be going home, his squad had gotten an order for recon in Gabon.

The pain slicing across his lower back stemmed from an old football injury. In the past if he ignored it, the pain would give up and go away. This time he'd had it for a week and it only got worse. Soon he might be forced to use a hot pack or buy, God help him, Icy Hot.

He squinted his eyes against the darkness. The heat of the tropics began to cool. Storm's search and rescue unit had been stalking for hours. The inch-by-inch crawl toward their target would have sent ordinary military forces packing for home, but his team of highly trained Navy SEALs was the best at what they did. As SEAL operators, they consumed a regular diet of search and rescue, demolition, and recon. His team was often called upon for search and rescue. The kind of dirty work he lived for.

He listened and slid forward another inch. His issued fatigues could barely be seen beneath the leaves and twigs he'd covered himself with. Any potential sweat or shine from his face was obscured by the black hue of burnt paper he'd covered his face with.

Another inch and they would be in range.

A twinge of pain vied for his attention. It had been years since he'd had any serious lumbar problems. Years. The slow, dull pain felt more like a warning, a premonition of bad things to come. On mission after mission, he'd learned to trust what his body told him. By the pounding, his body was preparing him for something out of the ordinary. He summoned his training and turned his mind from the ache. Just like a switch, he shut the pain off.

En route to the target, four of Storm's seven men swept the perimeter in preparation for their seizure of the building. They would ensure there were no outside threats.

Almost there now. He and his men inched closer and reached for their assault rifles, which they'd kept tucked beneath them. *War in slow motion,* he thought as each man drew up his weapon and took aim.

First, they would take out all personnel they could see, both inside and outside the building. Then, in a swift rush forward, they would advance.

Storm gave a barely perceptible nod. A thunderstorm of shots bombarded the still night air. Guards fell like targets on a shooting track. And those who didn't ran into the hills after seeing the bodies of their comrades shatter and explode with the barrage.

A short whistle, a sweeping hand, and they attacked. Scouts, patrolling the perimeter, became their cover as Storm and three members of his squad took up a snake formation and entered the building single-file.

Storm moved in first. Their mission was to search and secure the building where an American scientist was being held and bring him home.

Checking corridors. Checking rooms. Searching. Looking. Hands on weapon. Mind on mission. Haughton Storm had never lost a man during a mission and had very few wounded. His gut told him to make this quick or that fact might change.

His operators called out from above and below. "First floor, secure!" "Third floor, secure!" Check hallways. Check doors. *Gunfire!* He was being shot at. Storm got off a round, ducked behind a door, and slapped in another magazine. One operator was on his left. He signaled him to go around to the other side of the hallway and into the holding room.

The picture they reviewed in the mission briefing did not

do justice to the man they were sent to rescue. The photo was bad, but this guy looked worse. Storm could tell he was African-American. The problem was he looked as though a vampire had come along and drained all the blood from his body.

His second in command took out the last guard in the room.

Storm ran toward the pale man. "Are you injured?" he shouted.

The man shook his head and his eyes widened and seemed to dance a bit. Storm registered that the man had one gray eye and one ice-green eye.

"Then, down on the ground now!" As per his training, he treated all rescued personnel as hostile.

The man did as he was told.

"Put your hands behind your back!" Storm had drawn his nine-millimeter handgun and had it pointed toward the man's head. He patted the man down on all sides. "Are you armed or concealing anything that can be used as a weapon?"

"No," the man said, with what sounded like a smile in his voice. Storm was immediately distrustful. While one of his operators trained his weapon on the man's head, Storm put him in handcuffs and yanked him up.

"Let's move!"

Again, his men maneuvered into snake formation. This time the hostage was in the middle. With eyes like eagles, each one of his men checked side-to-side, above, and below. Their movements were precise, like the internal workings of the finest watch. The enemy could be anywhere.

When they reached the lower level, three men from his squad fanned out to sweep the area for their departure. They took the hostage with them.

There was a rhythm to mission deployment. Something a few soldiers could tune into like a sixth sense. Feeling like a hawk or panther, knowing exactly when to move, when to strike, when to retaliate. Many of his men said he had it—the rhythm. He wasn't sure what he had, but he knew it was like a pulse in the Earth pounding in his brain. A tremor only he could feel sometimes. It told him when to strike, when to stay put, when to lie low and when to take risks. And that tremor was telling him now that his squad was in danger. Maybe something in the orders they received was off, but the game had changed within the space of the last few minutes. And suddenly the whole thing smelled like rotten flesh.

Storm made a series of gestures with his hand. Closed fist. Open. Open. Point north. Three fingers, two circles. Closed fist.

They had to get out of there now.

The message traveled quickly, and the men of Cobra One fanned out one by one and pulled back from the edge of the enemy camp.

Storm's skin prickled. Closed fist.

Footfalls in the jungle. They were in trouble.

Shots fired. They hit the deck, each man rolling and scampering behind the shelter of the dilapidated building. The familiar surge of adrenaline charged through Storm's body and he barked orders through his headset. As customary, his team was in perfect sync. They followed his commands as if they had read his mind before he could think his thoughts.

Back out.

T formation.

If he could get the men back to the perimeter, they could return to the extraction point and be lifted out by helicopter.

"Alpha-Six, this is Cobra One!"

"Alpha-Six, over."

"Need extraction! ETA ten minutes!"

"Copy that."

Over a dozen enemy soldiers scrambled from the shadows, guns drawn.

Storm tagged a guard, who buckled with the impact and went down.

Gunfire filled the jungle night. The explosions lit up the sky like an erratic strobe. As his men fought for their lives and their country, Storm defended himself and swore that whoever was responsible for setting this trap would pay.

"I'm hit!" a voice said, slicing through the thunder of gunfire.

"Sharky!" Storm shouted, recognizing the call of his second in command.

A sniper pinned Storm down in a thicket. If Storm didn't take him out soon, he'd never get out of there to help Sharky.

Storm jerked himself against a tree for cover. His pulse pounded loud and hard. Jungle shadows provided some cover for him. His eyes swept the perimeter quickly. Bullets whizzed by on both sides of him. The enemy was behind them, stationary, not following—yet. He had to get to Sharky before that was no longer an option.

The footfalls and suppressing fire from his unit told him they were regrouping, but not fast enough. Without his men to cover him, he would have to run unprotected to where Sharky lay at the foot of a thick bush, unmoving.

He could see one leg. The rest of his comrade's body was motionless. A bolt of emotional pain struck Storm in the middle of the chest and he sprinted toward the man's location.

For years, he'd trained against letting the sight of injuries, wounds, or blood affect him. Every SEAL had. But for a millisecond, he lost his training as a sliver of remorse slid though him. Then it was gone and he knew that the man, shot in the side but still reaching for his gun, needed and deserved every bit of military training Storm had to get them out of the ambush.

"Just get me on my feet and put my gun in my hand," Sharky said, stark determination making his thirty-two years seem much older.

"You got it, sailor," Storm replied.

More shouts and bootfalls as the SEAL Team Cobra One aborted their reconnaissance mission. Storm hefted Sharky up and handed him his weapon. With a nod from the injured man they scrambled toward the extraction point, arm-in-arm, rifles drawn and blazing.

* * *

"SEALs, we are *lea-ving!*" Storm shouted when his unit had regrouped.

The enemy was following close now.

"Alpha Six, this is Cobra One, over."

"Alpha Six, go ahead."

"Zone is hot. Repeat, zone is hot, over."

"Roger that, Cobra One. What's your ETA?"

Storm tightened his hold on Sharky.

"Two minutes, and we got injuries, over!"

"Two minutes, chief. We'll prep for medical, over."

"Copy that. Cobra out."

Storm's breathing matched the pace of his run with Sharky through the heat and brush. He sensed the anxiety of his team. "Cobra team sound off."

"Sandman, on your six, sir!"

"Hardgrove, side-by-side, sir!"

"Mills, on the move, commander!"

"Fox, still in the pocket, commander!"

"Tuxedo, kickin' up dust, sir!"

"Faison, bringing up the rear!"

Good. His team was intact. He'd be damned if he'd lose any men to an ambush, which is what this was.

As the sound of gunfire grew behind him, he realized that what they'd experienced was a brush-off. If the guards had wanted a confrontation, he and his men would have done a lot more than simply retreat.

Why did this feel like a test?

When they arrived at the extraction point, the chopper flew in, cannons blazing. All seven of his men were by his side and ready to lift out.

"Go! Go! Go! Go!" Seconds into the helo and Storm issued the command to leave.

The helicopter lifted up and away sharply, guns still blazing.

"What happened back there?" one of the pilots shouted.

"Ambush. Somebody set us up." After making sure the

hostage was secure, Storm knelt beside his teammate. He and Sharky went all the way back to Hellweek in BUDs training. They had endured every horrendous test thrown at them. He was the closest thing Storm had to a brother.

Sharky was getting worked on pretty good by Doc. Raymond "Doc" Collins was the best corpsman Storm had ever worked with. If he couldn't save Sharky, no one could.

Doc looked up. "Punctured lung. I'm going to intubate and patch to keep his lung from collapsing. He's bleeding like a fat pig, but I'll get it stopped and he should be okay."

Relief slowed Storm's raging pulse.

Sharky trembled on the floor of the helicopter. His eyes widened. It was the first time Storm had ever seen anything close to fear in his eyes in all the years they'd served together.

"Suck it up, Sharky!" he barked. "That's an order!"

He touched Sharky on the shoulder. "You're gonna make it," he said.

"I gotta . . . gotta make it," Sharky replied, heaving with each word. "Or else there'll be no one who can keep . . . keep your . . . sorry carcass in line."

Storm grinned and nodded. Sharky was going to be fine.

Relieved, he sat back, reflecting. At the beginning of each mission, Storm would take a mental snapshot of his squad. Every time, he etched their faces into his memory.

Failure was not an option to a Navy SEAL. Each mission was carefully planned and rehearsed to be successful without casualties or injuries. If either occurred, the commander had made an unacceptable mistake.

His head rocked back and forth against the cold metal of the chopper. Vibration from the propellers strummed inside the vehicle like the heartbeat of a giant bird.

He shifted as his back sent out another twinge for good measure. The hostage hadn't said a word. Not thank you. Not much obliged. Not kiss my behind. He only sat in silence with a strange grin that gave Storm a jolt of unease.

He knew his men. Their body language was clear. Seven men, twitching and snorting like nervous bulls. The inside of the helicopter was uncharacteristically quiet and their gazes moved to and away from the man. Something about the man they'd rescued put them all on edge.

Storm closed his eyes and wondered why his green-faced warriors, a squad of the most highly skilled soldiers in U.S. military forces, were spooked by a tiny little man.

Two

Roxanne Allgood was on cloud nine—literally. As she checked the telemetry on the cockpit of the 757 she was flying, thoughts of home flooded her mind. Not home in the sense of her apartment in San Diego, but home to where her fondest memories lived.

Atlanta.

She switched on the microphone. "Ladies and gentlemen, we will be arriving in Atlanta International Airport shortly. Please notice I have turned on the *Fasten Seatbelt* sign and ask that you remain seated for the remainder of the flight. The weather in Atlanta is a cool sixty-eight degrees. And we will be landing in about fifteen minutes." She smiled. "Attendants prepare for landing."

She waited for the flight attendants to recite their familiar spiel regarding seat backs and tray tables.

She checked her instruments. A smile tugged at the corners of her mouth. Most landings she was all business. One hundred percent practiced captain with the safety of hundreds of people resting at her fingertips and residing in the standard operating procedures etched in her mind. This evening, however, something else was taking shape in her thoughts—something extra. She allowed the energy of it to add to her concentration and determination to have a safe landing.

The nose of the plane broke through the clouds. The lights of the city burned below her as if heaven and earth had been reversed and she was—as a result of some crazy twist in physics—headed down toward the night sky. But as she guided the iron bird closer to its destination, the sheer number of city lights betrayed that thought and the reality of a thriving metropolis replaced her fantasy.

The controllers cleared her for landing and she turned the yoke to make her final approach into the city. The reading on her altimeter and heading pleased her. Although cruising, her air speed was still several hundred knots.

Roxanne pulled the throttle toward her and began her descent.

With a nod to her co-pilot, she reduced her cruising speed by one-quarter and deployed the landing gear. Soon the precise lights of the airport replaced the general lights of the city.

Roxanne pulled the throttle again, steering the plane toward the landing strip. The back wheels touched down first and then the front. Roxanne pulled the throttle back all the way and used the floor pedals to steer and brake the plane.

Working for Delta had been a dream come true. They cared about people and made flying an airplane at thirty thousand feet fun. She'd actually built up quite a reputation as "The Singing Pilot." Jim Browning, her co-pilot, gave her a knowing glance. When the plane was safely on the ground and at the gate, she switched on the microphone and began her now-famous routine.

> *Time flies*
> *We'll never recall*
> *Each moment we spend*
> *When we spend them all*
> *Here's a wish*
> *For you my friend*
> *Remember this*
> *Until we meet . . .*

Deep breath.

> *Agaiiiiiiiiiiiiiiiiiiiiiiiiin!*

The applause was vibrant. She heard it clear through to the cockpit. That was the singing pilot. She'd always been able to hold a note. Five years ago, she wanted to see just how long she could hold it. To her astonishment, she ended up holding the last note of the "Star-Spangled Banner" for nearly a minute. Her discovery inspired her and, during solos in her church choir, she'd pushed herself and refined her abilities until now she could hold a note from de-plane to empty plane. A physical therapist who had been traveling on a flight once asked her how she did that. She smiled and said honestly, "Practice."

As passengers deplaned, many thanked her and shook her hand. She was happy to make their experience more enjoyable and grateful to have a job that allowed her to do so in her own way.

"Another excellent flight, captain," Jim remarked. "And that voice of yours is strong as usual. I still would like to know how you do that."

Walking just a few steps ahead of him, she shrugged her shoulders. "When I figure it out, I'll let you know."

Roxanne deplaned, bag in tow. She was staying with her sister Yolanda for a few days of much needed R&R. There were also some loose ends that she needed to tie up with her sister Marti.

She and Marti had been at odds for too many years.

She and Jim parted ways and Roxanne headed to the parking garage where her other sister Morgan was waiting for her. It was alright to stay at Yolanda's house, but her oldest sister refused to be bothered with trivial duties like meeting her at the airport. She claimed her schedule was much too busy.

Roxanne smiled into each face as if she knew it. She was home. Home! Now she understood why E.T. had been so fixated on going back there.

The Atlanta International Airport looked just as much like a shopping mall as it did an airline terminal. Every type of store one could imagine was there. From the obligatory book stands and coffee shops to clothing stores and a bar that for all intents and purposes equaled a discothèque. She could even buy produce from a small convenience mart.

On a whim, she stopped in a children's boutique. Marti's son would be ten months old soon. She could at least buy her nephew a new toy. And just maybe that new toy could double as a peace offering. She needed to be forgiven.

After realizing that everything in the store was not just expensive, but ridiculously overpriced, she settled on a cute little sailor's outfit. It was lapis blue with bright white stripes and a matching hat. She stepped out to the register knowing full well that Morgan the seamstress would have a cow. She could hear her now. "Girl, why did you buy that? I could have made that!"

"That will be $47.81."

Roxanne slapped down her green plastic. "I never leave home without it."

The young man behind the register smiled and hesitated. He pulled an item from a small display next to the register. "Can I interest in you a Light Bright?"

Roxanne frowned. "No, thanks. I had one when I was a kid. Lost all the little pegs. After a while, the only thing I could make was a smiley face."

The cashier smiled. "No, this is a light that you attach to your key chain." He turned the plastic container so she could get a better look. The small, thin object inside looked futuristic.

"Let me show you," he said, pulling out a mass of keys on a ring. "This little puppy is good for getting your key into your door lock at night. It's bright enough to light up your entryway once you get inside the house. The light on this bad boy is so bright, you can see it for a mile at night."

Roxanne marveled at how far technology had come. If the cashier turned salesman was telling the truth, that was. "Sorry. Not interested. Besides, I live in an apartment. I don't need a light to see my lock."

"You know, ma'am, it's only a dollar. A dollar for all this power."

"You must have an overstock," she said, raising an eyebrow.

"Actually, the store manager thought he was getting the deal of a lifetime on those old-fashioned Light Brights, like what you were talking about. But," he continued and lowered his voice, "instead of admitting his mistake and sending them back, he's making us push these off on customers for a dollar a pop."

He twirled the small plastic device between his fingers, eyes mockingly sad and pleading.

Maybe I could give it to Ashley. She lives in a house.

"Okay, I'll take it." She knew Ashley liked things that were different and the gizmo being scanned for her purchase was very different.

The cashier, whose name tag read Elbert, flashed her a grateful smile. She took her purchases and his have a nice day wish, and headed out to meet her sister.

"Hey sweetheart!" Morgan said and gave Roxanne a firm hug. "You've lost weight."

"Twenty pounds," she said, putting her things in the tiny space that passed for the trunk of her sister's Supra.

"Wow." The two women got in. "You look good. Especially in that uniform," Morgan said with a wink. "Have I ever told you I'm proud of you?"

Roxanne grinned. "Every time you see me."

As they sped off toward Casa de Yolanda, the sisters caught up on each other's lives and talked about their new nephew.

"There is no way I would have ever thought Runt would have a baby before us."

"I know," Roxanne said. "She's my kid sister and sometimes I forget she's not a kid anymore."

A wary silence passed between them.

"You going to see him?" Morgan asked.

Roxanne ran her hand across her hair, which was twisted against her head in thin rows. "Yep."

"Oh, Roxy. I'm so happy."

"Well, don't stomp your feet yet. It will probably be a while before Runt and I sing Kumbiya together."

Morgan whipped around a slow-moving car. "You know that girl. If there's one thing she can do, it's forgive."

"Amen!" Roxanne said, wishing she had some of whatever it was that allowed her younger sister to be so forgiving. Whatever that was, she didn't have it. Roxanne knew she could hold a grudge longer than Adam had been dust. But she loved Marti, and ever since her sister had the baby, she'd wanted to patch things up between them.

Morgan patted her knee. "Don't worry, Roxy. Everything will work out."

Her childhood home looked the same. Every time she visited Yolanda, memories of jump rope, Pitty Pat, Mary Mack, skinned knees, and her mother's homemade biscuits flooded her mind. *The march of time leaves footprints on everyone,* she thought. Morgan took her pulley; Roxanne carried her bag from the children's store.

"You ready for this?" Morgan asked.

She took a deep breath. Yolanda could be a pistol sometimes. Staying with her would be interesting. "No, but what am I going to do?"

Morgan knocked on the door. "Next time you'll stay with me."

"I always stay with you, so this time I thought—"

The door whooshed open and a woman who got all of their father's impatience and none of their mother's temperance stood fuming. "You said you'd be here by six. It's almost seven."

Roxanne stepped in. "Worried, huh?"

Morgan followed behind. "We got hung up in traffic."

Yolanda closed the door. "And neither of you has a cell phone?"

"Sorry. We just got to talking about KJ and I didn't think to call."

"Sorry, sis."

Yolanda Allgood stood in the middle of her living room, looking every bit like their mother. Same eyes, dark and inquisitive. Same cheeks, round and high. Same small chin, tapered and delicate. Out of all the sisters, friends and family claimed that she and Yolanda looked the most alike. Of course, neither of them agreed.

"You can put your things in the spare bedroom. You know where it is." Yolanda wiped her hands nervously against the pants she wore. "I finished cooking a long time ago, so the food is cold. You can nuke it if you like."

"You mean you have a microwave!" her sisters said simultaneously.

"Amara bought it for me for Christmas. I never use it though."

It figures, Roxanne chuckled to herself and went to go unpack.

"So, where's your husband? He's such a homebody," Roxanne said, after they had settled into dinner.

"I make him go out with his buddies once a month."

Morgan and Roxanne laughed.

"I have to. Otherwise, I'd never get him out of the house."

Morgan shook her head. "But you all are always so hugged-up. I'm surprised you let him out of your sight."

"After twenty-five years, that hugged-up stuff gets old," Yolanda said with a "girl, please" look on her face.

A ripple of understanding moved through Roxanne. "So I guess even a perfect marriage needs a little tweaking once in a while."

Yolanda nodded. "You got that right."

Roxanne had always admired her oldest sister's relationship. Yolanda had married her junior high school sweetheart. They'd been a loving couple for thirty years and married for the better part of it. She knew if her sister could find a good man like her brother-in-law, Cleon, and could keep him for this many years, then she could have that kind of life too. She needed only look to her immediate family to know that true love was possible. It would find her, or she would find it one day.

It was funny though. She thought she had found true love once. Ten years ago a man named Haughton Storm made her every wish come true before she wished them. If only Marti hadn't opened her big mouth.

"What are you thinking about?" Yolanda asked.

Morgan scooped the last forkful of jambalaya into her mouth. "I'll bet it's Runt."

"Don't talk with your mouth full," the eldest Allgood admonished, then a light of realization relaxed her features. "You going to go see Runt and the baby?"

"She said she is."

Irritation welled inside her. "I can speak for myself, Morgan."

Yolanda beamed. "You really ought to see him. He's so black and pretty. And he smiles all the time."

"And he's fat," Morgan said.

Roxanne sighed as the realization of all she'd been missing hit her soul. "Runt sent me a picture when he was born."

"Oh, no. You should see him now." Yolanda rose from the kitchen table and went into the living room. Within seconds, she returned with a blue fabric-covered scrapbook.

Roxanne flipped through the pages. A twinge of pain pierced her heart at all the memories she'd already missed. Pictures of KJ crying, laughing and drooling with everyone except her. Her callousness was unforgivable and she was determined to end it now.

"When are you going?"

"Tonight," she said.

Since Yolanda refused to buy a dishwasher, she and her sisters set about cleaning the kitchen. Roxanne washed. Morgan rinsed and dried. Yolanda put away. For Roxanne, their work brought back vivid memories. Her brother's smelly socks. Sunday morning haste to church. The ghosts of her parents. The house quaking as the planes passed overhead, the white doilies covering the arms of the chair. Her family had its moments, but all in all they were strong and loving. Something Roxanne was proud of.

"Can I borrow your car?" Roxanne asked, looking at Morgan.

"Sure. Where you going?"

"Marti's"

"I can just drive you."

"Look, I'm still a little apprehensive about this whole thing. If I get in a jam, I can tell Runt I have to leave because I have to get your car back to you."

Yolanda and Morgan exchanged glances. "It's been something like ten years. Let it go," Yolanda said.

Morgan chimed in. "Yeah. Lighten up."

Roxanne ruminated over her ability to hold a grudge about as long as she could hold a note. "That's easy for you to say."

She saw her sister dip her hand quickly into the water, but it was too late for her to prevent the dousing. Morgan grabbed a palm full of dishwater and flung it toward her. "I said lighten up!"

For the next four minutes Roxanne and Morgan engaged in a water fight free-for-all while Yolanda looked on, arms crossed, muttering, "Y'all better clean this up. That's all I've got to say."

Roxanne Allgood had summoned all the courage that had been missing from her life for the past ten years. She could remember the amount of prayers she'd sent to God asking him to cleanse her heart and make her a more forgiving soul. Of all the blessings she'd received in her life, her maker was taking his time with this one. There were people in Roxanne's past who she knew if she saw them today, she'd slap them on sight. More and more it was becoming clear that maybe God was waiting on her to show some sign that she really wanted to change.

She could think of no other place to begin her change than at home with her sister.

The weight of that realization lifted from her shoulders like a ship's anchor.

The conversation she was about to have brought with it memories of two people: Marti and Haughton Storm. She'd tried not to think of Haughton over the past ten years. She'd done a good job until recently. Since her decision to finally try to patch things up between her and her sister, she hadn't been able to get thoughts of her old flame out of her mind. If she were honest, she'd admit that he wasn't an old flame. He was an inferno that had burned savagely and unchecked within her veins. He was fire itself. Even his memory seared her. Made her glow tender and hot with longing and need. In his arms, she felt combustible; a fuse demanding to be ignited. Yes . . . those memories were dangerous. If she weren't careful, she'd set aside the brilliant pain he caused her and seek him out. Beg him to quench her once more.

She tootled along through the interstate and turned on the radio, hoping to get a chance to listen to her brother's latest single, when she noticed the gas gauge. It was getting low, so she decided to stop at the next gas station to fill up.

During her stop, she bought a few more things for the baby—a miniature teddy bear and a lollypop—and headed out. Before she made it to the end of the entrance ramp back on the freeway, a sound like a loud deflating balloon startled her. She uttered a few colorful expletives, pulled over, and stepped out to view the flat tire she anticipated.

The dark night surrounded her. Cars whizzed by just down the road on the interstate. The tire was definitely flat. She pulled her cell phone out of her purse and turned it on. When the large man leaned out of a passing van and grabbed her, the cell phone flew out of her hands with the first five numbers of Yolanda's phone number glowing eerily in the dark.

Three

Haughton Storm hated hospitals. He thought no one in their right mind would go to one voluntarily. No matter how custodians tried to mask it with antiseptic cleaners and Mop 'n Glow, he could always smell death and disease. It was as though an invisible cloud of sickness hung in the air. He was convinced that this floating mist of infirmity created more problems for patients than any medicine invented.

Today, he was determined to check his misgivings at the sliding door of the hospital and pay his teammate Sharky a visit while he recovered from his recent injuries.

He wasn't good at these things, visiting, paying respects, bearing glad tidings. He didn't remember most anniversaries or send cards to people on their birthday. Hell, he'd been known to forget his own birthday. He was a soldier. On call twenty-four hours a day. Most often, when he was called away, he never knew if it was a live mission or training for one. The government believed in keeping the activities of its most elite fighting force confidential in a most extreme way.

He entered an elevator and pushed the button for the fourth floor. Storm had on occasion visited his buddies in the hospital before, but no one this close to him. He felt like he should have brought something to cheer him, but nothing felt right. Finally, he decided he would just have to bring himself. He exited the elevator, hoping that would do.

Sharky was in good spirits when he arrived. The man had just suffered a dangerous amount of blood loss and major surgery, but he was sitting up in bed and smiling through the plastic mask covering his nose and mouth.

"Captain in the sick room!" Sharky proclaimed.

"At ease, soldier," Storm said, turning a small chair beside the bed and straddling it.

"How are they treating you up in here?"

"Like a hero, man. If I even breathe funny, there's a nurse in here before I can blink. They're faster than a speeding bullet."

Guilt riddled Storm like a spray of bullets. He came from a culture where failure was unacceptable. Navy SEAL missions were designed to be in-and-out with no traces. Unless they were doing demo, no one was ever supposed to know that they were there.

"So, how long are they going to keep you on lock down?"

Sharky took a haggard breath. "Whatever you do, don't make me laugh. That hurts like hell."

Sharky was a thin bolt of lightning. Out of all the operators Storm had ever worked with, Sharky had been the one who seemed tireless. He never wore out. Was always ready to defend his country, and never, ever complained of pain. It was a strange experience seeing him like this.

"That mission should not have gone wrong, Sharky. They were waiting for us."

The man sitting bandaged in the bed adjusted his breathing apparatus. "Sure seems that way."

His expression clouded in anger. "I told Shelton I was going to find out what went wrong."

"Don't bother. It's over. The hostage is safe." Sharky gave Storm a quick once-over. "And it's not your fault."

Storm wanted to believe his longtime friend, but he knew the truth. As commander of a SEAL team, it was his job to make sure each mission went off without a hitch.

He resigned himself to spending the afternoon with his buddy and never letting such a mistake happen again.

Storm stared at the invitation in his hand. His high school football coach was finally retiring after forty years at Buckley Academy. When Storm was a teenager, Clyde Foster had been a surrogate father to him and several other young men, especially his three closest friends.

The life of a SEAL meant that you never knew when you were going to be called to duty. When he received the invitation, he wasn't sure if he would be able to attend. But fate had made a way, and it looked like he would have some time after all. He packed an overnight bag and headed for the airport.

The flight from Washington to Texas was uneventful, except for the odd twinge of disappointment in the pit of his stomach. He told himself he'd flown Delta out of convenience, because of the price, because of the service, frequent flier miles, hell, anything.

But that wasn't true.

Recently his thoughts had turned to Roxanne Allgood, a woman he'd once loved more than life. It was as though someone had reached into his memory and brought her out screaming and kicking.

God help him.

The hardest battle he'd ever fought in his life was the battle to get over her. Their breakup was ugly. The sudden thrust of her memory back into his psyche unsettled him. So much so, that he'd booked this flight on Delta airlines. Hoping to get a glimpse of her.

What's wrong with me?

Not only was he misjudging missions, now he was conjuring ghosts.

Enough! he thought and took a magazine from the seat back in front of him and buried himself in an article he'd never remember reading.

Upon arrival, Storm rented a car and breezed through the Dallas traffic, brooding over his invitation to the retirement party. It was addressed to Haughton Storm and guest. The *and guest* part was almost laughable. Who would he bring? Let's see. There was the woman he'd met at Dillards. He knew instinctively that she was in the men's department shopping for more than socks for her cousin. After meeting her a couple of months ago, they'd spent the precious few days he had off from training together. It was carnal. What they'd done to each other's bodies were things he wouldn't dare brag to his buddies about. Wherever *there* was when people said, "Don't even go there," is where they'd gone. His body hadn't felt that ravaged since Hellweek back on the Coronado Strand.

But as soon as he left for a mission, she'd gone shopping again. *It's just as well,* he thought. He couldn't even remember her name now.

There was Karen. But he and Karen had never done more than a bit of rambunctious flirtation. They enjoyed trying to one-up each other. She was the only person in his life that he saw regularly. And that was because she took care of Jake. His half German Shepard, half coyote companion was particular about veterinarians. Karen was the only one he allowed to examine him without trying to dismember. Jake liked Karen. Storm liked Karen. But he also respected her. And he could tell that even though she might have allowed him into her bed, she would never have been comfortable with him in her life. She was the type of woman who needed a man to be around her. To be close. Like Yin and Yang. A man who wasn't around would never do. But he got a kick out of their friendship. She never backed down from him, and held her own with their verbal calisthenics.

Maybe he could take Connie. After all, that's whose house he was staying at while he was in town.

Connie Loghran.

She'd had a crush on him so fierce in high school, it scared him sometimes. He was too young then to understand how one person could love so hard.

She never said anything about it though. He thought of her as a sweet friend, attractive, but not his type. Connie was real close to being a pushover. And Storm liked his women tough and no-nonsense. He knew life was short and he had always wanted to be with someone who could yank life by the horns.

He could have called any of his hometown buddies to stay

with them. But the company he needed now was best described as feminine and soft.

When he'd called Connie after all these years, something told him she would be available and agreeable to him staying with her. He'd have someplace to crash for the days he was there to hang out with his buddies, and he could also get some much-needed sex from a woman who would never demand more from him.

It was perfect.

Haughton Storm thought he was dead. His body felt as though ten semis had rolled over it. His mind felt like oatmeal. The only thing he knew for sure was whatever had happened to him and wherever he was, it wasn't good.

His eyes peeled open and he struggled to pull a thought, any thought, from the soup that was now his memory. *What the hell happened?*

His mind cleared a little and then went black.

He came to again—seconds, hours, or days later. This time he brought a thought back with him. Like a videotape played too many times, the images were jumpy and slurred.

After that, nothing until waking up here. Wherever here is.

He groaned, then moved without knowing it. His feet. His arms. His breathing became more purposeful and he squinted to see. *Where am I?*

The last thing he remembered was the glorious feeling spreading from his groin. He was just about to have the best orgasm he'd had in months, when a bright light exploded at the back of his skull. After popping like an M-80 on the Fourth of July, the light winked out into darkness.

The headache accompanying his slow ascent to consciousness meant that he'd been struck. His severe grogginess and disorientation meant that he'd also been drugged. He worked to piece together the details.

He'd gone to Connie's. Unpacked, showered, and dressed for the reunion. He arrived at Buckley Academy and reminisced like crazy with his buddies. He wished Coach the best of luck on his retirement, gave him his gift, and made a promise to go bar-hopping with his old crew the next night. After that, he'd stopped at a convenience store, picked up a pack of condoms, then headed back to Connie's place and made no bones about what he'd wanted next.

He'd made love to her. She deserved it. All of the feelings she'd had for him welled up in her body like a fire that had been kept on simmer for much too long. He'd cooled that fire with a tenderness that surprised him. His last clear thought was of the tears sparkling in the corners of her eyes. He'd bent nearer to taste them when the light exploded, then went out.

He rolled over, wondering if a jealous boyfriend had caught them. Or if Connie had a husband that had come home from a business trip too early. Either one of those things would have made sense, except for the fact that Storm had no idea where he was. It wasn't Connie's bungalow, that was for sure. The room he was in looked clinical, sanitized. It was small, with bright white lights, white walls, and the table he was lying on. He got up, imagining some kind of accident. He must have been in a hospital. And if it was a jealous boyfriend, or husband, then there was a possibility that Connie was dead.

Four

It didn't take Storm long to change his mind. He got up, a little woozy at first, and then tried the door. It was locked. A bolt of adrenaline put him on alert.

He listened for any sound. There was nothing. He was in trouble.

He paced back and forth as much as his disorientation would let him. There was nothing he could lift and hurl to break the lock, and no matter how hard he shoved and pulled, the door would not yield.

He sat down, recalling his Navy procedures of only offering name, rank, and serial number when captured by the enemy.

"Chief Storm?"

Storm whirled. The voice came from all around him, as though the walls had pores and the sound was oozing through them. "Who are you?"

A cackle. He supposed it was laughter, but it sounded more like foil being chewed.

"They call me Amadeus."

The sound was deafening. Storm balled his fists. Someone was playing with him, and he didn't like playing games.

"What do you want, *Amadeus?*" he asked, words heavy with impatience.

More crackling. "Your. . . prowess."

Anger burned away his control. "You'll have to kill me, freak!"

"Maybe. But not yet."

Questions charged in Storm's mind. Where was he? How

did he get here? Who the hell was Amadeus, and what did he really want? The only thing Storm knew for sure was that he would do everything he could to extricate himself and maybe, just maybe, he'd take out Mr. Am-a-deus for his inconvenience.

"Have you had dinner, Chief Storm?"

Silence. Storm wasn't about to cooperate.

"No, I don't suppose you have. But of course you're trained to go without it, I presume. But I assure you, it's not necessary . . . at the moment."

In combat, Storm lived by one rule: never, ever give an enemy what he wants. Methodically, he went back to the bed and laid down.

The tin buckling replaced the sound of foil crunching. Storm gritted his teeth while he contemplated picking up the bed and hurling it against the door.

Storm sat up with a start. Shaking off the foggy remnants of sleep, he realized he must have dozed off. He looked around. Nothing had changed, except . . . the door he'd struggled against earlier was cracked. He hopped off the bed, wary of any sudden movement through the door.

He waited, poised beside the opening. He was ready to break a bone or two.

Nothing happened.

Obviously the door was ajar to entice him out. He took the chrome handle and pulled. Alarms of all kinds went off in his head. He knew he was violating a premium rule. He also knew that he had a better chance of facing whatever or whoever was holding him on the outside of the room rather than the inside. He swung the door open and swept the perimeter. Nothing. Only a tunnel, long, concrete, and apparently underground. So, he wasn't in a hospital after all.

He checked left, then right. One end was lit brightly, the other dimmed and bleak. He squinted and sprinted down the corridor toward darkness.

His mind worked. They must have wanted him alive, so he wasn't afraid for his life. But he did fear for Connie's life. He would find out what happened to her or die trying.

He was only in the darkness for a few seconds. Then the corridor lit up in front of him as he ran. He suspected he was being watched. Now he was certain. If he was being watched, he was probably being monitored as well. Storm stopped running.

"Where is she, Amadeus?"

"Who?" came the silvery reply.

"Connie! The woman I . . . the woman I was with!"

"Hmmm," the voice responded, vibrating like thin thunder all around him. "Let's discuss that after dinner."

A cold knot formed in his stomach. He had to find out what happened to Connie. And it seemed that despite his effort, his mysterious host had the upper hand. For now.

"Just follow the lights until you get to the big door. Don't get happy. It's not a door to the outside. Just a door to me."

Storm ground his teeth and followed the lights.

When he got to the door he waited, but not for long. A loud click and the door swung slowly open. In front of him was another tunnel, not quite as long as the one he was in. Blocking his path, but just barely, was a man of moderate height, but slender beyond what could confidently be called healthy.

"What . . . ?" Storm began and lunged toward the man.

Amadeus hopped backward and two large men stepped in front of him.

"Be careful there, Chief Storm," the thin man said. "Let's not get off on the wrong foot." Amadeus's cold smile made Storm's flesh crawl. "Let's walk and talk, shall we?"

They led him to an elevator at the end of the corridor. Storm made detailed notes in his mind of the turns he made, the paces they walked, the button pushed on the elevator. He would catalog every activity for use later.

The elevator opened into a hallway that angled up toward a door. When they reached the door, the man he assumed was

Amadeus passed his hand over an infrared sensor, and the door opened. The four men stepped inside a large living room. Like something you would expect in any residential district. But Storm's senses told him he was far away from that.

He had a look around. Amadeus's furnishings were like what you would see in a Victorian museum. The furniture—even Amadeus himself—looked like it should be roped off with signs posted on it that said DON'T TOUCH. A harpsichord was the only thing missing. Ostentatious. Stuffy and full of itself. Shiny wood with curves and flowers. Couch with fabric that looked more like wallpaper. The first parlor he'd ever seen that really was a parlor. Storm shuddered with disgust. Too many frills and froufrous.

The change in temperature from the tunnel to the living space told him that they had just come from underground. Even with the air conditioning on, the humidity was unmistakable. He was near water. Lots of it.

Amadeus's smile was crooked, as if the left side of his mouth wasn't working. "Trying to figure out where you are, Chief Storm? Let's just say . . . you're not in Kansas anymore."

A few more feet and they were in the dining room.

"I would be honored if you would have dinner with me. I can offer you a menu that you can hardly refuse. Twenty-ounce porterhouse, baked beans, Texas toast, Ice Mountain beer. Those are your favorites, aren't they?

"I'm honored to have you as a guest in my home, Mr. Storm."

Storm glared at the thin man, wondering how he knew so much about him. "What do you want with me?"

"Please," Amadeus said, his tiny teeth glistening with spit. "I hate to discuss business on an empty stomach. I'm sure a person of your background understands the importance of keeping up your strength."

Storm had already sized up the four men. Amadeus was a fragile twig that could be easily snapped in two. He was sure he could take the other three men individually, but together . . . ?

His muscles tensed. He had no choice. It was a chance he would have to try and take. If he was successful, there were all kinds of things he could do to the thin man to make him talk. Make him tell him how to get out of the building.

"I can see those soldier procedures whipping through your brain. Save your thoughts. You'll need them later."

Storm's eyes narrowed. "What do you mean?"

Amadeus's eyes grew wild and wide. He stomped his foot like a spoiled child. "You'll be civil, Mr. Storm, and cooperate, or you'll never find out what happened to sweet, little Miss Connie."

Storm clenched his mouth tighter and followed Amadeus to a long dining room table that was preset for two.

In short order they were served a meal much as Amadeus had described it. All of Storm's favorite foods. Even his favorite, chocolate ice cream, came as the next-to-the-last course, right before coffee.

An old woman wrinkled and bent with age traveled back and forth from the kitchen to the table, bringing food and filling their glasses with wine.

Storm had been quiet while his captor spoke in his tin can voice about military life and how fortunate Storm was to be able to use his brawn in service to his country. "Dinner's over, Amadeus," he said, irritation lacing his words.

Amadeus lit a cigarette, pulled a deep drag, and released it into the air. "Yes, yes," Amadeus said and flicked an ash. "Do I look familiar to you, Mr. Storm?"

"No," Storm lied. He'd recognize those mismatched eyes anywhere. He was the man his team pulled out of the jungle during his last S & R mission. The thought turned his blood to ice.

The old woman came in with a coffeepot, refilled their cups and lumbered arthritically out of the room.

"Twenty years ago, my name was Franklin Jones."

Storm sat up straighter in the chair. That name sounded familiar.

"When I was younger, I made a very good living playing

games. Video games. I won several championships. Actually," he chuckled, "I won them all."

Storm thought back. He remembered a time years ago when the media had a field day with a young kid they dubbed a genius. Storm's military career was just beginning then, so he couldn't recall many details, only that the kid had beaten every video game thrown at him. Storm didn't follow the story, but members of his training squad talked often about this strange-looking albino kid who was taking the gaming world by storm. Then one day, he just disappeared.

"After about a year, I was dubbed 'Amadeus' Jones because some reporter likened my mastery of video game playing to a symphony."

Amadeus's fingers were as thin as the cigarette he held between them, and his skin was just as white. A long ash dangled from the cigarette as Amadeus stared at a spot on the far wall.

"I kept hoping for a good game. One that would give me a challenge I couldn't predict. But each game I played was the same. It was as though I was plugged into the circuitry. I won every time.

"After a while, the sting of disappointment replaced the rush of victory I felt. There was no challenge. Meanwhile, I endorsed every electronic game accessory on the planet. I was the Michael Jordon of endorsements. Pretty soon the very thought of a video game or anything associated with it made me sick. I'd gorged myself for years and I swore I'd never touch another joystick or controller again."

"Don't tell me. You've changed your mind and need a 'worthy opponent.' Sorry. The last video game I played was Pac-Man."

"You almost had it, Storm. I have changed my mind about gaming. I never really got it out of my system. However, I don't want to play you. I want to *be* you."

Storm's stomach turned. Not only was he in trouble, he was in deep trouble. The man sitting across from him was definitely ill. He didn't know how the man knew so much about him, but now it didn't matter.

Amadeus stood. "Do you see this body?" He held his arms out to his sides. The bell-shaped sleeves of the ruffled shirt he wore hung down limply from his arms. His pants were skin-tight with large black and metallic gold flowers splattered against them.

Even in the flamboyant outfit, the man still looked as though he would become airborne from a good sneeze. "What about it?"

"I've always had the metabolism of three people. For years, I thought it had something to do with my albinism, but the doctors have never found any connection. The life of a skinny, geeky kid is hell, Mr. Storm. But I imagine you don't know anything about that."

Storm continued to look on impatiently. The old woman emerged again. This time she spoke.

"I'm going to bed now, Frankie."

The woman, who was every bit the epitome of an old hag, turned and headed out of the room, but not before stealing one last look at Storm.

Amadeus looked bored. "Goodnight, mother."

Storm's eyes widened.

"Everyone is always so surprised when they meet my mother for the first time. Don't let her appearance fool you. She's got a mind like a mathematician. And at a time when every bully in the school had his or her turn beating me up, my mother had the presence of mind to put me into a school especially for those with special intellectual gifts."

The three sidekicks at the table hadn't said a word and had barely blinked during this whole dinner and disclosure. They truly were minions.

"All of my intelligence and I've never been able to figure out a way to gain more than one hundred and thirty pounds. And I was only that heavy when I laid around for a month and did nothing but eat just to see if I could gain anything. I gained three pounds."

Storm was tired and bored with the story. "Amadeus—"

"No. You need to know this." He leaned on the table, his

chalky face inches from Storm's. "Playing video games always allowed me to do what my fragile body had never allowed me to do. Stand up for myself, lift things, break and smash things, stay out in the sun, beat a man to a bloody pulp, run like lightning. So, Mr. Storm, when I say I want you to save me, I'm not kidding. If I don't find some way to overcome the limitations of this . . . this body, I will truly lose my mind." Amadeus sighed and took a deep breath. "I'm going to do that, Mr. Storm, through you."

This time Storm laughed. It was like he'd been swallowed in a gothic dream. He eyed the kitchen. At least now he knew where the knives were. And although Amadeus didn't show much affection for his mother, she was still his mother. Somehow he would have to get to her and thrust a knife against her throat. Then Amadeus might be more agreeable to letting him go instead of taking his place. "There's only one me. Sorry."

Amadeus's lips peeled back into a skin-crawling smile. "That's precisely why I chose you. You see, I own an island. Therese Island, which is where you are now."

Storm's pulse quickened. He'd been more than kidnapped. He'd been abducted. He would need to do more than overpower his captor, he would have to figure a way to escape the island. He didn't recognize the name, but if it was within six miles from land, he could swim for it. SEALs were called frog men for a reason.

"I used the money I amassed from winning all those contests and endorsing all those products, to create the ultimate game, Mr. Storm. A game I call Asgard."

There was a bone-chilling iciness to Amadeus's words. The temperature in the room seemed to drop ten degrees.

"Asgard is —"

"The home of the Gods," Storm finished.

Amadeus's smile was blinding. "Very good, Storm. I see I've not only chosen wisely, I've chosen brilliantly!"

"High school mythology, Amadeus, now enough with the self-absorption. Why am I here?"

"You're here, my most revered warrior, because I've transformed this entire island into the ultimate game. Which . . ." Amadeus spun around in a circle then faced him again. "You are going to play for me."

Now he knew for sure. The thin man was a lunatic. Lunatics were best handled with kid gloves and walked around lightly.

Storm stroked his chin to feign interest. "What kind of game?"

"A quest, Mr. Storm. The only kind of game that matters. You will represent me and do the things I've dreamed of doing all my life. And I will watch you. From a safe distance of course."

"What am I after in this quest?"

"Your freedom."

Amadeus took his seat again across from Storm. His eyes flickered with delight. "There is a helicopter and a pilot at the far end of the island waiting to take you anywhere you wish to go. All you have to do is get there."

"I suppose there are obstacles."

"Yes. But nothing someone as highly trained as yourself can't handle."

All eyes were on him. Amadeus's and those of his three goons. They were cold, dead eyes. The eyes of people with souls that were easily co-opted. The eyes he'd seen in some of the enemies of America he'd come across on his missions.

He folded his arms. "Sorry to disappoint you, Amadeus, but I'm not good at games. So, you'll just have to let me go."

Amadeus sat forward and leaned on the back of his hands. "You can go at any time, Mr. Storm. My front door is unlocked. But I must tell you, as soon as you step through it, the Asgard mechanism is tripped and the game begins."

Storm ground his teeth in exasperation.

Amadeus turned to the man closest to him. "Go and get Professor Baer."

The large man disappeared in the same direction as Amadeus's mother. While Storm wondered what now, Amadeus gazed at him unblinkingly.

Storm might have won their stare-down if it hadn't been for

Amadeus's eyes. There was something about the man's eyes that had been bothering him all night. His eyes were two different colors.

Guido number one returned. A portly gentleman ambled alongside of him carrying a suitcase-sized metal box.

"Haughton Storm, may I present Carl Baer. Carly, show our guest our creation."

The round man placed the suitcase on the table and opened it. Storm noted the slight tremor in his hands.

Inside the case was what looked like a New Age backpack with a network of multicolored cords the width of a telephone cord. At the end of one cord was a gray plastic rectangle. It was flat and resembled a blank credit card.

"This is Odin's Eye. It's a device that will allow you to monitor your . . . strength level. But more importantly, it's a proximity detector. When the Adversaries are near, the screen illuminates and tells you just how near."

Storm stood. So did the two remaining goons at the table. "I'll bet my pension that it also monitors me."

The man nodded. His double chins jiggled against each other. "Yes. That's correct."

Storm moved closer and examined the device. It wasn't big, but still he didn't expect it to be as light as it was. If what Professor Baer said was true, there were plenty of organizations that would kill a small country to be where he was right now. He had to get away and tell his superiors what he'd seen. But he couldn't do that by risking his life in some sicko's warped fantasy.

He placed the contraption back in its box. "There's no way I'm going to do this. You can torture me if you like. All you'll get is my name, birth date, and social security number. You might even get my religion. But you'll never get my cooperation."

Baer's head snapped toward Amadeus, eyes bright with concern.

Amadeus's eyes hardened like two flint stones. He glanced at another one of his minions. "Get the woman."

Storm's heart beat normally for the first time since he'd come to. *Connie!* Connie was alive. Now all he had to do was figure out a way to get her safely off the island.

The thin man rose, clasped his hands around his back and walked toward the window. He stared out. "You see, Chief Storm, I already know your date of birth. Your social security number. And your religion."

Storm stiffened. "Bull."

Amadeus spoke without turning. "March 8th, 1964. 515-89-1234. And when you're not on a mission or training for one, you attend Holy Name Baptist Church on Meadow Street."

Storm's patience had worn away. He lunged at Amadeus. The minions caught him. He thrashed against them. One of them caught a right cross, the other a boot to the stomach. They released him and he headed for the man whose two different colored eyes he wanted to blacken. He drew back his fist to swing and a voice suspended him in time like a scene from *The Matrix*.

"Storm?"

The innocent brown face he'd expected, the delicate frame and demure countenance were nowhere to be found. "Roxanne!" he shouted.

The minions recovered from their beatdown and grabbed him solidly. He barely noticed. The only sensation he had was that of his heart beating like it wanted out of his chest. Of all the times he'd thought of her in the past ten years, she looked more beautiful than any image his imagination could create.

Amadeus turned slowly, as if spinning on a pedestal. His thin mouth grinned a nasty little smirk.

"You two do know each other, don't you?"

The biggest goon of the goons held Roxanne's arm. Her hands were tied behind her back.

"Let her go, Jones."

His pale skin flushed pinkly. "I'd be happy to. The moment you're safely on board that helicopter, I'll set her free."

Roxanne frowned. "Oh, no. Don't tell me you're here to rescue me."

Her words stunned him into silence.

She turned to Amadeus. "I'd rather die."

Storm's anger exploded and he pulled against the men holding him. Baer jumped aside. Storm's eyes narrowed on Roxanne. "You would rather die than have anything to do with me, wouldn't you?"

Her face clouded with anger. "If they don't kill me, I'll kill myself before I'd have anything to do with you."

Baer shot Amadeus a nervous glance. Amadeus's earlier glee faded fast into confusion. "But you, you said that you cared about her."

Roxanne's eyes widened in surprise.

Storm went still. His blood was chilling in his veins. "I would cut my tongue out before saying such a thing. Of all the things you know about me, you don't know anything important."

A frightening thought ran through his mind. "What happened to Connie?"

Roxanne recoiled. "Who's Connie?"

Storm ignored her. "Amadeus! What happened to Connie?"

Amadeus strode to a small cherry wood table near the living room. He opened a door and pulled out a photograph. He glanced at it, his face a tight pucker of frustration. He returned quickly and thrust the picture in front of Storm's face.

The pain was exquisite. A scream broke from his lips and his body went slack in the goons's arms. "You son of a bitch!"

Amadeus took long strides and stood beside Roxanne. He touched her hair. She jerked back. His slap came quickly across her face. She took it full force, never flinching. Her glare was hot enough to burn through steel.

A bolt of anger burst open in Storm and he propelled himself toward Amadeus with such force he dragged the men holding him two feet across the room.

"It seems there's something there after all. Well, my dear soldier. I think you'll be entering the world of Asgard very soon. Or else," he said, grabbing Roxanne's head and locking it under his arm, "I'll have another pretty picture for my scrapbook."

"No!" Storm shouted.

The bright glow of vindication showed all over Amadeus's face.

Haughton Storm's body went slack. He glanced at the woman whom he once loved more than life itself. Then he turned to Amadeus.

"I'll do it," he said, finally. "I'll play your game."

Five

"Nice of you to come around," Amadeus said. His words droned out calmly, but his expression held an overdose of glee. And somehow his wild hair seemed even wilder. An unruly celebration on his head. "We'll begin tomorrow. First light." He clasped the shoulders of Professor Baer, but kept his eyes on the large man holding Roxanne. "Take her away."

She eyed Storm suspiciously. "Don't give in on my account." Roxanne struggled. "What if he doesn't win?"

"For your sake, he better."

A sharp pain shot through Storm's heart as the minion manhandled Roxanne and led her back though the corridor. His anger flared. "Before this is over, I'm going to choke you with my bare hands. God help me, because I'm going to enjoy it."

Storm didn't think Amadeus's face could get any paler. He was wrong. The man looked as though someone had just dusted him with heavy flour. "Save your aggression, Storm. You'll need it later."

Storm glanced around, wondering what nightmare he'd been dropped into and what he could find to help him get out of it.

As they escorted him to the corridor, he spied a suit of armor in the corner of the room. There was a long axe in the armored hand. Storm wondered if it was real.

Guess I'll have to find out, he thought.

Just as they entered the doorway, Storm jumped up, straightened his legs into a sitting position and let gravity pull him down. The sudden move pulled his escorts into each other and they cracked heads. When their bodies parted, Storm propelled himself upward, prepared to battle, but the two had conked themselves out cold.

He dashed to the axe and snatched it from the armor along with a bronze shield.

He glanced in the dining room. Amadeus and Baer cowered in the corner. They were shaking against each other like two bug-eyed men suffering from an acute case of Parkinson's disease. Storm's first notion was to ram them through, but he had to get to Roxanne.

He sprinted toward the corridor, leapt over the two sleeping giants, and headed after the third.

"What the?" he heard the big man say as his footfalls grew nearer. The man turned then shoved Roxanne into a room. He heard a smack and the clinking of gears as the door began to close. Storm swung the axe into the air and brought the blunt end down against the man's skull. The crack echoed through the tunnel and so did the thud as the man hit the floor.

"Roxanne!" Storm shouted and rushed to the door just as it clinked shut. He threw down the axe and shield and pulled hard on the metal door. It wouldn't budge. He called out to Roxanne, but the quick glimpse of her he caught before the door closed told him she'd hit her head against the wall and was probably unconscious.

"I'm coming, Roxanne," he muttered, wielding the axe again. His aim was sure and it came down in the space between the door and the seal. The axe rocked vigorously back and forth then he forced it in further for leverage. Once it was in and angled toward the inside of the door, he leaned in, using all his weight to force the lock. His muscles burned with the strain. "Aaugh!"

The latch broke and the door slid open. Roxanne was sitting up and rubbing her forehead.

He ran to her. His hands roamed her body as he searched rapidly for injuries.

She slapped his hands away, disgust puckering her face. "Stop touching me! I'm alright!"

He jerked his hands from her as if she were on fire. "Then come on. We're getting out of here."

He extended his hand. She frowned at it first then offered hers. Their eyes locked for a brief exchange of frustration, and then they sprinted down the tunnel together.

She stumbled beside him, a fog of confusion wrinkling her face.

They continued down the corridor and through adjacent tunnels, quickly discovering that they were in a small catacomb of holding cells. Most of the doors were locked, and it became obvious the only way out was back the way they came.

"Hey," Roxanne said, shrinking away. "We can't go back there!"

"It's the only way out."

"Paleface and his goons will be waiting for us."

They came upon the shield. It was right where they'd left it, but Roxanne's escort was gone.

Storm picked up the shield. "You better take this. It's not much of a weapon, but at least it's something."

Roxanne took the shield then stared at him. The look she gave him would haunt him forever. She was afraid. Storm had never known her to be afraid of anything in her life.

"What's going on, Storm? What are we doing here?"

"I'm not sure I understand it all myself, but I do know this: you won't be hurt again. Amadeus and his cronies will all die slow deaths for hurting you."

"Haughton . . ." she said, touching his arm.

"First, let's get you the hell outta here."

He held the axe ready and pushed Roxanne behind him. Of course, she would have never been caught dead, or even in a crazy man's house, walking behind a man. So, they approached the entrance to the living area side-by-side.

Surprisingly, the door was open and the two sleeping beauties were gone.

"It's got to be a trap," Roxanne said.

"Shhh!" Storm admonished. "Stay here."

Roxanne walked right beside him. "You must be out of your mind."

Amadeus, Baer, and his muscle were gone. Storm headed for the kitchen, hoping against hope to get his hands on a knife. The door at the end of the hall was locked.

After a few minutes of careful searching, they found themselves confined to Amadeus's living and dining rooms.

"What the hell?" Storm said.

"Mr. Storm."

The voice came from all around them.

"Amadeus!" Storm shouted, looking around. "Your game was over before it started. Now let us out of here!"

"Like I said before. You can leave at any time. You just have to use the front door."

Suddenly, a place in the wall that he hadn't noticed before opened into a foyer, complete with a front door.

"Odin's Eye is still on the table, Mr. Storm. Take it and start the game. I promise I won't harm your lady love there. Unlike you with my staff. She can wait here until you make your way through the game and then when you finish, she's free to go."

His voice sounded tinny and made Storm grit his teeth.

"Come on," Storm said, grabbing Roxanne's hand. "Maybe there's a way to get around this game, disable it, or just not cooperate."

"What about that thing on the table?" she asked, walking with him.

"Forget that. I'm not going to let him think he's got the upper hand."

Roxanne stared at the open door, then she turned to Storm. "Amadeus wants you. So, if you want to go through that door, you go right ahead. I'll take my chances here."

Storm's frustration had reached a new level. One of the first lessons he'd learned as a SEAL was to never leave a teammate behind. While he wouldn't consider Roxanne someone on his team, she definitely wasn't the enemy.

"Not an option," he said.

"Look," she said, crossing her arms. "If I'm supposed to be the bait for this thing, then it would be better for both of us if I stayed here."

Roxanne thought of the thin man she'd seen. She'd bet that he didn't get many dates.

"Maybe I can work an angle from in here. Get under his skin somehow."

The sound of footfalls thudding their way interrupted their disagreement.

"This is nonnegotiable," he said, picking her up.

Roxanne struck him repeatedly as he hoisted her over his shoulder like a sack of potatoes. "Storm! You big lummox! Let me go!"

Their approach must have triggered a sensor. As soon as he stepped into the entryway, the vibrant timbre of a harpsichord filled the area and the door clinked open. Storm dashed through it.

The door smacked shut behind them, cutting off the concerto, but neither noticed. Roxanne's pounding intensified and one of her blows struck him at a sore spot on his back. He winced and tossed her off his shoulder. She hit the ground with a thud and glared at him. "You stupid—"

"Stupid! I just rescued your ass!"

"Do I look like a damsel in distress to you?" Roxanne got up and pushed the dirt off the back of her jeans.

He looked her up and down. "Damn sure!"

"Sorry to burst your bubble, but I can take care of myself. I'll find my own way off the island. You go play Amadeus's game."

Storm watched in disbelief as Roxanne headed back to the house. When she reached for the door, there was a pop and a loud buzzing sound. It knocked Roxanne all the way back to the spot where she originally landed.

He rushed to her side. A faint chemical smell rose from her pores. Her eyes were closed, but she was still breathing. A quick look at her hand showed her fingers already red and swelling.

Her head lolled to one side then righted itself. Her eyes peeled open. "What?" she asked.

"Nothing," he said, helping her up. "It's just that you may want to reconsider that damsel in distress thing."

Her eyes narrowed. She yanked away.

They both stood staring upward with wide eyes and mouths that were slightly open. Amadeus was right.

They weren't in Kansas anymore.

They took a few short steps, marveling at all the green they saw. Everything around them was off the scale. Enormous trees. Giant bushes. Overgrown brambles. Thick stalks of grass. Roxanne felt as though she'd just been miniaturized to squirrel size and placed outside.

Lush smells assaulted her. They were musty and dank like rotten mud and the potent aroma of living things. Roxanne wondered if they were in some kind of forest. Something stung her. She lifted her forearm to see the largest mosquito she'd ever seen in her life. *Jungle,* she thought and smashed the bug with her hand.

The busy and energetic sounds of Mozart were replaced by the sounds of animals, birds, and rustling leaves.

Roxanne caught up with Storm, who was already walking on the path leading from the house. "Where in the heck are we?"

He shrugged, still looking around. "He said an island. Therese Island. Ever hear of it?"

"No."

"That makes two of us. Look, I'm going to need you to stay close. Apparently he's rigged up this whole place as some kind of video game. No telling what might happen. The only thing I know about video games is Pac-Man, so who knows, there may be some goblins lurking around here."

Roxanne stared at Storm. "A video game? So is he watching us?"

"I am indeed, Ms. Allgood. I am indeed."

Storm stopped. "Jones. You said you would let me go if I made it to the end of the island. Which way is the end?"

The thin metal sound of his laughter echoed through the trees. "If you hadn't run off without the Odin's Eye, you might have been able to figure that out. I must admit, you've taken some of the fun out of the game for me. But not much. You'll just have to wing it."

"What do we do now?" Roxanne asked, hoisting the shield.

Storm's features remained stoic. "We find some water."

They trudged along in silence. Only the sounds of birds taking flight, insects calling out, and a strong wind broke the quiet. Roxanne's mind struggled to put meaning to everything that had happened so far. She had no idea how she got here, no idea where she was or how long she'd been here. She only knew three things. Her family had probably worried themselves into a tizzy about her; when she'd seen Haughton Storm for the first time in ten years, her attraction to him was still severe; and, thirdly, she was still as pissed at him as ever. The fact that she was stranded on an island with him was infuriating.

"What are we doing here, Storm?"

"You know about as much as I do. The guy's nuts. He wants me to be his guinea pig. And he thought threatening to harm you would do the trick."

"But that's what I don't understand. Why would he think that?"

Storm shook his head. "I have no idea."

He stopped at an area that wasn't as thick with vegetation. "Let's sit here for a while."

Roxanne took a seat. "I thought we were looking for water."

"We are."

Roxanne fingered a few blades of grass. They were sturdy, ribbed, and moistened by the humidity. "What do we have to do, wring the water from the leaves?"

"Shhh!" he said. "Watch the birds. They usually fly in patterns. From their nest to food. From their nest to water. If you watch the birds, they'll tell you where the water is."

Roxanne watched him closely, although he seemed to have no interest in looking at her or maintaining eye contact of any kind. A bird shrilled overhead and Roxanne realized she'd made a mistake. She was having a devil of a time looking away. Despite her anger, frustration, and the large grudge she still held on to, when she looked at Haughton Storm, she still saw the most handsome man she'd ever laid eyes on. The years had not been kind to him. They'd been golden, luxurious, and made him appear more refined than she remembered. Less reckless.

Hair dark and close-cropped, angular face, narrow, seducing eyes, bright white sexy teeth, and muscles stuffed tightly into his skin—straining to escape.

"Why would Amadeus use me as bait? I mean did you say something to him or hint in some way that—?"

"No. One minute I was . . . at a friend's house, the next I woke up here."

Two large white birds fluttered around each other and continued past the spot where Roxanne and Storm sat watching.

"Connie?"

Storm shuddered and rose to his feet. "Yes." He spat on the ground and slammed his fist into a tree. Then a man Roxanne didn't know came through Storm's facial features. This man looked as though he could kill coolly, without disturbing the rhythm of his heart. A chill moved through her.

"I'll find a way to punish him. She deserves that much."

"Was she someone special?" Roxanne asked.

Of course she was, Storm thought. She was sweet, demure, mellow. She was so giving, never thinking of herself first. If he hadn't been trying to use her, maybe she would still be alive.

"Yes," he said finally. "She was very special."

The twinge of jealousy surprised her. After all these years. Roxanne chided herself and reminded herself that she couldn't stand Haughton Storm and that she should act accordingly.

"It must be straight ahead," Storm said.

Roxanne nodded.

He held out a stopping hand. "Three things. First, pay attention to what you do. We are in the home of millions of creatures. Everything you touch, everything you step on, everything you sit on, lean against, is something's home. In this kind of environment, those somethings are often aggressive and will defend their territory no matter what the size of their enemies. Second, if there's a path, stick to it. Ticks tend to infest untraveled areas. So try not to brush against too many things. Third, we may be inside some kind of challenge zone. Be ready for anything.

"Oh, and one more thing, I'm in charge."

Roxanne stood then. "Says who?"

"I'm not going to repeat it."

Now all of the reasons why she disliked Haughton Storm came bubbling hotly up to the surface. "You're not the only person here with some rank. And I'm not some delicate little flower that needs protecting. I can take care of myself!"

"No," he mumbled. "You never were delicate."

"What?"

"You can talk that bull if you want to, but the truth is you're here, just like I am. Right now the only difference between us is that I'm trained to exist in any terrain against any enemy at all costs. And that means I might have a thing or two to say that you might benefit from listening to. Now are we going to stand here and argue or are we going to locate some water?"

They'd been in each other's company for less than an hour and already they were butting heads. The only thing that had changed about Storm was his looks. He was still stubborn and bullish. She would not be ordered around like some flunky under his command.

"You can bark orders all you want. I don't report to you. It seems to me we are *both* in a predicament here. We can either argue against each other or work in tandem to get the heck off of this . . ." She slapped another mosquito. This one on her neck. "Bug-infested island!"

Storm's eyes narrowed. He obviously was not used to being challenged. "Let's get to the water."

They trudged down an old footpath that was being re-claimed by vegetation. Some parts of the path were barely visible from the encroaching shrubs and underbrush.

They walked single-file, Storm in front. "Watch out for tree roots," he said. "They can jut up from the ground unex-pectedly. And so can branches that have fallen and are only partially covered by the ground." He turned around and gave her a quick, hot glare. "I wouldn't want you to fall into a mound of fire ants. *That* would be unfortunate."

The sarcasm dripping from his voice irked her. "Shouldn't we try to find shelter or make a fire?"

"If we don't locate a source of water, neither of those things will matter."

After fifteen minutes, Roxanne grew concerned. "How far do birds fly for food and water?"

"Miles, if they have to. But if this really is an island, then we shouldn't have to go too far."

Humph, she thought to herself. *Men always think they know everything. Especially this man.* The very first date they had ever gone on, he'd been driving a ramshackle pick-up. He didn't have sense enough to tell her that the darn thing had a slow leak in one of the tires. When she saw how low it was and suggested that they stop and fill it up, he'd taken some backwoods road claiming that a gas station was close by and that they shouldn't have to go too far. When the tire went completely flat, they ended up walking three miles on a dirt road at eleven o'clock at night. By the time she got home, it was after midnight. She was dusted with dirt and her feet screamed with pain. That should have been her first clue that Haughton Storm was about as hardheaded as they came.

Just when she was about to suggest that they try a different route, she heard the sound of water babbling just ahead and to the left. They veered a bit off of the main footpath and came to a small clearing. A tiny tributary of water meandered on their left.

Storm hunted around for a few moments, rustling through bushes, kicking over rocks. He grunted in frustration. He looked Roxanne up and down. The intensity of his scrutiny warmed her in the tropical climate.

"Where's all that stuff you ladies carry around? Most women keep an entire make-up case on them, don't they?"

"I don't know. When I woke up here, everything I had with me was gone. My purse, KJ's presents."

A thick onyx eyebrow lifted. "Who's KJ?"

"My nephew. Marti had a baby."

For a moment, he was thoughtful. "KJ? Hmmm. For Kenyon Junior."

She stared at him in disbelief. "How did you know that?"

He almost cracked a smile. "Unlike you and I, Marti and I have kept in contact. She called me when she had the baby."

"You're kidding!"

"As a matter of fact, I talk to Morgan and Ashley too. Just not as often as I talk to Marti."

"I don't believe this! They never said anything to me about it."

"I'll bet not. They probably thought you would blow your stack. Like you're doing now."

"I am not blowing my stack! I'm just . . . surprised."

"Why? Because someone in this world thinks I'm a nice guy?"

Her eyebrows rose. She crossed her arms. "Frankly, yes."

He turned away from her, kept his eyes on the foliage. "They seem to think I'm the one that got away." He turned back to her then, eyes dark and daring.

Handkerchief, wallet, lighter receipt from the drugstore. Condoms. He opened the pack of condoms and handed one to Roxanne. "Here blow this up."

"What for?"

"For the water. I'm going to fill these from that creek. Then we can set up someplace and purify it."

Roxanne sighed. Of course she didn't think that her ex-beau would have been celibate all these years since their breakup. She hadn't been. But she was angry with herself for feeling a tiny bit of resentment. It was like the fact that he had

a relationship with someone was being thrown in her face.
Then she reminded herself that that someone was now dead.

"I'm sorry, Storm," she said. "About your friend."

He nodded, fresh pain flaring his nostrils.

He filled three condoms and strapped them to his belt.
"Let's find someplace to camp and I'll get us some reason-
ably clean water."

Roxanne walked single-file behind him once more. Her
skin was clammy and the high humidity made her want to
suck air. They had probably walked a mile, but the heat made
it feel as though they'd been walking all day. Sweat glistened
on her arms, which were prickling up from all the bug bites.
She'd stopped killing the insects as they bit her and started
swinging her arms to keep them from landing on her skin.

Then the itching started. Like a blinding fury beneath her
skin, each bite welled up and was driving her crazy. At first
she tried not to scratch. When the itching became unbearable,
she started to gently rub at the areas. That wasn't enough, and
before long she was scratching both arms at once.

"Ooh!" she hollered.

Storm whipped around. "What's the matter?"

"These dad-gum mosquitoes and bugs. They keep biting
me!"

He grabbed her hands. "Stop scratching. If your bites start
bleeding, they could become infected out here. And that
would be bad." He moved closer and sniffed her arms and her
neck. "It's your perfume. They must be attracted to it. You'll
have to wash it off as soon as we purify this water."

He released her hands. And not a moment too soon. She
couldn't figure out what was making her more crazy, the itching or the familiar and protective sensation she got from his
hands holding hers.

"Here," he said, taking off his shirt. "This will make it
harder for the insects to get to you."

She slid her arms into the long sleeves of his shirt. "What
about you?" She took in the sinewy mass of his arms in the
white sleeveless tank top. "They will eat you alive."

"I'm not wearing any cologne, so it won't be as bad."

"If you say so," she said, and shooed away a large insect trying to land on Storm's back.

They found a clearing not too far from the stream. Storm took a twig and whittled the end against a boulder. Then he stuck the sharp end into his pant leg.

"What are you doing?" Roxanne asked.

He looked up, surprised that she might be the least bit concerned about him. "Just making some minor alterations."

After cutting off the bottom of his pant leg, Storm tied the end to make a funnel. Then he arranged layers of sand and rocks inside.

"Take off your bra."

"What?" she asked.

"Your bra. I need it to hang the filter."

"I know you, Haughton Storm. There's probably million ways to hang a filter, and using my bra is just one of them."

He stared unblinking in her direction. "You're right. But having something actually made with elastic makes it a lot easier to hang." His expression never changed.

She reached under the blouse she wore and unhooked her bra. Then she slid the straps down her arms and pulled it out.

"Here," she said, handing him the lilac, laced garment. He took it, but not before his eyes settled briefly where her breasts sat freely on her chest. She frowned and pulled his shirt tighter around her. "How do you know there's not some real water somewhere?"

"I don't know anything for sure, except that I'm not going to rely on Amadeus for anything."

Storm used the whittled branch to tear a small slit in the middle of her bra and then inserted the bottom of the filter through it. He used the straps to tie the contraption to a low hanging branch. Then he placed a makeshift trough directly beneath it to catch the water. He emptied the water from the condoms into the filter.

"We won't get much from that. Stay here. I'm going for more."

She nodded and swatted away the largest fly she'd ever seen.

Roxanne watched him disappear into the brambles, then turned to see the first drip of water from the filter. The first semi-calm moment she'd had since she'd been abducted. If she wasn't careful the audacity of it all would freak her out. Just a short time ago she was headed to her sister's house to heal a wound that had long been sore. Now she wondered if she'd waited too late to make things right.

Roxanne scratched her arm and winced at the sharp scratch of her nail and the warm trickle against her finger as a result. *Dear God,* she prayed. *Please let me live to see my family again.*

Six

Bali. Victoria's Secret. Halston. She threw them all out of her underwear drawer in handfuls.

"It's not here!" she shouted.

Roxanne Allgood gritted her teeth and charged out of the bedroom she shared with her sister Morgan.

"Morgan!" she shouted. She ran down the stairs and into the den where she knew her younger sister was probably hugged up with her latest boyfriend.

She stomped into the room and, sure enough, her sister and boyfriend number whatever were trying to choke each other with their tongues.

"Morgan! I know you hear me calling you!"

Her sister broke the spit fest she was having. "What!"

"Where's my new bra?"

"Iowno!" she said and rolled her eyes.

Roxanne stomped in the room and stood behind the couch. "You don't know, huh?"

"No! Now leave us alone." She smiled at Fred, Roger or whatever his name was.

A ball of anger exploded inside Roxanne. She grabbed her sister by the blouse and yanked a sleeve off her shoulder. Ignoring the rip, she focused on the midnight blue laced bra her sister was wearing. Her anger piqued.

"Take it off!"

Morgan jumped off the couch. "You tore my blouse! I just got this blouse!"

"And I just got that bra. You know I wanted to wear it tonight."

Roxanne had spent all of the money from her Burger King check on an expensive set of underwear. She was going on a date with a boy she met named Haughton Storm. He was so fine, she couldn't believe that he had asked her out, and she wanted to make sure that her underwear was extra cute *just in case* he got a glimpse. And now her sister had ruined everything. Haughton was a football star and those guys expected girls to go all the way on the first date. Well, if that's what she had to do to keep Haughton interested, then she would do it.

What would she do now? He was picking her up in less than half an hour, so there was no way she could wash her sister's funk off of her bra in time for her date.

She jumped at her sister and her sister lunged for her. They grabbed each other by the shoulders and tried to knock the other down.

"What's going on in here?" her uncle Sammy asked, rushing into the room and pulling them apart. Since her father had passed away, he'd been checking on the family now and then. This time, he might have come just in time to save her from slapping her sister silly.

He'd run into her hundreds of times since their breakup—in his mind that is. She'd been walking toward him on the street. Happy to see him. Forgiving. Ready to begin again. Or maybe just to go back to his place and have some "ask me no questions, tell me no lies" sex. He'd imagined her crossing the street in front of his car while he was stopped at a light. She'd turn, smile. He'd motion for her to get in and then while he cruised through the Seattle woodland park at eighty miles per hour, she'd give him a hand job or go down on him.

Once, he even imagined that his team was going into the desert on a search and rescue mission and the hostage they rescued was none other than Roxanne Allgood. A voice in his head whispered, "Be careful what you wish for."

He knelt down at the stream and dipped the condoms in, thinking that women like Roxanne had a way of sticking with a brother. Like home training. It's just always there. You don't even realize that it's become a part of who you are until the power of it surfaces at the most unexpected moments.

He dipped another Trojan, shaking his head, like she was a fog that could be shrugged off. The image of her braless in his shirt haunted his mind's eye. Keeping his thoughts on getting them to safety might prove to be difficult.

When Storm returned with the water, the filter was working like a faucet with a constant drip. He poured in what he took from the creek and sat beside Roxanne.

She sighed. "Now what do we do?"

He picked up the twig he'd whittled earlier and drew lines in the dirt. "After the water drops through it should sit for at least an hour. After that, it's drinkable. We can fill up the condoms again and take the water with us."

Roxanne cringed at the sound of the laughter. The sound was airborne and surrounded them the same way thunder would, or rain. "Very good, Storm. Very good. There are seven levels to this game, and you've just passed the first one with flying colors. Although I will admit that the next six are not nearly so easy."

Storm looked up and around as if he expected to see Amadeus perched in a tree somewhere or overlooking them on a hill. "I told you before, I'm not interested in your childish games!"

"But my dear soldier, I have something for you."

A metal cylinder rose from the ground. It was about the size of a public mailbox. The top of the cylinder was clear plastic and divided into two. In one side there was a large hunting knife. On the other side, there was a can of spray-on bug repellent.

"A reward for advancing to the next level."

Storm strode to the cylinder and reached for the knife.

"Wait!" Roxanne said. She got up to take a closer look at the device. "This is an either-or choice. We can't have both."

"Very insightful, Miss Allgood." He laughed. The sound reminded her of nails being scratched down a chalkboard. "And also true. You can have one or the other. Not both."

"No problem," Storm said, touching the side of the cylinder holding the knife.

Roxanne bristled. "Are you going for the knife?"

He turned to her with a frown. "Of course."

She rolled up the sleeves of the shirt he'd given her. Her arms were red and puffy with welts. One of them had obviously been bleeding. She looked as though she'd been beaten with a cat-o-nine-tails.

"Oh, Jesus," he mumbled.

"I've been christened dinner and the word's getting around. I can't take much more of this."

Her arms looked bad. But they couldn't defend themselves with an aerosol can. Storm didn't know what lay ahead, but whatever it was, he wanted to be as ready as possible. "We can't take any chances in this environment. We need the knife."

"You've already got an axe. And I've got a shield. At least that's something to defend ourselves with. But how can we protect ourselves against that?" Roxanne asked, pointing to a swam of gnats hovering to the left of where they were standing.

While they argued, the cylinder started a quick descent back into the ground.

Storm cursed and bent down. They had to make a choice before the thing disappeared altogether.

"Storm!" Roxanne shouted.

They needed the knife. For defense. For hunting. For clearing a path. For building a shelter. "Augh!" he grunted before the top of the cylinder descended away from him. He slid the panel aside to uncover the bug spray and snatched his hand out before his arm was cut off at the wrist.

Roxanne let out a deep breath. "Thank you," she said.

"This is better than I imagined," Amadeus's voice boomed. "Much, much better!"

* * *

They walked for an hour with their weapons and water. They'd given each other a thorough dousing of repellent and were strolling along bug-free. Before long, they came upon a mango tree and Storm pulled down two of the fruits for them to eat.

"Do you have any idea where we are going?" Roxanne asked.

"Amadeus said that there was a helicopter waiting at the other end of the island. That leads me to believe that it's probably straight ahead. All we have to do is prevent ourselves from walking in circles."

Roxanne swallowed a small bite of the fleshy fruit. "Why would we do that?"

"We wouldn't intentionally. But people have a natural tendency to veer when they walk. It happens all the time."

"We could leave a trail or mark our path somehow. That way we would know if we've covered certain ground already."

"Yeah," he said, chewing. "And lead whomever or whatever straight to us."

She nodded and took another bite.

"Weren't you ever in Girl Scouts?"

"Naw. I always thought that was sissy stuff. Plus," she said gazing up, "I always had my head in the clouds."

Storm's glance looked threatening. "You're telling me."

Roxanne blew a quick breath through her teeth and turned her attentions to the mango that was almost gone.

Storm bit his lip. That was one subject he wanted to avoid. Her career. Her focused determination on her career. To the exclusion of everything and everyone else.

All he'd ever wanted since high school was to be a SEAL, but he would have given it up for the family they could have had. Every time he thought of his seed growing in her womb, a pain greater than any he'd ever suffered on the field of battle gripped him and stole all his strength.

"Oom," he moaned.

"What?" Roxanne asked.

"Nothing," he said.

"I still hate that about you."

"Hate what?"

"The way you grunt and moan and puff air, and then when I ask you what's wrong, you say nothing."

"And you know what I hate about you? The way you zero in on minor things and shrug off the big things like they're nothing."

Anger rolled like a ball of flame through her veins. She stopped and slammed the shield into the ground. "You know what else I hate, the way you—"

"Shh!" he admonished.

"Don't tell me to—"

"Shut up," he said, grabbing her arm. The urgency in his eyes silenced her.

"Excuse me?"

The voice came from a cluster of bushes up ahead.

"Stay here," he commanded.

She stood still while Storm took slow strides ahead of her thinking that was something else she hated about him, his propensity for ordering people around, especially her.

In a matter of moments, the terrain swallowed Storm, and Roxanne stood alone with only the cawing birds, rustling leaves, and rasping insects to keep her company.

Storm followed the voice to a thicket of underbrush. He found Amadeus's mother beneath a canopy of leaves and branches. She appeared more hunched and haggard than what Storm remembered, "What are you—"

She held up her hand and silenced him. He could barely make out her form in the foliage. She reached beneath her cloak and pulled out the Odin's Eye. "Please, take this," she said, her voice barely audible in the noise of the jungle.

Storm, realizing that her concern was that they were being monitored, knelt before her and pretended to collect firewood.

"This will guide you through the island. It will tell you where the Adversaries are. It will protect you from their weapons. You can't win without it."

He gathered twigs and branches of all sizes. He discarded some randomly while the woman stretched out her offering.

"I have no intention of going along with this game. You can keep that contraption. We'll make it by wits and determination."

"Are you crazy?"

Storm whipped around to see Roxanne standing beside him, a look of impatience drawing up her typically beautiful face. "I told you to stay put."

"And I told you, you can't tell me what to do." She turned to face the woman, who shrank back into the cover of thick leaves and vines. "If she's got something that will help us, you'd be a fool to refuse it. If you won't take it, then I will. That way you can keep checking the environment to make sure we aren't going in circles, and I'll be on the helicopter on my way back to civilization."

"We don't even know if there really is a helicopter!"

"There is," the woman said, laying the Odin's Eye before her. "This will help you get there."

Roxanne reached for the device. Storm snatched it away before she could take it. "What do you think you're doing?"

"Using every resource at my disposal." Her face cocked in displeasure. "How about you?"

"I'm trying to figure out what the heck to do next."

Roxanne jolted as if a volt of electricity slashed through her. "What? The big bad soldier doesn't know what to do?"

He moved closer, anger driving him on. "I know that we are in a situation, and I'm trying to—"

Roxanne turned in the direction Storm was staring. The woman had gone. He rushed to where she'd been hiding. There was nothing. Like the old woman had vanished into thin air.

He did a thorough sweep of the area but she was nowhere to be found. "There must be a mechanism here." He checked branches and twigs. He pushed against tree trunks. Nothing on top. He dropped to his knees and felt around with his hands. Leaves, twigs, roots, dirt, rocks. Soft sand. Metal!

"Help me," he insisted.

Roxanne dropped the shield and the Odin's Eye and knelt to assist Storm.

They found a lid, cleverly disguised as underbrush. Storm inserted the axe around the edge and forced his weight onto it. Roxanne gave him a hand and they both grunted and moaned with the strain. When the axe started to bend, Storm called a halt to their efforts.

"It must be triggered electronically."

Roxanne wiped away the sweat forming on her forehead. "If this truly is a video game, this place is probably crawling with access tunnels. We're bound to get another chance."

He frowned. "How do you know that?"

"Amara. A few years back, she was addicted to video games. So much so that Yolanda put her in a special program to help occupy her mind with other things. I used to play with her a lot. We all did, until we realized it was getting to be a problem."

Storm picked up the mass of thin plastic tentacles that was the Odin's Eye and grabbed a hold of the axe. "I want to know everything you know about video games," he said.

They gathered their things and continued along the path. It was getting harder and harder to follow as they headed deeper into the undeveloped area of the island.

It was as though they had stepped onto a new world—a world filled with leaves as big a pillows and shining like verdant leather, trees and vines so intermingled you couldn't tell one from the other, and flying birds that sounded like motorized scooters zooming against the wind.

And so much green. Green everywhere. Roxanne was starting to feel swallowed by all of the green.

"It will be dark soon. Tell me about these games while I look for something to eat."

Roxanne thought back to all of the times she and her niece Amara had played together. She'd never quite gotten the hang of it, but when Amara had worn out everyone else, she would call on Auntie Roxy.

"I haven't played in a while, but when Amara was fourteen she—"

Storm stopped. "Fourteen! Is she that old?"

"I guess you haven't kept up on all the current events. Amara is about to be twenty."

Storm scratched his close-cropped head. "Man-o-man. I remember when she was born. It doesn't seem like twenty years could have passed since then."

Roxanne thought about the rollercoaster her life had been in the past twenty years. It was easy for her to believe it.

As they resumed walking, Roxanne told Storm all about her niece's fixation on video games.

"At first, she played all the innocuous games like Tetris, Donkey Kong, and Klax. Then she graduated to more aggressive games—Altered Beast, Out Run, After Burner."

As the path ahead of them became more overgrown with vegetation, Storm used the axe to push aside the encroaching canopy of jungle.

Storm turned over a few leaves and moved aside branches. "You know you're speaking a foreign language, don't you?"

"We didn't get worried until she started cutting off her friends, spending more and more time in her room. That's when I started playing with her. I tried to get her to be more social or to find out why she wished to be so isolated. By that time, she was playing games like Street Fighter, Mortal Kombat, and Killer Instinct. But it wasn't until she started playing the quest-like games that I kind of caught on to how they worked."

"And that is?" Storm asked, his dark eyes brimming with impatience.

"In most of the games Amara played, she was on a mission to get something or somewhere. Like we're trying to get to this helicopter."

"Missions I can handle," Storm said, pulling a fat caterpillar from a branch. "Hungry?" he asked, offering her the insect.

"No!" she said, flinching. "Aren't you going to trap a rabbit or catch a bird or something?"

"Maybe. In the meantime, we need to keep moving and keep up our strength. If there is a helicopter out there somewhere, I don't want to take all day getting to it."

She took one more look at the crawly thing squirming in Storm's hand and her stomach lurched. "You really aren't going to eat that, are you?"

Storm cracked a smile. The first since she'd seen him again. It looked good on him. She'd forgotten how much.

"Humph. Watch me."

She turned her head. "I don't think so."

"Insects are the most abundant food source on the planet. Eighty-percent protein. You can't beat it."

She shuddered at the smack of his lips. "You don't know what you're missing," he added.

"I'll take your word for it."

But she did look at him. He looked at her too, and something cold and frozen between them began to thaw.

"So, these video games . . . they have levels. Each one is more difficult than the last. And at the end of each one, there's always something or someone to defeat before you're allowed to go on."

Storm wiped caterpillar residue from the corner of his mouth. "So far it doesn't sound too bad."

"It's not, unless it takes over your life. Amara was a model child. She did what she was told; she got good grades in school. When most kids mess up, you can punish them by taking things away. But Amara never messed up, so Yolanda never had a reason to take the games away from her." Roxanne swatted away a gnat that got a little too close. She thought the repellent must be wearing off. "You know how strange my sister is. She liked the fact that Amara stayed cooped up in the house all day away from everything and everyone."

* * *

"What about that thing?" she said, casting her gaze toward the Odin's Eye, slung like a slingshot over Storm's shoulder.

He touched the tentacles almost absentmindedly. "I don't know."

"She said it would help."

"Yes," Storm said, slashing his axe against a grove of thin trees that blocked their path. "But she's his mother. She might say anything."

Roxanne sprayed herself with more bug spray. The more they ventured into the thick vegetation, the more carnivorous the bugs were. She was beginning to feel like dinner *and* dessert.

"Easy on the spray. You'll OD on the fumes."

"Well, something's gotta give. We're being swallowed."

Storm stopped. "Hold on," he said. "Let me have that spray."

Storm sprayed his arms and chest, which were swelling in places where he'd been bitten.

He gazed at Roxanne. She was staring at him with a look that gave his heart a familiar thud. He knew she was going to be uncooperative until he at least tried to figure out the thing he'd thrown onto his shoulder.

"All right," he said. "Let's find a clearing and see if we can hook this thing up."

Roxanne was grateful. They'd been walking for several hours and she appreciated the rest. Since Storm had dragged her from Amadeus's house kicking and screaming, she'd felt apprehension building. And it was something beyond them being stuck on the island. Something she hadn't felt for a long time. As the foliage thinned in front of them, she came face to face with the reason for her apprehension.

It was almost as big as her fist and sounded like a tiny jackhammer.

Roxanne shrieked and ran. Bug spray and shield forgotten, she took off in the direction they had come.

"Roxy!" Storm called, but it was useless.

Since she was nine years old, she'd had a paralyzing fear of bees. The one she'd just seen looked like it could kill a horse. How many more were there? They could be anywhere. There was no bug repellent on the planet that could keep a bee that big away. Oh, God! Why her? Why had she been brought here?

Storm arms grabbed her from behind. She fought, but Storm held her close to his body. When she settled down Storm turned her toward him. Tears covered her face and her eyes were wide with alarm. "What happened?"

"Bee," she said, trying to steady her breathing. "I s-saw a bee."

"Oh, Jesus," he said, remembering.

Just then she wasn't the thirtysomething woman who'd hated his guts for the last ten years. She was the teenager he'd met so many years ago who'd been so afraid of bees, wasps, and hornets. The sight of one sent her into hysterics.

"Come here," he said, holding her close. She melted against him, boneless and shivering from fright. "It's all right," he murmured. "It'll be okay. I give you my word."

"It's going to be okay," Haughton Storm said, applying aloe vera to his girlfriend's shoulder. Roxanne Allgood sat on his dorm room bed, balled up and shaking. She'd been stung by a bee and had freaked out. He'd never seen her so distraught.

"It was just a bee, baby."

"I hate bees!" she said through an onslaught of tears. He could tell that what she really meant was that she was afraid of them.

"That bee is more afraid of you than you are of it."

She stared up at him. Eyes liquid and sad. "When I was nine, my parents took me, Zay and Morgan to the grocery store. They left us in the car while they went inside." She smiled a little. "Back then it was safer. We knew to keep the windows rolled up and the doors locked until they came back, anyway. So we did it then and did what most kids do when their parents aren't around—fight. So we were into some serious battling, when Zay notices that there was a bee in the car with us."

Storm finished rubbing her shoulder with the aloe but continued rubbing it with his hand.

"Zay being Zay, he thought it was cool and tried to catch it. Well, that must have made it mad because. . ." Haughton had put the ointment away and moved his hands softly and sensuously across her neck and shoulders. The sensation took away her tension and panic. She closed her eyes and breathed slowly.

"I guess the bee got mad. It started attacking. It came after each one of us. Don't ask me why we didn't jump out of the car. Especially me. I was the oldest one in the car. Stupid kid stuff, I guess."

Haughton planted soft kisses on her throat. She moaned.

"Don't stop. Keep going."

She felt herself unwinding and wondered how much longer she could go on talking. "The more I tried to bat away the bee, the more it came after me. There wasn't much room to maneuver in the back of that station wagon. I backed up as far as I could, but it stung me anyway." She stared into Haughton's eyes. "I've had this thing about bees ever since."

Haughton settled into a place in the nook of her neck and sucked the area rhythmically. She tingled from his attention, and felt the tension building between her legs.

His breathing was heavy with need. "What if I promised you that no bee would ever sting you again?"

She touched his eyebrows with her thumbs. They were thin and always looked as though they'd been brushed. The hair was coarse beneath her fingers. "You can't promise that," she said, huskily.

She and Haughton had been dating for quite some time. Although he'd been trying to get her to sleep with him almost the entire time, at sixteen, she valued her virginity and feared her mother's wrath. But lately, Haughton had been more insistent. No matter what they were doing or talking about, he seemed preoccupied with getting her into bed. He was popular. Since his football days in high school, girls, even some Roxanne had thought were her friends, made it perfectly clear that they would do just about anything he wanted anywhere he wanted. She knew her time was running out and if she didn't give Haughton what he seemed to need so badly, someone else would.

In the back of her mind, she feared that maybe someone already had.

"Storm," she said, calling him by the name his buddies called him.

"Yes, baby," he answered, kissing her shoulders.

"Are you sure you haven't been with anybody?"

He continued to lick and suck her. "Not since we've been together. You know that."

"Are you sure?"

He stopped. "Yeah. Why?"

Fear resurfaced inside her. "Because I—" She looked up at him. "Because I don't want to lose you."

"He smiled. She loved his smile. He cupped her head in his hands. "Roxy. How many times do I have to tell you? There is nothing you could do or not do to make me stop loving you. I want to marry you. I wish I could do it today. But as soon as you're old enough—"

He peered at her intently and rubbed her bottom lip with the pads of his thumbs. His mouth softened and approached hers.

For her first time, Roxanne wanted to feel sexy, and alive, and like a woman—Haughton's woman. But all she felt was afraid. He touched his lips to hers. The usual slow golden warmth she felt from kissing him avoided her. She pulled back.

"You're shaking," he said. "What's wrong?"

"Nothing," she lied. "I just made up my mind." Roxanne squared her shoulders. "I want you, Storm."

He kissed her lips. "I want you, too, baby. You know that."

She stared up into his dark eyes and for a moment she wasn't sure she was breathing. "Then make love to me." The words trembled out of her mouth, but she was determined to conquer her fear.

Storm blinked, but the excitement on his face was unmistakable. "You're sure?"

She nodded her response.

Storm's heart charged like a cannon in his chest. *Finally,* he thought. He swallowed hard and glanced around his dorm room. Posters of Funkadelic, Klimaxx, and Navy Special Ops lined the walls. A half-eaten pizza lay in a box on his roommate's bed. His socks from yesterday rested on the floor where he'd removed them and hadn't bothered to pick them up. In the corner by the door, a cobweb that had been there since he'd moved in swayed mockingly.

He touched her face. "Roxy, baby. Your first time should be someplace special. Let's go to—"

"No," she said. "We do it here. Now. Or I'll lose my nerve."

Her eyes bore pleadingly into his. He let his hesitation go and crushed his lips upon hers. It was too fast. Too hard. Too wild, he knew. But he couldn't help himself. The thought of him inside her. . . . He pulled away. They both gasped for breath. If he wasn't careful, it would be over before it was over. It had been a long time since he'd had sex. Not as long as he'd led Roxanne to believe, but still for a virile male, it seemed like an eternity. He would have to pace himself, and be something he wasn't feeling right then. Gentle.

He undressed her slowly, though he wanted with everything in his soul to rip off her clothes, his own, and ride her with the fury that was his love for her. But she deserved so much more than that.

She deserved patience and tenderness.

He removed the last article of her clothing, and his manhood stiffened like an iron rod. He bit his lip. She was so beautiful.

He descended upon her and kissed her slowly. He rotated

his hips on her, grinding out a message that he intended to make it worth her while. He kissed her and with his lips and tongue tried to tell her that he knew the gift he was getting was special and he cherished it.

"Ow! Your belt."

He stopped, smiled at his foolishness, and removed his clothes.

"Do you have a rubber?" she asked.

"Yes," he said, lowering himself on her.

She squirmed. "Why?"

His guilt stopped his breathing. He couldn't hurt her. "Because I want this so badly. I just wanted to be ready."

He took a condom from his nightstand drawer and put it on. Then he did something he'd never done before and hoped he was doing right. He put his head between her thighs and licked the place that was soft and wet for him.

She gasped. "Storm! Don't!"

But he ignored her. He knew if he was ever going to be this intimate with anyone, it would be Roxanne Allgood. He wanted to explore each part of her body and started with the best.

He quickly discovered he liked what he was doing and lingered there while she wiggled beneath him.

Roxanne's mouth flew open and her eyes closed. She would never have imagined a feeling like the one coursing through her. She'd heard her sisters talking about it, but it was clear to her now. They didn't know what they were talking about.

The sensations grew like ripples in a pond. Each one more intense and taking her somewhere she was almost afraid to go.

But she had no choice.

Storm controlled everything. She felt outside of her body. Like she'd been splashed against a canvas of pleasure and she was dripping with delight.

Her eyes sprang open. Something was wrong. It felt too good. Her head was going to explode. No, not her head, but every part of her body was going to—

"Storm, I'm—" she began, and then a bolt of passion struck inside her like lightning and just as she feared, her whole body exploded.

Just then, Storm repositioned himself and entered her. He felt her interior walls shuddering and quivering around him. He moaned and bent his head toward her lips. She tried to turn her head, but he chased it. Finally, he moved his hips in a gentle ellipsis. Roxanne's eyes fluttered then rolled back. If the feeling of losing himself to her hadn't been so intense, he would have smiled. Would have beat his chest and called himself Billy Baad. She accepted him. And every reaction of her body told him he was a good lover. And that's exactly what he wanted to be for her. The best.

He took her deeply and she stared into his eyes as though she couldn't believe what was happening.

Roxanne didn't know how she knew to move the way she was moving. Her body was doing things she didn't know it could do. Undulate. Retract. Pump. Grind. She loved it! She loved Storm. Haughton Storm. Oh God, she loved him.

The room grew hot with their lovemaking. Droplets of sweat fell from Storm's brow and landed on Roxanne's cheek and chin and lips.

He clasped the headboard for leverage and drove deeper.

Roxanne gasped. She didn't feel sixteen anymore. And she never would again.

"I love you," she said, rubbing her hands up and down Storm's sweat-drenched back.

He moaned and bared his teeth. She opened wider for him. He sank deeper. Their eyes locked. "Say it again," he demanded.

"I love you," she said.

Pleasure played like pain across his face. The lines in his forehead deepened. He breathed harder. Panted. Then grunted.

Roxanne was transfixed—ecstatic that she could be the cause of his enjoyment. She never wanted to share this feeling with anyone except Haughton. And she never wanted him to share it with anyone but her. She tried to say so with her body. Mark him somehow. Claim him some way.

She thrust upward. She kept thinking and kept thrusting. *Mine. Mine. Mine.*

Storm growled. "Ah! Roxy . . . baby . . . damn!"

One last thrust deep inside her. He shuddered and cried out as he climaxed in a way he never knew existed. His body jerked with it.

He kissed her face. Every inch of it and down her neck to her shoulders. He lingered at the place where he'd removed the stinger from the bee. She stared at him with a sleepy smile. He kissed the tip of her nose, then rolled over.

Neither of them had realized the condom had broken until they saw it. His slowly retracting organ was smeared with their wetness.

And for an hour or so afterward, neither of them cared.

To catch up to Roxanne, Storm had dropped the axe and the Odin's Eye. When they retraced their steps, they discovered that the axe and shield were gone. The water that Storm had collected trickled down the sides of his jeans—the condoms had been broken open when he ran against the bushes after her.

Storm picked up the Odin's Eye and stared ruefully at it. "I guess you better help me strap this thing on."

Seven

She could land a 757 in snow, sleet, and driving rain, but a honeybee could derail her. The only other thing that could put her in such a tizzy was the man who'd just consoled her. Their breakup had sent her into a deep despair and had caused a rift between her sister and her. He had been the double-edged sword of her past unfathomable bliss and unthinkable pain.

Being in his arms again took her to a place in her life that she'd tried hard to discard. It was a warm place full of serenity and contentment. For years, he'd made her feel that way. And she remembered the details of it sharply. He'd held her so close. The way their bodies fit together—molded like putty. The way he smelled so manly and fierce, and the way her body lost cohesion and sank against him in submission.

It was all there, all the old feelings, all the old need, all the old anger, all the old lust. It had just been lying dormant like a sleeping giant, only to be awakened by an innocent act of touching. The thought turned Roxanne's stomach.

While he stroked her hair and told her everything was going to be all right, her mind screamed, "No! It's not! Nothing is going to be all right, because nothing has ever been all right since you left me!" But being stranded on an island was not the situation or the place for reheating the leftovers of their broken relationship.

Storm returned empty-handed. He'd left her in a clearing with the Odin's Eye to look for the things that they'd lost.

Disappointment cut harsh lines on his face. "He must have taken them."

Roxanne glanced around to all the trees and bushes surrounding them. "He's watching everything."

"I'm sure he can hear us, too," Storm said and joined in her perusal of the area.

Their eyes locked with understanding.

Roxanne grabbed the Odin's Eye and walked over to Storm. They both stared at it for a moment, then Storm nodded.

"Turn around," she said. "It must work like some kind of backpack."

Storm put his arms through nylon straps that secured the device to his back. He put his hands through extenders that covered his arms with cords and attached to his wrist. The cords were held in place by anchors—round disks the size of quarters that reacted to his skin on contact. At the end of the extender on his right hand rested a screen. It also attached to his skin on contact.

Storm turned to face Roxanne. She thought he looked like a New Age hiker with a funky piece of camping equipment. "Well?" he asked.

"Looks like that's it. I wonder—"

"Well done, Chief Storm! And may I say, it's about time."

They both twisted around to see if they could tell where the voice was coming from. Wherever Amadeus's communications devices were, they were well camouflaged.

"Looks to me like you are ready to get off the island. And believe me, I will be more than happy to see you leave."

Storm shouted up into sky. "I don't trust you!"

"If you get to the helicopter, that means you've beaten the game. Or to put it metaphorically, *I* will have beaten the game, since you represent me in this quest."

"All right, Amadeus. What now?"

He laughed and both Storm and Roxanne cringed. "Now, you let the Odin's Eye show you the way."

Impatience grew like a storm within Roxanne. "How?" she blurted.

There was no response.

"How?" Storm repeated.

Nothing.

"I guess he's through talking," Roxanne said. She looked at the apparatus. "Try pushing one of those buttons on the screen."

There were four buttons. Storm pushed the first one. The screen lit up and Storm's eyes grew wide.

"What?" Roxanne asked, rushing to his side.

The lines of typography were unmistakable.

Their eyes caught. "It's a map!"

"That red blinking dot must be the helicopter," Roxanne said.

"Yeah, but where are we?" Storm thought a moment, then it came to him. "Come on," he said.

They walked forward and Storm watched the landscape of the map change. He smiled despite himself and their predicament. "If my team had one of these . . ." He imagined all the possibilities. Then at the same time, he wondered where the technology came from and if anyone besides Amadeus had taken an interest in it.

"This way," Storm said, using the map as an electronic compass. It pointed a way straight to the helicopter—a way no doubt paved with dangers.

They walked along for a while, each preoccupied with their own thoughts. It was almost nighttime. They would have to rest.

"We'll have to find a spot to bed down for the night. I'll see what I can rig for a shelter and we'll get some sleep."

"Can we get something to eat first? I'm starving. And what are we going to do for water?"

Storm felt the place on his pant leg where the condoms had been torn open. The spot was dry—dried by the sun that was just starting to cool down. He hoped the days wouldn't get any warmer. Today had been mild, around eighty degrees. But much warmer than that, and he didn't know how much of the heat Roxanne could stand. He'd been trained to bare extremes of heat and cold. His methods for circumventing the heat would only go so far. Conditioning was a big part of survival. He was starting to think that rescuing Roxanne first might have been a bad idea. She might slow his progress through the game.

Well, he couldn't worry about that. He had to keep his mind focused on what was happening now. And right now, Roxanne needed to eat.

"How does it feel?" she asked, eyeing the Odin's Eye.

Storm wriggled his arms to his sides. He could easily forget he was wearing it. He imagined it had been designed for that purpose.

"Not bad, actually. I can hardly tell there's a foreign object attached to me."

"I wonder how you get it off."

Storm's eyes grew wide. He lifted one of the cords where it was stuck to his skin. "Ah!" he responded. "It feels like it's super-glued."

"There's got to be a way to get it off."

"If there is, only Amadeus knows it. And I'll bet he won't tell until he gets good and ready."

"Well, let's see what the other buttons do."

"Let's slow down, shall we?"

"Why?" she asked, walking beside him. "If the first button is a map, the other buttons could lead us to food, water, shelter, who knows?"

"Who knows is right. Nobody knows what's in the crazy man's head. For all we know those buttons could be self-destruct mechanisms."

"I don't think so. I don't think he would go to all this trouble just to blow you up. That would spoil all the fun."

Storm was about to suggest that since she wasn't wearing the device and he was, that he had more at stake than she, but something stopped him, stopped them both. Roxanne emitted a sharp intake of air. Until then the snake hadn't seen them.

Roxanne remained perfectly still. "Think it's poisonous?" she asked.

"Since I don't know for sure, the best assumption is yes."

The long reptile hung down from a tree branch in front of them and hissed rhythmically.

Storm glanced at Roxanne out of the corner of his eye. "Well, you said you were hungry. I'd say dinner is served."

"Cool," she said, keeping still. "You need me to do anything?"

"Naw," Storm smiled. "I think I can handle it. Just back up with me . . . very slowly."

They backed up about three feet. Storm knew that snakes had striking distance of up to half their body length. After they were at a safe distance, he waved his left hand slowly in front of the snake. The snake uncurled more from the branch. Storm continued waving his hand. The snake lunged toward it and missed.

"Be careful!" Roxanne shouted.

"Always," he responded.

The snake hissed and slithered closer. Storm made his movement more deliberate and inched a bit closer. The snake lunged once more. Storm grabbed it just beneath the head with his right hand and pulled it from the tree. It curled and snarled in his grasp. With both hands, Storm took it and twisted it like a dishrag. The snake stopped moving.

"It's not true what they say," she said, tearing a sliver of warm meat from her stick. "It really doesn't taste like chicken. It's close, but there's a little something different. Something . . . untamed."

"Yeah," Storm said after swallowing a large bite. "It's good, isn't it?"

Roxanne could kick herself. After seeing Storm manhandle that snake, something inside her went soft. He always was woodsy. Urban hunter material. In her younger days, she had been drawn to that mystique in him like a bear to honey. Now, he'd turned into a large barrel-chested man oozing enough testosterone to make one hundred women swoon. If she wasn't careful, she'd be caught up. Again.

She watched him get up and gather more wood. She didn't want to. She'd much rather seethe with fury. He'd walked away from her ten years ago. He'd accused her of telling a vile lie and then as if their relationship meant nothing, he'd left. She'd carried the anger from that incident around with her for so many years, maybe it was still there, but because she'd had it for so long, she didn't realize it. Or maybe it was the worst thing imaginable. Maybe it was gone.

His soldier's swagger was unmistakable. After feeding the fire, he sat next to her on the loose-dirt ground.

"So, tell me, Allgood . . . what's the last thing you remember?"

For a moment she thought he was talking about their relationship. Then she realized what he meant. "I was driving Morgan's car. I was on my way to see Marti, and I'd stopped to get some gas. When I got on the entrance ramp, a tire blew. So I stopped. Well, this van pulls up beside me, and these goons get out. The next thing I know a man paler than a corpse introduces himself and says he's got a surprise for me." Roxanne sucked her teeth. "I guess he meant you."

Storm cast her a scalding glance, then turned away.

"Well now we know how, but we still don't know why."

Storm grunted. "Obviously it was to goad me into playing his game."

Roxanne wiped her hands on her jeans.

"But why? Do you know Amadeus?"

"No."

"So how did he connect me with you?"

"That's a question we'd both like answered."

"We haven't been together in ten years."

"And counting," Storm said, taking the last piece of snake from the stick.

"He must have looked into your past."

"Obviously," he said, smacking.

"Surely there was someone else he could have chosen. Someone closer, more recent."

Now Roxanne was prying into an area he didn't want to go

into. The majority of Storm's life was spent in training or in action. He hadn't bothered to make time for a love life. At least not anything he'd call serious, or heaven forbid, romantic. If Amadeus wanted to threaten the life of someone that Storm would do anything for, he had chosen wisely. Somewhere in Storm's mind, in a place he didn't want to admit existed, his feelings for Roxanne Allgood smoldered like some long-forgotten brush fire. And if not kept in check in a state of dormancy, they would rage out of control and become inextinguishable.

He knew. Storm jerked up from where he sat beside Roxanne. Somehow that skinny madman knew that Haughton Storm only had one button to be pushed and Roxanne was it.

"What's wrong?"

"Nothing," he hissed through his teeth. He glanced down at his lopsided pant legs and his bare arms and snorted. "I'm going to see if I can find us some natural bug repellent. I won't be long."

"I'm coming with you," she said, standing.

Storm held up his hand. "Look, I'm a big boy. I can take care of this myself."

"What about the game? Shouldn't we be more cautious?"

"I've got a hunch that whatever Amadeus has got planned, it will start in earnest in the morning. He's probably getting some enjoyment out of making us wonder when something is going to happen."

"Well, never mind then. I was just going to tell you that—"

It was too late. He'd already made his way through the trees and was quickly engulfed by the thick foliage.

"Fine!" she said. Grateful for the privacy, she decided to take the opportunity to go the bathroom. *Only,* she thought regrettably, *there is no bathroom.* Only reeds and twigs. She hadn't relieved herself outdoors since she was a young girl and her worst enemy dared her to do it.

She had unfastened her jeans and was pulling them down when she heard a twig snap.

* * *

Storm weaved in and out of the trees, wondering why the entire island seemed to be filled with Roxanne's presence. Being near her was like having his breath stolen. He had to get away for a moment.

He thrust his fist against a lush baobab tree. Ten years. Ten long years, and he still hadn't gotten over her. From the second he saw her in Amadeus's house, a turmoil had started in his heart and in his mind. He was so offended by the thoughts in his head that if he'd been another person, he would have given himself a right cross.

She resented him. And she had good reason. He'd walked out of her life so abruptly, even he couldn't believe it. But the thought of her aborting his child without telling him, without even asking him what he wanted or how he felt, cut him in two just as surely as if she'd done it with an assault rifle. She'd been so single-minded about her career. He'd watched her move heaven and earth to get to where she was. He knew from the past that if she ever got pregnant, she wouldn't have the baby. But that didn't make it any less devastating when it happened.

Years later he found out that she didn't have an abortion. She'd had a miscarriage, but by then it was too late. She had tried to tell him she had a miscarriage before he left, but he hadn't believed her. He knew for a fact that she's had at least one abortion before, and he hadn't put it past her to have another one.

Storm blew a blast of hot breath between his lips. He tried to shake the torture of his memories out of his head and focus on his task. As soon as he did, he found the plant he'd been searching for right in the middle of a small thicket of bushes and brambles. He pulled off as many leaves as he could carry.

Suddenly, he felt like he'd been gone too long. He hurried back the way that he came and approached the clearing. The fire he'd built was almost out. He dropped the leaves on the ground, a knot of unease tightening in his stomach.

Roxanne was gone.

Eight

When Marti Allgood got the call about her missing sister, she was in the middle of painting a picture. She and her fiancé, Kenyon Williams, had just hired a nanny, so their ten-month-old son was being well taken care of. Because of that, they decided to spend some much deserved quality time together.

Marti had been asked by her friend Kathryn Runningbear to contribute a painting to her annual gallery exhibit on women. Marti had agreed and decided to create an abstract rendition of *love* as her contribution.

"Oh-oh," she moaned, reining in her concentration. The blue lines and shadows were starting to blend.

She sat naked on a chair in the studio Kenyon had built. Her palette was beside her. Her easel was in front of her. And her fiancé was prone before her with his lips and tongue causing the build of a wondrous commotion just below her abdomen.

She blended the colors mostly with the brush, but sometimes with her fingers. As the sensations rose and pitched within her, she created that feeling on the canvas. Swells of ochre. Billows of purple and gold. Waves of deep blue. An expanding riot of color as her practiced lover created a rainbow of emotion in her soul.

"S-s-s-uh-AH!," she cried out, dropping the brush onto the tarp-covered floor. At the peak of her sensations, she smeared the yellow into the red, and the result was an orange flare shooting up from the bottom of the picture.

"I'll get it," Kenyon said, standing.

Marti slumped back against the chair, so sated she hadn't

even heard the phone ring. Her arms dangled at her sides and her chest rose and fell. "Where're you going? Don't get up. The painting's not finished," she pouted.

He smiled and shook his head. His thick hair swayed against his face in long tendrils. "Take a rest, woman!"

"Hello," he said, voice deep and echoing in the sparse room. "Sure, just a moment." He covered the receiver with his hand and walked toward Marti. "It's Morgan."

Marti shook her head, quaking from the aftershocks of her climax and eager for more. "Tell her I'm asleep," she whispered.

He kissed her on the forehead. "She sounds upset, sweetie."

Marti pushed out her lips and wiped her hands on a Turpenoid-soaked rag. "Hey," she said. "What . . . ? She what . . . ? No, we haven't seen her. Oh my God! I'll be right there."

Marti's hand trembled as she handed the phone back to Kenyon.

"What's the matter?" he asked, stepping to her side.

"It's Roxy. She was on her way over here yesterday, but . . ." her voice faltered. "They found the car empty on the freeway, and nobody knows where she is."

Kenyon Williams reached over and touched his fiancée on the shoulder. "Marti . . ." he said tentatively.

She moved the phone receiver away from her mouth. "Just a minute," she said, then returned to her call.

They had been home for three hours, and she had been making phone calls the entire time. They'd spent the majority of the afternoon scouring the city, stopping at every place they thought Roxanne might have gone. Friends, family, old haunts. But they'd found nothing. When they got home, Marti pulled out every address book she owned and had been calling people nonstop ever since.

"I'm sorry to bother you at this hour, but I'm looking for my sister Roxanne. Have you seen her today? Have you seen or talked to her recently?" Deep sigh. "Okay, well if you see or hear from her, please ask her to contact her family immediately. Yes. No. Yes, please keep your eyes out for her. Yes. Thank you."

"Sweetheart?" he said, softly.

She turned to him. Her eyes were large and so full of pain it nearly stopped his heart. She'd looked that way ever since they left the police station. The officers had wanted photos of Roxanne and a description of her clothing. That had been ten hours ago. Since then, Marti hadn't eaten or had anything to drink. He guessed she was functioning on pure adrenaline and stark fear.

He knelt beside her. "It's after midnight. You need to rest."

"I can't," she said, shaking her head. "I've only made it to the P's."

Marti reached for the phone and her hands shook violently. She knew her sister was in danger. She knew it. Roxanne would never abandon a car like that. If only she could find someone who'd seen something.

Kenyon wrapped an arm around her shoulders and hugged her to him. "We'll find her. She'll be all right."

Their son's cry turned their attention to the nursery.

"Go," Kenyon said. "Take care of KJ." He took the address book from Marti's lap. "I'll finish the calls."

Sharky got a call from his commander on the morning he was released from the hospital. The news caused him to pace, however awkwardly, for nearly a half-hour in his apartment. Haughton Storm was missing. He hadn't reported for assignment and had not responded to any attempts to contact him. A couple of SEAL officers had gone to his home and it was obvious that he hadn't been there in days. His unit was about to classify him UA—unauthorized absence—but since Sharky was one of his closest friends, they wanted to know if he had any idea where Storm might be.

Sharky had no idea why he didn't tell them of Storm's return to Texas. It was the closest he'd come to an infraction since he enlisted. But a hunch rolling uneasily in the pit of his stomach told him that something was amiss and the best thing to do was to keep everything he knew to himself until he had a chance to investigate it.

Sharky took a deep breath, stopped pacing, and hobbled off toward his bedroom to pack.

Nearly twenty years in the military, and all of his training failed him. He was not calm. He was not detached. And by far, he was not levelheaded. Since Roxanne's disappearance, he'd behaved like a crazed man, searching frantically, calling out her name, cursing loudly, and wanting desperately to beat something or someone to a pulp.

He'd even accused Amadeus of doing more underhanded actions. But the jungle grew strangely quiet.

"I know you can hear me!" he shouted. "Now where is she?"

A heavy sigh came across the sky and ricocheted off the leaves and shrubs. "From now on, I'll have my meals brought up. That will allow me to monitor your progress in the game at all times."

"Forget the double-talk. Where's Roxanne?"

"If your girlfriend left you, don't blame me. But I *will* have a look around the island for her. We wouldn't want her to get into trouble prematurely."

"You tell me where she is, or I don't go on."

"My dear Chief Storm, whether you seek it out or I bring it to you, the game will continue."

Amadeus's maniacal laughter echoed like thunder. "The only way you can stop it now is to beat it. Get some rest, soldier. You'll need all of your strength tomorrow. And in the meantime, I'll be on the lookout for Roxanne, in case she decided to take her chances here with me."

Storm was beside himself. Roxanne couldn't have gotten any further than half a mile at a run, and he'd searched in all those areas. He'd found what looked like a trail, but then it just dead-ended. Something must have happened to her. Something Amadeus didn't know about.

His skin prickled with realization. He knew immediately that was either a good thing or a very bad thing.

The night came on with a vengeance. Shadows elongated and thinned out on the ground until the pitch of the evening swallowed everything. Storm fashioned a lean-to out of dry leaves and twigs like he had earlier and with some effort built another fire. He gathered enough kindling to keep it going all night. He could have used a knife to build something sturdier. He hoped this would discourage most insects, small reptiles, and who knew what other predators that might disturb his rest.

He bedded down. There was nothing he could do until morning, when Amadeus's game would begin in earnest.

He awoke the next morning with a start. He'd spent most of the night suspended in the twilight he and his comrades called "Warrior's Dream." Not fully awake, but not asleep either. He'd hovered in the midpoint of a self-induced trance that allowed him to rest yet be alert to any threatening sound or movement.

He sat up quickly and scanned the area. He got to his feet and shook himself to full consciousness. The sun was already climbing. Surprised that Amadeus hadn't taken his watch, he glanced at it.

Six-thirty a.m.

His pulse quickened and his senses heightened. Something was wrong.

He listened. It was as though someone had turned down the volume on the song of the jungle. His fire had long since died.

He looked around for a weapon. Surrounded by tall grass, dead leaves, twigs and tall trees, he ran, jumped, and grabbed onto a thick overhead branch. He held on. The branch bent and cracked with his weight. In seconds, it snapped away from the tree and Storm came down with it flatfooted.

He held it like a bat and crouched, ready for battle.

The sound came from out of the distance. Like a scuttling against the wind. It was unfamiliar and made Storm wish he'd spent more time playing video games with the kids in his neighborhood.

When the figure hovered toward him, he fought to keep from gawking. A silver-blue man in military fatigues ran in his direction, but his feet didn't quite touch the ground.

A hologram, his mind registered.

And damn if it didn't have a gun!

"Unah!" Storm grunted and rolled away from the volley of . . . something. Pulses of blue lightning whizzing by.

He ducked behind a tree and pulled the branch to his chest, thinking. A lot of good a physical object would do against a computer-generated one.

The whirring sound grew louder. Storm almost threw aside the branch, but something in the back of his mind told him to try it. When the sound was right beside him he stepped out low and swung. The branch passed right through the image. Without the contact of the blow, Storm lost his balance and tumbled forward. The soldier spun and fired, missing Storm within a second's movement. He twisted away and in his haste tumbled down a ravine. The soldier gave chase.

How am I supposed to fight this thing? he wondered, scrambling to his feet.

His mind flipped through all the information Roxanne had told him about video games. Nothing he remembered helped. As the soldier approached, Storm hurled large rocks, stones, and anything he could find at it. Everything passed through.

There's got to be a way.

His mind filled with images of teenagers riveted to their television sets, seemingly connected by a controller device they held in their hands.

Jesus, a controller!

There were four buttons on the Odin's Eye. Storm pressed each one in succession. The first three changed the image on the small screen. He was too busy darting between trees to buy time to know what to do. The fourth button sent a silver-blue charge running through the cords attached to the device and Storm's right arm warmed with the charge.

It was a crazy idea, but Storm believed he knew what it meant. He ducked around a large shrub and crouched in waiting.

When the buzzing sound was upon him, he jumped out and with all his strength gave the soldier a right cross.

The soldier tumbled backward and fell flat on his holographic behind.

Storm blew out a breath and glanced at his hand, which under normal circumstances would be smarting. It looked and felt fine. The soldier stirred and started to get up. Storm decided that one crazy idea deserved another. He picked up the branch that had tumbled down with him and held it in his right hand. His hunch proved true when the branch immediately emitted a silver-blue glow.

Before the soldier righted himself fully, Storm swung down and actually heard a crack as the branch connected with the hologram's skull.

The soldier closed his eyes and collapsed onto the ground. Storm prepared to deliver another blow, but the hologram was immobile.

He smiled as a rush of victory flooded his veins. "I could learn to like this," Storm said.

He bent to nudge the image with the branch. It disappeared before he had the chance.

"Bravo, chief! Bravo! I knew I'd chosen wisely. You are the perfect warrior. This game will be most interesting indeed."

Storm pressed the fourth button on the Odin's Eye. The device powered down. "What now, Amadeus?"

"Now I offer you a reward for your effort. You've successfully moved from Level Two to Level Three by defeating an Adversary."

"Adversary? Is that what it's called?"

"Not it. They. The Adversaries are the patrollers of the game."

Storm understood. If all of the Adversaries were like the

one he just faced, he would have no trouble advancing from level to level. He blew out a breath. He knew it wouldn't be that easy.

Another canister rose from the ground. It was identical to the one he'd seen with Roxanne. This one also offered two things. He walked closer.

"Just as before, chief. Make your choice."

Storm glanced at his choices and his head dropped to his chest. A bottle of antiseptic spray and bottle of water.

He needed water desperately. In this environment, he'd gone too long without it already. And after the physical exertion he just expended, it was even more imperative that he have it.

He also knew that the scratches on Roxanne's arm could become infected soon if they hadn't already. She needed the antibiotic.

The turmoil of his dilemma made him tense. He didn't even know where Roxanne was, and he had no idea if he would find her.

She was still with him and couldn't figure out why. Carl Baer had appeared almost out of thin air and taken her to a tunnel beneath the surface of the island. She hadn't wanted to go, but the gun he held to her head drew her cooperation.

She paced. Her nerves felt like a thousand small volts of electricity charging through her body.

She hadn't slept a wink.

Carl on the other hand was still sleeping. Her mind had been racing all morning.

She could try to incapacitate him and get away. She could try to take the gun away. He was sleeping on it, but the element of surprise might give her an advantage. Or she could just make a run for it. But none of those options seemed right.

He'd come to her asking for her help and in exchange for her help, he would help her and Storm.

The man lying near her in the cave was probably her same

age, but the wrinkles on his face and the shadow of anxiety in his eyes made him look much older. She also suspected that he was a little touched or just a tad bit crazy, unbalanced.

He'd taken her into a catacomb of tunnels. As soon as he fell asleep, she'd explored a few of them. They were like a web of networks below the surface. She guessed that's where the cylinder had come from.

His whole operation is probably powered down here. She could hear the whir and hum of a generator. It was either really big or very close.

She sat down on the concrete floor, recalling their conversation. At first she didn't understand what he was trying to tell her, but then everything started to make sense.

"You must help me," he said, holding Roxanne's arms behind her back.

She bent forward then lurched back, giving him a severe head butt. Carl screamed and let her go. She spun and put her fists up.

Carl tumbled backwards. "No! No!" he said. "I don't want to fight."

Roxanne eyed him suspiciously.

"As a matter of fact, I can't fight."

She kept her dukes up for a few moments, but the fearful look in the man's eyes told her that he was more alarmed by her behavior than she was by his.

"What do you want?" she asked, still on guard.

"I want you to deliver the Odin's Eye to a . . . colleague."

"A colleague where?"

"Don't mind that. He will find you once you're off the island."

"So, you're sure we'll make it."

"I have no doubt."

"I guess that means you're going to help us."

"I can't do that."

"Then you can forget about your friend ever laying eyes on the Eye. No pun intended."

Carl's round face scrunched into a pitiful pout. Like he'd just sucked on the sourest lemon. "You have to help me!"

Roxanne squared his shoulders. "Then, you have to help us."

Her comment seemed to pop him like a Mylar balloon. He exhaled and that's when the rambling began.

"Amadeus will skin me alive. No, he will kill me, re-create me, and then skin me."

At first, Roxanne was alarmed. She thought the man was freaking out. And in a way, he probably was. But the butterball of a human being before her appeared so disheveled and out of sorts, she felt sorry for him.

"So there really is a helicopter waiting for us on the other side of the island."

He looked up and appeared startled that she was speaking to him. "Yes, to be sure."

"And all Storm and I have to do is get to it?"

"Yes. Each level will bring you closer to your freedom."

"Why don't you come with us?"

Carl jumped as if he'd been prodded with a hot poker. "What?"

"Leave the island. Then you won't have to worry about Amadeus or anything he might do to you."

The sadness in Carl's eyes touched her.

"That's not possible. Amadeus and I, we're . . . doomed to work together." For a moment, he looked as though he might cry. "I'm sure I'll die by his side."

Carl was starting to give Roxanne the creeps. "Take me back to Storm. I'll make sure that the Odin's Eye gets to your, uh, colleague."

Carl settled down on the floor of the tunnel. "I'm tired now." He curled into a small ball. "Rest now. I'll take you back in the morning."

"Wait!" she said. "What are you going to do for us? How can you help?"

Carl stared up at the ceiling and steepled his fingers. "All quest games are based on a mythos. Usually that mythos is created specifically for the game. Asgard is based on an already existing mythology. As Storm moves through the levels, he will be awarded objects that will further his success in the quest."

Roxanne frowned. "I wasn't born yesterday. I could have figured that one out on my own. You have to give up something better than that. How do we turn off the game? Outsmart it? Circumvent it?"

"The only thing I can safely tell you without having to fear for my life is that the Odin's Eye is the key to your survival. As long as you have the Eye, the Adversaries can't hurt you."

"Is that the best you can do?"

He turned over. "Yes."

"Where've you been?"

"What do you mean where have I been? I'm a grown woman. I don't report to you!"

Roxanne put her keys in a ceramic dish she kept on the kitchen counter. Storm had let himself in with the key Roxanne had given him. He had just come back from training and wanted to spend time with her. He knew he didn't have long, so he'd called to tell her he was coming.

As in the past, he'd fly in and she would either pick him up from the airport or be waiting for him when we he got to her apartment.

This time, she'd done neither. And he'd just gotten a call that he needed to report for assignment tomorrow. He'd been at her apartment for a full three days and Roxanne was just now showing up.

His patience had boiled away hours ago. "I'm only going to ask you one more time. Now, where were you?"

The truth was that he'd called every hospital in the city to see if there had been some kind of accident. He'd called her family and they didn't seem to know a thing. He'd even phoned a few of her friends. It was no use. No one knew where she was.

The airline was not helpful. They wouldn't give him any details. So he had no way to know if she was working. Finally, he'd driven around the city to see if he could spot her car.

His mind pounded with every bad thought imaginable. She was hurt. She was injured. She was with another man. It made him crazy.

"Have you heard a word I said?"

He blinked and went to her. "No. I haven't." Then he grabbed her and kissed her hard. Smashing her mouth with his. His fear, anxiety, and dread plummeting him toward the depths of his love. He had no idea he could feel this way about a woman. The thought scared him.

Roxanne struggled in his arms. He continued kissing her. Punishing her for being so late. Celebrating her for coming to him. Confirming his worst fear that he was lost without her. And that now that she was here with him, he really didn't care where she had been. The only thing he cared about was the fact that she was here with him now.

She wrenched herself out of his kiss and gasped for breath.

His hands traveled through her hair, over her face, neck and shoulders. Feeling to convince himself she was really there.

His heart beat regularly for the first time in days.

"I love you woman, damn."

She hugged him. Her soft arm circled his waist. "I had to fly out at the last minute. I left you a message."

"Message? What message?"

What was he going to tell her, he wondered? *Excuse me, Roxanne. I know we've been kidnapped and brought to a tropical island. I know we're fighting for our lives here, but I just realized that I probably still love you. How do you feel about me?*

Maybe she'd seen it on his face and that's why she left. Out of all the thoughts fighting in his head, he was only consumed by one . . . finding her.

Instead of moving on to the next level in the game, he'd spent hours searching. He'd run through the dense vegetation almost blinded by the shade of green in front of him. He saw little else. More brushes, more brambles, more trees. Finally he'd come to a grassland, an open field that allowed him to see a ridge of hills and more undeveloped land. In one last attempt, he climbed the highest tree he could find and scanned the area.

He disturbed a different layer of life. A flock of parrots flew through the trees. Another bird in a nearby tree sang like a flute in the humid air. Animals he couldn't name squeaked and chirped in lower branches—no doubt sounding the alarm of his presence. And from way below, crickets called out to each other in the underbrush where it was always night. All of this he heard and saw, but there was no Roxanne.

Storm stared out into an azure sky as anger replaced his frustration. He'd been on countless missions. Most top-secret, most critical to the nation's security, and in all that time, nothing had ever gnawed away at his confidence like Roxanne's disappearance.

He took out the aerosol can that he'd stuffed into his jeans. A spray for her cuts and scrapes. Storm flipped it into the air, caught it. Then he put it right back where it had been and climbed down.

It didn't take Storm long to figure out what the other buttons on the Odin's Eye were for. As he made his way through Level Three, he pushed the second button and studied the change on the screen. The screen changed as he moved and he realized it was a proximity detector. He could see everything around him for a half-mile square. He wondered if the Adversaries would show up on the screen as they approached.

That would be too perfect. Just in case, he kept the tree branch with him for a little insurance.

The third button changed the screen in a way that confused him at first, until he realized he was seeing himself. Or inside himself actually. This screen changed and fluctuated with the rhythm of his breathing, his body temperature, his heartbeat. It was like watching a funky biofeedback readout. Colors, pulses, and lines converged like some New Age dance to the silent music of his life essence.

He knew Amadeus had a way to monitor what he was seeing. He had to have some way of keeping tabs on the well-being of his lab rat in case some physical affliction prevented him from making it to the end of the maze.

Hunger and thirst began to affect Storm's concentration. He picked a few gambaya fruit from a tree. He snapped a sap vine open and allowed the thick sweet liquid to trickle down his throat. Then, for protein, Storm searched for and found an anthill. He remained there awhile, ingesting fistfuls of the large black insects before continuing on.

"Chief Storm," Amadeus called.

Storm stopped. He checked the screens on the Odin's Eye to see if they had changed now that his captor was speaking to him. To his surprise, there was nothing.

"Don't bother trying to monitor me, Chief. You can't. But I'm having a devil of a time trying to monitor that woman of yours. Where is she, Storm?"

Storm cleared his throat. "If you recall, I was the one asking you that."

"Yes," Amadeus hissed. "An interesting ruse, I assure you, but I'm not interested in interesting. I want the truth."

"Do you think there is any way possible I would have left her on her own?"

Silence.

Storm rechecked the map. He knew that the area glowing several miles ahead of him was his target. He also knew something else. Amadeus was afraid. His concern over Roxanne's whereabouts had turned the tin undertones in his voice to a quivering twang. Whatever caused that turmoil for Amadeus, Storm had to find a way to use it to his advantage.

He resumed his trek.

"You know, Storm, Odin had several tools that he used to secure his reign in Asgard. As you make your way toward your freedom, you will gain one tool in every level you conquer."

"Fine," Storm said. One more complication in an already insane scenario.

Nine

"Get me out of here, Carl."

"Yes, yes," he said. "I'll get you out." He stared intensely at her arms, which were swollen, red, and oozing pus in some places. He'd given her food and water, but what he should have brought with him was soap or some kind of medicine.

"You need . . . attention."

Roxanne put Storm's shirt back on. "I'll be all right." She only hoped as much. She knew some plants were medicinal. She only hoped Storm knew which ones.

Storm.

She'd been thrown back into his life in some crazy way. Fate is a strange thing. Out of all the people possible, she was chosen to be with him here. She wanted to know why. If all things happened for a reason, what reason could bring them together here? Now?

"Take this at least," Carl said, handing her a canteen of water.

She took it and waited.

"Let's go," he said.

He led her through a long corridor. She heard the hum of machinery running all around her. It vibrated the tunnel and felt warm beneath her feet.

Soon they were in a room with a shaft that Roxanne assumed led up to the surface. "What is this?"

"It's a maintenance tube. Climb up. It will put you out half the distance between Level Two and Level Three."

"Where's Storm?"

"Don't know exactly. He should be at the end of Level

Three right now. As a matter of fact, he'll probably be quite busy when you find him."

She stepped onto the rungs and began her ascent.

Carl called up. "Remember, look to the Eye. He should never take it off until you're safely aboard the helicopter."

Marlowe "Sharky" Gilchrist stepped into Dallas International Airport with a duffel bag and a goal. He'd contacted the vet in Washington. She said Storm was three days late. He'd told her he was going to Texas and that he would be back in two days. That was five days ago. Something was up. Sharky could sense it.

His wound was healing nicely. The doctor had him on strong painkillers and an antibiotic to prevent infection. It was rough going sometimes. Walking. Breathing. But he was managing and knew that he wouldn't be alive to suffer through the pain of healing if it hadn't been for Haughton Storm. If his friend had met with foul play, he would do all in his power to make those responsible endure great anguish and torture. *Yes,* he thought. He would see to it.

His first stop was the home of Zurich Kingdom. Storm often mentioned him and a couple of other buddies that he went to school with. Said they were like the "Rat Pack." Always together. Always getting into trouble. Always trying to be cooler than they actually were. If half of the exploits he heard about them were true, they sounded like a great bunch of guys. A circle of friends he could easily fit into.

He knocked on the door. Within moments, a tall man answered. He was dark, and had a military stance and eyes that looked like he'd seen one too many painful things in his life. "Can I help you?"

Sharky flashed his military ID. "I'm a friend of Haughton Storm," he began, relaxing a little. "Actually, he's my commanding officer. He was—"

"Come in," the man said and stepped aside, motioning Sharky to enter.

He strode into a modest living room. Two other men sat around a cherry wood dinning room table. Their faces were acutely sad.

"This is a friend of Storm's."

The men rose, introduced themselves, and shook hands.

"We're trying to piece together what happened."

Sharky stiffened. "What do you mean?"

"The last time we saw Storm, he was headed to a friend's house. The next day we heard that friend had been murdered and Storm was nowhere to be found."

Sharky's resolve shattered. "My God!"

"He was supposed to hook up with us a couple days ago. No one has seen him. He never called."

"And he never flew back to Washington."

"We've got some critical connections. And we know that even though he disappeared, his personal belongings were still in Connie's house. We know something is wrong and we know something else—we're going to use every resource at our disposal to find out what happened."

Sharky smiled for the first time in days. He'd made the right decision.

Storm was enjoying another gambaya fruit when he heard the humming. It was louder than before. Checking the screen on his wrist, he saw three orange blips moving in his direction. He gripped the branch tightly. *Three of them,* he thought.

He ducked into a thick grove and watched until they were almost upon him, then he pushed button #4 and the branch in his hand began to glow. He had to be close to the first object.

The humming grew louder. Surrounded him. It seemed to be coming from all directions. If he switched the screen to see where they were coming from, he would lose the power he needed to defeat them. Instead, he waited just a few seconds and then jumped out from behind the covering and swung wildly. He struck one Adversary and missed the others. He ran to get a better position. Two Adversaries followed. He dropped to the ground and they flew right over him. Then he jumped to his feet and swung the branch forward. The blow dissected one of the Adversaries and it disappeared.

The last remaining one whirled around and fired a holographic rifle. The fiery blast struck Storm square in the chest. The force of it knocked him backwards. But surprisingly, he wasn't hurt. Garnering his wits, he scrambled away and ducked under a bush. The Adversary fired again, this time grazing Storm across the back.

"Careful, Storm. The game's just getting started."

"Amadeus!" he bellowed, darting forward. "What is this?"

"I told you, it's a game, and if you aren't careful, you're going to be out of energy."

The hologram had disappeared. Storm was alone with the voice of a madman.

"You must avoid getting hit, Chief Storm. Even though their weapons can't harm you physically, every hit registers through the Odin's Eye. Five hits on one level and you die, Storm. End of story. Game over. I'll get rid of you and your missing-in-action girlfriend and start all over with someone new. Maybe that Sharky you seem to be so fond of."

His anger became a scalding fury. "Don't worry. I'll beat your cursed game. And when I do, I'm coming for you!"

Silence. Then a wintry laugh that set his teeth on edge.

"Just worry about yourself, Storm. I can take care of me."

The sound of Amadeus's words faded away on a warm wind, and the humming sound resumed.

The closer Roxanne climbed to the surface, the louder the low rumbling became. When she reached the top of the tube, it was deafening. She twisted a lever on the hatch and slid it aside. As if it were waiting for her, a large spider scurried inside the tunnel with her and crawled down the tube wall. It was brown and furry with yellow spots. About half the size of her hand, it paused on the way down, as if to determine if she were a threat.

"Do you eat bees?" she asked.

It didn't answer, just scurried down the tube, and Roxanne hoisted herself out. She eased the lid back into place. If she didn't know what it was, she would swear it was just a green and gray patch of dirt and ground.

She stood, brushed herself off, and tried to get her bearings. Carl said she was halfway between two levels and that Storm was probably at one of them. But which one and which direction?

She turned in a circle. Nothing looked familiar. Nothing she'd seen before gave her a clue to where she was now.

Her heart raced. What if she never caught up with Storm again? A wave of apprehension swept through her, and her better judgment told her that the reason for it was partially due to the nest of feelings that had been uncurling inside her ever since she laid eyes on Storm again. Emotions came hurtling forward as if she'd packed them and held them in reserve for just this moment. A need she didn't understand urged her forward. She grabbed Storm's shirt tightly around her and sprinted into the dense wooded area.

The canteen slipped from her hands and she fumbled it like an awkward juggler. She'd been running only a few minutes, but it seemed like hours. Each crop of bushes looked the same. Each grove of trees looked like the one she'd just passed. Birds in the trees hurled mocking cries at her and her need to see Storm quickly turned into panic.

"Storm!" she cried out and disturbed a gathering of butterflies as she hurried into a clearing. They were everywhere—covering leaves, limbs, and her clothing. In any other circumstance, Roxanne would have been in awe of their beauty and their sheer number. Right now they were a hindrance, slowing her down and confusing her vision with their flight.

"Storm!" she shouted.

A strange sound accompanied by a glow in the distance caught her attention.

Storm!

She took off in the direction of the light. Although she'd run out of the flock of butterflies, a stubborn one clung tightly to her shoulder and held on for the ride.

She made it to the ridge in record time. She hunched over and grabbed her knees thinking, *Thank God for step aerobics.*

With her chest heaving, she scanned the area. She saw nothing. Then over the sound of her own breathing, she heard the sounds of a scuffle.

Roxanne slung the canteen over her shoulder and ran toward it.

The bright blue light flashed again and lit up the sky with its radiance and heat, irritating her arms that were already warm to the touch. The source was just beyond a ridge of leafless trees. She hurried toward it. Before she reached the grove, Storm came tumbling out and a man that didn't look quite real was in pursuit.

She blinked, not believing what she saw. The man-thing chasing Storm looked like a blue ghost in army fatigues gliding on air. Storm slid beneath a large plant just as the blue guy raised his weapon to fire.

"Storm!" she screamed and ran towards them.

Her voice must have startled him. He stared in her direction just as the blue man's shot ignited in the air like a brilliant flame and caught him on the shoulder. She watched in awe as Storm rolled away unaffected and came around to the other side of the grove.

Coming up behind the Adversary, Storm swung a branch and sent the "man" flailing to the ground. Then before he could recover, Storm ran up and pummeled it repeatedly. By the time Roxanne came up to where they were fighting, the Adversary disappeared right before her eyes and in its place was a golden spear.

She was so relieved to find him and grateful that he seemed unhurt.

His chest heaved, but his eyes softened. "Roxanne," he said, and they fell into each other's embrace.

She stared into his eyes and all the fear she'd held in check since her arrival bubbled up to the surface. Storm's face grew tender with concern and then he came for her lips and she gave them freely.

Sweet as their first kiss and just as intoxicating, Roxanne drank in the sensation as though her soul were parched and devoid of moisture. He brought a hand to her chin in a gesture that persuaded her to linger a while in his mouth—stay some moments with his tongue. Then his hands traveled across her shoulders and down to her arms.

"Ah!" she said, pulling away. She grabbed her elbows and winced in pain. Her cuts and scrapes were getting worse. She had to find medicine soon—natural or otherwise.

"What's wrong?"

"My arms," she said. "They're . . . they're bad."

He took one in his hands and rolled up a sleeve. Red, swollen, and infected. "Jesus!" He patted himself down. "I've got antiseptic. It's . . ." His shoulders slumped. "I must have lost it in the fight. It's probably under a bush or something."

They both crawled around on hands and knees searching the area. Storm went in one direction, Roxanne another. Then he heard a crumbling sound. "Don't get too carried away. We'll find it."

He searched in the spot where he'd lost his footing and tumbled beneath the large leaf of an enormous plant. "Found it, Roxy!"

No answer.

He stood and brushed himself off. "Roxy?"

Still no answer.

"Roxanne!" *Not again,* his mind screamed. He took off in the direction she'd gone and stopped just in time to avoid falling into a sinkhole. He knelt and peered in. He could barely make out what was down there. Shadows and roots from trees. The hole went down quite a ways. He swallowed hard when he saw the outline of a woman's body laying sprawled in the dirt. He pounded his fist against the ground and the ground collapsed beneath him.

He slammed into the dirt below with a thud. The impact forced the air out of his lungs. He looked over. Roxanne was only inches away. He reached out for her, then blackness covered him over.

Roxanne came around, not because she wanted to but because her head was throbbing out of control. She opened her eyes and sat up. She blinked to make sure that her eyes were open. They were, she was just in a dark cavern. In a few minutes, her eyes adjusted and she could see better.

Storm was out cold beside her. She rubbed the side of her head in an attempt to make the pain go away. It wouldn't.

She reached over and shook the large man sprawled beside her. He grunted and stirred, then grunted some more. Just then she was reminded of his snoring. Not too loud; not too soft either. She'd missed his night sounds. And smells and . . .

"What the hell happened?"

"Your guess is as good as mine."

"What do you remember?" he asked, sitting up.

"I remember you fighting. I remember us kissing." Her cheeks warmed. "Then us looking for antiseptic."

"That's right. You fell into a hole." Storm glanced skyward. "Looks like we both fell."

He rose and helped Roxanne to her feet. A glimmer of white in the dirt caught his eye. He bent and picked up the aerosol can. "Let's take care of those cuts."

Roxanne nodded and took off Storm's shirt. She held out her arms, and he sprayed them liberally.

The pain was excruciating. Roxanne bit down on her lip and a solitary tear escaped her eyelid and trickled down her cheek.

"We need to wash out those cuts somehow." Then he noticed the canteen around her neck. "Where did you get that?"

"From Carl," she said, fanning her arms beside her to cool them.

"There's water in it?"

"Yeah."

"Hand it over."

"After that fight you just had, I hope you intend to drink this water."

He took the canteen. "Give me your arms."

She slipped away. "We need that for drinking water. The antiseptic will do for now."

"Roxanne—"

"No. Who knows when we'll get clean water again?"

Storm had a feeling that Amadeus would give them a chance soon enough.

Roxanne frowned. "So what was going on up there? I mean, what was that?"

Storm pretended to survey the cavern. "That was me being a bit overzealous to see you."

She wanted to laugh. "No, silly. That thing after you. Was that an Adversary?"

"Yes."

"It's not real, is it? I mean . . ." She glanced at his broad shoulders. "It fired at you."

Now he inspected the area for real. Looking for footholds, trying to see how far the cavern went and in what direction. "It's holographic, just like the bullets it fires. It's clued in to this thing somehow." Storm raised his arm. Then he got an idea. He pressed the map button on the Eye. Nothing happened. He pressed the other buttons. The screen remained unchanged.

"Is it broken?"

"I don't believe so. It doesn't appear damaged." Storm glanced around. "I don't think it works down here. There must be some kind of range on the thing. Or maybe the rock in these walls is shielding it from reception."

The cavern stretched in two directions. Storm pointed them in the direction of the next level. "Let's go that way."

Roxanne walked, deep in thought. *Overzealous, my behind.*
That was more than a robust welcome back. The passion was
sweet and thick. It lay across her lips like honey. She knew if
she licked them, she would still taste it. If he was trying to
fool himself that was one thing, but he couldn't fool her.

Storm looked down at the Eye. "Ha! Maybe that means he
can't read me either. So, what happened to you?" he asked
after they'd squeezed through a narrow passage.

"Carl took me to an underground tunnel. He wanted to ask
me about the Odin's Eye. He wants us to give it to someone.
A colleague of his off the island. He said that the person
would be in touch once we get back to the real world."

Storm jerked as if he'd been punched. "No deal."

Roxanne stopped. "Why not?"

"This gizmo is evidence. You *do* realize that this man is
committing a federal crime?"

"Yes. But I think Carl is being coerced."

"Carl, Amadeus, the thugs. They're all going to jail if I
have anything to say about it."

"What about the help Carl is willing to give us?"

This time Storm stopped. "What help?"

"Carl said that you should keep the Odin's Eye on until
we are safely on board the helicopter."

"Part of me doubts whether there really is a helicopter."

"Carl said that there was."

Storm snarled. "And you believe him?"

"Why shouldn't I believe him?"

"How about the fact that we are stranded on a madman's
island, jumping through hoops like a lab experiment gone
techno? How about the fact that Carl is an accomplice? Unless I've gone crazy myself, those don't seem like good
reasons to be called trustworthy."

Roxanne blew a hot breath between her teeth. This was a
part of Storm she didn't miss. His bullheadedness. When he
got this way, the only way to prove him wrong was to let him
do things his way and watch him fall flat on his face.

"Come on," he said, taking her hand. "It looks like it's getting lighter up ahead."

She grunted. "Just remember how much I love to say, 'I told you so.'"

"Don't worry," he said. "Out of all the things I've managed to forget about you, *that* isn't one of them."

His words were so painful, Roxanne almost cried out. They certainly stung more than the Bactine spray. *But why?* she wondered.

The walls of the cavern were uneven and jutted out erratically like gray clay hardened and misshapen. As if on an obstacle course, they maneuvered and finagled their way through until they came to a chamber with more light. The illumination came from above through a similar hole to the one they'd both fallen through.

Roxanne sighed. "How do we get up there?"

Just as before, the walls, though uneven, were smooth and slicked by moisture.

"We can't," Storm said.

Roxanne hadn't been so uncomfortable in all of her days. The heat matted her hair to her head. Her clothes were sticking to her. Her feet ached. And her deodorant had failed some days ago.

Storm, on the other hand, couldn't look more appealing. The stubble of his beard growing in gave him a masculine edge. His clothing rippled with the activity of a man. And his scent was ripe with pheromones. He looked like he'd just spent all day making love. Furious, raging, molten love. He looked—

"What?" he asked.

An old familiar heat rose within her. "I was thinking that you look good."

He laughed. "If you think this is something, you should see me in uniform, ma'am," he said with a southern drawl.

The memory was pleasant. The first time she'd seen him in

uniform. Crisp bright white, so pristine and perfect it almost hurt to look at. To her, he was a grand representation of America. She cried with pride and couldn't stop touching the cotton creases and fresh-pressed lines.

Roxanne laughed then. Her laughter bounced off the cavern walls as they entered an area that tapered so narrowly, they had to pass through single-file.

Her pulse quickened. "How much farther do you think we can go?"

Storm checked the monitor on his arm. It still wasn't working. "I don't know. I was hoping there would be some kind of incline or we would come across a more porous surface to climb to the top. This cavern goes on for quite a while. The good thing is, there's another light coming from somewhere. If we find the light, hopefully we can find the way out."

Roxanne followed closely behind Storm. They moved along at a constant pace. Their footfalls echoed off the walls and sounded like a giant's heartbeat. Soon that echo stopped and the ground beneath them changed from damp to sticky to murky. After a while, they found themselves trudging through a thick grey sludge that was ankle deep.

"Ugh," Roxanne said, hearing the sucking sound that resulted when she lifted and set down her feet.

When Storm slowed, she almost ran into him. "What's wr—?"

"Shh," he said. He uttered a series of expletives under his breath. She couldn't see in front of him, so she had no idea why.

"Will this help?" she asked, handing Storm the Light Bright.

"Back up," he said, stuffing the plastic object in his pocket.

She did as he instructed. They moved back about ten feet.

"The first rule of cave exploration is beware of whose home you might be entering."

"What is it, Storm?"

"Bats," he said. "There's an entire chamber of them."

"How many?"

"Hundreds."

Roxanne tried not to panic, but the reality of their situation panicked her. If something disturbed those bats and they flew out, there was no way they would be able to survive the onslaught of their flight. They would be killed.

Despite her resolve, trepidation rose in her chest. She fought it back. Storm must have seen the alarm in her eyes. He grabbed her wrists.

"We can't go back the way we came. It's too narrow back there. We'll die for sure. We've got to keep going. The chamber opens up where the bats are. If we take our time and move quietly, we might not disturb them."

Her heart was pounding so hard it took her mind off her short breath. "What if—"

"No what-ifs. We're going to make it."

She stared into his hard determined eyes. The eyes of a warrior. Eyes that dismissed words like try and defeat. Ignored notions of danger and knock first.

He took her hand and together they entered the cavern.

Roxanne fought to keep from gagging. The odor was unmistakable. Urine. Now she knew the source of the filth they'd sloshed through. Mounds and mounds of bat droppings. Her stomach pitched and rolled with the realization of it. Storm tightened his grip as they traveled beneath rows and rows of bats hanging, squirming, scratching. Though most were asleep, even the still ones made her flesh crawl.

Storm turned to face her. He pointed to the light piercing the darkness ahead of them. His gesture was insistent. He was telling her to keep her eyes forward instead of looking up. But it was no use. As soon as he turned back around, her gaze crept upward. The sight of so many creatures held her mesmerized, transfixed. She couldn't tear her eyes away.

Something dropped on her face. It was warm and smelled strongly of the filth now covering them to their ankles. Roxanne shuddered and kept looking up, eyes frozen on the ceiling.

She didn't know what it was. Perhaps a root or maybe just

a thick glob of waste, but something tripped her. She toppled forward and Storm grabbed outward.

He missed and she slammed into the murk. It sloshed up over her and Storm squatted down to recover her. She trembled, certain the bats would fly out and smother them.

Aside from a few flutters and shifts of wing and position, the bats remained stationary. Grateful, Roxanne and Storm resumed their careful trek out of the cavern.

Ten

"Come on," he said, taking her hand and helping her out of the car.

She squeezed her eyes shut like he'd asked, but it took all of her resolve not to open them.

"Where are you taking me?"

"Someplace nice. Someplace . . . just come on."

She'd participated in trust exercises before. As part of Delta's team training, she and her flight teammates went to a weekend session at Camp Fontenelle. They had to move through hoops, walk on tightropes, scale walls, and climb down ropes. They did many of these activities blindfolded. She gained a new appreciation for individuals with limited physical abilities. But she still never got used to the idea of not knowing exactly where she was going or what lay ahead. That required a tremendous amount of trust. Storm was stretching her trust in him to its limit.

"How much longer?" she asked.

Even if she opened her eyes, the blindfold she'd been wearing for the past half-hour would probably prevent any light from entering her eyes anyway.

"Watch your step," he called.

"I can't watch anything," she shot back.

"Just be careful!"

Roxanne smelled water. And the concrete sidewalk they'd been traveling turned to rough uneven grass. She thought it could use a good mowing, as wisps of grass brushed like tiny fingers against her ankles.

Humidity thickened the air and the smell of moisture grew

stronger, as though they had just walked into the middle of a rainless storm.

Had he driven her to the coast? Where in the heck were they? Her body thrummed with nervous energy.

"Storm, I can't do this. I have to look. I have to see where I'm going."

He let out a deep breath. "If you insist," he said.

He moved behind her and untied the blindfold. After being light deprived for so long, she squinted her eyes to readjust. What she saw before her made her want to widen her eyes and stare. Not only did she smell water, but now she saw it, too. Lots of it. But the most impressive thing was the boat.

"What have you done?" she asked.

"You don't think I asked you to get all duded up for nothing, did you?"

It was true. Storm had a reason, usually a good one, for everything he did. When he showed up at her apartment in a tuxedo, he looked so handsome all she wanted to do was take it off and ride him until he screamed. But he would have none of it—even when he moaned for two minutes during a passion-filled kiss. Instead, he insisted that she put on something sexy and elegant and come with him without asking any questions. Any other time she wouldn't have minded, but she was just about to go to bed. Then he'd looked at her with those eyes of his—deep obsidian eyes that were used to getting their way, especially in matters of her heart. The next thing she knew they were speeding down the interstate—she wearing a royal blue satin dress and a blindfold.

"I wasn't sure we would get here in time."

Couples in exquisite finery boarded a fifty-foot yacht. She could hear soft jazz playing from the deck.

"A dinner cruise?" she asked, eyes sparkling.

"Not just dinner. There are thirty couples here tonight to go on an intimate cruise with The Temptations." As they approached the dock, a large poster proclaimed that they were about to board the "Temptation of Love" cruise, and bid them prepare for a night of "ballads and brilliance."

Roxanne couldn't have been happier. She stood on tip-toe, planted a lavish kiss on Storm's cheek, and took his arm.

They strolled onto the yacht, both walking on a little piece of their own cloud nine.

An array of sequined gowns, custom-made suits, and opulence surrounded them. Under a canopy of stars, Roxanne and Storm strolled the deck, drinking wine and talking about the future. Roxanne nodded and smiled as he told her of his desire to command his own SEAL team. Storm's eyes grew dark and intense when she spoke of her plans to move from the co-pilot's chair to the captain's seat. All the while Roxanne believed that she and Storm had their careers mapped to the last detail. She wondered about the details of their relationship. They knew where they were going with their jobs, but they barely made mention of each other.

She sighed, knowing that it was hard for two strong-willed people to admit their need, their dependence on something or someone outside of themselves.

But Roxanne couldn't deny it. No matter how many times she went up into the sky, flying an airplane only mattered now because she knew that on the ground, awaiting her return, was a man who loved her.

Everything he did precluded a military cadence. His mannerisms deliberate, controlled, precise, measured. His strides even, his back straight, his chest proud and large, eyes searching and alert. She wondered if he ever fully relaxed. Even when it seemed most unlikely, like when they were making love or now when they were sharing a meal on the yacht, he was still on guard, at attention. That part of him never switched off.

The gentle sway of the river lulled her into a relaxed state. During the five-course Captain's dinner, they were treated to sea bass, steamed asparagus spears and twice-baked potatoes, among other delicacies. The night was picture perfect. She felt untouchable and peaceful with the world floating by. In the midst of their hectic lives, she and Storm had finally found a quiet place. The *Queen's Legacy* sailed down the river. A cool summer breeze kept them company. The romantic and soul-stirring sounds of The Temptations drew them closer to each other. They held hands, stared into each other's eyes, shared discreet kisses. Roxanne was the happiest she'd ever been.

"Sempala?" he said.

Her eyes held his. She warmed at the mention of their pet name for each other. Once, when she'd had a little too much wine, she'd slurred the word *simply* into sempala. From that moment, they had called each other by that name, especially at the height of their sexual arousal. The word always sounded intoxicating and smoky when Storm said it. And sometimes having something special and secret between them reminded Roxanne how special their relationship was—more special than anything she'd ever experienced before.

"Yes, Sempala," she said in her most sultry voice.

He scooped her hands into his. "I love you," he told her.

She felt like satin.

On the way back to the dock, they found a secluded spot and made out like kids until their loins were burning with need.

By the time they got back to Roxanne's apartment, it was four a.m. Impatient to share the heat in their flesh, they took each other just inside the door. And there on the floor, Roxanne Allgood became pregnant for the second time in her life with Haughton Storm's child.

In her mind, she'd imagined that bats hung still in their sleep. She thought she recalled seeing a nature program, maybe *National Geographic* or something on the Discovery Channel, that showed the dark, furry creatures hanging motionless and wrapped in their own wings. She was wrong. The hundreds and hundreds of bats above her—some in solitary rows, some huddled together—jerked, scratched, and convulsed in ways that made her skin itch. Her eyes grew large as one bat stretched a long leathery wing straight out and then retracted it.

The closer they came to the light, the more they left the bats behind. Finally, they were at the mouth of the cavern and there were no bats at all, just jutting rocks, stalactites, and a growing warmth seeping into the cool of the cave.

Roxanne drew heavy breaths. Fresh air never smelled so good. Storm guided her through the passage into daylight.

Having been in the dim of the cavern, they both squinted against the sun and shielded their eyes until they adjusted. The break in the passage was a large one, but they could see that just a few feet ahead was an opening to another cave or perhaps a continuation of the one from which they'd emerged.

From the relative quiet in the cave, they stepped back into the noise of the jungle and the sound of things alive and growing. Surprisingly, the sound was comforting.

To Roxanne's surprise and delight they stumbled out onto a sandy beach and ice-blue ocean. They came out, and looked back on the plateau over the cave. Now all the thick greenery was swallowed in the majesty of the vast body of water.

Roxanne, still shaking from their ordeal, stumbled off and tried to get as far away from Storm as she could before her stomach turned inside out. She retched and heaved as great waves of nausea gripped her until the contents of her abdomen sprayed out at her feet.

She coughed, caught her breath, and wiped her mouth with the back of her hand.

Roxanne caught Storm in the corner of her eye, watching. He plucked a leaf from a plant and brought it to her.

"Here, suck this."

"What is it?" she asked, rubbing it between her fingers.

"A naje plant. It's like peppermint only not as gentle. It will get rid of the taste in your mouth, plus help settle your stomach."

She inserted the leaf in her mouth. The sensation was powerful. Her eyes widened.

"It reacts to saliva. Whatever you do, don't chew it or swallow it. Just hold it between your cheek and gum, like chew. Spit a few times if you like. When the flavor dies down, spit it out."

He took a breath, deep with concern. "I've never seen you so afraid."

Roxanne's eyes narrowed. "You still haven't. And don't you *dare* tell my sisters."

He grinned. "Don't worry. Your secret is safe." *And so was your love, once.*

She peeled his shirt from her body. It was damp and heavy with filth. She held it away from her as if her arm were an extension bar and her fingers were tweezers.

"You've gotta get cleaned up." He took the shirt from her and guided her toward the water.

"Strip," he said. He dropped the shirt at the edge of the ocean and undressed.

She nodded and quickly removed her clothes. She kept her eyes on Storm the entire time. He kept his eyes on her.

"Wait!" she said, as he peeled off the game equipment. "You're supposed to keep that on at all times."

He tapped a button. The screen fizzled briefly then winked out. "It's still not working. Even if I was wearing it, it wouldn't do me any good."

She looked unconvinced.

Thanks to their location, he was able to put the Eye on the ground far enough back from the shore so that it wouldn't be touched by the incoming waves. After Storm removed his T-shirt, he and Roxanne entered the ocean together.

The years had been kind to his body, she thought. Although it was clear that he'd gained weight, he carried it well. She, on the other hand, doubted that the few pounds that she'd lost brought her back to the physique she had when she and Storm were the best part of each other's lives. She hadn't let herself go, but she wasn't as diligent as she could have been. She couldn't believe how much that mattered to her right now.

"This isn't Six Flags. We've got work to do."

Roxanne realized that she'd done little more than wade out

until she was waist deep and stand in thought. Storm busily washed the grime from his body. Using his hands, he rubbed his skin thoroughly.

She cupped her hands in the water, drenched her arms, then worked off any dirt with her fingers. She was careful of the areas swollen and puffy. They weren't nearly as painful as they had been, but she was still concerned. She would spray them again when they dried off. *Dried off?*

"How are we going to get dry?"

Storm looked up and shielded his eyes from the sun's brightness. "The old-fashioned way."

"You mean the Cro-Magnon way."

"Stay here," he said, splashing toward the shore. He grabbed their clothes and brought them back. "Might as well get these clean, too."

For the next half-hour they rinsed out their clothes and rubbed them against rocks to remove the grime and feces.

The heat between their bodies pulsed and ebbed. Like a force alive and magnetic. It drew them closer. Their eyes caught. The familiar sense of being naked in each other's presence pulled them. The way he smelled manly, raw, sensuous. The way she smelled feminine, rare, alluring. They moved closer. The ocean pulsed between them and its current flowed with their own. An Eros as old as time itself.

Even if he made her angry and had said hurtful words to her in the past, she knew a night of his lovemaking had the power to make her forget them all.

She turned away.

"Why don't we put our clothes on those rocks to dry?"

He nodded, unable to speak. He could not hide his attraction, his need, as sharp and pungent as it had ever been. The years had not served to diminish his desire for her, only held it at bay until now. "Roxanne," he said, voice dark with lust.

She strode away toward an unusual configuration of rocks to the left of where they stood in the water.

He followed her around the bend in the shore. Storm's

mouth dropped and Roxanne gasped at the sight ahead of them. The waterfall had to be at least thirty feet high.

It sounded like a mighty rainstorm and was surrounded by long brown tendrils. Thin reeds hung down in cord-like fingers dipping from the cliff and touching their tips into the water below. A froth of white foam churned where the water beat steadily down into the ocean. They placed their clothes on the rocks and headed toward nature's natural shower.

Within seconds a swell of excitement burst inside them and they found themselves running toward the falling water. Whoops of excitement escaped their lips and the cold stream of wetness pounded down on them and stole their breath.

Roxanne stood under the strongest deluge, letting the water wash over her in great waves. She stretched her arms out side-ways and turned her face up to the water. She looked like a voluptuous water sprite being celebrated by a magnificent downpour.

Storm wanted to enjoy the refreshing drenching, but his mind was taken over by the sight before him. He felt paralyzed. Useless. His only freedom and salvation would come if he could somehow entice the beautiful woman standing in front of him to open herself, to let him unleash the tension building in his loins and in his soul.

After a few moments under the beat of the water, Storm ran his hands along the soft skin of Roxanne's back. She pulled her hair aside and lowered her chin, giving him full access. The cool water and the heat of his hands made an intriguing sensation on her skin. It awakened her and relaxed her at the same time.

For the next twenty-four hours, Roxanne would tell herself that what happened between her and Storm was a build-up of stress, frustration, and plain old lust. She would try to convince herself that her desire for him was nothing more than her surrender to the pulse of the jungle, the breath and cry of the wild, the allure of sand and sky. In the heat and humidity of the island, her need to mate was strong. It couldn't possibly be love.

Her eyes told him everything he needed to know. He could reach over, stroke her nipple, knead her flesh. She would moan and come to him. He could turn to her, press his manhood against her belly. She would open for him. His penis throbbed, ached ferociously for her. Coaxing her would be so easy. But he could not, or rather *would* not. The first move had to come from her. The chasm between them was ten years old. He had caused it. If the void was to be sealed, it would be Roxanne's decision. He wondered if her body would obey her mind and heart.

She turned to him, the flame of desire burning through her veins. "Let's get this lust thing out of the way."

Confusion furrowed his brow. "What?"

"We aren't going to be able to concentrate on the game until we get this lust out of our system."

She grabbed his face and pulled him to her. Roxanne reveled in the press of her lips on his. It had been so long. Oh God, too long. His arms came around her. Swallowed her. And for the sensation of his wet skin against hers, she would disappear in his embrace, only to reappear in his eyes and sparkle there like a diamond in the night.

Was it witchcraft? Surely some spell had come over her, for it was not Storm, but she who was the aggressor. Roxanne used her lips, her teeth, and her tongue to suck the very life out of the man trembling against her. Her gift was his whimper and the buckle of his knees at her deft assault of his mouth.

At that, she used her body and arms to swing him around and pin him against the rock behind the waterfall worn smooth by the constant pelt of the ocean.

His eyes fluttered open in shock. The cold stone against his back jolted him, but no more than Roxanne's power and possession. He had been the victor of military missions so top-secret, there was never any record of them. But with this woman, his heart was weakened by the mere bat of her eyes, a lick of her lips, the press of her thigh. If she wanted him supple and willing, he would be that or anything else.

But knowing Roxanne, she would demand what she wanted.

Storm returned quickly to the place on the shore where he'd dumped the contents of their pockets. He prayed for one more condom. When he found it, he wasted no time donning the latex sheath and joining Roxy before she could change her mind.

She pushed his hands up and pinned them over his head. He held them there while she drank the falling water from his skin. His mouth opened and a dozen moans escaped.

The waves of the ocean urged her on. Her heart beat with each crash of water against their legs. She rubbed her body against his. Thrilling him again. Claiming him again. The excitement of it made her crazy with need.

She reached on either side of her and wrapped her wrists in the hanging vines. Then placing her foot against the rock for balance, she pulled herself up. Storm bent his knees and grabbed her bottom. Then eagerly she lowered herself onto his hot and pulsing manhood. This time it was her moan that broke through the air.

Using the vines for leverage, she pulled herself up and down. Slowly at first, then the need grew like a sweet pain between her legs, driving her faster.

They both cried out in pleasure. Roxanne let her head fall back and panted through an open mouth. Water fell upon them both, but their desire soared unquenched.

Storm's hands descended upon her drenched breasts, kneading them and thumbing her nipples. His thrusts upward sent his hardness deeper into her core. She shuddered and gritted her teeth, preparing for the inevitable.

A tropical storm flashed through her mind and surged within her body. It was wild, intense, powerful, and frightening. Every inch of Storm's body came back to her in vivid detail—the muscular neck and firm shoulders she loved to hold on to, the well-built chest that pressed against hers, brawny arms that held her tight, sturdy legs that carried her, and on top of all this, dark eyes with a gaze so potent it stopped her heart only to make it beat more forcefully in her chest. She drew in quick breaths, besieged by pleasure beyond her imagination.

She ground her hips against him in a frenzy. Storm responded in kind. Roxanne let go of the long, thin tendrils and grabbed the sides of his face. Their mouths assaulted each other in a squall of desire. Tongues tangled and twisted like the vines of the jungle—together, inseparable. Their inhibitions came down, their self-restraint came down, the waters above came down.

Strokes on flesh, on muscle, against breasts and thighs melted away ten years of estrangement. The anger didn't matter. The hurt and disappointment didn't matter. Just the feeling rushing between them. Roxanne panted and groaned. It was too much and yet not enough.

Strength she didn't know she had propelled her on. She rocked and bucked with him—her hunger unbroken and raging. Craving the release only Storm could give her body, she yielded to his touch, beseeched him for more and greedily took all he gave.

Sweat fell from her body like tears. And instead of a volcanic eruption, the turbulence inside her suddenly slowed and felt suspended. Then a small break opened in her loins and expanded leisurely to the brink of her entire body. The sensation built as though each thrust from Storm inflated her lust like a balloon. But instead of bursting, her need grew larger. Unable to contain the emotion, Roxanne's scream filled the air and echoed throughout the canyon. It rustled leaves and drove Storm harder, faster.

Her strength drained. There was no end in sight. Her scream continued with the long and steady sensation. Like a jet during takeoff, she climbed with it, cried with it, screamed with it.

Storm watched her as long he could until ecstasy closed his eyes. He'd poured himself into her body. All that he was belonged to her now. He couldn't hold back his emotions and no longer wanted to. They belonged together. The last ten years had been a waste of time.

"What happened to us, Roxy?" he whispered, nearing the brink.

She couldn't answer. Didn't want to think about it. And didn't want him to ask it again. She plundered his mouth, hoping to silence him.

As Roxanne's womanhood tightened around him and her tongue ravaged his, he released his seed, determined that there would be no more time lost between them.

They uncoupled and a bird screeched in the distance. Roxanne steadied herself. They were both panting. Storm stared in her direction. She closed her eyes and stepped forward to let the waterfall wash over her. Roxanne willed herself to calm down or her heart would beat right out of her chest. The force of what had just happened scared her. It made her forget how much he'd hurt her. She couldn't let one sexual escapade blind her to the way he'd called her a liar and then refused to let her explain, and how easily he'd dropped out of her life. One physical exchange couldn't erase all that. But if she weren't careful, her heart would.

Storm tossed the condom into the water and stepped behind her. He reached out to hold her, but she moved away.

A shadow of anger crossed his face. "What?"

"Nothing," she said, rubbing the water against her skin. "I just don't want you to get all mushy on me."

He grunted. "When have you ever known me to get mushy?"

She trudged toward the shore. "You always get mushy after we make love. But don't twist things around. This was stress relief, that's all."

Storm couldn't believe what he was hearing. "I don't know about you, but . . . No. I take that back. I *do* know about you. I know *everything* about you. And that wasn't just sex. That was reconciliation. That was healing—mending. It went beyond making love. It was *making right.*" He caught up to her in the sand. "I know you felt it, so don't lie to me. It won't work."

"You haven't changed. Still accusing me of lying! Especially when you don't know what the heck you are talking about." She paced, although the sand made it slow going.

"This thing has been festering between us for too long. Let's just get it out in the open. Then we'll see who's been lying to whom."

She tore at him then. He caught her fists and held them above her head. She kicked at him. He spun her into his arms and held her while she squirmed against him.

"I know about the abortion, Roxanne."

"I told you I miscarried the baby, Haughton! Why couldn't you believe me?"

"Because I know about the abortion—the real one."

Roxanne went still then. After a few seconds he released her. She turned and blinked back the sting of his comment. "What?"

He walked over to a plant with elephant ear-sized leaves. After picking several of the leaves, he spread them on the sand, creating a makeshift pallet. He sat at one end and left enough room for her. Roxanne remained standing.

"I'll bet it was the first time we ever made love. And that wasn't sex either. I've always made love to you. We've always. . . . Anyway, we were kids—at least I certainly was. I had your periods mapped down almost to the hour. I know that was lustful, but I wanted you that badly. And you never let me . . . we never made love during your periods.

"But that August we had each other for six weeks straight. Then all of a sudden you had female problems. If only you'd seen your breasts. I know every inch of your flesh, Roxy. Every pimple, pockmark, and curve."

He knew soldiers didn't cry. But he also knew he could do nothing about the tear that pushed past his resolve and spilled down his cheek. He stared straight ahead. The ocean roared in front of him, a vast and powerful universe. But it seemed small compared to the pain he felt when Roxanne Allgood aborted their baby.

"For a long time—years—I held my tongue. I loved you, and I didn't know how to confront you without putting our relationship in jeopardy. So, I told myself that maybe you weren't pregnant. Maybe you did have female problems. And the biggest lie of all, maybe I meant more to you than your career."

Roxanne sat down then. Plopped down was more like it. The world had shifted beneath her feet. She no longer had any ground to stand on.

"Haughton—"

"I told myself lies for almost ten years. And then you got pregnant again. And you didn't tell me again. But I waited. I thought, 'This time surely.' And then Marti called to tell me you had an abortion."

He shook with rage. Roxanne reached over. He stood before she could touch him.

"I know I didn't hear you out. But it wouldn't have made any difference. You deceived me once. I believed you'd do it again. I couldn't live with the fact that twice you'd taken a life created from our love and for what? So that you could *make captain.* It went against everything I've ever believed about the union of a man and woman. To me, there's nothing more sacred than the fruit of that union."

He turned to face her. "So, I left. And I didn't look back."

Roxanne stood and went to him. "I did have a miscarriage. The second time—"

"I know. Marti told me years later. But by then it was too late. I knew you wouldn't forgive me for not believing you in the first place, and I knew I couldn't forgive you for not being honest with me all those years ago.

"I just figured we were destined to be apart."

Roxanne nodded in agreement.

Storm put a finger under her chin and lifted her head. "But being with you again . . . and I don't mean just the physical part although that's part of it . . . an emptiness in my life is finally filling. All these years, I've been functioning on auto-pilot. But now, it's like I'm alive again." He rubbed the pad of his thumb across her lower lip. "Maybe we can work through this somehow." He lowered his mouth to hers, but she turned away.

Roxanne was too devastated to be angry. He knew. All this time, he knew she wasn't lying. And he never told her. Never called her to say he was sorry for misjudging her. But then again, why would he? She'd betrayed his trust first. With a past filled with so much pain, what kind of future could they possibly have together?

She backed away. "I think we both learned some things today. Let's just keep it at that and focus on getting to the helicopter." She reached for her clothes. The cuts on her arms stung from being in the water. She would need an antiseptic spray again soon.

"Your clothes are still wet," he said.

Roxanne gazed up at the sky. They sun's rays were not as piercing as Storm's stare. "In this heat, they will dry soon enough."

Eleven

Amadeus sulked. For nearly an entire day, he had been unable to locate Storm or Roxanne. The helicopter was still in place, so they hadn't left the island. Unless they took leave of their senses and tried to swim to shore. Even so, his surveillance should have shown him something. As it stood now, it was as though they had vanished as part of an evil magician's trick.

Amadeus stood. He'd been sitting in his control station for hours. He'd pushed every button, pulled every lever, and turned every knob on his console. The Odin's Eye should have told him Storm's location at all times. Cameras strung discreetly on trees and inside some animals should have given him clear pictures of their actions. And his sound tracking system should pick up their movements, speech and breathing from miles away. He smashed his fist into the palm of his hand.

Nothing!

Even his bodyguards, which he preferred to think of as the three stooges, hadn't been able to turn anything up. The only thing they came back with was dirty shoes and mosquito bites.

He gnashed his teeth. Something strange was going on and he had an unnerving suspicion that Carl was in on it.

He headed out of his office, then stopped at the door. He was short of breath and dizzy. Thoughts collided in his mind. Was it his blood pressure? He knew he'd put too much salt on his bowl of corn. Maybe life on an island was finally catching up with him. He'd always been sensitive to heat.

God, he couldn't be having a stroke. Not now. Not when he was so close to seeing his ultimate fantasy realized.

For five minutes, he breathed into the palms of his hands in case he was on the verge of hyperventilating. When he felt steadier, he ventured out and strolled down the hallway and into his dressing room. Mirrors on every wall revealed everything he wished he wasn't—a tall frail man scared he would snap in two if the wind blew too strongly. All his life, he'd wanted to be a jock. Someone brawny and strong. But he was blessed with brains and not brawn. His success with games was nothing more than his attempt to flex the only muscle God had seen fit to give him. Each game he defeated made him feel stronger. But Carl's technology made him feel something far greater. When he was connected to his monitoring equipment, he not only watched what was going on with Storm . . . he could feel it. For the first time in his life, he knew what it was like to have untamed strength coursing through him. Storm's savage determination to fight, to defend, to win, charged through him like a brilliant and monstrous current. His breathing quickened as he realized the pleasure those thoughts of power gave him.

That Carl, he was up to something. He sneaked off to be by himself and disappeared too often. He seemed a little too eager to please and sweated a lot. He should have known that Carl would one day become restless. But he'd thought that if he gave Carl enough money and let him do all the strange techno-things that he did that he wouldn't mind doing a favor or two for his longtime friend. Besides that, they were the closest thing to family that either of them had.

Amadeus's mind flickered with the memory of his mother. She'd never quite known what to do with a genius child. So Amadeus had learned by age five that if anyone was going to be the parent in their relationship, it was going to be him. So he issued the orders and his mother obeyed.

It wasn't until he was a teenager that he fully realized his mother was afraid of him, and if it weren't for some thin strand of duty and obligation that connected them, she would have left when he was still a toddler.

For a time, he forgot about the man in the mirrors. But it was only for a time. He would find Storm and the woman. Whatever Carl knew, he would find out, or his longtime friendship would come to an unfortunate end.

Amadeus turned to face himself once more. He pulled his sweater around his thin middle and shivered. "Why is it so cold in here?"

They had little to say to each other after their self-disclosure. They worked in tandem to spear fish from the ocean, build a fire, and secure shelter. They shared sips of water from Roxanne's canteen and sprayed each other with a fresh coat of repellent.

Only they were quiet during the night. The full moon seemed to cause an uproar in the jungle. Like Amadeus had turned up the volume of the world around them. Roxanne thought it was just as well. That way she didn't have to listen to the thoughts churning in her head. It was enough that her body still thrummed from Storm's touch. But her mind was still reeling from it as well.

Their only discussion took place when Storm suggested that they make camp along the beach for the night and resume their journey in the morning. Roxanne agreed, and after a dinner of bananas, wild greens, and—heaven help her—roasted grubs, they lay side by side under the covering—together, but miles apart.

Brown crickets, grubs, diligent earthworms, and something Roxanne hoped was just a mouse kept her awake most of the night—that and the memory of her reckless tryst with Storm still burning every layer of her being.

She wished she could toss and turn, get up and pace, or better yet, take a cold shower. But the shelter she and Storm had built left little room to do anything but rest side-by-side or on top of each other.

Amid the night song of the forest, Storm's moderate snoring blended in to the sounds hitting her ears. She wondered how on earth he could sleep at a time like this. Who knew what animal could be lurking in the dark? What if an Adversary found them? Or what if she wanted one more taste of his luxurious body? What if—

"Go to sleep, Roxanne."

She stiffened. They'd been facing in opposite directions since they lay down. They said goodnight and, soon after, Storm had fallen asleep. So how had he known her turmoil?

"I know you're awake. You're fidgeting. Relax. We'll need every minute of rest we can get if we're going to make any progress tomorrow."

He turned toward her. "According to the last reading on that Odin's Eye, we're miles away from the helicopter. Even if we walk nonstop and don't encounter any craziness, it will still take us days to get there."

Roxanne sighed.

"I can't sleep," she said, looking out into the darkness. Living in the city gave her a different orientation with the night. With so many buildings, businesses, homes, and streetlights, she had never really known true darkness, with the exception of a power outage. But here, where gargantuan trees cut off the sun's rays and there was no artificial light, the night was pitch dark and frightening. It was as though she had her eyes closed when, in fact, they were wide open.

"Don't they ever shut up?"

His body contoured to hers. "No," he said.

One animal sounded like a man whistling. Another sounded like a broken car horn. Another sounded like a rusty gate.

"Every animal in the jungle must be awake."

"Not every animal. Just the ones that hunt at night."

Roxanne turned toward him. "Did you say hunt?"

He sighed. "Go to sleep, Roxy. I promise to kill anything that tries to eat you."

"Deal," she said, snuggling in.

She closed her eyes once more and tried to filter out the noisy dark. Maybe if she concentrated on the sound of the water. It was all around them. The downpour of the waterfall, the surge of the ocean. As a girl, she loved the sound of a steady rain. A lengthy downpour relaxed her, made her sleepy. Nowadays she never allowed herself the time it took to slow down and listen to the rain. She only paid attention to it when she had to—when she was piloting a plane over a storm or landing during one. If she'd learned anything from this experience it would be to slow down, thank God for her blessings, and appreciate those she loved. Never take a raindrop for granted.

Storm moved against her and draped a strong arm over her. She didn't flinch or try to move away. It felt good, safe, reassuring. "Focus on one thing—one benign thing. Just let it float in your mind unattached. If other thoughts try to enter your head, it's a sign that you're not completely relaxed. So breathe deeply and let the tension go. I can't have you weak or foggy because you didn't get enough sleep."

What could she think of that wouldn't add to her stress? She let out a slow breath and the image of her nephew came to mind. He had beautiful black skin and lots of hair. He had a big dopey grin in every picture she had. Roxanne said a prayer. *Dear God, please grant me the blessing of seeing my nephew in person. I promise I'll do whatever I need to do to fix my relationship with my sister. I promise.* She kept the image of KJ in her mind and said her prayer over and over. Storm stroked her arm softly and after a time, she drifted off to sleep.

The morning brought with it a white haze and the layered sounds of the jungle at daybreak—frogs croaking, trills of small mammals, the wind weaving through leaves. A chorus of forest songs surrounded them, brought them awake.

Despite the repellent and the tent-like covering Storm made out of branches and large leaves, they awoke with fresh insect bites.

* * *

Roxanne stretched the kinks out of her trying night. Once she finally fell asleep, she stayed asleep, cradled in a familiar contentment. She tried her best to shake it off before it set in permanently.

Her watch said seven a.m. eastern standard time. What she wouldn't do for a Spanish omelet, a cup of coffee, and the *New York Times*. She squinted up into the sun. Her heart lurched. She was missing her territory already. The air. The sky. She never liked being grounded for too long. Something told her that this escapade with Storm was going to cost her valuable flight time—that is assuming they survived.

"Give me a hand with this."

Roxanne did a slow motion about-face in the sand. "Yes, sir!" she said, saluting.

Storm came over with the Odin's Eye partially attached. She finished pressing the cords into place and liked the way his skin felt beneath her hands. For a second, she stopped and remembered. Her hands had once spent hours traveling the length and bulk of his body. Her fingertips burned at the memory. She shivered and looked up.

"Don't stop on my account," he said.

Maybe she didn't need a plane to fly. Her spirit soared with the mere thought of being with Storm again. They moved closer to each other, as if on autopilot. Storm's handsome face neared hers. He had the same chiseled features and sharp hard lines. His skin was the color of peanut butter and would have been just as smooth if not for the stubble darkening his jawbones. Frown lines at the corners of his eyes and a sprinkle of grey at the temples attracted her even more. In their years apart, he'd gotten even better looking.

Their lips touched. Her body went limp. He caught her with his strong arm before she could buckle under the power of his allure.

"Sempala," he said, voice quiet and hot against her mouth.

He drew nearer. She took a deep breath and prepared herself for his kiss and then—

"Uh-uh! Get back!" She pushed him away.

"What?" he said, blinking back his surprise.

She covered her mouth and nose with her hand. "You stink!"

His eyes rolled skyward.

He grabbed her then. Pulled her close. "You used to like the way I smelled."

She squirmed in his arms. The cords from the device rubbed against her in strange ways. "No. You're funky. That shower did *not* help you at all, brotha!"

He traced her shoulder, her throat, and her neck with his nose. A low growl rumbled in his chest. "You smell . . . wicked."

"Uh! I'm funky, too, ya nut!"

He spun her around to face him with a cocky smile plastered on his face. "I've smelled you much worse."

"You have never smelled me funky!"

"Don't forget who you're talking to. This is me, remember. When your temperature was one hundred and three and you couldn't move, I seem to remember—"

"Stop! Don't remind me." Roxanne shuddered. She'd had a virus that knocked her on her butt for a week. That whole time, Storm nursed her back to health, cleaned up some rather unsightly messes and bore all the odors her body oozed without cringing. It was one of the worst times in her life.

Roxy . . . once she made up her mind, she could be as stubborn as ever. He cast an admiring glance over the length of her body. He'd get nowhere with her now. But maybe later, when they were tired or excited and the aroma of exertion no longer seemed off-putting, when the attraction between them was as strong as it ever was—perhaps stronger. Then she would be his.

"Let's break camp," he said. "The end of the game is waiting for us."

"Where are you going?"

"Into the cave."

Storm shook his head. "We go up top. This has been a nice respite, but we've got to get back into the game."

"Why?"

"Because that's the way to the helicopter."

"This cave goes in that direction. If it's anything like the first part, we might be able to take it all the way to the helicopter. Then we can go up."

"Do you think Amadeus is going to go for that?"

She glanced at the Odin's Eye. "You said yourself that Amadeus can't touch us here. Nothing has registered on that thing since we entered the cave."

Storm stuck the end of the spear into the sand. "We don't even know what's in the cave. There could be animals, dead ends, or turns in the wrong direction."

"You didn't seem to be concerned about that while in the other cave."

"We didn't have a choice then."

"And we do now?" Roxanne kicked sand toward the ocean. "What's safer, Storm, going topside where we know that you will be in danger, or traveling through a cave where we know we will be bigger than any creature in there. I know you, Storm. What's up?"

Storm averted his eyes. "Nothing. I'm just trying to get us the heck off this island." He punched a few buttons on the Eye. "Now, come on!"

But Roxanne shrank back, suddenly aware of Storm's eagerness to continue. "You like this game."

His eyes widened, but his frown was insincere. "You're crazy."

"No, but maybe you are. You're enjoying this whole thing. Fighting, scrounging, roughing it. Not knowing what will happen next. You're enjoying it. You can't wait to get to the next level."

He took a step forward. "Roxanne—"

"No," she said with disbelief. "I should have stayed with Amadeus."

The pain in Storm's eyes hurt to her very core. She

shouldn't have said that. But it was hard to fathom the fact that Storm actually wanted to get back into the game. But when she thought about it more closely, she realized it wasn't so difficult to believe. Storm was a soldier, a warrior, a fighting machine. If he wasn't on a mission, or in training, he was unhappy. This is the life he'd been living for the past fifteen years. And from what friends told her, he was the best at what he did. She knew that to be the best, one had to immerse oneself in it. And a frightening truth rippled through her. If someone, however crazy, devised a game that challenged her piloting abilities in a new and different way, she might jump—no, bolt—at the chance.

In the space of a deep breath she realized that they were too much alike.

Maybe she understood after all. "Storm—"

"Look," he said, holding up a large hand. "We're beginning to sound like a married couple. Now, we're in a game. The only real way out is through this game. If you don't want to play, stay here."

She stepped to him. She didn't care how many missions he'd been on. He was still the same Haughton Storm that she'd met in school. The same square-faced guy who she saw being wheeled off the playing field the first time she saw him. "I was just going to say that you might be right."

His eyes grew intense with her eagerness. "Oh." He touched the side of her face. His fingertip traced the outline of her jaw. "Have it your way," he said.

With spear and canteen in hand, they both walked toward the cliff and climbed up.

As soon as they entered a grove a trees in a wooded area of the island, Storm checked the Odin's Eye. All systems were a go. They were five miles closer to the helicopter. There were no Adversaries in the vicinity, his vital signs were normal, and the next object in the level was less a mile away.

Roxanne was right. He did enjoy the thrill of the game. He'd built his reputation on outwitting the enemy. As always, thinking two steps ahead. From the moment he'd set the game in motion, a surge of power raced through him. The kind he'd fed off of during critical missions. The honesty of that fact made him feel guilty, but it also made him feel like whatever Amadeus could throw at them, he could handle. Not only handle, but conquer and emerge victorious.

"Where have you been?" Amadeus's tin-can voice popped out of invisible speakers like a blast of cold static.

"We fell into a hole," Storm said.

"All this time? A hole? You know you can't escape the game. I have painstakingly created this thing from one end of the island to the other. There's no way possible that—"

"Amadeus! We're back now. We got ourselves out of the hole, and we're back on track. So get off it!"

A tense pause passed between them.

"We're almost at the end of Level Three. Let us get on with this."

A warm wind rustled the many leaves and branches surrounding them. So many leaves, it sounded like rain instead of just air dancing on the green. Storm and Roxanne waited for Amadeus's reply.

"If I lose you again, the game is over. No helicopter. No pilot. No Odin's Eye. Nothing but you, the jungle, and my mercy."

The brush ahead of them thickened exponentially. Storm used the spear as a machete to cut through the dense vegetation.

"Are you sure it's this way?"

"Yes," he said, clearing the path ahead of them.

The jungle whizzed and screeched around them. An animal scurried off to their left. Roxanne followed the black-and-white blur until it settled in a treetop above them.

"A lemur. It's a lemur!" Storm called.

She shrugged at the animal that looked like a cross between a monkey and a raccoon. "Why are you excited by that?"

"Lemurs are native to Madagascar. We must be on an island off the coast. If we somehow get to a phone or computer or anything that would allow me to get a message out, I'll at least know where to tell them to look."

They'd been moving at a pretty good clip. Storm checked the Eye. They were getting close. He checked it again for Adversaries. There were none on the screen. Considering their distance, he'd expected to see something by now. Something was up.

"Let's wear a condom on this one," he said over his shoulder.

Roxanne fanned mosquitoes from her face. "What?"

"Sorry. That's the slang I use for taking it easy and using every precaution. It's automatic."

When the thick green parted abruptly, they entered a clearing and the locator on the screen blinked a furious red.

"It's here," he said, looking around.

Roxanne looked around also, not sure of what she was searching for but believing she would know it when she saw it.

Without the shade-producing covering of the bushes and trees, the sun beat down on them with full force. Knowing that they were so close to the equator probably added more temperature to the heat she felt. If she had to guess, she would have said it was one hundred degrees. She wiped the sweat covering her face. One hundred and ten.

Storm held out his arm and walked about, from bush to shrub to the tall tree towering above the tree line. Roxanne had noted that most of the very tall trees were about the same height, with a few exceptions. Periodically, out of the uniformity, there would be a mammoth tree that towered well above the others. Storm had stopped at the one before them and glanced up. After a few moment, he turned to her.

"I guess you don't need any artificial Adversaries when you've got gravity."

Roxanne joined Storm at the base of the tree. "What's up there?"

"I'm sure that's what I'm here to find out." He handed her the spear. "Hold this."

He walked around the large tree trunk to determine the best approach. One side seemed to be more amenable to scaling than the other.

"How will you know when you find it?" she asked as he started up.

"I'll know," he responded, keeping his eyes on the branches and footholds ahead of him.

Roxanne's heart pounded like a fist inside her chest. Each minute that Storm climbed higher turned knots of concern in her stomach. She hoped he was right. She hoped he knew it when he saw it. He was already up too high for her tastes. Any higher and he would look like a wild animal making himself at home in his own territory.

Watching him move up the tree reminded her of all the times she'd imagined him—in America, in other countries— doing all the things that made him part of the U.S. special forces. Her mind had pictured him in the water geared up in a wet suit and goggles, in the jungle wearing fatigues with his face painted black. He would come to her. Between assignments. After training. During a pause in her flight schedule. They would laugh, eat, and make love like teenagers. Their times together had been precious because they were so few. But when they were apart, her mind had seen him—leading his team, gathering secrets, saving lives. She never imagined that the real thing would be part of her life.

Now, it didn't seem so glamorous. Just incredibly dangerous. She blinked up into the sunlight, alone and afraid.

She could barely see him now. He'd been gone for almost an hour. The green swallowed up his slow march up the tree. Weary, she sat down on the dirt. By herself, her hunger surfaced and vied with thirst for her attention. Thirst won and she took a generous swig from the canteen. They would need more water soon. Very soon.

No sooner had that thought entered her mind did the first big drop hit her forehead. Then another plunked down and splattered like someone had thrown a tiny water balloon and it had struck and burst over her right eye. Thunder rumbled above her. She glanced up, wondering where the signs of this rain were. The sky was relatively clear, just a few billowy clouds.

Is the devil beating his wife? she wondered.

Maybe rain rolls in differently on this side of the world. Maybe—

Another rumble in the air. More big drops. She shuddered nervously and glanced at the tall tree.

Storm.

Marti watched her niece Amara while she held her son KJ. Amara had turned out to be a wonderful young lady. For a while, the family was worried about her. But she'd managed to turn her life around and was like a godsend. She was so good with kids, it was uncanny.

The four men in the living room with her husband glanced in her direction. She kissed her son and touched Amara's arm. "Will you play with him in his room?"

"Sure."

When they disappeared into the hallway, Marti turned her attention to the topic she'd been dreading and anticipating at the same time.

The whereabouts of her sister.

Roxanne had been gone for several days. No one had seen or heard from her in all that time. In her desperation, Marti had called everyone she could think of, including one of Roxanne's old boyfriends, Haughton Storm. She'd left a message on his answering machine telling him of Roxanne's disappearance and pleading with him to call her. Six hours later, she'd gotten a call from a Marlowe "Sharky" Gilchrist, a friend and team member of Haughton's. He said that he had something he needed to discuss with her and requested a meeting. That was yesterday.

Today he'd shown up with three others. She could tell they were all military. Their stance, their walk, they way they'd addressed her and her fiancé, Kenyon. Before they'd gotten settled into the living room, Marlowe told her that Haughton was missing too and a feeling in his gut told him that the two disappearances were too uncanny to be a coincidence.

That's when she'd called Amara to come over and watch KJ while they talked.

"What can we do?" Kenyon's deep voice asked when she came into the room.

Sharky spoke while the others looked on. "After your call, I checked something out. The witnesses from the gas station described a man in a van. The description of that man matches one given by a resident in a neighborhood where Storm was staying."

The ground shifted beneath Marti. Kenyon rushed to her side and held her up. She covered her mouth with her hands, in more pain than she ever remembered feeling. "Why did you come to us?" she asked.

Marlowe stood. "Because we believe we might be able to track them down, but it takes . . . resources."

He looked directly at Kenyon. "People have to be convinced to look the other way while we investigate or are persuaded to give us information, equipment, and anything else we might need." His eyes narrowed with determination. "We need—"

"Baby?" Marti said, feeling like someone was drowning her heart. But he was already nodding. Her fiancé had connections to just about anyone and anything.

"Whatever you need," he said. "Whatever you need."

Twelve

The rain wasn't so bad. Now. The thick canopy of leaves from the tree provided some covering from the deluge.

If he didn't find whatever it was soon, he wouldn't be able to see above him. And worse yet, the rain made the tree trunk and branches slick and hard going. It was all he could do to keep himself from falling, let alone climb higher.

He'd kept the Odin's Eye on the locator screen. He could tell by the reading that he was getting close.

His hands ached. They were scraped and cut from climbing.

Thunder shook the heavens. Finally the rain came down between the covering of leaves and soaked him. He continued up, slipping at times and scrambling to keep himself against the tree. A faint voice below caught his attention. It was Roxanne. He hoped she wasn't in trouble. If she was, there was nothing he could do about it now. Besides, he saw something large directly above him. And the red pulsing light on the screen grew bigger and flashed erratically.

He wanted to answer her. But calling down would run the risk of moving in a way that might cause him to lose his footing. Right now, he needed all his concentration to get to his goal above and descend back to the jungle floor.

So far, he'd disturbed several species of birds, two lemurs, an owl, and more insects than he could count in a lifetime. Had he been thinking, he would have sprayed himself with repellent before embarking on this vertical journey. Rough and jagged bark scratched his chest and arms. Up here, the jungle sounded different. Not so distant, but right next to him. Pulsing all around him. Inside him. So many living things. It would be easy to feel insignificant among so much life.

A couple of times he'd stopped his ascent to stare out over the jungle. At first, he'd just wanted to see if he could spot the helicopter. But the beauty of all he saw overwhelmed him—the magnificence of the island and the expanse of the ocean. He squinted through branches and leaves to see it. His heart beat like a hearty drum—hollowed out of the very wood upon which he stood. The world was a complex and amazing place. When you look at it through the eyes of a soldier, that was sometimes a hard fact to see. But he was seeing it now. And it was spectacular.

Finally, he trained his eye on the end of the island where Amadeus said a helicopter and pilot were ready and waiting for them. His heart strummed even faster when he saw it. From his vantage point in the tall traveler's tree, the helicopter looked like a toy—something a child would play with alongside Hot Wheels and small metal tanks.

They'd come a long way and weren't that far from the end of the island. As long as they moved through Amadeus's crazy levels, they would be airborne in two days, three days tops.

A shield.

Storm ground his teeth, thinking that Amadeus was one crazy mother. . . .

He reached up. "How in the heck did you get this up here?"

"That's not your concern. Just get it, so you can move on to Level Four."

"I should have known you'd be listening."

"Listening, watching. I plan on keeping an eye on you from now until the end of the game."

Storm pulled the flat metal object from the overhead branches. "Just as long as you keep our agreement," he said.

He could barely see now. The only thing coming into focus was the bark inches away from his face. The jungle quieted a little, replaced by the sound of a million drops of water falling on a million leaves. The temperature had already dropped at least ten degrees. He would have been grateful for that if it didn't feel like a giant had taken a tremendous bucket of oil and poured it onto the tree. Every foothold, every branch, every crevice was slick with rain. It would take him twice as long to get down as it did to climb up.

He'd slid his left arm into the shield hold and pushed it up against his shoulder. He was tempted to toss it to the ground. But there was no way the wide metal could fall through the branches without getting trapped.

He was better off carrying it down.

He hoped that Roxanne had gotten out of the rain. It would be bad if she caught a cold. He wondered what Amadeus would do then. Offer them a choice of cold medicine or a hot meal?

He hated climbing. That was his least favorite part of his military training. Anytime he'd been required to scale a rope, net, wall, or anything vertical, his feet always did strange things, like try to make doubly sure they were planted in the right spot. Only this usually resulted in a misstep. If he would just trust his judgment and go with his instinct, he would do a lot better.

Maybe.

He inched down branch by branch, wondering what his instincts told him about Roxanne.

When his foot slipped, he was deep in thought. Concerns about Roxanne bombarded him from all directions. But they were quickly taken over by the fact that not only had he missed the branch below, when he recovered, he stepped in a weak spot and the foothold was splitting.

He would have to move more quickly. Because of the shield, he weighed more now coming down than he did going up. He would be unable to take the same route downward.

Another slip sent him hurtling toward the bottom. A thick branch broke his fall and caught him solidly on the back. He lay there for a moment, dazed and angry that he could be so careless. A warm pain throbbed just above his buttocks and he wondered if it might be a better idea to stay put until the rain died down.

Suck it up, soldier! The voice in his head was loud and clear. He'd been behaving like a cream puff instead of a commissioned officer in the U.S. Navy SEALs. *What's wrong with me?* But he knew the answer before he even asked the question.

Roxanne.

She always had a way of mellowing him out. Her challenges and stern demeanor always softened him somehow. Made him a little less tough to chew.

When they were alone, he didn't mind. In the past, his capacity for tenderness surprised him. But as long as Roxy was the only person to see it, he didn't care. As long as it was in service to their relationship, he welcomed it.

But now, it was doing neither of them any good. He was taking this game far too easy. He was too relaxed. And now, when he needed the wits of a warrior, he did something stupid, like almost fall out of a tree.

He righted himself and secured his gear. Climbing up wasn't exactly a piece of cake, but climbing down was out of the question.

He stood and took stock of his surroundings. From here, which seemed like halfway to heaven, he could literally go out on a limb. Once there, he could descend through the trees using the thick branches like monkey bars until he reached a point where he could drop to the ground without being harmed. Several of the numerous vines caught his eye. Some of them extended almost to the ground. He could use one or a couple of vines like ropes to rappel down the side of the tree.

He liked that option.

The rain came down steadily now. He'd grown accustomed to it and had already begun to ignore it. Repositioning the items, shifting the shield to where it could hang against his back, he tested the dangling vines.

Right away, some snapped before he could give them a good pull. Taking three of the thicker cords, he twisted them together like a rope and tugged. Nothing. No sounds of tearing, snapping or ripping. He measured the distance between his position and the ground. Forty feet, he guessed, and started his careful rappel downward.

He pushed out, gently at first. The vines held and he slid down about six feet.

He hissed at the burn in the palm of his hands. Much more of that and his palms would be raw and eaten away by the makeshift rope.

Once he settled onto a solid brown branch, Storm ripped off pieces of his undershirt and stuck his fingers into holes he tore with his teeth. Then he resumed his descent.

Push off. Swing out. Slide. Plant. Push off. Swing out. Slide. Plant.

Five feet. Six feet. Seven feet.

It was difficult going, maneuvering through branches and between long-reaching leaves. Spindly twigs and slippery bark.

His jump was carefully controlled. He knew that at any time his rope could pull apart and he'd plunge to the ground.

Push out. Swing. Slide. Plant. He was getting the hang of it, despite the obstacle course of foliage. He'd be on the ground soon.

"Storm!"

Roxanne's voice broke his concentration. He looked down, searching through the branches for a bit of blue or spot of white. *It couldn't be,* he thought. Her voice was too close.

"Storm!"

"Roxy!" he called, rappelling a few more feet. Quicker this time. A bad feeling demanded his haste.

"Roxy?" he called out again. He saw her now. She'd climbed up nearly one-third of the tree and was still coming. He didn't know if she saw him, but he was furious.

He slid down to where she was stepping onto on a branch.

"Where do you think you are going?"

"You were taking too long," she panted. "I thought something had happened."

The feeling in his chest rumbled with concern. "What possessed you to—"

"Never mind!" she said, holding on for dear life. "Let's just get down from here."

"Grab hold of this," Storm said, ducking tree limbs to hand her the vine.

She slid the arms of his shirt down to cover her palms. Concern darkened her eyes. She'd been worried about him. He'd ponder that more when they were both safe and on the ground. "Go on," he said.

Roxanne nodded and with a quick push of her legs, she was on her way toward the ground. The thought of her climbing up to . . . to what? Save him? He could see she was going to be a liability in this game.

A hard rumble of thunder shook the tree. Roxanne's hair and clothes flattened limply against her. He steadied himself against the trunk.

In minutes, her frame was a small doll-like presence at the base of the tree. As soon as she was clear, Storm continued his climb down.

The palms of his hands throbbed like the strikes of lightning in the sky. The rain was turning into a storm. The sky darkened and the wind picked up, making Storm's footing on the tree trunk difficult at best. He followed Roxanne's path down and finally joined her at the foot of the tree.

"Are you crazy?" he shouted.

"Are you?" she shot back. "I know you heard me calling you. All you had to do was answer, and I would have known you were all right."

"I was concentrating on climbing. Besides, what were you going to do up there?"

That question silenced her. After a few seconds she responded, "I don't know."

Storm took the shield from his shoulder and placed it on the ground near the spear. "No? Well, I do. You were going to get yourself hurt or killed!"

A SPECIAL "THANK YOU" FROM ARABESQUE JUST FOR YOU!

Send this card back and you'll receive 4 FREE Arabesque Novels—a $25.96 value—absolutely FREE!

The introductory 4 Arabesque Romance books are yours FREE (plus $1.99 shipping & handling). If you wish to continue to receive 4 books every month, do nothing. Each month, we will send you 4 New Arabesque Romance Novels for your free examination. If you wish to keep them, pay just $16* (plus, $1.99 shipping & handling). If you decide not to continue, you owe nothing!

- Send no money now.
- Never an obligation.
- Books delivered to your door!

We hope that after receiving your FREE books you'll want to remain an Arabesque subscriber, but the choice is yours! So why not take advantage of this Arabesque offer, with no risk of any kind. You'll be glad you did!

In fact, we're so sure you will love your Arabesque novels, that we will send you an Arabesque Tote Bag FREE with your first paid shipment.

Call Us TOLL-FREE At 1-888-345-BOOK

* Prices subject to change

THE "THANK YOU" GIFT INCLUDES:

- 4 books absolutely FREE (plus $1.99 for shipping and handling).
- A FREE newsletter, *Arabesque Romance News*, filled with author interviews, book previews, special offers, and more!
- No risks or obligations.

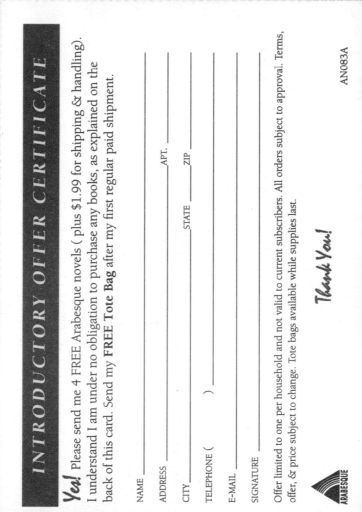

INTRODUCTORY OFFER CERTIFICATE

Yes! Please send me 4 FREE Arabesque novels (plus $1.99 for shipping & handling). I understand I am under no obligation to purchase any books, as explained on the back of this card. Send my **FREE Tote Bag** after my first regular paid shipment.

NAME _____

ADDRESS _____ APT. ____

CITY _____ STATE ____ ZIP ____

TELEPHONE ( ) _____

E-MAIL _____

SIGNATURE _____

Offer limited to one per household and not valid to current subscribers. All orders subject to approval. Terms, offer, & price subject to change. Tote bags available while supplies last.

Thank You!

AN083A

ARABESQUE

Accepting the four introductory books for FREE (plus $1.99 to offset the cost of shipping & handling) places you under no obligation to buy anything. You may keep the books and return the shipping statement marked "cancelled". If you do not cancel, about a month later we will send 4 additional Arabesque novels, and you will be billed the preferred subscriber's price of just $4.00 per title. That's $16.00* for all 4 books for a savings of almost 40% off the cover price (Plus $1.99 for shipping and handling). You may cancel at any time, but if you choose to continue, every month we'll send you 4 more books, which you may either purchase at the preferred discount price. . . or return to us and cancel your subscription.

* PRICES SUBJECT TO CHANGE

THE ARABESQUE ROMANCE BOOK CLUB
P.O. BOX 5214
CLIFTON NJ 07015-5214

PLACE
STAMP
HERE

"I can climb a tree better than anyone you know. Better than you!"

Storm thought about that. When they first met, he discovered that she had a thing for trees, climbing in them, that is. Always trying to get close to the sky. She had no fear of heights whatsoever. But that still didn't mean that in a world controlled by a madman, she couldn't be injured.

"It was a stupid thing to do!"

"Really?" she asked, pacing in front of him. They were shouting above the deluge as the sky erupted above them. "Next time," she said, eyes full of fire, "you're on your own!"

"This is better than I thought. I should have made this a two-player game."

Amadeus's laughter angered Storm even more. "This *is* a two-player game, Amadeus. You against me."

The silence comforted Storm, and let him know he'd struck a blow in a sensitive area.

"You're mistaken, Chief Storm. We are not at odds, you and I. We are alike. Very much alike."

Storm stood with Roxanne under the canopy of large-leafed trees. "We have nothing in common!"

"Oh? Roxanne . . . if you've had your fill of roughing it in the wild outdoors, I can arrange for you to come back inside." More twanging laughter. "Just think, you could be here where there's no rain, no frustrating macho man, and no bees. Whatdayasay?"

He hissed the last word and Roxanne felt as though snakes were slithering on her skin. She knew without a doubt that she would much rather take her chances in the game with Storm than be locked up with a crazy man. She tossed Storm a look of frustration. Not thirty seconds ago, she'd proclaimed her independence and determination to rebel against Storm. Now slapped with the cold, hard truth, she knew she couldn't leave him or betray him.

Storm waited. His eyes narrowed. He expected her to take Amadeus's offer. She turned from him and spoke above the thunder. "I'm staying here," she proclaimed. "With Storm."

"The loss is mine," Amadeus responded. "You see, chief, you and I do have something in common."

And then in the middle of a nerve shuddering cackle, his voice stopped as if it had been cut in half by giant scissors of silence.

They found a stone overhang and waited out the storm there. Roxanne thought her game companion looked pretty much the part of the warrior when he carried the spear and shield. The heat of the jungle had cooled at least twenty degrees now and Roxanne shivered with the change in temperature.

She noticed Storm noticing.

"This rain might be over soon."

She shrugged. "And then again, it may not. This could be the beginning of the rainy season here and we could be in for it."

"Thanks for your positivity."

"You're welcome," she said.

"You know, you didn't have to stay."

Roxanne snorted. "I don't know which creep is worse—you or Amadeus!"

"You didn't think I was so creepy when you pinned me up against the rock under that waterfall!"

"And you didn't seem too eager to leave my side!"

"By the expression on your face, you didn't seem too eager for me to leave!"

The stratosphere boomed and clattered above them. A thick contingent of clouds rolled in, changing day to night.

"No, Ms. Allgood. You're here for a specific reason."

Roxanne and Storm whirled in the direction of the voice. They saw nothing, but there was no mistaking it. The voice in the dark belonged to Carl.

The inside of the tunnel was cool and dry. While Roxanne shivered in a corner, Storm leaned against the cool concrete wall, arms folded in disbelief.

As soon as Carl led them away from the downpour and into the tunnel, things started to make sense to Storm.

"I assume she told you about the Eye."

"She told me," Storm said.

Carl eyed him pensively. "And will you help?"

Storm pushed off the wall to his full height. "No."

The color in Carl's face faded to a grayish-tan. "You *have* to."

Carl had towels and water for them to drink. Storm wondered if the man's generosity would change now that he knew he wouldn't be helped.

"You've seen for yourself the Eye is a success. As you progress through the game, you will face greater challenges, but I'm confident that the Eye will prove invaluable. As long as you use it."

"And when I'm finished . . . when Roxanne and I leave this godforsaken rattrap, I will turn this device over to the military police, who will no doubt have questions for you to answer."

"I can help you, Mr. Storm. You don't know what the next levels are. I could tell you. Warn you. Prepare you."

Roxanne's eyes widened. "Storm?"

"We've done just fine, so far."

"So, that little tumble you took on the tree—that was planned?"

"Roxanne and I are in one piece and that's how we plan to stay."

Carl's laugh was even worse than Amadeus's. There was nothing happy about it. The deep rolling sounds were obviously caused by anger and desperation. It was a dead laugh that confirmed Storm's suspicions.

"What will Amadeus do when he finds out he's being manipulated?" Storm asked.

Carl's fake smile disappeared and Roxanne stopped drying herself with the towel.

A cold silence fell between them. Bright realization shone in Roxanne's eyes, and her mouth dropped. "You're responsible . . . for all of this."

Carl's sinister gaze on Storm never faltered. He neither

blinked nor missed a beat. "Amadeus is a man who never grew out of his Underoos."

Carl walked away from them then. Paced in the round concrete tunnel. Seemed to draw himself up. "He's not even a man. I've given him more credit than he deserves. He's a tall, pale boy. A toy freak."

"Who just happens to be wealthy," Storm said.

Carl spun, eyes wide and greedy. "Yes," he hissed.

"And who is so caught up in his fantasy that he never noticed yours."

Now the man's smile was authentic. "Yes," Carl hissed again.

Roxanne's anger was palpable. "Amadeus is a pawn, just like we are."

Carl reached out to stroke Roxanne's damp hair. She frowned in disgust and jerked away.

"Amadeus is surely a pawn. But you two are no doubt king and queen."

Roxanne would have shivered anyway, but Carl's words made her shiver even more. All along, Amadeus wasn't the one they should have been concerned with. It was Carl.

"What a clever ruse. To bury your own scheme inside the plans of a maniac, where no one would find them. You *promised* the technology, didn't you?"

"I've made arrangements," he replied.

"So you thought I would exchange, turning over the Eye for information about the game."

Carl smiled broadly, revealing two rows of tiny white teeth. Roxanne found his glee appalling.

She turned to Storm. "All right, we need a game plan."

"Does that mean you want his help?" Storm asked, turning toward her.

"It means we need to decide. Frankly, I don't trust him. And we've come this far."

"Affirmative."

The two carried on for a few more moments as though Carl were no longer there. The tunnel hummed with their conversation. They kept a keen eye on him. He was not at all pleased with their behavior.

Carl stamped his foot. "You cannot refuse me!"

"On the contrary, Carl," Roxanne remarked. "That's exactly what we've just done."

Eyes narrowed, Carl pressed a combination of numbers on a keypad, too rapidly for Storm to discern.

A door slid open. Steps led to the outside, back into the jungle.

"Then you've made a grave mistake."

Roxanne and Storm looked out to where the rain had slowed to a drizzle.

"You *will* regret your decision. My influence with Amadeus is immeasurable. This game can be challenging or it can be . . . vicious. As you will soon see."

Storm escorted Roxanne up the stairs. "My team calls me Cobra. Rest assured, there is a reason."

And with that, Roxanne and Storm gathered their resolve and reentered the game.

They had been traveling for days. Storm was starting to wonder if part of the holographic technology was being used to make them think they were getting closer to the other side of the island, when in fact they were walking in circles. A stone of dread fell into his stomach. If that was the case, Amadeus or Carl could keep them on this quest for weeks and they would never see the end.

He stole a glance at Roxanne. He couldn't believe how well she'd ridden out this whole ordeal. She had the strength and tenacity of men on his team. She refused to give in even when they ran out of water and bug spray. She had snapped vines with him until they found one with a reservoir of water. She'd taken the plants he'd shown her and used the sap in their veins as a salve for her mosquito bites. And when he'd stopped trying to protect her, as she so vehemently asked time and time again, he'd found that she made the perfect partner—breaking through thick brush, sometimes with her bare hands, helping to construct their shelter at night, and catching small animals so they could eat.

"I know I look terrible, but you don't have to stare," she said, frowning.

True. Even though they bathed every time they came upon a fresh-water spring, her hair had sweated into clumps, and her pants and the shirt he'd given her bore numerous rips and were stained with grass and dirt. The mint they'd shared for their breath did nothing for their other odors. Casting a glance at himself, he saw that he looked even more ragtag than she.

But after all they'd been though on the island, she looked more beautiful to him than he'd ever seen her.

"Don't give me that look, Storm. I know how I look and it ain't good."

His laughter disturbed a few birds in the tree above them. They took flight as his hearty chuckle prevented him from saying what he was thinking: *If she only knew how good she looked to him.*

But somewhere beneath the deep brown of her eyes burned the truth. He could tell that on another level she felt the same about him. And it stopped him in his tracks.

She stopped, too, and it came to him that in another time this could have been a serene place. Expansive leaves from the trees interwoven above them created a splendid latticework of green-green enchantment. A kaleidoscope of vibrant color surrounded them. He touched her face. Stroked it. And this time he said what was in his heart.

"We'd better get this over with."

"I thought we already did," she said, voice silky with need.

He took her hand and led her into a thickness of vegetation where even the most high-powered camera would have trouble penetrating. He sat down, pulled her onto his lap, and sated the need that had been building between them for days.

* * *

He felt twenty again. A young man. Smitten. The sweet nervousness of love making him glow. It was as if he'd never told her goodbye. Never left her to go fight invisible wars. Never gone days without food. Never painted his face jungle black. Never killed anyone.

He'd never had his heart broken or slept with other women. Never.

Their love was still fresh on his lips, like a whisper at midnight, full of promise and possibilities.

She'd swept him away. Being raised by a single-parent father, he hadn't realized how wonderful a woman could truly be.

Roxanne.

His heart had been uncapped by her presence. Thawed. Made new. They navigated through vegetation, greener than anything he'd ever seen. They pushed past brambles toward who knew what. Storm wore a mask of concentration, but inside he smiled. Happy—truly happy—for the first time in a long while.

How strange that they had been walking for days, neither one exactly sure of where the Eye was leading, and instead of feeling like he was on an impossible mission, Storm felt like he was on some kind of bizarre date.

Suddenly, the forest didn't seem so overwhelmingly green. He discovered that if he paid attention, he could see other colors, too. Yellow streaking through the veins of enormous leaves. The fiery red vines of tulip plants. A barely pink orchid. Or the sun striking a bush so sharply the verdant color turned white. They were all there as though God had dipped the tips of his fingers in a rainbow and lightly touched the jungle ahead of him.

Love was a wonderful thing.

He hummed as they pushed their way through the foliage.

"I remember that song," Roxanne said. She kept her eyes ahead.

"What?" he said, not realizing he'd been humming anything in particular.

" 'I'll Be Good.' My cousin made me listen to that song over and over. That was when—" She looked up, a half smile curling the corners of her mouth. "That was when Edwin Holloway ran you over."

Storm slid a glance in her direction. "That was also when we met."

She nodded, not wanting to warm at the memory, but acknowledging the heat already rising to her cheeks. It was the summer she, her brother, and her sisters had been shipped off to family members in Texas. They'd all gone down on a Trailways bus and spent two months with Aunt Stella and Uncle Charlie in Dallas. She and her siblings had paired up with cousins of similar age and interest.

Deborah was a cheerleader. Roxanne had always wanted to be a cheerleader, but there was so much work for her to do at home helping her mother that she'd never had the time or opportunity.

In Dallas, she followed Deborah everywhere, especially to cheerleading practice. Her tagging along had paid off and led her to the boy of her dreams.

He was the most perfect being she'd ever seen. His skin was a creamy brown color, and his narrow eyes were set deep and serious, as though his mind were in a constant state of reflection. His cutting cheekbones tapered to a mouth with lips that appeared pursed and ready to be kissed. His chin jutted out just a bit in a way Roxanne thought looked strong and daring. He also had the prettiest, whitest teeth she'd ever seen. In all of the short years of her adolescence, she'd always had crushes on guys with cool teeth. It looked like her heart was at it again.

It wasn't the seriousness in his eyes that caught her attention, but the spark she could see in them. A burning light just below the surface made her believe that a genuine person lived beneath all the padding, uniform, hype and bravado. One who was as excited about life as she. The air was charged with her attraction to him and it became clear to her that the reason she came to Texas for the summer was to meet the guy with the last name of Storm stitched on the back of his jersey. Somehow, some way, she had to meet him. And if his occasional glances in her direction meant anything, she would meet him sooner than later.

"Storm! You're in!"

Haughton Storm snapped his chin strap and jogged into the huddle. He'd played safety for his high school team for two years and he was good at it.

Not just good. He was the best.

His match-ups had contributed to more goals than any other team in the history of football at Buckley Academy. Energy ricocheted in his body.

Concentrate. Watch their eyes. Be mobile. No mercy.

Unlike most players who focused on winning the game, Storm focused on winning the play. Every play. Coach Foster told him once, "If you can do that, the game will take care of itself."

His limbs tingled with excitement.

The ball was snapped. He charged toward his receiver. He would hear the coach's admonition, "Always check your peripheral," after the ringing stopped in his ears. But before then, his eyes were fixed on the ball and a possible interception, not the receiver angling toward him.

Storm guessed their collision could be heard for miles. All he would remember would be a sound like a gong being struck inside his head and the scream of the girl who had been watching him during the entire game. After that, it was lights out.

When he awoke about an hour later, his family, his best friend, his best friend's sweetheart, and the girl that had been watching him were in a hospital room with him.

"What are you all staring at?" he said, and tried to sit up. When the room spun upside down, he closed his eyes and stopped moving.

"Damn," he moaned.

"Haughton! Your language," his mother quipped.

"Sorry, Ma, but my head feels like crap."

The canister rose from the leaf-covered ground and startled them out of their thoughts. Storm glanced at Roxanne, wondering what spoils Amadeus would offer them this time.

The same cylindrical shape. The same compartment-sized storage areas, the same sliding plastic front. The container whined to a halt.

A gallon of water on one side, a book on Nordic mythology on the other. Roxanne's reaction mirrored his own.

"Thank God!" she said, reaching for the water.

"What are you doing?" Storm responded, grabbing her hand.

"What does it look like?"

"It looked like you were going for the water."

"I was."

He maintained his hold on her wrist. "We need the book," he said, releasing her.

"You're crazy!" she said, lifting up the canteen she carried. "We are a few swigs away from being dried up."

"This is an island, Roxy. We can always get water. But that book can give us insight to this whole game."

He took a deep breath. "The story of Odin is in there. This whole game is based on that story. That book probably has clues . . . clues that we will need since Carl is now an enemy."

Roxanne slid a glance at the fresh canteen of water just waiting for their consumption. Her mouth would have watered if it hadn't been so dry.

Her gaze returned to Storm. "I can tell you everything that's in that book."

He remembered Roxanne reading stories to her niece. Amara had probably been about six at the time. From time to time, Marti would even sit in. She was a teenager, but she still loved being read to. He never imagined that Roxanne's steadfast determination to expose her young relative to literature also held a selfish bent. Her fascination with mythology.

She'd never admitted it to anyone. Hell-bent on maintaining her practical, strong black woman front, she didn't want anyone to know that stories of goddesses, faraway lands, and mythical beasts turned her on. She shared her knowledge of Viking gods with him until she ran out of stories to tell.

Thirteen

This morning she'd watched him wash the sweat from his body and get dressed. Sunlight glistened on his damp skin. He looked like a gladiator, preparing for battle.

Her hair was almost matted against her head from the heat and humidity. If today was anything similar to yesterday, she and Storm would be able to *see* the humidity by midday. She rescinded her original wishlist. Now she wanted a comb, some soap, and a personal air conditioner.

"Remember that power outage at the dorm?" he asked.

Roxanne would never forget that weekend. Storm had been his usual amorous self—always trying to get her into bed. He was a good lover, so she never balked. Except when *Star Trek* was on.

Roxanne was a *Next Generation* junkie. Every time Storm came for her when her show was on, she always refused him, to lose herself in the compelling world of space flight.

One Friday night, when they were lying on the bed in his dorm room, he slid his hand beneath her shirt and massaged a nipple with his fingertips—one of his many signals that he was ready for love.

She groaned angrily and pushed his hand away. He was not dissuaded. He tried again and murmured coaxing words from his lips. To no avail. Commander Worf was about to take The Oath with his Klingon girlfriend. Nothing could prevent her from seeing how it all turned out.

"Stop!" she ordered.

That's when the argument started.

"Is this fantasy bullcrap more important than me?"

Roxanne blew a short wind through her teeth and kept on watching. "Of course not."

"Prove it," he said, sliding off the bed. He stepped in front of the television with his arms crossed.

"Hey!" she said. Roxanne sat up. "Get out of the way!"

"No."

She pushed him and tried to look around his thick body. "Move!"

"No," he repeated.

She couldn't tell what was happening. Were they going to go through with it or not? Worf really needed a mate. "Storm!"

He grabbed her shoulders and stopped her movement. "I hate this show. At first, I tried to tell myself that I didn't like science fiction. But that's not it. When *Star Trek* is on, it's like nothing else in the world matters. It's the same with your flight training."

He let her go then, but kept talking. "You get fascinated with things—at the exclusion of everything else. Roxy, your interests should add to your life, not take it over."

She was listening, a little. She was also noticing that they'd gone to commercial and she didn't know if they had actually taken the Oath or not. "Darn it!" she said, sinking back on the bed.

Storm recoiled, realizing what had happened. "You know, all I have ever wanted is to be the best at whatever I do. But being the best for me *includes* you." He swallowed. "When you think about being the best, am I anywhere in that definition?"

He left the dorm room then. Five minutes later, the lights went out.

Roxanne was outraged that she would not see the end of her favorite show, until Storm started kissing her. Soon she forgot all about Worf and his love interest and focused on her own.

They'd been spending more and more time reminiscing. They'd filled hours with recollections of the past. The activity brought on a strong longing for the comfort of her sisters and a memory she wished she could erase.

During a Christmas party at Yolanda's house, Roxanne had let her grudge-holding hit an all-time high. She remembered circulating in the living room, determined not to stand in one place for too long. The family had gotten together for another big Christmas celebration. Her siblings were there with their respective significant others. She was there alone. She'd spoken to everyone. Carried on conversations, made small talk, and spent quality time with her niece. But when her sister Marti approached her, her desire to converse fizzled. The words wouldn't come. She forced a smile and gave closed answers. Her sisters knew what was going on. They tried to get her to be more civil to her sister.

"It's been five years," Morgan said. "Why are you still acting like this? She's your sister for God's sake!"

"A sister doesn't ruin another sister's life," she shot back.

By then everyone in the room had turned to watch the exchange.

"I never meant to ruin your life!" Marti shouted from across the room.

Roxanne slammed down the drink she'd been carrying. Apple juice spilled over the sides of the glass and left a yellow stain to spread on the white linen cloth. "Yeah, well, ya did!" she shouted.

Roxanne gathered her things from a bedroom and hurried out of her oldest sister's home. She'd ruined the gathering. She knew she had. But she didn't care. Nothing could change her heart regarding Marti's irresponsibility. Nothing.

Roxanne shuddered, floating from her painful memory back to the present. She decided to fill her mind with more pleasant thoughts. "You used to let me do freaky things to you," she said.

Storm smiled his tough-guy smile. Half cocky, half verve, all man. His almond eyes, two smoldering ellipses, urged her to continue through the pause.

"Things I've never done with anyone else. Things no one else would understand."

He pulled her to him. "Things no one else would let you do." He kissed her deeply, wetly, urgently. Images flashed through her mind. Two creamy brown bodies naked. Bumping together. Grinding together. She slid her body against his. His thigh. His side. His perfectly round backside. She remembered lingering there. Rubbing herself against him. The friction sending shivers through her. Sliding. Rubbing. Grinding. Coming.

His kiss deepened. Her body jerked with the memory of taking him from the back.

She could taste his soul then. Every time they made love, Roxanne heard funk music full of drums and horns and a moody bass. She smelled incense—blue Nile, musk, and rain. She felt like a bold black sister in a crushed velvet painting. Her insides throbbed like strobe lights. And she flew sky-high.

They resumed their trek and her eyes smiled as she remembered another time. He had come to her, in his clean and crisp Navy uniform. The white was so brilliant she blinked at the brightness. His medals gleamed in her living room like tiny headlights.

His poise and strength stirred her. Roxanne's physical need for Storm was immediate and acute. She grabbed him by the collar and pulled him on top of her. Down onto her couch. Down into her lust. She tossed her finely detailed pillows to the floor and went for his zipper.

They had said nothing when she opened the door. They had spoken no words when he'd walked in and she'd closed the door behind him. And now, as she reached through the opening in his trousers and stroked him with a practiced lover's rhythm, they kept silent and still, and let their eyes do the talking.

Their gaze transmitted a tempest of emotions and thoughts whirling between them. *I missed you. I need you. We must have this joining. I'm incomplete without you. I can't live without this feeling.*

I love you.

Storm reached for the buttons on his shirt, but Roxanne stopped him. "No," she said hoarsely. "Make love to me like this."

Maneuvering beneath him, she removed her clothing, but she wanted him to keep all of his on—a potent aphrodisiac and reminder that the man she loved was a soldier, a warrior. Among the most elite that America had to offer. And he was hers. In her mind. In her soul.

In her body.

Storm removed a condom packet from his back pants pocket, opened it, and handed it to Roxanne. He knew she loved to put on their protection. Any excuse to touch his manhood—to caress it just the way he liked it. He moaned at the warm slide of her hands down the length of him. He couldn't wait to be inside.

When he pushed into her—into the sweet space between her thighs—she moaned again. Even with the condom, he could tell she was wet for him. Drenching like a summer rain. He shuddered at the steady downpour of her arousal. The sensation more like falling than entering.

Their gazes caught and held. There would be no close embrace. No neck-to-neck nuzzling. There would be no closed eyes. The spell between them was too strong to be broken.

Their bodies moved together and apart. Toward and away from each other. Just like their touch-and-go relationship. Conjoined for only brief moments in time. Long enough to renew their bond, stoke their fire. Their gaze grew more penetrating, as did their thrusts. Each conveyed to the other how time apart had created an urgency that had only just begun to be satisfied.

Storm was so heavy on her, crushing sometimes. And she loved it! He pressed his body down her, dipped himself into her core as if she were a well, bottomless, yet brimming with water. Unbridled heat overwhelmed her and for a moment, her eyes snapped closed.

"No!" he ordered.

Their gazes locked again and they stared trance-like as shadows of ecstasy played on their faces.

"What are you thinking about?"

Roxanne wanted to ignore Storm's question. If she could just stay a few more moments in the heaven of their past . . .

"Us," she admitted. "I was thinking about us."

He reached over, fingered one of the many tousled strands of hair on her head, then slid the backs of his fingers down the side of her neck. He massaged the knob of her collarbone, causing circular heat to rise within her, matching the heat of her memory. "What about us?" he asked.

"How good we used to be together," she said, realizing that she hadn't been as good in or out of bed with anyone since Storm.

He kissed her cheek. "Better than perfect," he replied, then went off to scout the trail ahead of them.

When he returned, they continued their journey into the past.

"I knew you were a good lover when I saw you eat those peaches," she said, grinning.

He showed his teeth then, in a bright warm smile that lit up her insides. "What peaches?"

"You know what peaches. The ones you fawned over when you got out of the hospital."

After Storm's injury on the football field, he was in the hospital for two days. When he finally got released, a handful of friends and fans showed up at his parents' house to celebrate his homecoming. With the small throng of adoring fans, Roxanne felt snuffed out by all the older girls who'd obviously come to catch Storm's eye. Being sixteen and pre-growth spurt, she felt the tall, lanky, and heavily made-up girls squeezed her out of Storm's line of sight.

Zurich Kingdom carried a small bag with him and handed it to Storm as soon as they walked into the house.

"Got somethin' for ya, good buddy!" he said, handing over the package.

"My man!" Storm said, opening the bag. Walking toward the living room, he pulled out a plump peach.

Friends and fans talked at once, all vying for Storm's attention. Roxanne stood next to her cousin, ignoring the girls and keeping a keen eye on Storm.

For a moment, he seemed to be taken with the giggly schoolgirls crowding around him. They laughed and fawned. He smiled and flashed and his pearly whites. Roxanne melted.

She watched as his eyes darted and searched. She wondered if he could be looking for her. When their eyes caught, she had her answer.

Storm's vision had threaded through the throng and found her. Once found, his stare held fixed and bright.

Time slowed. Roxanne's heart leapt to her throat. He turned the peach automatically between his fingers, then slowly, methodically, he brought the fruit to his lips and bit softly.

The bite left peach juice and pulp at the corners of his mouth. Even with her inexperience, she knew that if she had been older, licking away the remnants of his treat would have been an appropriate, maybe even expected, thing to do.

God, to be eighteen!

The obvious pleasure on his face radiated against her skin as if she were radar and he'd just entered her scope. He chewed like the meat of the fruit in his mouth was the most delectable thing he'd ever tasted. He savored it, like he would a lover's kiss. And just when she thought his actions couldn't get any more sensual, he licked the places around his lips where the juice had begun to run. Roxanne felt things she'd never felt in her life. Excitement prickling her skin. Warm pulses pooling below her stomach. Attraction collecting in her heart. She knew then and there that when she decided she wanted to offer her virginity, it would be Haughton Storm who would take it.

After that, her mind was consumed with thoughts of him. His mouth on her like it had been on that peach, devouring, sampling, tasting.

When he'd showed up at her cousin's house with his best friend, she hadn't let nervousness or apprehension rule. Even though she had felt them both. A guy like Storm would only be bored with another groupie type. And she'd never been like that anyway. So she'd treated him like he was just a regular Joe High School instead of one of the stars on the football team. She didn't bat her eyelashes or laugh at all of his jokes. And when he tried to kiss her, she refused.

At first.

He'd settled for holding her hand and sitting close beside her on the back porch. Her cousin Deborah had no qualms about French-kissing Zurich. Roxanne had only heard her older sister Yolanda talk about that kind of stuff with her friends. But she knew that before the summer was over and she and her siblings returned to Georgia, she would let Storm French-kiss her.

She would find out what it was like to be a peach.

"Why did you zero in on me?" she asked.

Storm trailed the middle finger of his large, calloused hand down her sideburn. "How could I not?"

In all his life he'd never known a woman like Roxanne All-good. She was made of more mettle than some of the men he trained and served with. Strong-willed. Downright aggressive when it came to what she wanted.

Since their breakup he hadn't been with a whole lot of women. There'd never been time. But he'd been with a few.

Why did he always seem to find the ones who had no clue how to make a decision? And they all had timid little voices that sounded like they were either too happy or on the verge of crying. These kind of women always said things like, "I don't care. What do you want to do?" He could live his entire life without hearing another woman say that. Please, God.

Now Roxanne, on the other hand, not only knew what she wanted, but she tried to tell him what he wanted as well. She always wanted to call the shots. Always thought she knew better.

Which, if he admitted the truth, was precisely why he

gravitated to women who seemed just a tad bit vacant. No other kind of woman would settle for what he would offer them. Sex and just sex on his terms. Only when he was off duty. And sometimes not even then.

They didn't ask questions. They better not. Not if they knew what was good for them, or rather the quasi-relationship they had.

He settled back against the tree, away from the sap draining and the single-file trail of ants marching into the trunk.

His attention fell upon the ants. Single-minded in their purpose. They didn't have to think about what they wanted as individual ants. Only the good of the colony mattered.

She was still staring at him. Still waiting for an answer. Why did he chose her? What made him turn away from so many other girls in high school who would have sucked his dirty toes if he'd asked them, to focus on a girl who wouldn't even kiss him?

It was simple.

Back then he'd known. Roxanne was his girl. She was the one.

He returned her gaze, the pain of his mistake rearing up anew like a thumb-struck match.

"Because I was supposed to," he said.

"How much time do we have?" he asked.

"Three days," she said.

He closed the door behind her and, not wanting to waste another minute, had taken her on the floor of the entryway of his apartment.

She'd stopped to see him on the last leg of her flight schedule. Instead of going home to her apartment, she'd come to Washington to be with him.

He had been determined to show her just how grateful he was for her visit.

Afterwards, they'd eaten dinner and then gone outside to watch the sunset. His apartment building was set on a hill on the edge of a wooded area. An important part of their ritual together was sharing the setting of the sun and making love until the sun rose again.

The light summer breeze cooled her skin and moved through her hair. Crickets chirped and the heavy smell of moisture hung in the air, foretelling of the imminent rain. They leaned against each other in the moonlight, calm, relaxed, and content.

The sound they heard made them both sit up. They stared at each other and waited. It came again. Unmistakable. A coyote howling.

Storm rose and stared out between the trees. He could see nothing moving, but the animal sounded close.

"Come on," he said. "Let's get you inside."

Roxanne huffed. "You don't have to play protector."

"I know. But I am. Now come on, before it gets any closer."

Roxanne stood. "I'm sure it can smell us. It wouldn't dare come over here."

"Under normal circumstances, I agree with you. But this thing could be rabid, hurt, or just plain hungry. A hungry animal will do strange things to feed itself. Including walk up on us. Understand?"

She nodded her head and walked with him away from the benches and toward the door.

Another howl. This one much closer. Right behind them. They walked faster.

Storm took out his keys to unlock the door, but Roxanne could sense what he wasn't telling her.

"Storm," she said quietly.

He turned around to where she was already looking.

The animal on all fours behind them looked like it was part coyote and part something else—collie maybe. It was definitely a half-breed.

Storm put his hand to her back and pushed her more urgently toward the door. The animal followed, head lowered, but eyes on them.

Roxanne gasped. She could see the poor thing's ribs. It was either sick or just plain starved.

She wondered if it had once been a pet. It could have been released back into the wild, but having been domesticated, it was having trouble feeding itself. She imagined all sorts of things. When the animal growled, her thoughts turned to calling the police or someone to come and get the mongrel.

Once inside, she watched it from the window. Storm riffled through his pantry, cupboards and refrigerator.

"What are you doing?"

"It's hungry. I'm getting something for it to eat."

Roxanne grabbed his arm. "You are not going back out there. I'm going to call the police to come and get it or shoot it."

Storm put some leftover hamburger, hot dogs, processed turkey, and a raw egg in a large bowl. "In the meantime, anyone coming home or leaving runs the risk of aggravating the thing and getting attacked."

"That includes you!" she said, surprised at the rise of her voice.

"Stay here. I'll be back."

"Storm!" she said, but he ignored her. He'd stepped out of her grasp and took his offering outside.

She looked on from the window while dialing 911. When they answered, she knew her story would sound crazy, but she had no choice.

"Yes, I'd like to report a wild animal." She gave them the address and asked them to hurry.

Roxanne breathed a sigh of relief. As Storm walked outside, he held a revolver in one hand and the bowl of food in the other. He placed the offering away from the apartment building, close to the edge of the wooded area.

The coyote stared, eyes piercing, nose flaring and pulsing. It must have caught a good whiff of what Storm carried. It growled and bared its teeth. Storm held the revolver with both hands, aiming directly for the animal's head, and walked backward to the apartment building. Roxanne ran downstairs to let him in.

He stepped inside, gun still drawn, the animal still growling. A wave of relief washed over Roxanne when she closed the door behind him.

They walked upstairs arm in arm, entered his apartment and watched as the coyote wasted no time going to the food. He ate ravenously, periodically glancing in their direction as if he knew they were watching.

By the time the police had arrived, it had eaten most of what Storm put in the bowl and darted back into the wooded area when they approached.

Storm went out to get the bowl and to talk with the police.

The coyote came back each of the two nights Roxanne was there with Storm. And each night, Storm fed him. When Roxanne left, the animal didn't look so mangy and fierce. Just hungry and tired.

The next time Roxanne came to visit Storm, the animal had gained fifty pounds, was well-groomed, and had a pallet in the corner of Storm's apartment labeled "Jake."

"You know what I remember?" Storm asked, pulling Roxanne out of another personal memory.

She slid a sly glance his way. "What?"

"You singing our song." His eyes smoldered with lust. "Sing for me, Roxy."

"This is not the time or the place for—"

"Please," he said, running a finger up and down her forearm. "It's been so long."

She sighed deeply.

His eyes beseeched her. Her heart thudded against her chest. Roxanne had sung in front of many audiences—hundreds of people at a time. But this audience of one made her more nervous than she'd been in a long time. She closed her eyes, knowing what he wanted to hear. Their song. "Feel Like Making Love."

The first words came out tentatively. As she gained confidence, she sang a little louder. A bit stronger. When she opened her eyes, Storm was gazing at her or through her. She couldn't tell which. What she saw in his expression was warm and comforting. Encouraging. Somehow her voice had been able to soften features hardened by the life of a soldier.

She sang on.

With soft rain as her orchestra, her voice moved forward through the verses, yet transported them both back in time. Back to when she sang to him frequently, but rarely finished. Because her melodies served as preludes to their kissing. Aphrodisiacs. She always picked a song with lyrics that explained how she felt about him. He always responded to her selection by showing her physically how he felt about her. It was musical foreplay then. What was it now?

Storm couldn't look away. He breathed harder. His whole body flooded with the memory of their life—their love—together. He'd been shot at, knocked down a cliff, almost drowned, and struck by strong fists, but nothing he'd ever endured compared to the pain caused by listening to Roxanne sing their song. The wounds in his heart opened afresh. The anguish of not having her in his life burst open like shrapnel in his veins.

The acuteness of it made him stand up. "Stop!" he said. He didn't remember her voice being that resonant, that precise. The song touched him in a way he couldn't allow himself to experience right now. Its sting was too sharp.

He walked away, a string of curses trailing behind him.

It looked like Storm had as much difficulty hearing the song as Roxanne did singing it. Memories and feelings she didn't know she still had crowded into her voice and added a layer of honesty to her voice she'd never heard before. But instead of startling her or making her uncomfortable, it felt . . . right, somehow.

She went to him.

"I'm sorry I didn't tell you about the baby. Babies. I'm sorry about the abortion."

His back was turned to her. She touched his arms. Wrapped her arms around his waist. Pulled herself close.

To her delight, he didn't move away or tense.

"You were right about me. The only thing I could see back then was my career. I thought . . ."

Her emotions got the best of her and muddled her speech. "I thought a child would ruin my plans."

"What about *our* plans?" Storm asked.

"We didn't have any plans then."

He turned around, his face a mask of pain and regret. "We could have . . . if you would have told me."

"At that time, that's not what I wanted, Storm."

"And now?" he asked, holding her gaze. "What do you want now?"

She backed away. "Do you think a week can change ten years?"

His eyes grew dark with seriousness. "Yes."

"Well, you're wrong."

"Am I?" he asked, closing the distance between them. His thick arms encircled her waist. "Finish your song," he demanded.

She blinked in surprise.

"No," he corrected. "Finish *our* song."

Roxanne opened her mouth to protest, but Storm was wearing his man-in-command face. He was a man used to giving orders and having them obeyed. A dissention on her part would only prolong the inevitable.

She reached down into the well of emotions created by their excursion to feelings gone by and started where she left off.

This time her voice wavered, then trembled. She was shaking and not sure why. When she finished, there was one question nagging her that she had to have answered.

"Did you ever *once* think of calling me?"

Storm slid a glance in her direction. "Every day."

Fourteen

"You know what else I remember?"

"What?" she asked.

Storm finished the chunk of mango he was chewing. "Twister."

Roxanne laughed. When her laughter subsided, her cheeks warmed at the memory. She gave him a lingering glance then returned her attention to the fruit.

"Did your family have enough games?"

"No! There was always something out we wanted that for some reason we had to wait for. Like UNO and Trivial Pursuit. By the time we got them, they were outdated." She pinched off a piece of mango. "We took care of our games though. When we played Twister that time, it was like new, wasn't it?"

"Yeah."

Roxanne shook her head. "I can't believe I almost gave it up because of a game!"

"Umm-umm-umm," Storm mouthed. "How old were you? Eighteen?"

She punched him in the arm. "You know darn well I was sixteen. You should have been ashamed of yourself!"

"Why me? You fell on top of me, remember? And when you felt my reaction, you didn't seem to mind."

She remembered that day clearly. Her parents weren't home and she and Storm had been talking for about a week. When he came over, she took him to the basement, where she and her siblings always took company. Except she knew she wasn't supposed to be alone with a boy down there.

But Haughton was different. And by then, she'd started to call him Storm like everyone else.

Storm hadn't tried to do anything nasty. They'd only held hands once. But the electric attraction between them was strong. They spent a lot of time bumping into each other and brushing against one another. So when they were twiddling their thumbs for something to do in the basement, Twister seemed like a great choice. They could play an innocent game and still have a reason to touch each other.

The game started off. Left foot, green. Right hand, blue. They were laughing and shoving each other in no time. When an impossible combination of spins entwined them like two pretzels, Roxanne lost her balance and tumbled down on Storm.

They giggled for a while. A short while. Then the realization of her position hit her. Their eyes locked and Storm's reaction was immediate.

Sarah Allgood's voice stomped around in Roxanne's mind. "Don't let a boy touch any of your private parts. If a boy gets fresh, you let me and your father know." But as she lowered her head to Storm's, she knew she was the fresh one.

She'd never kissed a boy before. When he stuck his tongue into her mouth, she was appalled. She drew away, but he stopped her.

"Wait. It's okay."

She shook her head and trembled with uncertainty.

"Let me show you," he said.

She trusted Storm, and if anyone was going to teach her about kissing, she wanted it to be him.

For the next ten minutes, he explained the concept of French-kissing and gave explicit, lengthy demonstrations. Roxanne caught on fast.

She also remembered her older sister saying that for guys, kissing is always *part* of something. It's always the beginning of something and to never start something she couldn't finish. With all this kissing she was doing, she wondered if she'd headed down the wrong road.

Her sixteen-year-old body felt like it was waking up. Like it had been asleep or resting and was now coming to life to do what it was supposed to do.

Everything on her felt strange. Her arms and hands. Her thighs and legs. All tingly like a million sparkles were dancing inside them. She didn't want that feeling to go away.

When Storm cupped her breast in his hand, she didn't stop him. She thought he was a little rough but liked his touch just the same. Before she could think coherently to say, "Maybe this isn't such a good idea," they were both naked to their underwear and Storm had a hard-on that felt like a pipe in her hands. She couldn't believe she was going to go through with it.

She'd forgotten all about Twister.

"Such a smile!" Storm said, interrupting her reflection. "Was I that good?"

"Of course not!" she protested. But he *had* been that good. He conjured sensations inside her body that would have caused her to defy her parents. If it hadn't been for . . .

"Marti, Marti, Marti." Storm was smiling as well and looking in her direction. "If it hadn't been for her, I would have ridden you into the sunset."

Roxanne made a dismissive gesture with her hand. "Please. You were eighteen. What did you know about riding anyone anywhere?"

His eyebrow rose. Smug confidence turned his smile into a broad line. "I was your first. You tell me."

Just two years after Marti caught them buck-naked on the Twister game, Roxanne and Storm consummated their relationship in his dorm room. By then, he knew exactly what he was doing. There was no youthful fumbling like some of the other guys she'd made out with. Storm was sure and determined. He loved her slow and long.

No matter how many times they made love after that, or how many lovers she'd had since Storm, her first time was the most special time. He truly made her feel like a woman. She would never, ever forget it.

He was waiting for her response.

"Maybe," she said. "You know what *I* remember?"

"What?"

She tucked in her lips and licked them pensively, suddenly reluctant to speak. A feeling greater than her reluctance propelled her to continue. "I remember when you cried."

Storm made a sound like an agitated stallion. "You have never seen tears fall from these eyes."

"No. You don't cry with tears. You cry with silence. You cry when your body becomes stiff and unyielding. You cry with your teeth when they gnash against each other. You cry with your fists balled and ready to strike."

He remembered. It was after Hell Week. He'd successfully endured unimaginable tests to become a Navy SEAL. He was ecstatic that he'd reached his ultimate goal. He was also devastated because he'd be gone from Roxanne for a long time.

Not knowing when they would be together again, he'd spent all day making love to her. Imprinting his desire for her. He wanted her to have no doubts. She understood his urgency and had responded in kind, so much so that during that exchange he could have sworn he could taste her soul.

When the night came, he held her without talking. Without moving. He stayed awake all night, suffering with the realization that he would be leaving her. He stared at her feet, her hands and face. Committing them to memory.

She was right. He had cried that night. In his own way, he'd wept desperately.

He'd spent the next day finalizing his plans to leave for good. He'd taken a station in Washington State and all too soon he would call Seattle his new home. He'd also asked her a million times to go with him. To marry him and be by his side. But men like him didn't have wives, and women like Roxanne didn't give up or change their career plans for a man.

He knew that.

But it still hurt.

Roxanne said he was disgusting, but that day he'd refused

to shower. He wanted her scent with him all day. He'd wanted to drown in it. Make it a permanent part of his physicality. He willed it to sink into his pores and be with him any time he got lonely for her. Little did he know that a part of him was doing something similar inside Roxanne's body.

Marti contacted him two months later with news of Roxanne's pregnancy or, rather, her abortion. When he'd confronted her about it, she denied it at first. Then she admitted to being pregnant, but said that she'd lost the baby.

All of the feelings he'd put on lockdown from the first time she was pregnant vaulted to the surface and darn near choked him. He didn't believe her. Knew that she would lie for her career.

He looked at her. The fire in his gaze cooled with sorrow. He knew his own grief, she imagined, but he could never know hers at the miscarriage of their son.

She'd named him Pearson, after her father. Even though he was only in her body for four months, she still felt his presence in her life as surely as her own breathing, her own soul. It was the first time she had ever questioned God's judgment. Not even when her mother had been called to heaven, had she doubted God's eternal wisdom. But when she miscarried Haughton Storm's child, she hurled anguished shouts of "Why!" to her lord and Savior.

Only one answer came.

She had been punished for aborting her and Storm's first child. Roxanne's foolish fixation on her career in aviation blinded her to the reality of what was truly important in life— people who loved her and those whom she could love.

After her miscarriage, she'd immediately written a letter of resignation. She carried it around for days, wondering if she was doing the right thing. Then an explosive argument between her and Storm nearly finished her. He'd accused her of getting an abortion and lying to him. He'd said that he never wanted to see her again.

Her life was over.

Instead of quitting her job, she'd thrown herself into it.

She'd requested odd shifts, took on the itineraries that no one wanted. It was her punishment for betraying Storm early in their relationship. And it was her penance to cool the anger she felt when he accused her of lying. After all the years they'd spent together, she was devastated when he didn't believe her. And for that, she never wanted to see him again.

Storm's suspicions about holographic augmentation to the jungle were confirmed when they came into a clearing and there, hovering without explanation, was a golden ring.

He and Roxanne glanced at each other, then walked tentatively toward it. About twelve inches in diameter, the golden ring hung in the air, suspended without wires, ropes or cords. It was as though someone had attached it to the sky with an invisible nail.

Roxanne took small steps around it. "That's got to be fifteen feet up."

"Try twenty," he said.

Roxanne glanced around. "Of course there's nothing around to climb on to get it."

"And of course Level Four is whether or not I find a way to add that to my collection."

"I've played enough video games to know that this is here for a reason. This ring will come in handy in another level."

Storm's eyes narrowed. "I want to try something." He searched the ground and found a rock that fit his hand nicely. Standing like a baseball pitcher, he hurled the rock at the ring. With a reverberating clink, the rock hit a golden side and bounced away.

Roxanne's eyes traveled the length of his body, then settled on his bicep. "Nice arm."

He almost smiled. "Thanks," he said. "Now you."

She shrugged. "Okay." Roxanne grabbed a similar rock and hurled it toward the hovering circle of gold. Instead of hearing a sound of contact, they hear the whoosh of the rock as it sailed straight through the golden ring and landed yards away.

Her head snapped toward Storm, confusion wrinkling her brow. "I was dead on!"

He nodded and raised the arm that was hardwired to the circuitry of the game. "But you don't have the Eye."

"Amadeus is either a genius or a madman."

"What concerns me is that he's probably both."

"Flattery will get you nowhere," a sinister voice said, uncoiling from hidden speakers like a snake disturbed from slumber. "I just popped in to say how well I think you're doing and how much closer to getting off the island you've come."

Storm wished Amadeus was standing in front of him. Then he'd show him just how close.

"And I must say bringing your ladyfriend along for the ride was a stroke of brilliance. It makes the game much more interesting. I should have thought of that myself."

"What do you want, Amadeus?" Roxanne asked, strain and annoyance tightening the sound of her words.

"Why, nothing more than to give you two a pep talk. If Storm is successful in capturing the ring, the game will get very interesting. Very interesting indeed. So I'm rooting for you, chief, I really am. I just wanted to make that clear."

"Is that why you've been so generous with the water lately?"

For the past few days, they would come upon canteens of water sitting on rocks and hanging from trees. At first they'd been skeptical, but their thirst overwhelmed them. Then Storm realized that it would defeat the purpose of the game to have them weakened or perish from dehydration. It was in Amadeus's best interests to help them at least that much. Although his generosity was sometimes a long time coming and they went back to cutting vines and binging on fruit, he hadn't let them go to far without replenishing their water supply.

"Amadeus!"

Roxanne huffed. "You know he only talks when he gets ready." She glanced up. "Besides, we've got bigger fish to fry."

For the next few hours, Storm tried without success to free the ring from its place in the sky. Since the spear was too short to reach it, he'd climbed the nearest tree, gone out on a limb, and jumped toward it. That had landed him empty-handed in the leaves he and Roxanne had piled to break his fall.

He'd even tried swinging, Tarzan style, from a vine. When he grabbed at the ring, it wouldn't budge. He returned to the forest floor without his prize once more.

He paced beneath it. "What will it take? Some stairs so I can just climb up to it? Some kind of golden lasso? I feel like Batman without his utility belt."

Roxanne laughed. "You look more like Captain Cave Man."

"This isn't funny!"

"Yes, it is, Storm. I mean, you should see yourself, jumping at the sky like a maniac. It's real funny."

"You got jokes while some sicko keeps us prisoner on God knows what island."

Roxanne walked over to a flat boulder and sat down. "Come sit next to me," she said.

"Roxanne—"

"That's an order, soldier."

If he had been a fire-breathing dragon, he would have roared a tornado of fire at that moment and lay waste to a mile of land in front of them. He wasn't, though. He was a man trying to protect the woman he loved. The knight rescuing the damsel in distress. Only she didn't appear to be in too much distress and he was too in love with her to refuse her anything.

He sat down next to her.

"Never forget that this is a game, Storm. Games are supposed to be fun."

"This game—"

She held up her hand. "This game is no different. When Amara got hooked on these things it was because playing stopped being entertainment. It became her world. It consumed her. She was so serious about video games, she couldn't see two feet in front of her."

Storm released a long breath.

She put an arm around his shoulder. "Relax a little. The solution will come. Besides . . . we ain't going nowhere. What else have we got to do, but figure a way out of this level?"

He slid her a sly glance.

Her libido ebbed. "Besides that," she added. "Now, let's get something to eat. Sometimes the best way to solve one problem is by working on another."

They feasted on a dinner of roast rabbit, greens, and mangoes. After dinner, they built a shelter for the night, built up their campfire and reminisced about the good old days.

Roxanne had a memory like a steel trap. He couldn't believe all the details she was able to add to his sketchy rendition of their past. Just another thing about her that he found remarkable. Suddenly, he jumped to his feet and started walking.

"Where are you going?" Roxanne asked.

"I'm going to get you something. Going to get us something." His voice trailed behind him in sultry waves. "When I get back, I want you in that shelter. Naked."

"Are you crazy? No telling what these insects will do!"

"It's not the insects you have to worry about."

He disappeared into a thicket before she could protest.

"Naked!" he called in the darkness. "That's an order!"

At first, Roxanne had reservations about Storm's request. Before, their intimate interludes had been obscured by caves and thick brush. Their shelter was out in the open and Amadeus would most certainly know what they were doing.

Could he use that information against them somehow?

She certainly hoped not. Because with all her heart and soul, she meant to fulfill Storm's wish and be naked and ready for him when he returned. She wondered what he was bringing her.

She didn't have to wait long to find out. He returned with a long flat rock, a smaller round rock, an assortment of fruit and a handful of reddish yellow flowers.

The flowers were defiantly a romantic gesture for Storm.

She was grateful and reached out for them when he entered the shelter.

"Storm! They're beautiful!" she said.

"Uh-huh. Tear the tops off, will you? We're going to eat them."

"What?" she asked as he settled in next to her.

"I promise you, you'll like it. Now tear them off while I get out of these clothes."

In minutes he was naked and smashing the fruit into a fine pulp with his bare hands. Then he asked Roxanne to add the flower tops. He sprinkled them over the mush he'd created and she watched as he kneaded them in. After working the mixture for a few moments, he pinched off a bit of it and lifted it to her lips. "Taste," he said.

She stared into his eyes, hesitant for a moment. But the intensity she saw in his face made her trust him and his intensions. She opened her mouth.

He placed the mixture on her tongue. She closed her mouth around his fingers and he drew them out slowly.

She chewed carefully, trying to discern the taste. Mango. Plantain. And the sweet smoothness of the flowers. Not great. But not bad.

She nodded.

He followed the pinch for her with one of his own.

"What is it?" she asked.

"Litchi," he said, taking another pinch. Then he offered her more. She took it, enjoying the pleasure of being fed.

"If we had a still, we could make wine from the petals."

"Really?" she said, helping herself to more.

"Really. But if you crush it up and eat it like we're doing, it just gives you a buzz. Like a wine cooler."

Roxanne stared at him in wide-eyed disbelief. "Are you trying to get me drunk?"

Storm smiled and showed a beautiful row of gorgeous teeth. "Yes."

Roxanne giggled, already feeling a little warm in the belly.

"You wouldn't believe how much pharmaceutical knowledge a unit of soldiers can amass over time."

"You're crazy, you know that?"

"Only when it comes to you," he admitted.

She snickered and decided to indulge herself in the promise of sweet intoxication.

"You said relax. So, we're going to relax."

"We could have done this with our clothes on," she said.

"Yes, but it wouldn't have been as much fun."

They both laughed. The effect of the flowers was swift. She felt woozy.

"Are you sure this effect is only a buzz? I f-feel more than that."

"Well, according to my guys, it's also an aphrodisiac."

Roxanne's belly wasn't the only area of her body warming up. "You don't say."

"Keep eatin', Allgood."

She ran the tips of her fingers against the hard muscle of his upper thigh. His hot glance traveled from her hand to her eyes.

"Just hold on," he said. "I want you good and toasty before I take you." He motioned to the fire burning just outside their shelter. "And I'm not talking about the campfire."

Storm made another batch of the fruit and flower mixture. They finished it off in no time and started giggling like teenagers at a party.

But unlike when they were teenagers, Roxanne's feelings for Storm had matured. The force and severity of them shocked her. Made her tremble and shake with their power. She knew it wasn't the flowers totally. It was her inability to keep the wall between her and Storm intact. The layers of resentment she'd built over the years had melted away like ice in warm rain. And the repercussions of that scared her.

"Hey, hey," he said, cradling her. "Maybe you should slow down on the flowers."

Their eyes locked. "Maybe I should slow down on you."

"I'll never let that happen." He bent over and kissed her cheek. "No about-face, all right?"

She was too frightened to move, to talk. And fear was a foreign emotion to her.

"Roxy," he said, voice as sultry as the night.

She turned to him. More open and exposed than even her nakedness could reveal. He laid her down against the pallet they'd made from clothes and leaves.

She must have been drunk because she could have sworn that Storm had six hands instead of two.

"Storm," she whispered, trying to catch her breath. "This is too intense."

"Baby," he growled brazenly. "That's the whole idea."

And she was the whole idea of his existence. As he washed her face with his kisses, he was grateful for the way fate had brought them back together. Like equal parts of the same life they loved and lived better together than apart. They—

He rose up from her. "What did you say?"

Her eyes fluttered open. "I didn't say anything. But if you want me to talk dirty, I will."

"No," he said, sitting up fully now. "About working on one problem to solve another."

"What?" she asked, sitting up with him. Her breasts throbbed with need. "That was yesterday."

"But I just now heard you."

Storm planted a big juicy flower-induced smack on her lips then got up.

"Where are you going now?"

"To get the ring."

"Right now? Like that?"

Storm glanced down at the area of his body that seemed to be getting the most attention from Roxanne. "Fifty percent of the world's population has one of these." He smiled at her and she returned his gaze.

"Not like that," she said, letting the wine cooler plus sensation speak her thoughts.

He picked up the spear and shield and headed out of the shelter.

Roxanne watched from the obscurity of the shelter. Storm's naked body bathed in moonlight flared her ebbing lust. With the spear and shield and the lush backdrop of the jungle, he looked every bit the African warrior. *Chief* African warrior. She willed her heart to slow its thunderous beat. It ignored her.

The ring was still where she'd last seen it, hanging mid-sky. It shone like a second moon. Storm stood yards before the golden disk and, with shield in hand, hurled the spear like a javelin toward the ring. The spear flew through the center of the ring and landed in bush. Storm grunted, grabbed the spear, and tried again. This time he placed the shield directly beneath the ring and threw the spear. Again the spear sailed through the hole in the ring. The spear landed in the bushes in almost the same spot, but the ring landed in the shield.

Roxanne whooped like a cheerleader celebrating a touchdown. Storm gathered all three items and walked back to where she stood waiting. "You really have had too many flowers."

The heat between them was too much for her to bear. She wrapped her arms around his neck. "On the contrary, I haven't had enough."

Storm entered the shelter with her and set the items to the side. "Now, where were we?" he asked, and settled himself on top of her.

Roxanne reached over and scraped the last morsels of Storm's mixture with her finger. She licked them off the tip of her finger and smiled. "Level Five," she said eagerly.

Fifteen

Amadeus stared down at the small bulge between his legs. It surprised him. He didn't feel aroused sexually. But he was aroused in every other way possible. The final levels of the world's ultimate game were about to begin.

The blue button on the control console called him, beckoned to him. "Here," it whispered. "Press . . . here." An action that he'd been waiting years to perform came with brilliant tenderness. He lowered his trembling index finger to the button and pressed it down.

Four-foot panels on the wall in front of him slid away and the screen behind it showed Asgard in dazzling digital color. "Marvelous!" he said, and licked back the bit of saliva that had trickled out of the corner of his mouth. "Carly, you're a genius!"

Carl, who'd been huddling in the background, allowed his face to break into a smile, and said, "Thank you."

Amadeus came around from the console, walked to Carl and extended his hand. "You did, Carl! You did it!"

Carl cast a disapproving look at the small round puff in Amadeus's trousers. He wasn't sure, but he thought that if he didn't get out of that room soon, he would throw up all over the alabaster-skinned man. "I'd like to watch from the tower if you don't mind."

Amadeus's eyes narrowed. "No, I don't mind. Just so long as that's where you're going . . . to the tower."

"Yes, that's where I'm going." The hairs on Carl's back stood at attention. A few more seconds and everything he'd had for lunch would—

"Go then," Amadeus said.

Carl sighed. "Thank you," he said. As soon as he stepped out of the control room, he bolted for the bathroom. Amadeus's cold, thin laughter filled the hallway behind him.

When the Odin's Eye vibrated on Storm's wrist, he tensed immediately. That sensation, coupled with the forewarning that he always got when he and his squad were in deep danger, prompted him to grab Roxanne by the arm.

"What?" she asked.

They had been walking side-by-side as enormous leaves and branches thinned out ahead of them. He had calculated that they would make it the five miles to the next level by mid-afternoon.

He stepped in front of Roxanne. "Something's up."

"Something like what?" she asked, stepping beside him once more.

"This is not the time to be difficult. Now get behind me."

Roxanne relented with a huff and the two walked a few more feet. Then the entire area ahead of them warped. Like mirages of wet road on a hot day, the path in front of them quivered like a vortex of heat.

She stepped solidly to Storm's side again, mouth agape. "What the . . . ?"

"I don't know," he said.

"Can we go around it?" she asked.

Storm checked the map on the screen of the Eye. It registered rough, uneven, and hilly terrain on either side of them. "Negative. Going around would take too long and be too dangerous."

He gave her a look of brown-eyed reassurance and they stepped forward.

The closer they came to the disturbance, the more it changed. Became clearer.

Rising out of the mist of distortion was a large stone castle gray with age. A high wall of stone blocks surrounded it. An abode fit for Goliath.

They glanced at each other a few times in their progress. The expressions on their faces confirmed that they were indeed seeing the same thing.

Roxanne nodded in recognition. "Asgard."

"If this is Asgard," Storm said, glancing back toward the jungle, "then where have we just come from?"

"Valhalla."

"So all of that was just—"

"Preparation for this," she said.

Now the past week was starting to make sense to Storm. Amadeus had been fine-tuning his game. Since he hadn't actually built a program for the game character, the game had to learn about him. How did we think? React to stimuli? How good were his motor skills? Could he do battle and if so, at what level? Then the game would adjust itself to him and create worthy opponents. That's why Amadeus had been so generous with water. He needed to keep them alive until they reached this stage.

Roxanne studied Storm, eyes wide and inquisitive. "Ahead full?" she asked.

"Aye-aye," he responded and moved closer.

The image before them grew in greater detail. It seemed to be part of the ground and rose up out of it like a palace that was as much a part of nature as the birds, trees, and wind.

It was made entirely of stone—a polished limestone shining brilliantly in the afternoon sun.

"Asgard was built by a giant. That's why it's so big and tall."

The enormous gate gapped open in menacing invitation. A long corridor stretched out deep and wide before them—the end of it still materializing as they stood in blinking awe.

"Oh my God." Roxanne said. "Do you see it?"

Storm nodded. "I see it."

They both stared on as the end of the corridor materialized to reveal a Black Hawk helicopter straight ahead of them.

"Is it real?"

Adrenaline started its familiar buildup in Storm's veins.

"There's only one way to find out. I've got a feeling that this is where the rubber meets the road. You really should stay behind."

"Why don't you admit for the first time in your life that you need me?"

His head snapped in her direction. "I never said I didn't need you."

"You've never said you *did* either."

"Look, you've told me all about this mythology stuff. I can handle it from here."

Roxanne stared at a place in the middle of the long corridor before them. "Do you know what those are for?"

Storm turned in time to see two ravens circling the interior of the palace. "No."

"Then you'd better take me with you."

Muscles in Storm's jaw flickered angrily and, after a growling sigh, he replied, "All right. But before we go in, you have a few things to learn."

Roxanne's eyebrow rose as she folded her arms. Storm pulled her aside and gave her a crash course in the special hand signals he and his team used to communicate silently during missions. He cautioned her against doing anything foolish and made her promise that she would do her best to stay out of harm's way—even if that meant leaving him behind.

Roxanne's heart fluttered at his last request. Now that fate had seen fit to thrust them back into each other's lives, she wasn't sure if she could ever leave him behind again.

His eyes bore the heat of determination into hers. He would accept nothing less than a yes from her. Finally, she nodded her head in reluctant agreement.

They approached the enormous stone structure. The screen on the Odin's Eye beamed a bright red. The three large blips blinking against his wrist could mean only one thing. Levels Five, Six and Seven lay dead ahead.

As they came upon the opening to the structure, another materialization took them aback and halted their progress. The gates, which had been open, disappeared and reappeared—only now they were closed.

"A strength test?" Roxanne asked.

Storm kept his vision straight ahead. "We'll find out."

He rubbed his hands together and then placed them against the wrought iron poles. Pushing against the metal, which was surprisingly cool beneath his fingers, he groaned in strain against the blockade.

The gate remained secure.

Storm spoke through gritted teeth. "You said you wanted to help."

Roxanne lifted her arms to brace against the gate and add her own leverage, but something she found unbelievable happened. Instead of leaning her weight into the iron, she simply fell through to the ground.

Storm took a step back. "It's the Eye."

He banged on the poles. The sound of vibrating metal filled the air. "It's only real to me."

Roxanne rolled her eyes and gazed skyward. "Then how can we open the door?"

"There must be a key."

"Yes!" Roxanne said, her face brightening. "In Amara's video games, there's always some kind of object that serves as a key to enter locked places. It's usually something you have to acquire."

They both stared at the objects Storm had acquired: the spear, the shield, and the ring.

"It has to be one of these," he said. "The Eye shows that everything else is inside the fortress."

Storm took another step back and examined the gate. He considered trying to pick the locking mechanism with the spear or using the shield as a wedge to pry the gate open. Then the shape of the gate caught his attention.

"It's the ring," he said, and placed the flat edge of the ring against a circular groove on the lock.

The gate glowed a bright yellow and swung open. But the hall of Asgard changed dramatically, so much so that

Roxanne grabbed Storm's arm and said, "There's got to be another way."

He was surrounded by high walls of closely fitted stone blocks. He knew Roxanne kept a close pace behind him, but the only footsteps he heard were his own.

"We're reaching the end," Roxanne said.

"It can't be. There's supposed to be three more levels."

"Yeah," she said, staring anxiously at their surroundings. "But this has got to be the final battleground."

"I don't know what that is, but the sound of it puts me on full alert."

"Good idea," she said.

It looked very much like a mythological home for giants. Seven-foot dancers on stilts would have room to spare in the doorways, arches, and ceiling. They made their way down a columned hall, flanked on each side by rows of doors and cement benches. His soldier's instinct told him whatever Amadeus had planned lay straight ahead. If only he had a clue to what it was.

The screech sent a jolt of surprise through both him and Roxanne.

"What now?"

Soaring above his head, yet inside Asgard, were the two ravens. They took turns cawing back and forth.

Roxanne looked up. "Those belong to Odin. They are the real eyes of Odin."

He stopped and stared at her. "How do you mean?"

"They're like scouts. They go before Odin and warn him of his enemies."

Storm blew hot breath between his teeth. "Where were they last week?"

They walked further and the ravens kept circling.

"Wait," Roxanne said, pulling on his arm.

"What?" he asked, all his senses on alert.

"Do you hear that?"

Storm listened. "Besides the ravens, I don't hear anything."

"That's what I mean. Whatever this is, it's major. Amadeus has cut us off from the jungle."

Roxanne was right. And he was ready. Everything they had experienced on the island up until this point had served to build his adrenaline. He wanted this whole ordeal over now. And he would do everything in his power to end it as soon as possible.

"There's something about the ravens. They're the key to the next level."

Roxanne nodded her encouragement.

Storm had spent the entire game acquiring the tools of Odin. He knew he had to acquire the ravens, too. His gut told him each one represented a new level. *"They* are the next level," he said. "Do they have names?"

Roxanne frowned. "I don't remember that much detail."

"I've got to get up there and get them."

Then he got an idea. "Or bring them down to me."

"How are you going to do that?"

"Hell, I don't know. I'm supposed to be Odin up in here. Maybe I'll call 'em."

Roxanne rolled her eyes. "Yeah right."

"Let me have my shirt back." She did as he asked and he put on the shirt. Storm, who felt a little cocky, thrust his arm out and waited. The only thing that happened was a spontaneous burst of laughter from Roxanne.

Undaunted, Storm put two fingers in his mouth and gave a loud whistle. Roxanne's laughter stopped abruptly as the large black birds stopped circling and dove toward them. Miraculously, they landed on Storm's arm and before they could settle down, a canister rose beside them.

Unlike previous canisters, this one was dim. At first. When the interior brightened, Roxanne gasped and Storm sent the ravens flying back to the ceiling.

"I'll be—"

"Oh God, Storm!"

There, side by side in the canister, was a cell phone and Storm's pet, Jake.

He pulled Roxanne close. "Just when I was about to say how easy that level was."

Tears formed at the rim of her eyes. "I have to call my family," she said.

"And then what happens to Jake?"

Roxanne turned to face Storm. "I can't believe that Amadeus would harm him."

A muscle twitched at Storm's jaw. "Look around, honey. Does this look like the creation of a sane and rational man?"

"Then we should call for help."

"And tell them what?"

"I don't know! That we're kidnapped on an island somewhere. Maybe they can trace the call."

"And maybe the phone doesn't work. Or maybe it's not charged. Or it's only good for about fifteen seconds' worth."

Roxanne pulled herself away. Storm followed and spun her around.

"Roxy . . . Amadeus is not stupid enough to allow us to call anyone that matters."

"Speak for yourself!" she challenged, thinking of her family.

At the sound of his master's voice, the dog barked and became agitated.

"Look, Jake is a live animal. No telling what will happen to him if we take the cell."

Roxanne looked unconvinced.

"You said yourself this is the final battleground. We are almost out of here. Home free. Then you won't have to call your family. You'll see them."

Roxanne wanted so badly to call her sisters, to tell them she was all right and to hear the voice of someone that could reassure her that civilization still existed. Without that ray of hope, Roxanne was afraid she would go crazy. Lose what remained of her resolve.

"Storm—"

"I can't believe we are even having this conversation. We're talking about a—"

"All right!" she said, giving in. "Get Jake out of there."

Storm said nothing, simply went to the canister and slid aside the plastic door. Jake bounded out and into Storm's arms.

Roxanne's hopes sank with the canister as it disappeared into the floor of Asgard.

"Well I must say, Chief Storm, it's been a great game so far. And now the best is yet to come. Or, dare I say, I saved the best for last.

"Everything has been leading up to this, you know. Your actions up to this point have been digested by the computer. Your reflexes, your battle tactics, your physicality, your reasoning, your ingenuity, your sense of compassion. It's all become part of the game. And the last level will test them all."

Storm put Jake down and Jake sat back on his haunches.

"Well, let's get on with it," Storm ordered.

"As you wish," Amadeus said.

"Why *Jake*, you sick maniac? First Roxanne . . . now an innocent animal! What's next?"

"You shall see," came Amadeus's tart reply.

Roxanne tugged on Storm's arm. "Jake fits," she said.

Storm's chest was heaving with anger. "None of us fit here, Roxanne."

"In the legend, Odin had two wolves in addition to two ravens. It's the last piece. It's got to be."

He spoke through clenched teeth. "So what now?"

"Now is the culmination of all the game has learned!" Amadeus bellowed. "Now . . . Level Seven!"

In an instant, they could see the helicopter more clearly. For the first time, they got a good look at the man standing next to it. But he didn't hold a close resemblance to a pilot. He looked more like an Adversary.

Storm picked up the spear and the shield. "Stay here," he told Roxanne. "Keep Jake out of the way."

Roxanne knelt down and held Jake by the neck. He licked her inner arm. Then they both looked on as Storm made his way down the corridor. Each one seemed to sense impending danger in their own way.

Storm marched deliberately toward the last thing standing between him and his freedom. With each step, an unfamiliar unease crept up his spine. He couldn't remember the last time he felt anything so powerful. And it wasn't fear. It was more like an acute sense of foreboding that let him know that Amadeus did indeed have something up his sleeve.

The Adversary approached as well. There was a familiarity in his gait. As if they'd met before. As if they knew each other somehow. When Storm saw the face of the man-thing coming toward him, he nearly dropped the shield in front of him.

The face coming toward him was his own.

"No!" he said, at a dead stop.

"Storm! What's wrong?" Roxanne called behind him. Jake barked incessantly, but Storm heeded neither.

The proximity screen on the Eye lit up in a blazing red. It flashed wildly and he knew this was the last stand. Since the game began, he hadn't paid much attention to the energy readout. But a quick push of a button switched the screen. Each blow from this Adversary would cost him dearly. He needed to monitor his vital signs on this one.

He and the Adversary circled each other, feeling each other out. The Adversary held up the palm of its right hand. At first Storm thought it was to stop the game for a moment. And then he saw. Imprinted in the palm of its hand was the key to the helicopter.

His combat training gave him a precise way to size up the enemy, pursue, and defend. At the sight of the key, all that went out the window and Storm lunged at the Adversary.

The sound of metal against metal reverberated in the great hall. Shields and spears collided in a loud crash of physical force. Storm discovered quickly that it would be hard, if not impossible, to outwit and outmaneuver himself. His every move was anticipated and countered.

A quick glance at the Eye told Storm that his energy level was already down by twenty-five percent.

Determined not to come this far and be defeated, Storm

changed his strategy. If fighting the thing head-on wouldn't do, maybe he needed some assistance. He drove a crushing blow down against the Adversary's head and leapt toward the limestone benches. Once there, he lifted a stone seat and hurled it toward the Adversary. The heavy stone left a gaping hole in the floor and smashed against blue armor, staggering Storm's opponent. Storm then moved down the row of seats, throwing each stone block until his muscles ached in complaince. Now the Adversary's energy level was even with his own.

Jake's barking sounded more ferocious by the minute. He was not a small animal. Storm came around to his enemy's side, hoping that Roxanne could hold on to the canine.

She couldn't.

Jake bolted from her arms and headed straight for the Adversary. He leapt over the chasms in the floor caused by Storm and with one last powerful jump, he lunged. But instead of landing on the Adversary, he fell into one of the holes. They heard a tormented wail of anguish and then silence.

"Jake!" Storm cried. When the sky exploded in Storm's head, he was trying to get to his dog. He never saw the blow coming.

He hit the ground with a crash.

The impact jarred the shield and spear from Storm's hands. The Adversary closed in. It raised its own spear and just before it came down, Storm put up his arm to block the strike.

Instead of smashing into Storm's skull, the spear struck the Odin's Eye. The Eye shattered and the lights on the screen fizzled, then went blank.

Momentary relief washed over Storm. Without the Eye, the hologram wouldn't be able to harm him.

The second blow to Storm's head told him otherwise. He scrambled to get up. Backing away, he realized that Amadeus's technology had transcended mere three-dimensional imagery. Somehow the thing he was fighting was *real*.

From her place at the mouth of the hole where Jake had

fallen, Roxanne grabbed a granite brick and ran toward the Adversary. Once she realized that the thing wasn't just a projection and that some of the things she saw were real, she knew she could help Storm.

Jumping onto its back, she pummeled the Adversary again and again with the brick. It flailed wildly, trying to throw her off. She hung on, but just barely. Roxanne managed to get in a few more hits before she was bucked off. She hit the ground and a bone in her forearm snapped.

Luckily she'd given Storm enough time to get his bearings. He got up, grabbed his spear, and threw it into the Adversary's neck.

The armor-clad giant staggered backwards, dropping its spear and clutching frantically at the one Storm had thrown. Storm picked up the shield and followed the Adversary as it tumbled back toward the shore.

Swinging wide and hard, Storm brought the shield down again and again. He didn't need the Odin's Eye to tell him that the Adversary's energy level was decreasing with each wallop. He backed the thing up to a rocky cliff that hung over the water, continuing his bold assault. He'd had enough of Amadeus's games and evil Frankenstein-like creations. The monster he fought was neither alive nor dead. But it would stop functioning. Storm would see to that.

With his remaining strength he meant to sever the thing's arm and toss it into the ocean. He brought the tip of the shield down once more, but the Adversary jerked and the shield slammed down into its chest, cutting through its armor.

Immediately, it stopped moving. Then a blue light flashed and the metal body went limp.

Whatever intestinal fortitude held Storm up vanished and he collapsed to the ground. His chest heaved. He could barely catch his breath. He forced himself to glance in Roxanne's direction. She was holding her arm, but she seemed to be fine. Until . . .

"Storm!" she cried, pointing in his direction.

He turned just in time to see the helicopter key dangling

from the Adversary's hand. He bounded up to get it. The motion jostled the arm and the key fell from the cliff and into the ocean.

"Oh God!" Roxanne shouted, and before Storm could dive in himself, she had gone after the key.

By the time Storm stumbled to the shore, Roxanne had been underwater at least three minutes. His heart slammed into his rib cage. "Roxanne!" he called. "Roxanne!"

Nothing. No answer. No movement from the current. No bubbles. Frantic, he dove in after her.

The ocean was a cold, dark place. He swam past schools of fish, plankton, coral, algae. But that's all he saw. There was no trace of her or the key. His frogman training was useless. He couldn't calm down. He had to come up for air.

Roxanne loved her family with all her heart. She constructed the faces of her sisters in her mind. Saw them floating before her. How much time had she actually spent with them recently? How much *real* time? Quality time? Meaningful time?

The most important thing she'd done with them recently was to come together with her sisters to make sure that Marti's boyfriend did right by her. A crisis had to bring her back into the bosom of her family.

If it hadn't been for the water she was swimming through, one could have seen the tears streaming down her cheeks. What a waste her life had been recently. She had a life, but no love. Or not much love.

Still holding her breath, she realized that her parents would have been ashamed of her behavior had they been alive. They would have called a family meeting and resolved her rift with Marti immediately, before it spread to ten years long. The thought made her gasp. She lost some of the air in her lungs.

Dear God. She hoped she had enough air left to get to the keys . . . and enough time left to reconnect with her family.

Storm bobbed on the surface of the ocean like a top. "Roxanne!" he called. Still nothing. He went under again and searched the area where the key had fallen. The current was strong there. Dread filled him and he came up for air once more. Please. Please God. Don't let me lose her now. Not when I've just found her again.

He climbed onto shore and pounded his fist in the sand. "No!" he screamed.

At first, he could barely make out the coughs because of his own haggard breathing. Startled and hopeful, he turned to where Roxanne was hoisting herself out of the ocean and onto the shore. He looked closer and realized she had the key.

With only determination and love as his strength, he went to her. He grabbed her up and crushed her to his chest. She was all right. Now he knew he would be all right.

"Roxy," he whispered, overwhelmed by the sensation of her body—warm, wet, and boneless—in his arms. He kissed her face. Stared into her deep brown eyes. Traced his hand over the smooth skin of her cheek. "I thought, I thought." He dared not consider it again. All that mattered now was that Roxanne was safe and they were together.

The ocean roared in mighty waves around them. There was only one thing left for Storm to do, and their journey would be complete.

Sixteen

Roxanne's jaw swung open. "You're what!" she exclaimed.

"I said I'm going back. I can't leave without knowing that Amadeus has been stopped—that this whole game has been dismantled."

Even out of breath, even soaked to the bone and exhausted, Roxanne knew that was a foolhardy idea. "What do you think you can do? You're only one man."

Storm's body cocked like a shotgun. "But I'm the baddest thing walking. Ask anyone in the Navy." Then his eyes softened from the hard pebbles of determination they'd become. "Ask your heart."

"Storm you—" but she was cut off. By searing lips and a heat-seeking tongue. By a mouth on a mission.

By a man who had never taken no for an answer.

She lost her soul to his pursuit. For the first time in years, she was flying without the help of an aircraft.

She was airborne.

He wrenched himself away with a growl of remorse. Their eyes locked.

"Storm you can't—"

"Don't worry. I have a plan." He touched her face. Her cheek quivered beneath his fingertips. "For us as well," he finished.

He tore the Odin's Eye from his arm. "Hold on to this. I know some people in high places who'll want to make sure this never gets in the wrong hands ever again."

She took the device and clutched it to her breast. Tears threatened to spill from her eyes, but she held them in check—she thought. One tear betrayed her. Storm wiped it away with the pad of his thumb.

"I was born to do this. I *will* be back."

He picked up the spear. "In case something happens, I have to tell you that I love you. Always have, Roxy." He looked away for a moment, then looked back. "Always will."

Storm sprinted toward the other end of the island. "Just don't leave without me."

Roxanne watched him run away and hugged herself. She turned his last remark over in her mind, knowing that she would never be able to do anything without him ever again.

Storm ran to the place where Jake had appeared. He shoved away surrounding bushes and brambles and tore off grass from the top of the platform. With a grunt, he inserted the tip of the spear into the rim and pushed down.

Within a few short sweat-and-strain-filled moments, the top of the canister snapped off, revealing a shaft leading down into the depths of the island. Storm tossed down the spear and, with a swing of his legs, followed the weapon down into the darkness.

Storm fished the tiny light out of his pants pocket and snapped it on. The room instantly flooded with purple-blue light.

Roxanne was right; he could see for at least a mile ahead of him. And what he saw pleased him. As he'd suspected, the game was connected by a labyrinth of tunnels. That would allow Amadeus, Carl, or any of their henchmen to move freely throughout the island to set and repair holographic equipment, surveillance equipment, and offer tempting choices for passing each level. He picked up the spear from the floor, remembering the last compass reading on the Odin's Eye. He'd bet a boat-load of gold that the tunnel he was standing in led straight back to the house.

He jogged down the corridor, determined to prove himself right.

Storm passed more electronic technology than he'd ever seen in one place. Most of it was encased inside glass partitions that probably slid aside with a key or a code.

As intricate and detailed as a cockpit or a submarine studio. A fleet of buttons, switches, levers, and small lights. A keyboard control panel signaled every juncture.

Storm huffed, turning his jog into a hard run. The swift hum of the machinery urged him on. He couldn't allow this kind of atrocity to ever happen again. His footfalls echoed in the concrete tunnel. The heat of the computers mixed with the cool of the corridor, creating a cold sweat on his arms, chest and face. Images of Roxanne waiting for him at the chopper flashed like strobes in his mind.

Storm drove on.

When he reached an all-too-familiar portion of the tunnel, he slowed to a quick walk.

A shudder of anger reverberated through him as he passed the room where he was held when he first arrived on the island. A few more feet and he passed the room he'd broken into to get Roxy. Each step ratcheted his anger—his fury—back, building like a five-alarm fire.

When he reached the door leading to Amadeus's house, his fury had reached his peak. He tried the door, knowing it would be locked and anticipating a message from the pale insane man. He was not disappointed.

"Haughton Storm. I've watched your return with curious fascination."

Storm ignored Amadeus and shoved the spear into the crack of the door and into the locking mechanism. He pushed against it with a grunt, hoping the spear didn't snap in two.

"Why, my dear Chief Storm, all you need do is say the word and the entrance shall be made available."

Storm glanced up into the camera in the ceiling. He spat out a few choice expletives and returned to his work. But true to his promise, the steel door swung open with a creak and Storm, wasting no time, rushed in.

* * *

She'd never taken time to enjoy a paradise like this. Sandy beach, tropical breeze, lush vegetation. She'd always been too busy with what she thought was living. Remembering the violet-red sunset and the bright orange sunrise, the waterfall, and now being at the ocean's edge . . . the slow turn of nostalgia in her belly. This is the kind of place where fond memories were made. A place where people giggled, fed seagulls, hunted for seashells, marveled at stingrays. She could have been laid out on a soft, thick terry cloth towel or let the sun warm her skin while she sat under an umbrella; or better yet, slept as the loud and gentle wash of the ocean lulled her, relaxed her, to sleep. How ironic to be here with Haughton Storm. The man who'd meant everything to her. They should have been able to share a perfection like this without the manipulation of a madman. Roxanne felt a sadness in the breeze. A sadness and a regret for her past and her present.

Last week, she couldn't see the sky. She and Storm had been alone, strolling along the path of a tropical island and all she could concentrate on was how much she missed the clouds. The encroaching plants and shrubs had made Roxanne feel claustrophobic. She'd felt shut in, closed down, sewn up. She'd moved, very well in fact, but it was as though her feet were shackled. With so many overgrown leaves, even the sun was denied her here. But like a miracle, they'd made it through.

Now, in the stillness of day, the awe-inspiring track of the sun reminded her of God and miracles. She hoped God heard her today, granted her one more miracle, and brought Storm back to her safely.

Roxanne wrung the last of the water from her top and hung it to dry next to her pants. She tucked the key to the helicopter into her underwear and headed toward the cockpit. It had been a few years since she'd learned to fly a helicopter. She hoped the skills would come back to her.

In the time that it took Storm to get back to shore, she hoped to reacquaint herself with the instrumentation and be ready for takeoff.

The wind blew across her bare skin. Her legs prickled with goosebumps. When she heard the voice behind her, she knew the bumps weren't just from the wind.

"Now I understand exactly what Storm sees in you."

Roxanne whirled around to see Carl standing behind her, eyes smiling with mischief.

His lips peeled back to expose two rows of tiny teeth. "Bringing you here was a smart move and a wonderful boon for the game. I don't think Storm would have performed as well without your presence."

Roxanne's modesty only stayed long enough for her to consider covering herself and then she shoved the thought away. She was too angry for modesty. But she knew Carl could provide her with answers to questions swirling in her mind.

"Why was I brought here, Carl? Why me?"

Obviously the man had been taking too many cues from Amadeus. His laughter held a smattering of metallic sound in the choppy air. "You were a special request—from the man himself."

"Amadeus?" she said, confused.

"No! Amadeus isn't that smart. Your loverman, Storm."

Roxanne shook her had. "That's not true. Storm said he didn't know why I was here."

"Well, he may not remember. Of course he doesn't remember. I drugged him. Then I got him to talk about himself, his life. Pretty soon it was obvious. Even above his precious military career, he cared about you. He kept talking about you. Every now and then he'd mention the mutt. That's why he's here."

"Jake," Roxanne insisted.

"Whatever. But when he would mention you, he became even drunker than the drug could possibly make him. That's when we knew we'd struck pay dirt."

Carl laughed again. This time heavier, stronger. It curdled

the breakfast she had in her stomach and made her nauseous. "Getting you here was not an option. It was a necessity."

A sense of awe quickly took over the sickness in her belly. All this time, Storm had still cared for her. Still loved her. Just as she had him. A renewed sense of love and devotion bathed her body like liquid sunshine. More of Carl's horrid laughter interrupted her revelation.

"You didn't know, did you?" He doubled over and rubbed his portly belly. "Oh, this is too precious. You had no idea. What a gold mine we struck with you. I couldn't have planned it better!"

Roxanne's anger returned. She leaned against the helicopter to keep from choking the man. "What do you want, Carl?"

Around them, tribes of birds screeched and howled. The chorus of living things echoed against jungle walls of raffia, baobab and steppe—boulders, high cliffs, and roaring ocean. Carl seemed an inordinate spectacle against the majesty of nature—something abominable and sorely out of place.

"I want you to reconsider my offer," he said, closing the distance between them. He spied the Eye on the pilot's seat, then returned his cold gaze to her. "Can't you see? Amadeus would get suspicious if I delivered the package. Heck, he might even figure the whole thing out. In which case he'd shut down my little experiment, and all of my years of work would be for naught. I can't have that, Ms. Allgood. I *won't* have that!"

Despite the shadow of fear threatening to eclipse her anger, she stood her ground. And when he came within a few feet of her and the hairs on the back of her neck stood at desperate attention, she squared her shoulders and lifted her chin. "Why are you doing this, Carl? How can either Storm or I possibly help you?"

"I've made certain promises. Promises that I intend to keep. And they all ride upon my ability to deliver this technology. People have been waiting."

"So you used Amadeus to provide the financial means for you to create this game?"

Carl stepped closer. "Not the game. The game was only a toy to keep Amadeus distracted. That last Adversary. The only one that looked and acted like your Chief Storm . . . he *was* Chief Storm. In every sense of the word. Haughton's feelings for you weren't the only things we extracted that day. I also took samples of his DNA. Then I combined those samples with the holographic technology. I won't go into particulars, but suffice it to say that with the success of the experiment on this island, man has truly become God. He can create any person he so chooses, at will."

Roxanne's eyes widened at the realization of Carl's statement.

"That's right . . . Roxy . . . to use terminology you'd be more familiar with, I've soared far beyond the clouds of cloning. This little marvel will earn me a place beside the giants of history."

Then Carl's gaze clouded over and his voice lowered as though he'd forgotten Roxanne was there. "No one will ever make fun of me again. No one will ever underestimate my genius. I'll be crowned king of genetic engineering. History books will record my story for millennia."

He snapped out of his reverie and took one step closer to Roxanne. "My 'friends' will come looking for you, Roxanne. You and your lover. So if you want to live, you'll cooperate and give them the Eye."

She wished she'd paid closer attention when she was younger and Storm tried to teach her self-defense moves. She could use a good one right now. The only thing that came to mind was a move all mothers taught their daughters. She envisioned a swift kick to Carl's most sensitive area.

He had to have sensed her mood or motive, because suddenly he backed away.

"You're a fighter, Roxanne Allgood. Storm has chosen well. And you needn't worry. He will return to you. I've already seen to that."

Carl turned and disappeared into the thick of the jungle with Roxanne fuming and more determined than ever to get off the island.

The inside of the house was dim. Unlike the tunnel which had grown in illumination the closer he came to the house. He switched on Roxanne's tiny light again and crept through the darkness.

His battle-intuitive antennae went up and he was ready for anything. As if he were on a search and destroy sweep, he moved room by room through the house, checking hallways and securing areas.

He finally wove his way through to what he realized was Amadeus's control room.

He blinked and halted his charge. What he saw in the room spoke to Franklin "Amadeus" Jones's warped perception of reality.

In the center was a chair that looked more like a throne with its high back, red velvet upholstery, and gold ornate trim. A control panel surrounded the chair in five sections. Each section was a battalion of knobs, levers, and buttons. The front panel came equipped with a microphone and on the wall in front of it was a wall-sized flat screen that showed him lurking in the doorway.

He raised the spear and tapped the top of it in the palm of his hand. "The game is over, Amadeus."

"On the contrary," a thin voice boomed, "It's only just begun."

Storm was determined to destroy the computer-generated game and all its technology. After seeing the many offshoots and remote units underground, he'd guessed that destroying the command center in the house would only be the first step in the process. He'd have to see to the destruction of each node. Remembering the underground cave he and Roxanne had traveled through days earlier gave him the perfect idea. But for now, he had to tackle the task at hand.

He rushed toward the large chair. When he was only inches away, he hit an invisible wall and was propelled backwards by a jolt of current stronger than anything he'd ever felt. He landed on his haunches with a thud. The blow knocked the air from his lungs and the spear from his hand.

He shook his head, trying to regain his coherence. His eyes narrowed with anger. Now he was irate.

"You've proven that my game works, Haughton. The technology works. Now, it will only get better."

That tin voice sliced through Storm's soul like a hot knife.

"Of course, I'll have to choose a new location. By the time you get back to civilization, I'll be long gone."

The picture on the screen changed and Storm got to his feet and watched as Amadeus's thugs hauled equipment down a long corridor.

"As you can see, I'm packing up. I'll be out of here before you can say Odin of Asgard. You can go, too, chief. You can turn around and head right back to the helicopter. Otherwise . . ."

The view on the screen changed back to the interior of the room. He saw himself standing near the center of the room and two large men behind him in the doorway.

"Otherwise, Roxanne will be leaving without you."

Unassuaged, Storm readied himself for battle. But he had to find a way to short circuit the forcefield. There had to be something he could do to get to the control panel. An idea came to him and he prayed it would work.

Slowly, he backed away from the center of the room, back toward the entrance. Then, with all the force of his anger, he threw the spear like a javelin at the main console.

The tip of the spear hit the forcefield and sliced through it like a hot knife through butter. The contact made a crackling sound. Then the sound of circuits shorting out filled the air as the spear slammed into the control panel and pummeled into its circuitry.

Storm turned his head as a light flashed and sparks flew from the gaping hole caused by the impact.

"You idiot! You could have gotten away! Oh well,"

Amadeus's voice whined as the two men from the doorway rushed in and grabbed Storm. "I guess you've used up all of your lives in this game."

Storm struggled against the two men.

"Sorry, no bonus points," Amadeus said and cackled wryly with that tin can laughter of his.

Storm gnashed his teeth and struggled against his captors. Their grips were strong and he made no headway. They escorted him out into the living room and shoved him toward the front door.

Storm prepared to charge the two goons when one of them held up his hand. "Stop!" he said. "You're free to go."

Confusion flooded Storm's mind.

"What? Why?"

"Don't ask," the other one said.

Then they turned and went back the way they'd come.

At first, Storm thought it might be a trick. Then he recognized what must have been Carl's handiwork.

"Predictable to the end, eh, Carl?" Storm asked to an empty room. He looked around and searched for something he could use, something that could help him fulfill his plan of destroying every part of Asgard the game. He wished he hadn't left the spear in the control room. It would have made a fine torch.

He swept a glance over the room. Quickly, he ripped part of a drape from a window, then grabbed two tall cast-iron candleholders from each side of the couch and rushed out the door.

Moving directly toward the first canister he and Roxanne had come across, he pried the lid open and jumped inside.

Once in the tunnel, he rushed down the corridor until he came upon a place in the wall where a computer console had been recently removed. Storm took a breath and hoped his hunch was correct.

With the force of all his might, he slammed one of the candleholders into the empty space against the wall. By his calculations, this would be where the wall was thinnest and it would also be where this man-made tunnel would connect to the natural cave he and Roxanne had traveled through. He continued swinging, sending chunks of cement and dirt flying with every blow.

After several hard contacts with the wall, Storm created a hole. Swiftly, he thrust an iron holder into the hole and used it as leverage to create an even larger opening, one he could squeeze through.

Once on the other side, he switched on the mini-light. A purple glow illuminated the path in front of him. He wrapped the cloth from the drape around the end of one of the candle-holders and charged down the cave.

Adrenaline surged through his veins. He had a feeling— a strange feeling. Similar to the sensations he got during a mission, but this one was different as well. His feeling told him that he would be successful, that his plan would work, his beloved Roxanne was waiting for him, and that upon leaving the island, they would have a wonderful life together.

He smiled and ran faster.

Storm came upon the bats faster than he'd anticipated. He slowed his progress so as not to disturb the sleeping mammals.

Carefully, he slogged through the puddles of bat waste. Then he took the tip of the candleholder that was wrapped in the drapery cloth and dipped it into a slush of guano until it was covered. Afterwards, he crept toward the cave exit quietly.

He knew that in some parts of the United States bat droppings were used as a potent fertilizer. But he was more interested in its second most popular use—as an explosive.

At the mouth of the cave, Storm pulled a lighter out of his pocket and did something he hadn't done in a long time— said a prayer, set the makeshift torch on fire, then held it to the trail of droppings at the opening of the cave.

The guano ignited with a flare and a hot whoosh of flame. Satisfied, Storm bounded up the hill and headed toward the woman he wanted to see more than anyone else in the world.

* * *

Amadeus howled with grief. Smoke billowed into his house through every vent and he choked on the dry air.

Anger curled his toes and made him curse into the darkening room. In anguish, he threw himself over the console in the control room and screamed. "Carl!"

Storm couldn't have escaped without Carl's help. He couldn't have been able to ruin ten years of work without the assistance of one fat, pathetic, Humpty Dumpty too smart for his own good—"

"Yes?"

Amadeus's body jerked up at the sound of Carl's voice. He turned toward Carl, teeth bared like a rabid animal.

"Before I have you drawn and quartered, I just wanted to know, why? After everything we've built together?"

"We?" Carl shouted. "We've done nothing! I, on the other hand, have created the greatest technology the world has ever seen." Carl's face wrinkled with disgust. "All you've done is . . . fantasize."

Amadeus clawed at the air. "I made you!" The words erupted from his throat like a blood-curdling scream. "When no one would even be associated with a spineless, sociopathic—"

"Spare me the projection, Franklin. You think you used me? You think you're the only one with dreams? I used you, or rather, your money. And your grandiose fantasies are nothing compared to what will happen once I sell the Eye."

"Sell the—" Amadeus's words were choked off by smoke.

Within seconds both men were doubled over by coughs. Carl dropped to the floor and covered his nose and mouth with the upper part of his shirt. Amadeus clutched madly at his control panel, pushing buttons, flicking levers.

Sparks flew from the panel and a motor hummed to life then sputtered and popped like a block of C-4.

Amadeus coughed and gagged for breath. Tears sprang to his eyes. The room spun and went black.

* * *

Just as Storm had suspected, Amadeus had manipulated the island using holographic technology. The days they'd spent traversing the jungle could have been traveled within hours. While the program that controlled the game continued to explode around him, Storm ran at top speed through bushes and thick greenery, not so much to escape the island but to get back to Roxanne.

After the first explosion, Roxanne's typically calm demeanor wilted away. As if the detonation had taken place within her body, she slumped to the ground and struggled to think clearly.

God, please don't take him from me now. Please not now when—

At the second explosion, she closed her eyes, wrapped her arms around herself, and shuddered.

"I'm not leaving without you, Storm. Do you hear me?"

Her arms were still swollen and puffy from welts and bites. A few mosquitoes attacked her skin through the tears and rips in Storm's shirt. She exhaled long and slow, no longer caring to swat them away or prevent their feast on her body.

The largest mosquito she'd ever seen hovered over her wrist like an Air Force bomber coming in for a landing. The sound of someone running toward her startled her. Roxanne jumped before the insect could alight and it buzzed away.

"Roxy!" Storm's voice called. It sounded strange. Not real. She looked at him as if he were a mirage.

Gasping for air, he called again. "Roxy!" He sprinted toward her.

Relief washed over her. She jumped to her feet and broke into a run to meet him.

The two lovers slammed into each other. Their embrace was crushing and life-giving. They kissed reverently. She assaulted his face with an onslaught of kisses. The energy of her

welcome renewed his own. He supported her soft buttocks
with his arms.

"Well, well, well. Maybe I should go away more often."

She gazed at him, eyes intense with determination. "I don't
want you to ever leave me again."

Her admission touched him, and he kissed her without
restraint.

A loud blast shook them apart. They nearly fell to the
ground as the results of Storm's plan exploded around them.
Tongues of fire leapt into the air from underground tunnels
and passageways. Storm hoped that the same was true for the
house as well.

He gripped Roxanne's arm and ushered her toward the helicopter. "Let's get out of here."

Roxanne raised her hand in salute. "Aye, Sir!"

Just like making love with Storm, the rhythm of flying a
helicopter came back to her in every detail. Within minutes
of his return, Roxanne had the helicopter prepped and ready
for takeoff.

Without head gear, the loud motor and whir of the blades
made it difficult for them to communicate without shouting. But little had to be said as each settled into bucket seats
and strapped in. One last look at the island, one more intense look at each other, and Roxanne steered them up into
an azure sky.

The helicopter teetered off the ground, a bit shaky at first,
and then grew more steady with altitude. A familiar sound
muffled in the hum of the motor compelled Storm to place his
hand over Roxanne's.

He listened in between the whoosh of the blades. His nerves
jumped to sharp alert. "We've got to go back!" he shouted.

"What?" Roxanne responded, already angling away from
the island.

"Set 'er down!"

Roxanne couldn't make sense of Storm's request and then

her eyes widened with alarm when she saw Jake running along the shoreline, chasing after them and barking like crazy.

She swallowed the relief she felt for leaving the island and landed the chopper just a few yards from Storm's pet.

Storm unbuckled and jumped out. He squatted down and patted his thighs. "Jake!" he called. "Come here, boy!"

The grey-eyed canine stopped and sniffed the ground, then stared eagerly in Storm's direction. Thinking that the helicopter might be a bit intimidating, Storm moved closer and continued to call his companion.

Suddenly, the animal broke into a run and headed in his direction.

"That's it, boy. Come on!"

Storm stood anticipating Jake's jump into his arms. Then a rustle from the bushes startled him and Carl lunged from behind them and grabbed Jake.

The animal squirmed and growled for a few moments, but Carl's hold, which was more like a cradle, calmed him. And the strong and steady strokes on his forehead quieted his growl.

Storm's eyes blazed murderously. "Carl—"

"No," he said, calmly. "You listen. No more games, Chief Storm. Just the truth. The truth is that my friends are on the way, and you are going to give them the Eye or I will tie a piece of the computer core to your furry friend's waist and toss him into the ocean."

Storm strode toward Carl, swagger thick and forceful. "You're only right about one thing. This game is over. It's time for the real deal."

He rolled up his sleeves. His eyes narrowed to slits. A vein in his forehead pulsed angrily.

Carl lumbered backward, clumsily struggling to keep Jake in his embrace. "Stay away!" he shouted.

Storm marched on and witnessed the transition of Carl as he changed from a man swollen with false power and full of demands to a person cowering behind a domesticated coyote.

Storm towered over him. "Let him go," he demanded.

Carl glanced up, face bright with fear. His hands shook as

he released his grip on the animal. Jake licked his lips, sniffed Carl's face and jumped to Storm's feet.

Storm's fists opened and closed. Roxanne called Jake from behind him. He looked down at the dog, looking pleadingly at him. "Go on," he ordered. Jake took off toward the helicopter. Storm's hot gaze returned to Carl. He grabbed him by the scruff of the collar and hoisted him to his feet.

"I have half a mind to beat you unconscious," he said.

Carl was speechless and shaking.

Storm's fury abated. He smiled instead of striking the man. "Don't you ever threaten me or mine again. If you do"—he tightened his grip, causing Carl to gasp a bit for air—"I won't be such a good sport."

"Storm!" Roxanne's voice beseeched above the loud helicopter.

He spun around and his concern matched hers.

Another helicopter approached their position. He wondered if it carried the friends that Carl spoke of. When the ground exploded next to Roxanne, he had his answer.

"I told them you might need some . . . convincing," Carl hissed.

Fed up, Storm gave Carl a swift right cross and knocked him out cold, then he sprinted back toward Roxanne.

Seventeen

Storm dashed into the helicopter cockpit and strapped himself in. "Get this bucket moving!" he shouted to Roxanne, who was already maneuvering the flying vehicle up into the air.

Storm tried as best he could to secure Jake, but the canine barked and pranced in response.

"Down, Jake!" Storm ordered.

Instantly Jake lay flat against the cockpit floor.

Storm scanned the interior of the chopper while Roxanne steered them into evasive maneuvers. Bullets whizzed past and a small missile exploded beside them.

"We've got no cannons!" Storm shouted.

"No kidding!" Roxanne responded as she swung the chopper erratically above the high tree line of the island.

"We're low-hanging fruit out here!"

Roxanne flicked a glance his way, then returned her attention to the sky in front of her. "Not if I can help it! Hang on to something!"

Storm wrapped one hand around a grabber and the other around Jake. Roxanne maneuvered the chopper up and above the tallest trees. She wound around canyons and through gorges.

The other helicopter continued to fire. A shower of bullets sideswiped their chopper and suddenly the helicopter wouldn't respond to the controls.

"I can't steer!"

"What!"

Roxanne unhooked her seatbelt. "We've got to bail!"

Storm filled the cockpit with expletives and unbuckled his seatbelt.

The helicopter teetered dangerously. Roxanne, Storm, and Jake slammed into the side of the cockpit.

"Can you get us back toward the shore?"

"No way!" Roxanne shouted. "The controls are frozen."

"Try!" he insisted.

Reluctantly, she returned to the pilot's chair. Her hands flew over the console, making quick adjustments. Her arms bulged with the strain. Storm soon joined her and together they guided the helicopter inches closer to the shore.

"Ah!" she said when all her strength was spent. "That's it!"

"All right," Storm said, scooping Jake into his arms.

The helicopter pitched and slammed them together. Jake yelped but the shift brought Roxanne and Storm face to face.

"I love you," he said. "Now let's blow this bucket."

"Yes, sir!" she said and jumped into the water.

Storm followed close behind and splashed into the water seconds behind her.

Wet again, she thought about swimming towards shore. Storm and Jake were right on her heels. Unfortunately so was the other helicopter. They all ducked under as bullets cracked like sharp thunder in the sky and drove up the water around them.

Then a loud explosion took them off-guard. The chopper they'd spent days trying to get to slammed down into the hillside and burst into flames.

Roxanne summoned energy she didn't know she had to get her to shore. She wanted nothing more than to crawl up and sink into the sand, but she knew she, Storm, and Jake would have to scramble for cover.

The three of them broke into a run. The Eye dangled precariously from Storm's grasp.

Roxanne dared to look back, and out of the corner of her eye, she saw another helicopter approaching from a distance.

"Storm!" she cried.

He glanced up as well. "Could be more of Carl's friends," he said, ushering her and Jake into the cover of trees.

Bullets and missiles slammed into the ground all around them. Roxanne covered her ears and Jake barked angrily.

"These trees will provide us some cover," Storm said. He held up the Eye that was dripping with water. "They don't want to take a chance on damaging this device, so that will buy us some protection."

Storm looked on as the helicopter hovered at the shore. Two ropes uncurled and two armed men climbed down.

Just as he was about to urge Roxanne and Jake into deeper cover, shots from the other helicopter rang out into the air. But they weren't aimed in their direction. They were aimed at the hovering chopper at the shore.

The armed men scrambled back to the ropes and climbed up as the chopper closed in. It continued firing until the enemy chopper was out of range and traveling fast out of sight.

"Stay here," Storm ordered and headed toward the shore.

The new chopper hovered in the position of the previous one, the door slid open, and a man with a big wide grin and an M-16 rifle leaned out.

"Sharky?" Storm said in a voice just above a whisper. "Sharky!" he called out. "You bloodhound!"

"Chief!" Sharkey bellowed. "You look like you've been through World War Three *and* Four!"

"Get us off this godforsaken island and I'll tell you all about it!"

"Woo! Get this man some Zest and some Right Guard!"

Roxanne looked on as the reunion with Storm's best friends ensued full force. Spirited greetings, quick embraces and hearty pats on the back made the atmosphere inside the helicopter lively and buoyant.

Among the soldiers in clean and freshly pressed uniforms,

she and Storm looked haggard, worn, and in need of a long hot bath.

After the boisterous reunion, Storm's three friends gathered around her while Jake panted and wagged his tail behind them.

One by one they all gave her firm hugs.

"Roxy, it's been a long time," Neal Allen said.

Zurich Kingdom planted a kiss on her forehead. "Yes, it has."

"Hey!" Storm protested. "Don't get too close to my woman!"

Nelson Wainwright handed her a blanket. "Whatever, Aquaman."

Roxanne shuddered. The dampness of her skin and the air conditioner in the helicopter chilled her. But her mind came to a single focus on one matter.

"Does somebody have a phone? I have to call my sister."

Marti Allgood sat in the den of her house, still and quiet. Roxanne had been on the missing person's list for just under two weeks and since then she'd been able to do little more than mope around the house.

Thank God for Amara. Her niece had stepped in and helped to take care of her son, Kenyon Jr., just when she needed it.

Her fiancé was out of town conducting a visiting lecture at the Smithsonian Institution on genealogy research. One of his friends had contacted him in hopes that he could persuade her to do a portrait of him. She'd tried for hours to busy herself with sketches of the man. But no matter what she did, her mind always returned to thoughts of her sister.

Marti and her other sisters called each other several times a day to keep their spirits up and sometimes to pray together. When the phone rang, she assumed it was Yolanda or Morgan calling for their daily dose of support.

"Hello?"

"Runt?"

"Oh my God," she said and her legs ceased their ability to

hold her up. She tumbled to the floor. "Roxy?" Her hands and voice trembled fitfully. "Roxy?"

"It's me, sweetheart."

"Where are you? I can barely hear you! Are you all right?"

"I'm fine, Runt. Dirty. Funky. But I'm fine and I'm coming home."

Marti's joy overwhelmed her and she sobbed into the phone.

"Marti, I love you. I'm sorry it's taken me so long to say it." Roxanne's voice faltered. "I love you."

Amara rushed into the den with KJ in her arms. "Aunt Marti!"

Marti held up her hand. It was still shaky and so was she. But her sister was all right. And she'd forgiven her. And everything was going to be okay.

The engine of the Apache helicopter roared like a freight train. Jake stared out of the open door, tongue lapping, eyes eager. Her rescuers had settled toward the front of the aircraft and spoke in low voices. She and Storm, huddled against each other in the back, remained silent while the severity of their situation sunk in.

She realized that their ordeal may have caused them both to react out of character, to say things that they might not have said under other circumstances. They'd been thrust back into each other's lives for several days and had made promises, shared memories, and created fantasies. Now, as they flew back toward reality, she realized how out of proportion everything had been. How unrealistic it was to believe that after only a few days, their lives could be changed forever.

She sighed deeply. Her life, however, *had* been changed. Like a miracle, every feeling she'd ever had for Haughton Storm came galloping back to the surface. And now it burned like a sun in the sky. She sighed again.

"Stop it," his voice growled.

"Stop what?" she asked, turning in his direction.

"You're thinking too hard. You always do that double sigh thing when you over-analyze."

Tired, embarrassed, and found out, Roxanne looked away.

Storm touched her chin and turned it back to him. His fingers were covered with dry dirt and calluses, but to her at that moment they were the sweetest things on Earth.

His gorgeous face neared hers. "I don't know what force brought us together again, Roxanne. But I'm not about to lose you now. I'm not going to walk away. You can't get rid of me this time, Roxy."

She must have been more tired than she thought, because instead of holding back the tears she felt, she let them go. They spilled freely down her cheeks.

Storm kissed and swallowed each one. "I meant what I said. Here and on the island." He took a deep breath. "What about you?"

She touched his face, his shoulder, his chest. "I love you, Haughton. Real bad. God help me. I do. And I'm sorry about—"

His lips captured her apology and burned her with passion. She gave in to every pull of Storm's urgency. Every tug of her heartstrings.

He pulled away and pulled her to her feet. "Look here," he said, pointing toward the open helicopter door.

Jake jumped to his feet and wagged his tail. His friends stopped talking and looked on.

Storm finally knew the meaning of honor, the meaning of pride. He'd been chasing glory all his life. But true glory was in the love he had for the woman standing by his side. He pointed toward the horizon and the land appearing out of the distance.

In the west, the sun was beginning to set and bathed everything in a golden-red light.

"You see that?" he asked, extending his hand.

Roxanne nodded.

"Our future is as vast as that horizon. Just as full of possibilities." He turned her toward him. The wind blew her hair about her face in long wisps. "I don't want to face that world without you. Understand?"

Roxanne raised her hand in a trembling salute. "Aye, Aye, sir," she said, and a smile broke out on her face.

Storm enveloped her in his arms and held her tightly against his heart, in contentment and in love.

"I know this isn't a fancy restaurant or a cruise ship. Hell, it isn't even a sandy beach." His heart slammed against his chest. "I know that we're ten thousand feet in the air and I can barely hear myself talk." He wiped the nervous sweat forming on his brow. "I know that we both are funkin' up this camp and that, along with the exhaust fumes, make for a pungent memory. But there's something else I know."

His eyes darkened with determination and he stood a little straighter. "I know that I love you. And I know that ten years is a long time and I don't want to spend another moment apart from you."

Roxanne blinked in awe.

"I know that I want you in my life—for the *rest* of my life." He paused and took a deep breath. "As soon as we get back to civilization, I'm going to ask you to marry me, Roxanne Allgood, and when I do . . . what will you say?"

She folded in her bottom lip, letting the reality of his words wash over her. The game was over. The fantasy that they could ever be apart from each other and live happy lives had ended. This moment with Storm was her only truth. She smiled with the setting sunlight glowing on her face.

His eyes grew tender. "Sempala?"

"I will say, yes."

For a sneak peak at
the first book in the
At Your Service series

Top-Secret Rendezvous
by Linda Hudson-Smith

from BET Books/Arabesque

Just turn the page . . .

One

"Hi, beautiful, what are you drinking this afternoon?" Smiling at the rare beauty daintily perched on a high, cane-back barstool at the Hotel Meridian's poolside bar, Zurich Kingdom lowered his hulking frame down onto the stool next to hers. "I'd love to buy you a refill when you're ready for one."

Hailey Hamilton took her good old time in sizing up the newcomer. Her amber eyes shamelessly roved his physical attributes with a definite spark of interest. As her gaze came to rest on his sun-bronzed face, she decided that she loved the warmhearted smile still pasted on his sweet, juicy-looking lips. As his smile broadened, she got a good glimpse of tooth-paste-white teeth, all of which appeared free of cosmetic dentistry. His twinkling sienna-brown eyes appeared sincere, but she didn't know if she should be flattered or annoyed at the reference to his opinion of her looks. It had slipped off his tongue a little too easily for her liking.

"Would you like me to supply my measurements for you?" he asked.

"That won't be necessary, since I've got twenty-twenty vision. But you can tell me your name if you like." She playfully purred from deep within her throat. "I bet it's a strong one."

"Zurich Kingdom." He grinned. "How's that for strength?"

"It's packed with power and it personifies your physical make-up—tall, strong, Marine-like build—yet you seem so tender and sincere. There are a lot of manly powers packed into your six-foot-plus physique. I would be surprised if your ancestry didn't include royalty. I can imagine you running an entire *kingdom* single-handedly or commanding an entire army of men and women. Zurich brings to mind the majestic ambiance of the Swiss Alps. That thought definitely conjures powerful imagery. I can see you raising the flag of victory after your strength and fortitude has allowed you to scale your way to the very top. However, your approach needs a little polishing." Smiling smugly, Hailey was pleased to share her own brand of bull.

"Please don't stop, lady, now that you have me falling in love with myself. No, I'm only kidding, but enough about me for now. What's your name?"

"Beautiful! But I thought you already knew that since you said it when you first sat down." Her amber eyes flickered with devilment.

He nodded, smiling broadly. "Okay, okay, you got me there. Sorry for being a little overly flirtatious and forward, but I certainly wasn't lying. You *are* a very beautiful woman." He quickly arose from the stool and walked away. He only took a few steps before he turned around and came back to claim his seat. "Hi, I'm Zurich Kingdom. Mind if I join you for a drink?"

She tossed him a dazzling smile. "Hailey—with an 'i'— Hamilton won't mind if you do."

"Now that name certainly speaks to mystifying allure. I like it way more than *Beautiful*. How is it that your name is spelled like that? Isn't it different from the normal spelling?"

"I think some people spell it the same as I do."

"I don't know why, but I'm fascinated with the spelling. Is there a story behind it?"

"The story on the origin of my name is a long one."

"Am I already running out of time in your engaging company?"

"We've got a little time yet, Zurich."

"Good!"

Zurich summoned the cocktail waitress. Upon her arrival, he found out what Hailey was drinking and asked that the waitress keep both of their glasses refilled. It surprised him to learn that Hailey was only drinking lemonade, the same sort of refreshment that he enjoyed. A glass of wine or two was the only alcoholic beverage he ever indulged in, and even that was infrequently.

"Ready to tell me your name-related story, Hailey with an 'i'?"

"I guess I can tell you the story without going into all the boring details, which my parents, Martin and Marie, love to do. They lived in the small town of Palatka, several miles from the hospital in Gainesville, Florida. A horrible hailstorm had hit the morning my mother went into labor. As the conditions worsened, my father pulled off the road to help me into the world. I was born in the backseat of his car. From what I'm told, I was also conceived there. That's a longer story; another weather-related one. To finish up, my father decided to name me Hail. When it was typed into the official records, two additional letters were accidentally inserted. But I think someone felt sorry for me and decided to show some mercy, thus, Hailey."

"After hearing the story, I'm even more intrigued than before."

"Daddy wanted to change it when he first saw it, but Mom loved it. She wasn't too keen on Hail from the beginning, but there are times when she and Dad shorten it to just that."

"A beautiful story befitting a beautiful lady. In what twentieth-century year did that miracle of miracles occur?"

"In 1975. So, what's your story? What are you doing here on South Padre Island?"

"Vacationing. But I never thought I'd find literal paradise in my favorite Texas coastal city. Silky auburn hair, sparkling amber eyes, an indescribable figure packaged in a hot tangerine-orange bikini, soft-looking burnished-brown skin; all highlighted by a winning smile and a bubbling personality add up to my definition of a living, breathing paradise. Earlier I was in Dallas to honor my old football coach, Clyde Foster, during a special weekend event at my alma mater,

Buckley Academy. I always make the Meridian Hotel Resort my playpen when I'm here in my great birthplace of Texas. That is, after a couple of days at my mom's modest ranch."

His loquacious description of her didn't earn him so much as a blush. Referring to her as *paradise* had awarded him the same number of points as his earlier reference to her as *beautiful*—zilch. "I've heard a lot about your alma mater. Buckley Academy is the most prestigious prep school in the country."

"So I've been told. I attended Buckley from 1981 to 1985. I also played football for the Buckley Eagles. It was sort of a reunion for all the students, especially the football team, though we were really there to honor our coach. Three of my friends, Neal Allen, Haughton Storm, and Nelson Wainwright were on the team with me. We're still the very best of friends. All of us live in different parts of the country, and travel extensively, but we always manage to stay in touch. It was good to see them again."

"I'm glad your reunion was a success. Mind if I refer to something you said earlier?" After his replying shrug she asked, "You used the word playpen in reference to the resort. Now that's an interesting choice of words. Do you consider yourself a playboy, a player, or just a mischievous baby boy needing a safety net in the form of a *playpen* for security?"

"None of the above. But that was kind of cute if it wasn't meant as an insult."

"No offense intended, Zurich."

"No umbrage taken. To answer your question, I'm no player. I came here to relax and thoroughly enjoy myself. I want to have lots of fun without any emotional entanglements. Whatever I get into in the next couple of weeks will definitely end when I leave here. I have the kind of job that keeps me moving. I'm single and I want to keep it that way, that is, until my professional obligation is stable. I wish I knew how not to come off so direct, but I don't."

"A man after my own heart. It seems like we have a lot in common; I'm here for the very same reasons you are. I like all the cards to be placed right out there on the table where I can see them. I'm leery of people who keep less-than-desirable traits hidden and then spring them on you after you've given them your complete trust and loyalty, usually based on their false representation of self. I like to refer to that kind of person as the poker-playing hustler. I don't play cardshark-like games with others' emotions and I don't allow anyone to play me, period. What profession are you in, Zurich Kingdom?"

Zurich's eyes narrowed. "That's highly sensitive information, classified as top secret."

Zurich was surprised and pleased by her mature attitude. But in no way did he think she was the kind of woman who was going to take pleasure in having a physical tryst with someone for a couple of weeks only to have it end abruptly. In his thirty-five years he'd run into every type of woman imaginable. After numerous failures to read the signals right, he had finally learned how to easily differentiate between the women who were in the game strictly for pleasure, the ones in it for money and prestige, and the ones who weren't interested in either. The kind of woman who loved without reservation, without expecting anything in return, was a rare find indeed. That's the same sort of love Zurich wanted to offer to his wife when his career finally allowed him the freedom to marry.

It was his opinion that Hailey belonged to the latter group. He'd be willing to bet the ranch on his hunch. He might be eight years her senior but she seemed to have as much savvy as he had in how the game of life was played.

"Wow, we really do have a lot in common. I have the same type of job as you do. Maybe we're both members of the FBI, the CIA, the Secret Service, or some other covert organization. This vacation is suddenly starting to look up. I never thought I'd meet a very interesting man here at the resort, let alone one as fine as you. What's so amazing to me is that you like to play by the very same rules as I do: no hang-ups, hassles, or heartbreak."

He didn't know whether she was kidding. Her expression gave nothing away, and there hadn't been a hint of sarcasm in her gentle tone. Zurich didn't know what to make of her, but he couldn't recall a single female whom he'd ever been more impressed with or totally intrigued by. Hailey Hamilton had already scored an exorbitant number of points with him, effortlessly. Zurich was truly hoping that they could spend more time together.

As he studied her alluring profile, he cursed his profession under his breath. That was something he couldn't ever remembering doing, since he was extremely proud of his chosen field. In fact, it was all he knew, the only job he'd ever had. There were countless married folk in his line of work, but he wasn't the type of man who could divide his loyalties. Plain and simple, Zurich was married to his job and he loved it as much as he could ever love a woman.

"Hailey, are you saying that you and I can hang out and have a good time without having any hang-ups or hassles when the vacation is over?"

"That all depends on your definition of hanging out."

"Dinner, a movie or two, dancing, and enjoying the sunsets. And, if I'm really lucky, perhaps we can even share in a few sunrises."

"Sounds like you're making a bid for exclusive dibs on my time. Are you?"

"As much of it as you're willing to share with me."

"That seems like a great way to spend the next two weeks. However, if at any point I decide that I'm not having such a grand time, I'm back on my own. Okay?"

"As long as it cuts both ways."

"Absolutely. I believe wholeheartedly in equal opportunity and treatment. As for the sunrises, don't count on Lady Luck. The odds aren't in your favor."

He grinned. "Don't be so sure about that. I don't have any aces up my sleeve, but I think you'll be genuinely pleased with me as a date. I'm a man who knows how to treat a lovely lady. By the way, sunrises can be enjoyed from a variety of locales. So if you're thinking I'll be trying to get you up to my room, you're probably right, but not for any X-rated activity. I only make love to a woman when there's mutual consent. Love-making can't possibly be the beautiful, intimate experience it was intended to be if both parties aren't willing participants."

"My instincts tell me that I'll be completely safe with you. If they somehow fail me, be forewarned. My feet are registered as lethal weapons." She winked at him as she got up.

He laughed heartily. "I thought we had more time. Where are you off to all of a sudden?"

"Up to my room to get a few winks of beauty rest before our first dinner date. I'll meet you in the main restaurant at seven. You can have the hotel operator put a call through to my room should you need to cancel. I'm registered under my intriguing name. No aliases or secret code names were used this time around. I save those babies for when I'm on a special undercover assignment." *If only he knew the truth, he'd probably run.* She laughed inwardly.

"Lady, I do like your style. You're utterly fascinating! The only call you'll be getting from me is the one I'll make if you fail to show up at the appointed time and place."

"In that case, see you at seven sharp, Zurich. It's been such a pleasure."

"You can say that again." He stood and then leaned down and kissed her cheek. "So long for now, Hailey Hamilton. This is one evening I'm more than looking forward to."

"The feeling is mutual, Zurich Kingdom."

Totally intrigued, Zurich stood stock still as he watched Hailey disappear into the hotel. The woman had certainly left him with a lot to think about. He didn't know if meeting her was luck or a curse, since their relationship wouldn't last beyond the next two weeks. A blessing was a more accurate description of his first-time meeting with one Hailey Hamilton. It had felt like the angels were smiling down on him the entire time they were together. Grinning, Zurich prayed that the angels would continue to smile on him for the duration of his vacation.

* * *

Hailey awakened to a loud knock on the door. Wondering who could possibly be on the other side, she looked at the clock. She'd been asleep a lot longer than she'd intended. The steaming-hot shower had relaxed her completely. As three short raps sounded on the door, she thought of Zurich. No, she mused, he wouldn't come to her room, not without calling first.

Quickly jumping out of the king-size bed, Hailey slipped on a loose-fitting cover-up, dashed across the room, and asked who was there. Upon learning that it was a hotel service employee, she became a little leery. She hadn't ordered anything from room service. Further inquiry let her know that the gentleman had a package to deliver.

Curious as to who'd sent her a package and why, Hailey flipped the locks and opened the door. Her eyes grew bright with surprise when the deliveryman handed her a large, white wicker basket wrapped beautifully in lavender cellophane and tied with a huge purple bow and curly streamers. Since the basket was done in her favorite color, she suspected her parents. It had to be from them. They were the only people who knew where she was. Smiling, she thanked the young man and closed the door.

The sensuous smell of Tresor perfume wafted across her nose. Body lotion, shower gel, and a host of other fine toiletry items in that same heady scent filled the basket. The lavender heart-shaped candle touched her deeply. Looking at the accompanying card, she saw that the gift wasn't from her parents. Zurich was the one who'd sent it to her. That made her smile.

As she thought about his statement, *I'm a man who knows how to treat a lovely lady,* she laughed. He certainly hadn't been lying about that. This was such a nice way to start a first date, as well as the gift being such a lovely gesture. After all the cards had been laid out on the table in front of them, she'd felt relieved. His plans fit perfectly into hers—no hassles, hang-ups, or heartbreaks. Once the vacation time was up, she and Zurich would go their separate ways. Her next mission was far away from home; she had to be fit for duty, both mentally and physically.

Hailey didn't know if Zurich was serious about his job, but she certainly was about hers. She was so close to her ultimate goal, so near to fulfilling her lifelong dream. If all went as she hoped, a promotion was imminent. Six more weeks of intense technical training would be no problem for her. She never once regretted all the blood, sweat, and tears that she'd already poured into her job. Hailey was extremely proud of her career.

Hailey decided she wanted to look extra special for Zurich. What to wear out to dinner wasn't a problem for her. Everything she'd brought along with her was versatile. Hailey had chosen articles of clothing fashioned in fabrics of linen, silk, spandex, or pure cotton in soft but bright colors, solids, subtle prints, and basic blacks. She could go casual, classy, or dressy by simply adding or subtracting an accentuating piece or two. A couple pairs of denim jeans, linen blazers, lightweight shells, and sleeveless tops completed her fashionable wardrobe.

Since the basket was cellophane-wrapped in her favorite shade, she decided to wear her lavender silk dress with the bandeau top, which was classy and sexy with or without the matching jacket. If Zurich had chosen the color scheme for the basket, then he just might appreciate her wearing the same hue to show her appreciation of his choice.

Hailey plugged in her portable steamer after filling it with tap water. While waiting for the small appliance to heat up, she sat down on the side of the bed and put on fresh silk undergarments. She then seated herself in front of the mirrored dressing table and applied a fresh layer of foundation to her face. Earlier, before her nap, she had given herself an herbal facial.

After steaming her silk dress, she slipped into it. Her jewelry, a pair of diamond dewdrop earrings and matching pendant, came next. The two-carat diamond tennis bracelet she had a hard time fastening was a gift from her parents when she'd recently earned her college degree. Cute lavender-and-white medium-heeled sandals were her choice in footgear. While dabbing the Tresor on her pulse points, Hailey made a mental note to leave for the date early in order to purchase a thank-you card for Zurich from the hotel gift shop. She suddenly realized that she hadn't given the delivery guy a tip. Hailey recalled what he looked like, so she could easily remedy her mistake the next time she saw him around the hotel.

There were numerous first-rate hotels on South Padre Island, but the Meridian was Hailey's choice because it was smaller and more intimate than the larger resorts; it was also easier to recognize the staff and get to know them. There would be no touring or other outside activities on this trip since she planned to stay inside the self-contained entertainment complex and get caught up on her rest and relaxation, just another of her reasons for choosing the Meridian. Her next work assignment would take her far away from the comforts of home—and her next opportunity to take a vacation wouldn't come anytime soon.

A last minute glance into the mirror left Hailey satisfied with her stunning appearance. Smiling smugly at her image, she reopened the bottle of Tresor and dabbed a bit of the engaging scent onto the base of her throat, just in case Zurich desired to shower one of her more sensitive pulse points with his affection. He seemed like the romantic type, and she couldn't wait to find out if she was right. She needed a little romance in her life; romance without the worry of commitment was the best kind. But she definitely had her boundaries preset.

The thank-you card she chose for Zurich was lightly humorous, but with a sincere message of gratitude. She had purposely looked for a card in the same lavender color he'd chosen to have her gift wrapped in. Hailey felt really lucky when she'd found the cute one done in lavender and white. Two boxes of chocolate-covered raisins, one of her favorite treats, and a roll of wintergreen Lifesavers completed her gift-shop purchases. Hailey had less than two minutes to make it to the restaurant, but it was just a few steps away and around the corner from where she was. She wouldn't have to run, but she'd have to step lively.

Zurich's sensuous smile caused her pulse to quicken. All this man wore was a crisp white shirt, dark pants, and a designer blazer that defined his broad shoulders, yet he looked the part of a highly successful businessman. Zurich also seemed extremely relaxed.

His hand came up to her face and tenderly stroked her cheek. It was an innocent enough gesture, and certainly brief, but it made Hailey sizzle. The pleasurable experience lit up her eyes like sparklers.

"You look radiant, Hailey. And I just love a woman who's punctual. Did you bring a good appetite along with you?"

She smiled sweetly. "A ravenous one." She handed him the special card. "This is for you, Zurich. I hope you like it as much as I loved the gift you had delivered. Thank you so much."

Zurich was taken by the way Hailey showed her appreciation for the gift. He raised an eyebrow. "My thanks to you, as well. Mind if I open it once we're seated?"

"Not at all, Zurich."

He took her hand. "Let's go inside and get our table. I reserved one by the window. We should have a great view of the Gulf. It won't matter once it gets dark, but we still have an hour or so of daylight left."

Zurich gave his name to the willowy, blond hostess, and she instantly directed them to the cozy, elegantly set window table. The restaurant was practically empty, but Zurich knew it would quickly fill up with patrons. With that in mind, he hadn't objected when Hailey had chosen a time for their date that was about thirty minutes earlier than the most popular dining rush hour. Le Meridian was one of his favorite places to dine when he visited the island.

Hailey gave Zurich a dazzling smile as she sat down. "Did you arrange for this little surprise?" She picked up the placard with her name on it. "Miss Hailey Hamilton," she read aloud, "AKA Beautiful."

He seated himself directly across from her. "I'll only 'fess up if you're impressed."

"Intrigued is more precise. It's also a very sweet gesture. As I looked around at the other tables, I didn't see any other placards, so that's why I asked. When did you request this little extra nicety?"

"Right after our first date was set up. Glad you're not offended by it."

"Quite the contrary. Why would you think I'd be insulted?"

He grinned. "Earlier, you weren't too thrilled at being referred to as beautiful, so I thought I'd like to show you that I wasn't using the term flippantly. As I said earlier, you *are* beautiful, Hailey, and I am being sincere."

"Thank you, Zurich." Hailey looked up at the waiter as he appeared at the table. "Looks like it's time to order dinner." Hailey positively loved Zurich's unique way of expressing himself, as well as his seemingly romantic nature. She could hardly wait to see what else he had up his expensively tailored coat sleeve. He seemed as sweet as he was handsome.

"What do you have a taste for in the way of appetizers, Hailey?"

She picked up the menu. "Maybe I should first take a quick peek at what they have to offer. It'll only take me a minute or two. This is my first time eating here."

"Take your time, Miss Hamilton. I have no desire to rush us through our evening." Zurich looked up at the waiter. "We'd like a couple of more minutes to look over the menu, please. In the meantime, I'd like to request a carafe of chilled sparkling cider."

The waiter nodded at Zurich and then quickly moved away from the table.

As his eyes zeroed in on his lovely companion, Zurich's breath caught. Bathed in the soft glow of the candlelight, Hailey's near-flawless complexion had an angelic appearance. Her full, ripe lips were the next of her delicate features that caught his eye. Zurich imagined that a lot of women would love to have a sensuous mouth like hers. He could almost taste its sweetness.

Hailey made eye contact with Zurich. The softness exposed in the depths of his eyes made her heart tingle. "I'd like a shrimp cocktail for my appetizer, Zurich. What about you?"

"I love their stuffed mushrooms and fried mozzarella cheese. I even order the same from room service every time I stay here. This is my favorite restaurant in the hotel."

"How often do you come here?"

"Every time I visit my mom; at least twice a year. I love visiting this island. It's so quiet and peaceful here." He removed a couple of colorful brochures from the inside pocket of his jacket. "I picked these up from the hotel lobby so we can decide on a few fun things to do. I used to venture outside of the complex for my entertainment pleasures, but on my last few visits I've just stayed around here. I'm sure there have been a lot of changes on the island since then, and I'd love to re-explore this paradise with you." He handed the brochures to her.

She laid the pamphlets next to her place setting when the waiter reappeared with Zurich's beverage order. The young man removed the carafe of cider from the tray. After pouring the liquid into the crystal goblets, he set them in front of the couple.

"Are you ready to order, sir?" the waiter asked, dining check and pen in hand.

"Appetizers first." Zurich wasted no time filling in the waiter on their pre-dinner choices. Zurich then decided they should go ahead and order their entrees at the same time.

Once the waiter took the meal orders, he hurried from the table.

Hailey picked up one of the brochures and glanced it over.

"I had actually made up my mind not to leave the hotel complex. I planned on catching up on my reading and relaxation. A lazy, daily stint of lying out by the pool was also on my slate of things to do. I want to get my tan on, too," she joked, laughing.

He smiled at her. "Your coloring is already perfect. But I'd love to rub the suntan oil on your body for you. Interested in my hands-on services?"

"Maybe, maybe not. However, I do have a hard time reaching my back. I just might let you handle that area for me, but only if you can control your hands and keep them from roving into the 'no trespassing' zones." Her smile was a tad smug, but the laughter within was joyful.

The waiter's arrival kept Zurich from responding verbally, but the responsive thoughts in his mind had him laughing inwardly. Controlling his hands was the easy part. It was his inability to exercise restraint over the lower part of his anatomy that had him worried. Just the thought of massaging oil into Hailey's sexy body already had him physically aroused.

Hailey hadn't expected the pink, plump shrimp to be so large. After squeezing lemon on her appetizer and then dipping one into the cocktail sauce, she bit into the seafood delicacy. Her taste buds instantly went wild. The red sauce had a tangy, gingery flavor to it, different from anything she'd ever tasted. She could barely refrain from moaning with pleasure, but her amber eyes had the tendency to give away even her simplest thoughts.

Zurich was mesmerized by the expression of utter satisfaction he saw in Hailey's eyes. "You look like you're having a divine culinary experience over there. Is it really that good?"

"Hmm, you'll have to see for yourself." Taking another shrimp from the glass rim, she dipped it in the sauce. With a slight arm stretch across the table, she held up the shellfish to Zurich's mouth. Hailey's heart rhythms accelerated when his tongue made slight contact with her fingers. Wondering if the look on his face matched the one he'd seen on hers, she laughed. "What do you think, Zurich?"

"I think I need to place another order. From the heavenly look I saw on your face, I get the feeling you may not want to share another one of those delectable shrimp with me."

Repeating the same steps as before, she offered Zurich another one of her appetizers. The totally unselfish gesture caused him to eye her with mild curiosity. This time, he allowed his tongue to linger a little longer on her fingers. His attempt to effect a tender moment between them didn't go unnoticed, nor was it unappreciated by Hailey; her smile told him at least that much. The sensuous connection had been made, and each of them was feeling it.

"Thank you. That was very generous. There are people who don't like to share."

"I guess you could say that, but since you're the one paying the bill, I can afford to be generous." Although she was joking with him, she kept a straight face.

"Oh, it's like that, huh? How is it that I'm paying when you're the one who asked me out to dinner? Or was I mistaken in my assumption, Hailey?"

"I know I don't have amnesia, but you're remembering something that I'm not."

"I distinctly recall someone saying they were going to their room to rest before our first dinner date. Does *I'll meet you in the main restaurant at seven* ring a bell?"

Hailey couldn't have lied even if she wanted to. There was no denying what he'd remembered. Her own words rung in her ears with such familiarity. "Well, in that case, it looks like this dinner is my treat. But I don't mind if you order another appetizer. What's a few dollars when you're having a wonderful time?"

His eyes fell softly on her face. "It's nice to know you're enjoying yourself, Hailey. And I wouldn't think of having you pay the check. I realized you were joking when you made the statement about me paying. The laughter in your eyes allowed me to ignore the poker-bluffing look on your face."

"Oh, so you think you can read me that easily, Mr. Kingdom?"

"No, but I'd like to learn how." His expression turned pensive. "I know you and I have already set the ground rules, but what happens if one of us falls in love?"

She raised an eyebrow. "One of us? Why can't it be a mutual thing?"

He shrugged. "It can be. It happens all the time. I didn't come here looking to fall in love, but I didn't know I was going to find you here, either. We said a lot of things earlier about what we are and aren't looking for during our vacation time and what we're going to and not going to do. I'm now wondering if perhaps we made a mistake by doing that. What's your take on it?"

"We made those comments because we both knew that we weren't in a position to look back when it's time to go our separate ways. I think we're the type of people who have to keep it real. I know that every comment I made earlier about my life was an honest one. What about you, Zurich?"

Zurich gave Hailey's comments a minute of thought. "It has often been said that I'm too honest. But in my opinion, honesty is the only way to fly. The story will always be the same when you're telling the truth. Lying is the most confusing to the one doing it. You're right about keeping it real. It's easier that way. To answer your question, I was honest with you."

Zurich definitely knew how to keep it real. But what he didn't know was if it was going to be so easy to leave Hailey Hamilton behind without looking back. Their imminent separation might indeed be a hard one to pull off, especially without bringing about some sort of a change in him. For the better or the worse? He just didn't know. But this woman was truly different.

"I wish I knew how not to be so direct, but I don't. Do you remember who said that?"

He cracked up. "Sounds just like me. Well, here comes the waiter. We'll have to get deeper into this conversation after we eat. Okay with you?"

She nodded. "Fine, but what about ordering another appetizer?"

"It was good, but I really had enough. The main course is here now, so I'll be just fine. Thanks, Hailey."

Zurich quickly picked up the envelope he'd received from Hailey. He then opened it and read it. The simple words of thanks put a smile on his face. "This was really nice of you. I appreciate the way you show your appreciation. You're very thoughtful."

"I'm glad you like the card. It was the least I could do to show how much your gift meant to me." She stretched her arm across the table and put her wrist under his nose. "How do you like the perfume on me?"

His heart raced as he traced her wrist with feathery kisses. "It smells divine on you. It looks like I picked out the perfect scent for you. You two were definitely made for each other."

Seated across from one another in one of the popular lounges inside the hotel, where a live band played top-forty tunes, Hailey and Zurich had yet to experience an awkward moment as they enjoyed getting further acquainted. It was a little difficult to communicate above the loud music, but they somehow managed to converse despite the noise level.

His lips grazed her ear as he spoke into it. "Do you want another ginger ale, Hailey?"

"That would be nice. While we're waiting for the waitress, I'm going to slip into the ladies' room." She stood and reached for her purse.

Smiling, he got to his feet until she walked away.

After coming out of the stall, Hailey washed her hands. She then stood in front of the mirror as she freshened her lipstick and dusted her nose with corn silk. A slight smile appeared on her full lips as she thought of the good-looking man waiting back at the table for her. Zurich came off as a very genuine person, and she had to admit that she already liked him a lot.

Too bad they only had two weeks to click with each other. She could really get into Zurich, but when duty called she had to be ready and all set to go. Even if they did make a love connection, they'd still have to go their separate ways. Each of them had laid down the ground rules from the start: two weeks of fun in the sun and then it would be all over for them. The fact that Zurich thought they might've made a mistake in laying down the rules surprised her. Sighing with dismay, Hailey picked up her purse and left the ladies' lounge.

For a sneak peak at
the second book in the
At Your Service series

Courage Under Fire
by Candice Poarch

from BET Books/Arabesque

Just turn the page . . .

Prologue

Ronald Taft wore dress blues. Although his wife couldn't see the shoes, she knew they were spit-shined black.

The officer's dress blues were his favorite Army uniform. He wore them with a sense of pride and honor for his country and for the fact that he—a black man who came from little—had progressed so far. He loved the Army and even more, he loved his status as an officer.

Arlene Taft remembered when Ronald had taken her to her first formal military function. Since it was his ball, she'd elected to wear a blue gown instead of her dress uniform.

Just a smattering of African-Americans had been in attendance.

"We'll go far in the military," he'd said to Arlene. They were both stationed in the Washington, D.C. area. Although it was unusual to get assigned to the same location for years, he'd lucked out with his posting at the Pentagon. Since she was a nurse, staying in one location wasn't unusual for her. She'd been at Walter Reed Army Medical Center for years.

As the years passed, Ronald's postings required more and more travel—so much, in fact, that it was easy for him to take a vacation with a mistress without his wife's knowledge.

Arlene sat through her husband's funeral with strained emotions. What was she to feel except betrayal, disillusionment, and a deep burning anger that she couldn't appease?

Her mother-in-law sniffled and moaned her grief beside her. She held on to the woman's hand, perhaps too tightly at times, but Nancy Taft didn't complain. She was swallowed up in her own grief and she didn't even notice. The nurse had already revived her once with smelling salts. Ronald had been Mrs. Taft's only child—a truly beloved son. And somewhat spoiled. But she didn't blame Mrs. Taft for being a loving and giving woman. She'd accepted Arlene into the fold as if she were her own child. Nancy was a rarity. She seldom spoke a disparaging word against anyone.

Arlene's father was present with his new wife, a woman who was merely a few months older than Arlene. She was so unlike Arlene's mother that Arlene wondered what he saw in her except for the obvious appeal of a younger woman. Arlene's mother had died three years ago, and Arlene supposed this was his way of moving on. He certainly dressed younger. His wife stood out in her lavish black attire. The skirt was higher and tighter than Arlene thought appropriate, but who was she to judge? She only wished she could see more of her father. Their relationship hadn't been the same since her mother's death.

The preacher's words droned on. They could have been disjointed ramblings, because Arlene didn't hear any of it. She didn't know why she was grieving.

Her husband died on a boating trip with his lover—a lover Arlene must have subconsciously known had been out there. Did she have blinders on? The reality that he spent so little time with her should have been one clear indication. Randy army officers rarely went without physical pleasures. She'd only deluded herself into thinking that her man was made of sterner stuff.

Arlene shook with his betrayal. She wondered if his army buddies who laughed and joked in front of her knew of his exploits behind her back. Had their wives, who called themselves her friends, also been privy to the information? The military community was small. People knew each other's business, and they told. Yet no one had seen the necessity of informing her.

Somehow Arlene got through the funeral. She barely startled at the gun salute, and made polite conversation at the reception held after the gravesite service. Her father and his wife left.

Arlene stayed on for a few days to console her mother-in-law. Then she flew back to Washington, D.C., telling Mrs. Taft that she would stay in touch and that she would send her mementos of her son.

It was Friday night when she unpacked her suitcase in the row house she'd lived in for years. The message machine was beeping. Ignoring it, she stood under the shower a long time, then went to the closet to pull on a robe, even though the outside August temperature hovered in the nineties.

Ronald's suits and clothes hung in the closet beside hers. What happened next seemed to be outside of her control.

She came back to her senses when she heard the doorbell ring. Shelly Bailey, her girlfriend since kindergarten, stood on the cement steps, a suitcase beside her.

Arlene glanced around the room. It was a disaster. Every piece of Ronald's clothing was flung about the room. A stack of black garbage bags was hidden under more clothes on the cocktail table.

Shelly glanced at Arlene's ravished features. Then she glanced around the living room, a worried expression on her face.

She tugged Arlene into her arms and held her tightly. "Girlfriend, I'm here. We're going to work this through together."

One

Some days were better than others. Arlene wanted to pull the covers up to her neck and spend the next few hours in her warm bed.

At nine she made an effort to rise, but never made it up. She dozed again, off and on for two hours. A siren blared from afar, but that wasn't so unusual in the city.

The clock closed in on eleven when she finally considered actually getting up. She didn't feel too guilty. After all, she'd worked the eleven-to-seven shift at the hospital the evening before.

Arlene contemplated calling in sick—perhaps to spend the rest of what was left of the day in bed. Half of it was gone anyway. This was totally out of line for her. She'd never called in sick when she wasn't. But many things had changed in the last month and she didn't feel quite herself.

Suddenly the phone rang, a loud and unwanted sound in the quiet of her bedroom. Lazily she reached out a hand, plucked up the receiver, and barked out a groggy "Hello."

"Lieutenant Colonel Taft, we need you here stat!" the hospital scheduler told her.

Now! Was that woman crazy? Arlene wanted to avoid the day altogether, but she wouldn't dare say so out loud. A soldier was on call twenty-four-seven. If they needed her, she'd have to go.

"Due to the disaster, we need more nurses, especially specialists," the woman said.

"What disaster?" Arlene asked.

"Haven't you seen the news?"

"No. What happened?" Sitting up in bed, she reached for the remote. It was too far away. Now that she thought about it, she had heard more sirens than usual, but it hadn't pierced the fog that had settled on her.

"The Pentagon has been bombed. And both towers of the World Trade Center are gone. And that's just the beginning."

"Gone? *Impossible.*"

"Just turn on the TV. Every station is broadcasting. We need you here. Now."

"I'll be there as soon as I dress." Arlene fumbled the receiver back onto the hook and scrambled for the TV remote to press the power button. Every channel focused on the tragedy. It didn't take long for her to get the gist of the earth-shattering disaster. A deep sense of dread and sorrow flowed through her for the suffering these people were experiencing and that someone would dare do this in America. She saw it in the news when it happened in Europe and Israel. *But here?* The U.S. seemed isolated from all that, but global involvement had brought the entire world closer—for the good as well as the bad.

With a quick prayer, she rushed out of bed so fast her head swam. Tugging off her nightgown and thrusting it aside, she headed to the shower. After taking the fastest shower in history, she listened to the news as she quickly donned her uniform. Her new hairdo of short red curls only took a moment to rake a comb through. Turning off the TV, she paused only long enough to grab a bagel and cream cheese to eat in the car as she drove the short distance to the hospital. Depending on the number of injured, finding time for a break once she arrived could be next to impossible.

At the hospital, she was quickly directed to the trauma section. It was a beehive of activity.

"Lieutenant Colonel Neal Allen is one of your patients," she was told. "He has multiple fractures, scorched lungs and throat, and internal injuries. Right now we're trying to keep him breathing on his own to clear his lungs and increase his chances of survival."

Arlene recorded his vital signs on his chart. He was still heavily sedated from surgery.

Neal Allen. That name was indelibly etched in her mind. Could this be the Neal Allen who lived next door to her in middle school? Arlene shook her head at the foolish thought. It couldn't be. Of all the people for her to run into.

The Neal Allen she'd known back in Texas had been the bane of her existence. She would never forget the time he'd taken her red-and-white panties off the clothesline, attached them to a piece of cardboard, scribbled her name in huge bold letters across the front, and hung them on his father's flag-pole. Her panties had flown for hours where the man had so proudly flown his American flag. All because she wouldn't walk to the movies with him. She'd already accepted a date with someone else, but even if she hadn't, she wouldn't have gone out with Neal. *What was that boy's name?* she wondered. Perhaps she hadn't been the most diplomatic with her refusal, but she didn't deserve that.

As Arlene looked at him, she realized he was that Neal Allen. Determined to find something to dislike about him, she noted his physical appearance had changed a lot in the last twenty-one years from the gangly youth she'd known.

It was immediately evident that he worked out regularly. His relaxed state failed to mask his underlying strength. His chest and shoulder muscles were amazing. She felt the steel beneath soft skin when she attached the blood-pressure cuff. His dark lashes covering his closed eyes were much too at-tractive. His hair was cut short, yet still managed to look striking. As Arlene gazed down on him, she wondered if his character had changed as much as his appearance.

She shook the memories away and got back to the business of keeping Lieutenant Colonel Neal Allen alive.

* * *

The next day, when Arlene reported to duty, the patient was looking better. She wondered if he remembered her.

"How are we feeling today, Lieutenant Colonel Allen?" Arlene asked him as she slipped the pressure cuff on his arm.

"Good to be alive," he whispered in a raspy voice she could barely hear. It was tinged with the smoke and heat damage from the fire.

"Oh, you'll be feeling better in no time." After making a notation of his blood pressure, she slid the thermometer into his ear, then recorded his temperature. It was only slightly elevated.

"How did the others—"

"You saved quite a few people. They've been calling about you."

"But—"

"Don't try to talk. Save your throat." She smiled. Whatever their past, he was her patient and she was determined to give him the best care. "You're a hero."

"No . . . So much destruction. So many people injured—" he whispered.

"And many generous people who are out there offering help. You did your part; now let us help you."

"It wasn't enough."

Arlene patted his hand, wanting to ease his distress. "You gave all you could. No one could ask for more."

He closed his eyes.

Arlene didn't know if her words had had any effect. She only hoped they eased his pain.

She kept peeking at him as she attended to his injuries. His concern for the others touched her more than she wanted. Could he have changed so drastically from that obnoxious kid she knew so long ago?

"Well, Little Miss Leave-Me-Alone."

Arlene stopped in her tracks, her hackles rising. She forced herself to present a calm front. "We must be feeling better."

"Thought I'd forgotten you, didn't you?"

Arlene had hoped so.

"Were you trying to hide your identity?" His voice rose barely above a whisper. She strained to hear him, but she heard nevertheless. His cute brown eyes were dancing with merriment for the first time. Even though it was at her expense, she was glad for it.

She'd hoped he'd forgotten about her past, darn it. After all, she couldn't look the same, and her last name had changed. Back then, he'd loved to tease her. "I don't have anything to hide. My life is an open book. I see you haven't changed from that obnoxious kid who lived next door to me."

"In some ways—in many, many ways—I hope I have. Changed, that is."

"Hummm." He had changed, all right. Even with his numerous injuries, she hadn't missed the striking proportions of his body. As his nurse, she'd seen all of him, and to her chagrin, she liked what she saw.

"We'll just work on getting you healed right now, okay?"

His smile faded. "How are the others who were brought in?"

"I don't know. I'm sorry. They were taken to hospitals all around the area." She pulled the sheet up to his chest. "I want you to rest your voice. Your throat is still raw. It must be painful for you to talk."

He clasped her hand in his, imprisoning it with a grip that belied his condition. "I need to know."

"I know you do. Believe me, we're all doing our best for all the injured. Trust me."

"Can I trust you?" The seriousness of his tone surprised Arlene.

"Why wouldn't you?"

His stare was intense, as if his eyes spoke words he wouldn't say aloud. Then suddenly he glanced away from her to the picture beside his bed.

She regarded the photo, which a nurse had found in his pocket. A pretty young girl with two thick pigtails. Arlene had brought a frame for it and put it on his bedside table, hoping the photo would give him pleasure. From her conversations with his mother, who called often, she'd garnered that the child was his niece, a cutie named April.

"Your mother and your niece have called several times. They're very concerned about you."

"What did you tell them?"

"That you're better, and that we're taking excellent care of you. As soon as your voice heals, we'll let you talk with them. But right now, I want you to rest your vocal cords."

He glanced at the clock. "It's time for you to leave?"

"Yes," Arlene said. "My shift is over."

"Can't you stay a little while?"

"Why?"

"I don't know. To talk about home. To read to me. Something—anything. I can't sleep."

She stopped the urge to stroke his forehead. "They'll give you something to help you sleep," Arlene said softly. "You need your rest."

"I don't want any more medication."

Arlene knew very well that she had nothing to rush home to. Her husband was dead—had seldom been around when he was alive. Since his death, things hadn't changed that much, actually. Except for the expectation of his arrival. When she looked back on her marriage, she saw that it hadn't been that great. She'd been complacent. And that was sad.

Arlene had nothing to go home to.

"All right. I'll read to you. What kinds of books do you like?"

"Anything will do." Neal just wanted to listen to her voice. Her soothing voice intrigued him, not the story. He was disgusted with himself for wanting her near. Most of his waking hours were spent watching the disaster on TV. His unit would be one of the groups dispatched to Afghanistan. He was disappointed that he wouldn't be among them.

Now he was punishing himself by listening to Arlene's

voice, even though he knew she'd been responsible for his sister's, and thereby April's, unhappiness and pain.

But Ronald Taft *had* been Arlene's husband. He'd already been married, and Bridget had no right to him.

Arlene smiled—a smile he remembered so well from when she was up to mischief. "Would one of my romance novels work?"

He smiled, and the image was amazing.

"How about a mystery?" Arlene amended, knowing the skewed notion men had of romance novels. "I'll find one that will keep your heart pumping for hours. Or I might get you something soothing enough to help you sleep. What's your preference?" She found herself stroking his hand even though she'd cautioned herself not to.

"Excitement, please."

There was that smile again—the one he'd used just after he'd teased her in middle school. Back then, Arlene had hated that smile, but now she found it sexy. She chuckled. "I'll be back soon," she said, and went to meet with the nurse who would replace her.

"Arlene, we're transferring a call. This kid insists on speaking to you and only you."

For a change, Neal was sleeping peacefully. Arlene's hand hovered over the phone so that she could catch it before the ring woke him.

"Nurse Taft?" a young voice asked in a firm tone.

"This is Lieutenant Colonel Taft," Arlene responded.

"Good. I'm calling about Uncle Neal. I'm worried about him. When can he come home? I miss him. I *need* him." The little girl sounded as if she were near tears.

"Are you April?"

Silence greeted Arlene. Then a hesitant, trembling voice said, "Yes."

"Your uncle is much better, April. He's responding well to

the medication. But he needs time for his body to heal. It might take a little while."

Arlene heard sniffles on the end of the line, and her heart cracked.

"Is your grandmother there, or your mother?"

"My mommy's dead. Uncle Neal is supposed to take care of me now."

"I'm so sorry, honey." Arlene's heart went out to the motherless little girl. She remembered Bridget well, and was saddened to hear the young woman was dead. Neal seemed to be the child's security blanket.

"Grandma's worried about Uncle Neal. She wants to come there but Grandpa's too sick. Grandpa wants to come, too. But he can't."

"It won't be easy catching a plane right now, anyway. Maybe it's best they stay home. Anytime you're worried about him, just call me, all right?"

"Will you tell me the truth?"

Arlene closed her eyes, moved by the hope in the child's voice. "Always."

"Uncle Neal's really doing better?" she asked with a skepticism too old for one so young.

"Yes, he's much better. I promise." That much wasn't a lie. Arlene wouldn't lie to her.

"He's really not going to die? Grandma said he wouldn't, but I thought she was just trying to make me feel better."

"No, he's definitely not going to die. I wouldn't lie about that."

"Thank you."

"You're very welcome, dear. Did you get your grandparents' permission to call?"

"Uncle Neal gave me lots of phone cards so I can call him anytime I want to."

"And you know how to use them?"

"Sure," she said with a confidence that belied her age. "He showed me how to use them. And I've been reading for years. I can read directions."

Arlene smiled. "You're a big girl, aren't you?"

"Yeah. I can do lots of things."

When Arlene hung up the phone, she caught Neal's steady gaze as he watched her. He was always watching her in that strange way. Why? What was he looking for? "I didn't know you were awake," Arlene said finally. "I'm sorry I woke you."

"It's okay," he whispered. But a deep sadness seemed to steal over him. She understood some of what he felt, only her grief was different. Her sorrow was tinged with adultery, mistrust, and hurt. The loss of a beloved sister was so much worse.

"I'm so sorry about your sister," Arlene told him.

He nodded and turned away from her. Nothing could be said to ease the sorrow of a loved one's death. She wouldn't even try to ease what she couldn't anyway.

She thought of Bridget again. She'd been five years younger than Arlene. They'd known each other, but their ages were too far apart for them to run in the same circles. But Bridget had looked up to Arlene. And Arlene sometimes baby-sat for Mrs. Allen. Bridget had been as full of energy as her precocious brother, but not quite as mischievous. Their mother was practically useless when it came to handling two such active kids. Sometimes it seemed she didn't even try.

Arlene glanced at the photo on Neal's bedside table. "April is very pretty. She resembles you."

"You think so?"

"Yes. Although she also reminds me of Bridget at that age. She definitely has your nose and your smile."

His smile was not filled with humor.

"Are you comfortable?" Arlene asked, straightening his covers.

He nodded.

With nothing more to offer, Arlene touched his hand and left the room.

Considering the meticulous care she gave him and the gentle comfort she offered his family, it was difficult to believe that Arlene was the vindictive woman who wouldn't give her husband a divorce, even after she'd already agreed to do so, simply because she discovered another woman was pregnant with his child. According to Ronald, his relationship with his wife had been over years ago. He'd finally decided to end it, and she'd agreed. Then, when she discovered Bridget was pregnant with his child, she refused to give him the divorce, threatening to ruin his career if he tried to get one.

Ronald and Neal were both Army career men. The threat of adultery could damage a black man's career in a heartbeat. White officers could sometimes get away with unsavory behavior. Even with the barrage of publicity, only a few cases actually amounted to anything. The press usually died down after a short while. Besides, officers protected each other. Today as much as in the past, black men lived by a different, more cautious code.

Another worry nagged relentlessly at Neal. He was responsible for raising his niece. Would he heal well enough to return to his post so he could properly care for her? He wasn't ready to retire. But if his body betrayed him, he would have no other recourse. He wanted to expose her to the world. There was so much for her to learn—so much to see.

April had lost a mother and father only a month ago. And now her guardian was in the hospital. His parents were too infirm to care for a rambunctious eight-year-old. And April had always been full of energy. Every week since his sister's death, his mother had called to tell him about some mischief April had gotten into. He'd lecture the child, but her deeds weren't that serious, and Neal didn't put that much energy into the lecture. She'd lived through enough traumas. He wouldn't make her life any more unbearable than it already was. He needed to be with her.

Neal had paid for a live-in nanny to care for her until he could take the responsibility for her.

She was on her third nanny so far. The second one had been frightened away when April put her hamster in the woman's bed. The woman had woken in the middle of the night to find the hamster crawling up her leg.

Neal had hoped to get April in a few weeks. Now, there was no telling when he would be able to return to the real world and care for her.

He could imagine the frightening thoughts running through her head, especially with his accident so close on the heels of her parents' deaths.

It was Saturday. Neal had been in the hospital for two weeks now. It was Arlene's day off, and she debated going in to visit him. He expected to see her every day. They had fallen into a routine of sorts, although sometimes his mind seemed to wander. Some deep, dark secret from the past, perhaps. Arlene got the feeling he didn't like her for some reason. But she certainly couldn't be part of whatever troubled him.

When she arrived, the phone in his room rang. By now it was second nature for her to reach for it.

"It's time to send Uncle Neal home," April said, when Arlene answered it.

"He's healing very nicely," Arlene told her. "But he isn't quite ready to return home."

"But I need him *now*." Every situation was urgent as far as April was concerned.

"He misses you, too, sweetheart."

"My nanny is a witch." A long, labored breath followed that pronouncement.

Arlene smothered a laugh.

"How so?" Arlene couldn't help but ask.

"She doesn't understand me."

"Maybe if you explained your problem to her—"

"She doesn't understand, though. She's too old. I need help!"

"Honey—"

"Can you believe she got mad because my guinea pig got out of the cage and went to her room?"

"It just happened to get out?"

Silence greeted her. Arlene surmised the rodent had had plenty of help.

"I may have *accidentally* left the door open when I took her out to play with me. Maybe I didn't latch the door good enough. But it was an *accident.* Everybody makes mistakes. Why can't I make them?"

"I see," Arlene said. Evidently Nanny didn't like little animals scurrying around the house.

"And my hamster won't stay in the cage. Nanny keeps calling it a mouse and threatening to kill it. Can you believe she'd kill my hamster? I told Grandpa on her too. He told her not to kill my animals. She's a mean old lady."

"Let me get this straight. The hamster gets out of the cage on its own. You didn't give it any help?"

"No. Never."

I just bet it did, Arlene thought.

"Is it my fault he keeps getting out? I do everything I can to get him to stay in, but every morning when I wake up he's gone. And he stays away until he gets hungry. Then he comes back looking scrawny and starved."

"So after the hamster got out of the room on its own, it found its way to your nanny's room, too?"

"What can I do about *that? "* April asked, affronted. "He got out on his own. It's the hamster's fault. Why doesn't she blame him?"

"She can't exactly talk to the hamster."

"I talk to him all the time. But does he listen when I tell him to stay in a cage? Nanny's mean. He's got to be careful around her, and I told him that, too. But Grandma says that's a man for you. They never listen."

Arlene couldn't contain her laugh.

"And then there's my dog."

Did the child have a zoo in that house? Arlene wondered. "A dog?"

"Nothing worth getting mad about. It just chewed on her raggedy old house shoe. And then it peed on the carpet in her room. But that was her fault. She shouldn't have scared him. If I was a baby, I would have peed too if that old hag had frightened me. It's just a puppy."

Arlene peeked at Neal to make sure he was still sleeping. "I take it she doesn't frighten you."

"Not really. I hate her!"

"Have you spoken to your grandparents about this?"

"They don't understand because the mean witch always gets to them first before I even get a chance to tell them *my* side." A long, defeated sigh came over the phone. "Now I'm stuck in my room until I learn to behave. I'm going to spend the rest of my life cooped up in this room. Can I come to Uncle Neal? Please? Please? I'll take care of him. I won't bother him. I promise to be good."

Arlene's heart clenched. April desperately needed her uncle. "Sweetheart, you *are* good." She was just an eight-year-old acting her age.

Early Monday afternoon, General Ashborn presented Neal with the papers and eagle for his promotion to Colonel. He also received a special commendation for his rescue efforts.

Arlene borrowed a disposable camera from one of the nurses and snapped pictures.

"Congratulations, Colonel," Arlene told him once the general had left.

"Thank you," he said.

"This is absolutely wonderful."

He studied the commendation as if it held the secrets to the universe. "So many people were hurt far worse than I was. So many lives lost. I don't feel I deserve this."

"That doesn't mean we can't recognize our heroes. You deserve your commendation, Neal. You have something to be proud of."

Neal's phone rang, and Arlene picked it up as if it were her own.

"My hamster's dead!" April wailed over the phone.

"What happened?" Arlene asked, ready to go to battle with the mean old nanny who had the nerve to kill a child's animal.

"My dog bit it."

"Your dog?" Arlene pressed a hand against her chest to still her quickened heartbeat.

"It got out of the cage again. It wouldn't listen to me. And Pickles ate it. He was bloody and dead on my carpet this morning. I didn't even hear him last night."

"Oh, I'm so sorry, honey."

"I want Uncle Neal. Please can I come?"

"Honey, your uncle is improving daily, but it will take some time before he's ready to come home. You can't stay in a hospital."

"I'll be good, and I'll be quiet, too. I promise."

Arlene's heart ached for the little girl. "Who will keep your animals if you leave?"

"I'm mad at Pickles. She ate my hamster."

"It's not quite Pickles's fault, honey. His natural survival instinct encourages him to eat animals. Dogs are made that way."

"It's mean."

"It seems like it. But those instincts keep them alive when they don't have someone special like you to take care of them."

"I feed her. I even give her food from my plate sometimes, even when Nanny gets mad."

"I'm sure you take very good care of her. And you must continue to do so until Uncle Neal is well. Okay?"

A few sniffles came over the wire before a weak, "Okay."

"Good."

"I buried him in a shoe box in the back yard. Grandpa said a prayer over his grave."

"That's good."

"I made a cross out of some sticks, and planted a flower by his grave. My mama's flowers were prettier. You think he'll like the flowers?"

"I'm sure he loved them."

"I miss my hamster and I miss my mom."

"I know you do, sweetheart." Arlene struggled to hold back tears.

A couple of sniffles preceded, "My friend Keanna has a boyfriend. I'm never going to date a boy."

Arlene smiled and swiped the wetness away from her eyes. "You might feel differently when you enter high school."

"They're so hardheaded. Grandma said that's why my hamster's dead. Because boys are hardheaded. They're the devil's spawn, she said. They always do what you tell them not to. I don't want any hardheaded boys. It hurts too much. I'm not getting any more boy animals."

"Oh, sweetheart. They aren't all bad." Thinking back on Neal when he was a boy, Arlene thought April wasn't too far off the mark.

"Grandma says they are. Nanny agreed, but I don't believe anything she says. She wanted to dump my hamster in the trash. Can you believe that? She wanted to treat him like he was trash."

This woman was toast if Arlene had anything to say about it.

"Grandpa wouldn't let her. He made her keep him so we could bury him."

Arlene closed her eyes briefly. So much grief for one so young. First she buried her mom. Now her pet. Arlene's own pain seemed minuscule in comparison.

"What's the devil's spawn? Nanny called me that, and I'm not a boy."

"You're not the devil's spawn. Put your nanny on the phone."

"She'll be mad at me."

"Right now."

A few seconds passed before an older woman answered the phone. "Hello?"

"Mrs. Carter, I'm Colonel Allen's nurse. He has asked me to speak to you about April."

"She's a handful, I'll tell you that."

"All little eight-year-olds are handfuls," Arlene said.

"Mine weren't."

Did the woman think she'd raised angels? They were probably just good around her. "You do understand that she's just lost her mother, and her uncle who is now her guardian is gravely injured. He would appreciate it if you can keep things calm for her and give her a little consideration."

"He wants me to spoil the child?"

"Consideration means not calling her bad names that might label her for life. Children are very sensitive about that. She also loves her animals. If you could be a little generous toward them, he would be grateful." Arlene chose her words carefully. After all, Neal couldn't search out a new nanny in his condition. Still, the nanny should show some kindness toward the child. No child should be labeled the devil's spawn. Of all the nerve!

When Arlene hung up, she wondered if she'd overstepped her authority. She glanced at Neal. He was watching her, his emotions unreadable. Even regarding his illness, she couldn't always read him. He hated taking pain medication. He was so good at hiding emotions that she couldn't always tell when he was in pain. What else was he covering up?

"I hope you don't mind," she said.

He shook his head.

Neal seemed always to be thinking, always considering some matter. Arlene wondered what was going through his mind. Sometimes she felt he was measuring her, and wondered why. She wondered if she came up lacking.

Near the end of Arlene's shift, as she recorded Neal's vital signs on a chart, a gorgeous, honey-brown–hued woman wearing an Army uniform entered Neal's room.

"Hello, Neal. I was told you were improving," the woman said as she walked to the bed.

He nodded.

"Just ring the bell if you need anything," Arlene said to Neal, and prepared to leave.

"Hello, I'm Natasha, Neal's wife."

Wife. A ring hadn't been among his possessions, and he'd never mentioned a wife.

"Nice to meet you," Arlene said, and left the room.

Neal's wife *would* be what men considered a knockout. Why hadn't Natasha visited him before? Or called him? Perhaps she was stationed elsewhere and had trouble getting to D.C. April called every day. Surely the wife could have called him once.

For some indescribable reason, a shaft of disappointment swirled through Arlene. *You weren't falling for your patient, Arlene. So what's going on?* She took a deep breath and continued the last of her duties of the day. Neal was thirty-six—certainly old enough to have married at least once.

Neal watched Arlene leave the room, surely thinking he'd lied to her.

"Why are you here, Natasha?"

Natasha approached his bed. "I know this is bad timing, but the sooner we get this divorce moving, the better. If you sign the papers now, the divorce will come through in six months. I got the papers a couple of weeks ago, but I wanted to give you some time."

"How generous," he whispered. His voice was a little stronger than it had been, but not much.

"Give me the papers."

Natasha took a manila envelope out of her huge purse and retrieved the papers.

"The lawyer tagged the areas where you should sign," she said.

Neal activated the remote for the bed so he could sit up.

"I'll help you with that."

"I have it," he shot back. If he could handle a divorce, he could damn well handle a remote. He scanned the papers, making sure he wasn't signing away everything he'd ever saved. A five-year marriage that only halfway worked for the first three years wasn't worth everything he'd ever worked for.

Now Neal was grateful Natasha had insisted on a prenuptial agreement, fearing that if things didn't work out, he'd end up with the little her father had left her. He knew very well his assets amounted to more than hers. He wanted to keep it that way.

Neal signed the papers and handed them to her.

"How is April?" she asked, as if she really cared.

"She's fine."

"Good." Natasha checked the clock. "Well, I have an appointment. I hope everything turns out well for you."

"You, too," Neal told her, knowing very well that she was rushing off to be with her new boyfriend.

Now uncomfortable with him, she quickly left. A part of Neal's life was nearing a close. He shouldn't feel anything, should be grateful to see the last of her. Still they had been married for five years, and parting wasn't easy.

He glanced at the clock and wondered if Arlene would stop by once again before she left. He was falling for her, just as he had as a lovesick thirteen-year-old. Every time she came in the room, his system went into overdrive. He had to work at keeping his emotions contained. She was forever leaning over him or touching him in her warm manner. And her touches set his heart thumping. He watched the clock, waiting for her to return.

She didn't, and he was even more disappointed than he'd been with the ending of his marriage.

Arlene had the next two days off, and for the first time since Neal had arrived, she didn't go by the hospital to visit him. They were the longest two days of Neal's life.

She returned on Thursday. When she came into his room, she was very businesslike. She did the chores she usually did, and was about to leave the room when he grabbed her arm.

"What's going on?" he whispered.

"Nothing. Did you have a good weekend?"

"I expected to see you."

"Wasn't your wife with you?"

Neal sighed. He needed to clear the air. "We're separated. She brought the separation papers by for me to sign."

With an unbelieving glint, Arlene's eyes widened. "She brought you papers while you're in the hospital?"

Neal shrugged. "They needed to be signed. My marriage has been over for years. We're just getting it done legally."

"I'm sorry, Neal."

"I'm not."

"Are you okay?"

Neal nodded.

Arlene squeezed his hand and went about her rounds, wondering at the cruelty of people, or was it just that they didn't care anymore as long as their needs were taken care of. She hoped she would never be that uncaring.

April had called practically every day since Arlene's conversation with the nanny. Somehow, the energetic child brought Arlene out of her own grief.

"Are your bags all packed?" Neal asked.

"They are. Most of my things have been shipped to Korea," Arlene said. Korea was her next tour of duty. She was scheduled for a short stay there.

"Aren't you going to miss this place?"

Arlene nodded. "I'm definitely going to miss the D.C. area. The beautiful old homes. The rhythm of the city. The museums and activities on the Mall. The theaters. Cherry blossoms in the spring. The restaurants. But it's time for me to see other parts of the world." The things she'd mentioned were only a few of the activities Arlene would miss, but the day after she returned to work after burying Ronald, she'd asked for a change in location. She realized she'd grown stagnant. She was pleased the change had come through quickly.

Neal was leaving the hospital today. He was taking a flight to Dallas to finish his recuperation near his family. April needed to see that he was still alive and recovering. Arlene had halfway fallen in love with the child over the last few weeks. She would miss their lively conversations. If she'd had a child, she would have wished for one like April.

She would also miss Neal. Darn it. Tears clogged her throat. How had she fallen for him so quickly? She hadn't fallen in love with him or anything stupid like that. It was just . . . in their month and half together, they had formed a bond of sorts.

Neal, too, had mixed feelings about Arlene. He'd grown to respect her skills, and had even fallen in love with her a little over the last several weeks. It was difficult to reconcile the vindictive woman Ronald had described to Bridget, with this tender, caring woman who dealt so well with April, his parents, and his concerned friends.

Perhaps Ronald had been wrong. It was possible that Arlene had refused to give him a divorce because she was in love with him. After all, he had been her husband. She had first dibs on him. Bridget, the baby sister whom Neal had loved so much, had found her happiness on the dregs of another woman's lost dreams.

It hurt to think about his sister. The two of them had always been protective of one another. It seemed his connection to family stability had been broken with her death. Family was special to him. Sometimes he thought the only thing keeping his life in perspective was April, simply because she needed him.

For the last month she'd called almost daily, wanting him home with her. The doctors wanted him to stay in D.C. another week or so before he went to Texas, but he couldn't. He was going home.

Arlene drove him to Dulles International Airport. The trip on 66 West was almost bumper-to-bumper traffic. Normally he would have flown from Washington National, but their full flight schedule hadn't resumed yet. From Dulles, he wouldn't have to change planes.

From the passenger seat he assessed her. He was accustomed to seeing Arlene in her nurse's uniform. She was beautiful today in dark blue slacks and a matching V-neck top and gold necklace. She looked elegant and fetching.

"Thank you, Arlene, for all you've done for me and my family."

"You're very welcome," she said.

Words couldn't express his gratitude. He'd received many letters of good wishes from the families whose loved ones he'd saved, and his friends from Buckley Academy had called him often—even sent flowers and cards. But Arlene had been his steady champion. And he couldn't think of the words to express how indebted he felt.

When they arrived at the airport Arlene let him off at the terminal and requested a wheelchair. He went through check-in while she parked the car. The lines were long due to increased security. Although he could stand for short periods, he was glad she'd insisted on the wheelchair, as much as he hated it.

An athletic man his entire life, an Airborne Ranger, even, he found it humbling to be pushed through the airport to his gate while Arlene walked beside him carrying his cane. He shouldn't complain. After all that had occurred, he was grateful to be alive, and well enough to even take the flight.

"Can I get you anything?" Arlene asked him. "A sandwich, maybe?"

"Nothing. Thanks. Just sit and relax."

She sat in a chair by his wheelchair. He took in the beautiful elegance and warmth of her face, the tenderness in her eyes, and wondered if he would ever see her again. He hoped that another twenty-one years wouldn't pass before their paths crossed again.

He started to ask for her phone number—ask if he could visit her once he healed, but decided against it. April was his responsibility now. And he couldn't ask Arlene to be a part of her husband's baby's life, to have her pain thrown in her face on a daily basis.

The fact that he had gotten custody of April had been the final breaking point of his marriage. Natasha had made it clear that she didn't want a kid of her own, much less to take care of somebody else's. He certainly couldn't expect Arlene to care for her husband's child.

This would be their final good-bye.

Preflight boarding for his flight was announced, and Arlene started to stand. Neal caught her hands, leaned toward her, and, with a gentle tug, pulled her toward him until their lips touched.

He expected her to jerk away from him. When she didn't, he swiped his tongue over her lips. Her sweet essence mingled with a touch of perfume and the sweetness of the kiss was almost painful.

She opened her mouth to him, and for the first time in his life, he kissed the lips that had tempted him as a horny fourteen-year-old, standing on the cusp of tomorrow without a clue about how to deal with the girl who'd snubbed him. Even now she enticed the full-grown man. The emotional distance between them seemed as palpable as it had years before.

With a pressing need to touch her, he captured her warm face in his hands, tasted her, felt her soft skin—knowing this was all they would ever share. The realization was heartrending. A knot rose in his throat.

"Thank you," he whispered, while gazing into her eyes. There, he saw the same need that held him in its grip. Slowly, he slid his hands down her arms. Holding both her hands in his, he carried them to his mouth and gently kissed her knuckles, closing his eyes against the strength of his need.

They had come so close once again, only to have the future snatched away. When she opened one hand to caress his cheek, his gaze jerked to hers. All that he felt was reflected in her pretty brown eyes. There was so much he wanted to say, yet he felt compelled to remain silent. With hundreds of words left unspoken between them, the attendant wheeled him away.

He'd been given a commendation for courage, but he felt far from courageous when he caught one last glimpse of Arlene looking after him. The attendant whirled the wheelchair toward the gate. He didn't dare glance back with longing for what he could never have. Dear Lord, fate would have it that he could only move forward—toward April.

For a sneak peak at
the fourth book in the
At Your Service series

Flying High
by Gwynne Forster

from BET Books/Arabesque

Just turn the page . . .

One

Nelson Wainwright, Colonel, United States Marine Corps, glanced at the overcast sky, dropped his briefcase, and switched on the television. He hated getting wet when he was fully dressed; in fact, he disliked untidiness and considered a wrinkled uniform its epitome. He turned on the television to check the weather, and read the news beneath the picture: Sixty-eight and cloudy. Rain likely. Cooler than usual for May.

"What will a man endure to achieve his aims?" the motivational speaker said, as Nelson reached to switch off the television. The question mocked him, enticed him to linger and listen. "How much will he sacrifice? What will he give? What will he gain? And what can he lose?"

Ordinarily, Nelson did not allow media gurus or other self-styled motivators to impress him, but those words hounded him as he drove from Alexandria, Virginia, to his office in the Pentagon. He had spent eighteen of his forty-one years in the Marine Corps, and as recompense for working so hard and shaking hands with death more times than he wanted to remember, he intended to retire with four silver stars on his collar. He'd love to retire with five stars, but nothing less than four-star general would satisfy him.

Nelson knew two reasons why, even with good fortune, hard work, and shrewdness, he had a less-than-even chance of retiring as a full general. His superiors did not know that an injury to his neck pained him sufficiently to make him unfit for duty, nor did they know of his failure to report a corporal whom he'd discovered sleeping while on guard duty in Afghanistan. He didn't doubt that if his superiors knew of the unremitting pain he suffered, they would force his immediate retirement. And if he managed to camouflage that, he could be dismissed, or at least disciplined, for not having reported that marine's misconduct. Either meant he would finish military life as a colonel.

He parked in the space reserved for officers of his rank, and as light raindrops spattered his shoulders, he dashed inside the Pentagon. But as he entered his office, an eerie feeling settled over him, and the very pores of his skin jumped to alert as if he were back in Afghanistan anticipating a missile. He rushed to answer the telephone even as dread washed through his system.

"'Morning. Wainwright speaking."

"Good morning, Sir," a female said. "This is Lieutenant McCafferty in the Commandant's Office, and I'm sorry I have to give you this sad news."

Nelson leaned forward, mentally bracing himself, and listened as she told him that his brother had perished in an automobile accident that morning.

"You're listed as next of kin, Sir, and as guardian for Commander Wainwright's child, Richard Wainwright. Let us know what we can do for you. This office will send you an order for two weeks' leave beginning now."

He sat there for an hour dealing with his emotions and collecting his thoughts. Joel, his younger brother and only known relative other than little Ricky, had been looking forward to a great future in the Navy, and now . . . Well, what was done was done. The navy would take care of Joel; he had to look after four-year-old Ricky.

As the days passed, Ricky didn't respond favorably to the succession of foster mothers with whom he placed the boy, and he couldn't help noticing negative changes in the child's behavior, from bright and cheerful to sullen and quiet.

"That does it," he said to himself when, on one of his daily visits, Ricky clung to his leg in a fit of tears and wouldn't let go. He picked the child up, paid the foster mother for the remainder of the month and took Ricky home with him.

He wasn't a religious man, but he gave sincere thanks when Lena Alexander, whom his secretary recommended, walked into his house. She greeted him, looked down at Ricky, who loitered behind, dragging a beach towel, and her face lit up with a smile as she bent to the child and opened her arms. "My name is Lena, and I love little boys. What's your name?"

When Ricky smiled at her and told her his name was Ricky Wainwright, Nelson relaxed. Seconds later, Lena was giving Ricky a hug, and the child was telling her about his imaginary friends. The next morning, he moved her personal belongings to his home and settled her in a guest room.

It had been years since he had shared his living quarters, not since the four months during which he lived with Carole James, the woman who had brought another man—his closest friend—to the bed they shared, and had cared so little for him that she let him catch her cheating. The woman who would have been his wife within six weeks. In the more than five years that followed, he had enjoyed the quiet, though not the loneliness, and hearing Ricky's joyful noises and Lena's humming as she worked and her laughter with Ricky buoyed his spirits. Home was suddenly a pleasant place, especially at dinner when he had company for the delightful meals Lena prepared.

"What's the matter with your neck, Colonel?" Lena asked him at breakfast several days after joining his household. "Looks to me like you always favoring your neck. Better get it looked after. Trouble don't stand still in this world; either gets better or worse. You know what I'm saying?"

He did, indeed. Didn't the pain in his neck get worse daily? "I'm dealing with it, Lena. Don't let it bother you."

"Ain't bothering me none, Colonel. You the one that's uncomfortable. I declare, I wish somebody'd tell me why men so scared of a doctor. In the almost thirty years that I worked as an LPN—you know, licensed practical nurse—I never yet saw a male patient who didn't wait till he was half dead before he went to the doctor. You better do something before you get a problem with your spine."

He didn't have to answer her because she left the breakfast room humming what he suspected was her favorite hymn. "What's the name of that tune, Lena?" he asked when she came back with a carafe of hot coffee.

"If you don't know that song, you in trouble. Even the devil knows 'Amazing Grace.'"

He held his breath, watching while she filled his cup to the brim. When it didn't spill over, he bent over and sipped enough so that he could raise the cup to his lips without spilling the coffee.

"That surprises me, Lena. I would have thought the devil was more creative than to . . ."

He stopped. Her expression amounted to wonderment at his low level of intelligence. "Colonel Wainwright, I never said he sang the song; I said he knew it."

She walked with him to the door, holding Ricky, who enjoyed telling him good-bye and getting a hug. "You go see a doctor today, Colonel."

"See a doctor, Colonel," Ricky parroted.

"Ricky, you have to call him Uncle Nelson," she heard Lena say as he headed for his car.

"You sit down here and build your castle or read your book while I tend to a little business," Lena said to Ricky one morning about a month later as soon as Nelson left home. Ricky talked to the pictures in his books and pretended to read.

She dialed the hospital. "Let me speak to Dr. Powers, please."

"Dr. Powers speaking. How may I help you?"

"Audrey, honey, this is Aunt Lena. I love my boss. He's a wonderful man, so good with his little nephew. I wish—"

"Aunt Lena, I am not interested in your matchmaking. I'm glad the guy is a good father, and I'm glad you like your job. Now—"

"Hear me out, Audrey. Something is wrong with this man's neck. If he's not holding it and rubbing it, he's got something wrapped around it, and I can't get him to see a doctor. It's free for officers at Walter Reed Hospital, but I can't get him to go. Last night, he stopped eating his dinner, got up and put something around it. I hate to see him suffer like this. Come over one night, or maybe this Sunday when you're off, and have a look at it. He's such a good man."

"If it bothers him enough, Aunt Lena, he'll do something about it. I'd rather not meddle in that."

"Well . . . I, I just don't know what to do. It's not like he was hiding from the law." Lena hung up. She would find a way to get him to a doctor, he could bet on that.

"You didn't commit no crime, did you, Colonel?" she asked Nelson one night at dinner. When he stopped eating and stared at her, she pretending not to notice. "I mean, you not hiding out or something. You know what I mean, don't you."

He half-laughed and pointed his fork at her. "No, Lena, I don't know what you mean, and stop needling me." Then he laughed outright. "It just occurred to me that you're a blessing to my ego. I get so damned much deference in the Pentagon that I've started to believe I deserve it, but I can count on you to bring me down front and keep my feet to the fire, so to speak."

She turned her back in order to get the piece of celery that had lodged in the gap between her front teeth, then turned back to him. "I didn't mean to get familiar, but—"

He laughed. "I don't believe you said that."

"Well, truth is I care about what happens to you, and I've

had plenty experience with people who've been injured, so I know that neck of yours is a serious problem."

"That's right. Sometime I forget you're a nurse. Lena, I'm not entirely foolish. A missile hit the helicopter that I was piloting in Afghanistan, and when the copter crashed, I got some injuries, and this whiplash was one of them. My other injuries healed; this one is taking a little longer. That's all."

"Hmmm. You had that before I came here, and I've been working for you over three months. That's more than long enough for a whiplash to heal. Why don't you go over to Walter Reed and let them take care of it?"

"I can't do that, Lena. If my superiors find out that my neck is still giving me trouble, they may force me to retire. It's bad enough that I'm still on desk duty."

"Oh, dear. I see what the problem is. And if you go to a private doctor, it'll be reported. Well, I'll pray for you. I sure will."

He seemed relieved to get that subject out of the way, but he didn't know that she wasn't used to accepting defeat. She put Ricky to bed, and while Nelson read the child's favorite story to him, she figured it was a good time to call her niece.

"Audrey, could you do me a favor?" she asked, after they greeted each other. "I want to go on my church's outing Saturday, day after tomorrow. They're going to Crystal Caverns down in Strasburg, Virginia, and I always wanted to go. Year before last when they went, I couldn't get away from work. Could you look after Ricky"—she didn't dare mention Nelson—"for me Saturday? Just give him lunch and read him some stories. He's no trouble, and sweet as he can be."

She listened to the silence until she thought she would scream. Finally Audrey said, "What time do you think you'll get back there?"

"Around seven."

"All right. I'll do it this once, but you know I don't cook."

"Sandwiches will do just fine." She hadn't planned to take the excursion, but she phoned the organizer and got her seat.

Maybe she could kill two birds with one stone. Nelson Wainwright was a catch for any woman.

Audrey Powers did not relish the thought of baby-sitting, not even for half an hour. But her aunt had been so supportive during her struggles first to get through college and then to complete her medical training that she could hardly think of anything she wouldn't do for Lena. She stuffed half a dozen Chupa Chyps into her handbag, and stepped out of her house at barely sunup. Owing to the sparse traffic, the drive from her house in Bethesda to Alexandria, circling Washington on the Beltway, took her only twenty minutes early that Saturday morning. She parked in front of the beige-colored brick town house at 76 Acorn Drive. Lena greeted her at the door. "You're just in time. My taxi will be here in fifteen minutes." She turned around and pointed to the little boy. "This is Ricky. Ricky, Audrey is going to stay with you today."

Audrey looked down at the child who stared at her with an almost plaintive expression, and her heart seemed to constrict as she knelt beside him. "Hello, Ricky."

"Do you like little boys? Miss Lena loves little boys." His expression had changed to one of challenge.

"I love boys, especially little ones, and since I don't have a little boy, I can love you, can't I?"

He nodded, but kept looking at her. Suddenly, he smiled. "You can play with my bear and my blanket."

Realizing that that meant acceptance, she hugged and thanked him.

"Nelson will be down for breakfast around eight-thirty," Lena said as the horn blast signaled the arrival of her taxi.

"He'll be . . . Well if he's here, why am I . . ."

Lena closed the door.

Audrey took Ricky's hand and followed him to the refrigerator. When she opened it, he pointed to the milk. "Chocolate milk, please."

She poured the milk, thinking that she couldn't wait to give her aunt a piece of her mind. "I've been had," she said, when she didn't see any cooked food in the refrigerator. "I'm thirty years old, and I let my aunt hoodwink me."

He held the glass up to her. "Sugar, pease."

"I don't believe anybody puts sugar in your milk, but since nobody gave me any instructions, have a field day."

She put a teaspoon of sugar in the milk, stirred it and watched his eyes sparkle with delight. Now what? Her search for cereal or anything else a child would eat for breakfast proved futile.

"What do you eat for breakfast, Ricky?"

"Cake."

"Don't even think it. Try to bamboozle me, will you." She found some bread, toasted it, and, aware that he had a passion for things sweet, slathered the toast with butter and raspberry jam, poured a glass of orange juice, and sat Ricky down for breakfast.

"How old are you, Ricky?"

He held up four fingers. "Five."

She wondered if that was another of his games aimed at addling her, and it occurred to her that she might have to spend ten or twelve hours dealing with Ricky's little shenanigans. While he ate, she looked around for a coffee pot and the makings of a good cup of coffee. She didn't remember having gone so long after awakening without her caffeine fix. As soon as the smell of coffee permeated the kitchen, Ricky held out his glass.

"Can I please have some coffee, Audie?"

She would look back one day and know that that was the moment when he'd sneaked into her heart. "You little devil," she said as laughter spilled out of her. A lightheartedness, a joy, seemed to envelop her, and she lifted him from his chair and hugged him.

"No, you can't have any coffee, and you know it."

His lips grazed her cheek in a quick, almost tentative, kiss, delighting and surprising her. "Now be a good boy and finish your milk."

"Okay. I'm four."

She was about to thank him for telling the truth when the sound of heavy steps loping down the stairs reminded her that they were not alone, and her belly tightened in anticipation.

Nelson stepped out of the shower, and as he dried his body it occurred to him that a man of his height had to spend twice as much time on ablutions as a did a shorter man of slight build. But he wasn't complaining; he liked his six-feet-five-inch frame. He slipped on a red, short-sleeved T-shirt and a pair of fatigues and followed the aroma of coffee, his spirits high as he anticipated getting in a solid day's work at home.

He was used to Ricky now, and thought nothing unusual as he strode down the hallway enjoying the sound of boy's chatter. He stepped into the kitchen.

"'Morning, you two. What's for break . . . What the? Who are you, and where's Lena?"

"Unca Nelson, Audie gave me toast. I love toast, Unca Nelson."

She looked up at him, her lips parted in what was surely surprise, and immediately her lashes covered her remarkable dark and luminous eyes. *Who was she?* Jolts of electricity whistled through his veins, firing him the way gasoline dumped on a fire triggers powerful flames. He thought he would explode.

"I said . . . who are you?" Her grudging smile sent darts zinging all over his body. Poleaxing him. He groped for the chair beside Ricky where Lena usually sat, and slowly lowered himself into it.

"What are you doing here? If I may ask."

"I'm Audrey Powers," she said. "My aunt Lena had to go on a church outing today, and asked me to fill in for her. I can't believe she didn't get your approval."

Dignified. Well-spoken. Yes, and lovely. "Lena get my approval for something she wants to do? She tries, and if she doesn't succeed, she deals with matters in her own way.

Thanks for helping out. I have a lot of things to do around here today, and it's good that you're here to look after Ricky. Any chance I could get some breakfast?"

Her reticence didn't escape him. "Cooking isn't something I'm good at, Colonel. I noticed some grits in the pantry. If you can handle grits, scrambled eggs, and toast . . ."

She let it hang, and he knew it was that or nothing, so he didn't mention the sausage or bacon that had to be somewhere in that refrigerator.

"I'd appreciate it, and if you wouldn't mind sharing your coffee . . ."

As if seeing him for the first time, or maybe questioning his temerity, her eyes narrowed in a squint, and suddenly he could feel the tension crackling between them. *Good Lord, I don't need this. I don't know a thing about this woman.*

She got up from the table, exposing her five-feet-eight inches of svelte feminine beauty, rounded hips and full bosom emphasized by a neat waist. He gulped air as she glided toward the kitchen counter, got a mug of coffee, and handed it to him.

"If you want a second cup, the carafe is over there beside the sink."

Her message didn't escape him; she wasn't there to pamper him, but to take care of Ricky. "Thanks. I'm not much good before I get my coffee."

"Somehow I find that hard to believe, Colonel. I'd bet you do what you have to do, no matter the circumstances."

His left eyebrow shot up. "I try to do that, but how did you know?" He gripped his neck with his left hand as the familiar pain shot through him, took a deep breath, and forced himself to relax. Thank God Lena wasn't there to start her lecture. "When it comes to duty, a man ought to set personal consideration aside. And call me Nelson. Do you mind if I call you Audrey?"

"No, I don't."

"I like Audie, Unca Nelson."

"After conning me into putting sugar into your chocolate

milk, I guess you do." She looked at Nelson. "He told me he eats cake for breakfast."

He couldn't help laughing. "Ricky is skilled in getting what he wants. He doesn't get sugar in his milk, and I hope you didn't give him any cake."

"He got the sugar, but I knew better than to give him cake."

"I like cake, Audie. Miss Lena makes cake, and it's good, too."

Her gaze lingered on Ricky, and it was clear to him that Ricky had won her affection. "I'm sorry, Ricky, but I have never made a cake in my life. Excuse me, Nelson, while I get your breakfast."

"It's okay. Miss Lena will make the cake," Ricky called after him.

If only his neck would stop paining him. He had to finish installing the bookcases in his den and get some work done on the paneling in his basement.

He finished his breakfast, started upstairs to his den, and glanced around to see Ricky following him with his "blanket," the navy-blue beach towel trailing behind him.

"Rick, old boy, you're going to have to give up that blanket. Wainwright men do not romance blankets." He looked up to find Audrey's gaze on him. "They romance women." Now, why the devil had he said that? He whirled around and dashed up the stairs feeling as if he'd lost control of his life. And he always made it a point to control himself, and, to the extent possible, his life and everything that affected him personally.

"She's not going to detour me," he told himself, "I wouldn't care if she was the Venus de Milo incarnate. And I'm going to give Lena a good talking-to when she gets back here."

Damn! He jerked back his thumb, dropped the hammer and went to the bathroom to run cold water on the injury. If he had been paying attention, if the picture of Audrey Powers sitting at his kitchen table smiling at Ricky hadn't blotted all else out of his mind . . .

I don't care who she is or what she looks like, I'm not getting involved with her. He laughed. Getting involved was a two-sided thing, and she hadn't given any indication that she was interested. He corrected that. She'd reacted to him as man, that was sure, but the woman displayed her dignity the way the sun displays its rays. And she kept her feelings to herself. He'd give a lot to know who she was, but he was not going to let her know that. She was here for one day, and he'd make sure that was all.

Audrey cleaned the kitchen, something she seldom had to do at home, and tried to figure out what to do with Ricky. Finally she asked him, "Where's your room, Ricky?" Perhaps she could read to him or he could play with his toys.

The child beamed with glee, grabbed her hand, and started with her to the stairs. "Up the stairs, Audie. I have a big room."

She started up with him, and stopped. She did not want to encounter Nelson Wainwright right then, for she hadn't reclaimed the contentment that she'd worked so hard and so long to achieve, the feeling that she belonged to herself, that her soul was her own. One look at Nelson Wainwright, big, strong, and all man with his dreamy eyes trained on her, and she had nearly sprung out of her chair. Like a clap of thunder, he jarred her from her head to her toes, an eviscerating blow to her belly. She thanked God she'd been sitting down.

"Can you play my flute?" Ricky asked her as they walked into his room, a child's dream world.

Her gaze fell on a full-size harp, and her heart kicked over. She had studied the harp and once played it well, but hadn't touched it since her father died. He'd loved to hear her play it and would sit and listen for as long as she played.

"I'm sorry, Ricky, but I've never played the flute."

"Unca Nelson can play it. Can you read me Winnie-the-Pooh?"

She told him she could and he handed her the book, surprising her when he climbed into her lap and rested his head on her breast while she read to him. The prospect of motherhood didn't occupy much of her thought, because her one experience with love and loving had erupted in her face. And since she wanted nothing more to do with men, certainly not to expose herself to an intimate relationship, she blocked thoughts of motherhood and children. But she couldn't deny that Ricky stirred in her heart a longing for the joy of a child at her breast.

When the story ended, Ricky scampered off her lap, ran across the room, and put a compact disk on his player. Then he ran back and looked up at her, waiting for her response as Ella Fitzgerald's "A Tiskit A Tasket" filled the room. To let him know that she appreciated his gesture, she sang it along with Ella, while he clapped his hands and jumped up and down laughing and trying to sing along with her.

"Hey, what's going on in here?"

She settled her gaze on the door and the man who stood there wearing a quizzical smile and a soft, surgical collar around his neck.

Ricky ran to his uncle and tugged at his hand. "Audie read my book for me and I'm playing my CD for her."

He picked the boy up and hugged him. "Don't wear her out, now."

"How old is Ricky?" Audrey asked Nelson.

"He'll be five next week." His left hand went to the back of his neck. "He's made tremendous progress since Lena's been with him. I had him in foster care for a couple of months after my brother died, and that experience set him back considerably. I brought him here to live with me, and I could see an improvement within a week."

She watched as he held his neck without seeming to give the act conscious thought. It was not a good sign. "I'm sure he feels the difference. Some foster parents give a child love and understanding as well as care; others don't, often through no fault of their own. Tell me, do you play the harp?" She pointed to the instrument there in Ricky's room.

He lowered his head. "Wish I could. That one belonged to my brother, Ricky's father. He played it very well indeed. I put it here in case Ricky takes an interest in it."

Speaking of his brother obviously saddened him, and she found that she wanted to know more, but she didn't dare invade his privacy with a personal question.

"I'm hungry, Audie. Can I have some ice cream?"

"May I have some ice cream?" Nelson said, correcting the child. "No, you may not. You get ice cream after you've eaten all of your lunch. You know that."

With innocence spread over his face, he turned to her. "Don't give me much lunch."

She stifled a laugh and got up, surprised by the realization that she had spent half a day enjoying the company of a four-year-old. Still holding Ricky in his arms, Nelson didn't move from the doorway as she attempted to leave the room. Her nerves skittered as she neared him, and when she couldn't help glancing up at him, he looked down directly into her eyes and caught his breath. She managed to pass him, but only the Lord knew how she did it.

Something in him, something hard, and strong, blood-sizzlingly masculine clutched at her. An aura like nothing she'd experienced before jumped out at her and claimed her. And all he'd done was stand there. How she got downstairs she would never know; he blurred her vision and sabotaged her thoughts. Worse, her heart threatened to bolt from her chest. She leaned against the kitchen counter. Nelson Wainwright was just another man, and she had no intention of making a fool of herself over him. A long sigh escaped her. One piece of her father's wisdom claimed that the road to hell was paved with good intentions.

"Girl, you need to get out more," she chided herself. "Stuck in that hospital all the time, you forget what it's like out here."

Within a few minutes, she called up to him. "Lunch is ready, Nelson, such as it is."

He took a long time getting downstairs, and she couldn't help wondering why. "Thank you for taking care of this, Audrey," he said. "I get the feeling this is aeons away from what you normally do."

He stared at the food before him. "I take it you don't cook much. These look good, though," he said of the tunafish salad and cheese sandwiches.

"I cook not at all."

Ricky clapped his hands and laughed. "No potatoes and no veggies, Unca Nelson. I like this. I want Audie to stay with us all the time."

Nelson seemed to wince as his hand went once more to his neck, and this time there was no mistaking his pain. Without considering her action, she rose from the table, stepped behind him and examined his neck.

"What the . . . what are you doing?" he demanded as her fingers began the gentle massage that she knew would bring him relief. "I said . . . Look here. You're out of line."

"No, I'm not," she said without pausing in her ministrations. "I'm a physician, Nelson, and physical therapy and sports medicine are my specialties. This will make you feel better."

"You're a *what?*"

"A physician. I can't help noticing your problem, and it's clear to me that the pain is killing you."

"Look here! You can't—"

"Don't you feel better already? Fifteen minutes of this and you'll feel like a different man. Just relax and give yourself over to me."

"What kind of—"

"Shhh. Just relax."

"Does it hurt, Uncle Nelson?" Ricky's voice rose with anxiety, and she hastened to assure him that she was helping, not hurting his uncle.

"I'm making him feel better, Ricky. Go on and eat your sandwich. Isn't the pain easing already, Nelson?"

Her fingers, gentle yet firm, kneaded his flesh. "Relax," she'd said, but how could he, tense as he was with the pain that was his constant companion. He thought of pushing back his chair and leaving the table, but if he did that, he could hurt her. How could Lena betray him so blatantly?

"Relax. Drop your shoulders," she whispered.

No one dictated his life, as Lena was trying to do, and he wouldn't have it. He attempted to move, but with deft fingers Audrey soothed him, easing the pain, giving him the first relief he'd had in nearly a year, reducing the throbbing to a dull ache. Her hands massaged him with soft circular movements, squeezing and caressing. He lowered his head and luxuriated in the relief that her gentle strokes gave him. Then, with his eyes closed, he saw her fingers skimming his entire naked body, caressing and adoring him, preparing him for the assault of her luscious mouth.

Good Lord! His eyelids flew open, and he gasped in astonishment. He'd been within seconds of a full erection. Better put an end to that bit of heaven, and fast. He put both hands to the back of his neck and gripped her fingers.

"Thanks. You're right, I feel better, but can I finish my . . . my sandwich now?"

She went back to her chair, but she didn't sit down. "You're not angry, are you? I know it made you feel better. The problem is that the relief is very temporary. Massage is not a cure."

He didn't pretend, nor did he attempt to deprecate the comfort she gave him; Audrey Powers obviously knew her business, and anyway, he didn't want to seem ungrateful. "How could I be angry? I feel better right now than in a year."

She sat down, her eyes wide and a look of incredulity on her face. "You've been suffering like this for a year? How could you stand it?

He let the shrug of his shoulders communicate his feelings. "You do what you have to do. Simple as that."

She leaned toward him. "But it isn't necessary for you to suffer like this."

"It is, Audrey, believe me. The Marine Corps is a unit of men in perfect physical and mental condition. We are the crown of the Service, the cream of the crop. If you can't hack it, you get a letter of thanks, and that's it. I can handle it, and I will."

"But can't you go to Walter Reed, or the Navy Medical Center?"

"Sure, if I want an honorable discharge. I'm not ready for that."

"But . . . You mean your superiors don't know about this?"

He stared at her, and if he seemed threatening, he didn't care. "No, and nobody's going to tell them."

Not many men stood up to him, but he could see from her demeanor that if he pushed her, she would shove right back. Apparently having thought better of an alternative response, she nodded and said, "I see. What a pity."

Even at the tender age of four, Ricky appeared to sense Audrey's concern, for he attempted to pacify her.

"I'm eating all of my sandwich, Audrey."

She smiled and stroked Ricky's cheek, though he could see that her thoughts hadn't shifted from him to the child.

"Am I going to get my ice cream, Audie?"

It amazed him that Ricky had so quickly handed over his care to Audrey. Maybe he just liked women; if so, he wouldn't blame him, and he certainly understood Ricky's preference for this one. She'd gotten to him the minute his gaze landed on her. Not that it would make a difference in his life. He meant to give Lena a stiff lecture about her underhanded little trick, and he didn't expect to see Audrey Powers again.

"If your uncle Nelson says you may have ice cream, I'll get you a nice big scoop," he heard her say to Ricky.

With a smile obviously aimed to captivate Audrey, Ricky said, "Miss Lena always gives me two nice big scoops."

Laughter rumbled in his chest, and he felt good. He couldn't remember when he'd had such a light . . . He pushed the word back, but it returned, and he admitted to himself that he felt happy. He looked from Ricky to Audrey, and tremors shot through him at her unguarded expression. It was there only for a second, but he didn't mistake it; she wanted him. It had been there when they met. He'd had enough experience to know that an attraction as strong as what he felt for her couldn't be one-sided.

Questions about her zinged through his mind. Why would a medical doctor baby-sit even for one day? Where was her office? She wasn't wearing a ring, not even a diamond, so why was a woman with her phenomenal looks single? He voiced none of them. He didn't like revealing himself, and therefore he didn't request it of others. He pushed back his chair.

"Thanks for my lunch, and especially for that great massage. I'd better get back to work while I'm still pain-free."

He looked at Ricky and marveled that the child didn't jump from the chair and trail after him as he usually did. Ricky ignored him.

"After you give me my ice cream, Audie, you can play with my robot."

He went upstairs, almost reluctant to leave them. As he worked, their chatter and laughter buoyed him, but after a time a quiet prevailed. He walked over to Ricky's room to find them both asleep, Ricky in her lap with his head on her breast and she with both arms around him. The longer he stared at them, the lonelier he felt. Disgusted with himself, he put on a leather Eisenhower jacket, went out in his back garden, and busied himself building a fire in the brick oven. He couldn't say exactly why he did that, but he was certain of his need to change the scene and recover the part of himself that, within a split second, Audrey Powers had stolen. He sat there in the cool and rising wind until after dark warming himself by the fire and reminding himself of Carole James, the one woman, the betrayer, he'd allowed himself to love. Thoughts of her brought the taste of bile to his mouth.

"I'll die a bachelor," he said aloud, shoveled some dirt on the coals, and went inside.

Audrey prowled around Ricky's room, fighting the vexation at her aunt that was rapidly escalating into anger. It was time Ricky had dinner, she didn't know what to give him, and his hotshot uncle was nowhere to be found.

"I wanna eat, Audie. I'm hungry."

She looked at her watch for the nth time. Seven-fifteen. Of course he was hungry; so was she. She heard the back door close, grabbed Ricky's robot, and rushed to the top of the stairs.

"Who's there?"

"Sorry, Audrey. It didn't occur to me that I might frighten you. Lena isn't back?"

"No, she isn't, and Ricky's hungry. Maybe you'd better phone a restaurant and have something delivered."

He reached the top of the stairs where she stood holding Ricky's hand, or maybe Ricky was holding her hand. The cloud covering her face and the set of her mouth told him to tread carefully. He didn't enjoy tangling with women in the best of circumstances, and this one was angry. Moreover, she had a right to be.

His hands went up, palms out. "I'm sorry about this. I was out back, thinking Lena—"

"She isn't here, and—"

He wasn't accustomed to being interrupted, but he thought it best not to tell her that. "As I was about to say, if you'll tell me what you'd like to eat, I'll order dinner. I know a great seafood restaurant that will deliver full-course meals within forty minutes."

"I'll take shrimp and whatever goes with it."

A deep breath escaped him. Thank God for a woman who didn't feel she had to wash his face with his errors. "Great, so will Ricky. Be back shortly." He went into his room and ordered dinners for the four of them. He had a few things to tell Lena, but that didn't mean she should be deprived of a good meal.

His hunch told him the less Audrey was required to do, the better her mood would be, so he set the table in the breakfast room and opened a bottle of chilled chardonnay.

"Would you like a glass of wine while we wait for dinner?" he asked Audrey.

Suddenly, she laughed. "I may be furious with my aunt, Nelson, but I won't bite off your head."

"Thanks for the assurance. You had such a dark look on your face that I wasn't sure I should say a word to you. This wine is usually pretty good."

"Thanks, I'll have half a glass. I don't drink when I have to drive. Say, that's the doorbell, isn't it? Mind if I answer it?"

"Uh, no. If it's Lena, give her a chance to explain before you blow her away."

She rushed to the door with Ricky and his "blanket" trailing behind her. "Oh. It's the food," she called to Nelson, looked up and saw that he was beside her. He paid the deliveryman and took the food.

"Come on, you two, let's eat."

They sat down, and the doorbell rang again. She moved as if to get up, but he raised his hand. "I'll get it. You should have cooled off by now."

"I never cool off till I get my due," he heard her say as he headed for the door.

"How you doing, Colonel? I know Audrey's mad by now, but I got back quick as I could."

"Audrey? What about me? I'm the one you've got to reckon with."

"Now, now, Colonel. Give me a chance to get in. I bet your neck feels better."

The audacity of the woman! "Dinner's on the table. I'll speak with you later."

"Miss Lena, guess what? I had toast this morning, and I didn't have to eat any veggies for lunch. Audie gave me san . . . sandwiches"

"I bet she did. Audrey, honey, I'm so sorry."

"No problem," Nelson said. "Audrey's mad at you, but you two can deal with that later. Right now she's going to smile if it kills her. We're going to enjoy our food."

They listened to Lena's tales of the famous Crystal Caverns and her picturesque account of the scenery during the drive.

He knew she meant to placate both him and Audrey, but he didn't think she achieved either.

"I'd better be going," Audrey said when they finished eating. "Be sure and take care of your neck, Nelson. My judgment is that if you don't, you will have serious trouble down the road."

It struck him as silly; he didn't want her to leave. "Uh, thanks. I . . . It was good to met you, Audrey."

"I want Audie to stay," Ricky said. "I don't want her to leave, Unca Nelson. Please don't let her leave."

Audrey knelt beside the child and placed an arm around him. "I have to go, Ricky. I hate to leave you, but I have to go home."

"No!" Ricky ran and stood with his back against the door. "No, you can't go."

He looked down at his nephew and wondered whether Audrey had sprinkled some kind of dust over him and the boy. Then, he reached to lift Ricky into his arms, but the child evaded him.

"I don't want Audie to leave." Ricky sat down on the floor and began to cry. "Unca Nelson, don't let her leave. I don't want her to go."

Lena bent to take the child into her arms. "Ricky, darling," she said. "It's time for bed. Kiss Audrey good-bye and off we go to bed."

He twisted away from her. "No. I want Audie to stay."

"I'll come back to see you, Ricky. I promise."

He stared at her. "Don't tell him that, because you don't mean it."

She squinted at him, and a frown clouded her face. "I wouldn't dare lie to a child. If you don't want me to come see him, say so."

"I'm sorry." He picked up the recalcitrant boy, hugging and comforting him. "It's all right, Ricky. She said she will come to see you, and she will. Now give her a big kiss and let her go home. She's tired."

Ricky reached out to kiss Audrey. "I'm sorry you have to go, Audie. Bye."

Ricky didn't usually hold on to him so tightly, and it struck him with considerable force that the effect of so many losses in the child's young life lay close to the surface of Ricky's emotions. He wondered if Audrey reminded Ricky of his mother. She didn't bring to his own mind any other woman he'd ever met, and he doubted he would forget her soon, if ever. He remembered her promise to visit Ricky, turned, and, still holding the child, loped with him up the stairs to his room. Who was this woman who had changed both their lives? He put the boy to bed and stood looking down at him as he dozed off to sleep. *You will forget her long before I will.* For the first time in seven hours, pain streaked through his neck.

Dear Reader:

Thank you for going on this most unusual journey with me. When I first thought about the story I wanted to write for Roxanne and Haughton, there was a large question mark in my mind. I knew I didn't want to do anything "safe." So I let the question rest in my brain's computer and one day when I wasn't thinking about it, the answer appeared like a flash of daylight.

I've always been fascinated with mythology. So, I combined that with my son's love of video games, and my interest in adventure sagas. The result is the romantic-technofantasy you hold in your hands. I felt that after all the pain Roxanne and Haughton had experienced in their previous relationship, nothing short of something spectacular would serve to bring them back together.

I hope you continue to be engaged in the Allgood series as I endeavor to bring you stories about Amara Fairchild and Ashley Allgood.

As always, I love to hear from readers. Please contact me by mail or Internet at: P.O. Box 31544, Omaha, NE 68131, http://www.kimlouise.com, or MsKimLouise@aol.com.

Until next time, peace and blessings!

Kim

ABOUT THE AUTHOR

Kim Louise resides in Omaha, Nebraska. She's been writing since grade school and has always dreamed of penning "The Great American Novel." She has an undergraduate degree in journalism and a graduate degree in adult learning. She has one son, Steve, and in her spare time enjoys reading, card making, and watching the sun set.

The Arabesque At Your Service Series

_Four superb romances with engaging characters and dynamic story lines
featuring heroes whose destiny is intertwined with women of equal
courage who confront their passionate—and unpredictable—futures._